CHAPTER 1
RAGE OF THE JINN

PARIS, FRANCE

2022

THERE SHOULD NOT HAVE BEEN a body under that floor.

It already felt like a desecration to Antoine, to tear up the base of the great cathedral. Notre Dame was the holy heart of his country and the icon of his own faith, however loosely he held that. Yet here he was, an hour before his lunch break, working to clear the broken pieces of stone flooring. So much had been destroyed when the great roof collapsed.

That fateful day in April, Antoine had been watching from across the Seine. He had stopped to pick up dinner at his favorite Chinese restaurant on Rue Hautefeuille. Fried rice and crispy chicken spring rolls. It was a greasy and guilty pleasure, but he resolved to give up smoking the next week for balance. That was certainly the vice that needed to go first.

When he stepped back out onto the street, plastic bag in hand, everyone in sight was staring off across the river, toward

Île de la Cité. He lifted his eyes to see smoke billowing up into the cool evening sky.

He started walking, then running toward the Seine. There were already people gathered along its banks, watching the flames rise from the spire of Notre Dame. Astonished horror rippled through the crowd. Within an hour, it looked as if the great cathedral was burning with the fires of hell itself. Antoine stood there, grief welling in his gut. The bag hung limp in his hand. The rice and spring rolls went cold.

He had not imagined that years later, he would be standing in the scarred bowels of it all, repairing the eight hundred and fifty-year-old monument. The heart and soul of his country.

Above him now, a web of silver scaffolding stretched along vaulted arches, up to the temporary aluminum roof above that rolled open during the day. Hundreds of workers milled in and out, dangling from ropes, hauling away debris, and cleaning every inch of the limestone with handbrushes. They had only recently finished clearing the lead dust from the interior, with teams wearing full protective suits and special breathing apparatus. Long gone were the smells of incense and oak. Since the fire, the place had smelled of charred wood and choking stone dust.

It was a relief to everyone on site, to finally do away with clean zones vs. polluted zones. Polluted zone workers would have to check in with a Health & Safety operative each day for underwear, overalls, boots, helmets, and gloves. At the end of the day, they'd shower in a designated trailer to scrub away any remaining trace of the poisonous dust.

Today, Antoine and his crew of seven were bare-faced, wearing the standard white helmets, picking away at chunks of stone. They had seen the Chief Architect of Historic Monuments striding about the transept area that morning, assessing every

RAGE OF THE JINN

OX DEVERE

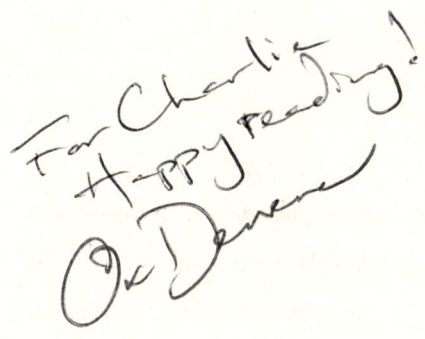

www.oxdevere.com

ISBN: 979-8-9895424-0-6

❀ Created with Vellum

for Granjan

unit in their progress. Most of them felt the weight of the work. Notre Dame needed to be brought back to life.

Antoine was still looking forward to the ham panini that he had waiting for him at lunch. And he was itching for a smoke. The morning had felt endlessly dull, with his work team trading tired jokes. Pascal had spent the morning grumbling about his wife, Jean was fishing for gossip about the latest health inspector, and Luc was hungover.

None of them were prepared for what they found that morning.

"Hey, look!" exclaimed Pascal.

He was down in the broken recess of stone pieces, beckoning for anyone. Antoine climbed down to see what he was staring at.

"What is that?"

Antoine bent down, confused by what he was looking at. It was a long container of some sort, covered in dust. One end of it was still stuck under a ledge of stone. He swept a gloved hand over the edges, and then realized: the shape was vaguely human.

"Oh, my God."

CHAPTER
TWO

———

BASKETBALL WAS MADE for days like this.

The asphalt was drenched in warm afternoon sun, and a breeze from the nearby Potomac whirled across it. The game was three on three, shirts versus skins.

Ridley Samaras had chosen to keep her shirt today, which was now damp with sweat and clinging to her stomach. The only other woman on the court, a five-foot-seven scrapper with an outlandish vertical jump named Lilah, had gone skins in only a sports bra. It was probably the better choice.

One of her teammates snapped off a chest pass toward her. She caught the ball and faced up to Lilah, then feinted a shot. When she leapt at it, Ridley pivoted to the outside and shot. The ball nicked the inside of the rim with a soft *clunk*, then slipped down through the net with a satisfying *swish*.

"Aright, Kobe, aright!" yelled one of her teammates, Nate, as they tracked back.

Some took the transition time of crossing down-court to get a few seconds of mental and physical relief. Ridley needed it to refocus.

They'd been playing for thirty minutes, and while she knew four of the other players from regular neighborhood games, the fifth was new. Though fairly quiet, he had put her on alert. At nearly six-foot-one, in his late thirties, he had cropped short hair, a torso of sinewy muscle, and a sharp jawline. He spoke with a faint Haitian accent and played ball like he was getting paid for it. He'd said his name was Henri.

She took it as a personal challenge when she realized how good his balance was, how measured his defense. He kept low, his hands out wide, ready to grab the ball from either side. And those hands were fast.

Now as he went on offense, she found herself guarding him. Her height made her formidable, all five feet and eleven inches of it. Her athleticism made her something of a freak.

About to make you uncomfortable.

Henri wasn't dangerous in every moment the way some players were. He was more calculating, picking his moments to go, to get aggressive. Those would be her moments, too. As he started to move, dribble, and spin with the ball, she went low, jostling hard into his legs and hips.

It gave her a rush when she saw how much he hated it. He stumbled and nudged back, losing concentration on his own play.

His teammates were calling for the ball. He finally got off a sloppy pass—*intercepted*. She grinned and tore down the court with her team. The ball thief, a Dominican-Italian named Pete whose agility and shooting more than made up for his lack of height, took a clear run-up and looped a shot in off the backboard.

"Fifty-eight, fifty!" called Ridley.

She was backtracking down the court again when she caught sight of someone taking a seat nearby on the picnic table. A broad-shouldered, silver-haired man who looked right at her and grinned.

"Hundred bucks on skins!" he shouted.

They all heard it. Some laughed.

Oh, let's fucking go.

"Who's this guy?" said Pete, jogging past her.

She shook her head, calling over to the table, "Save your money! Buy glasses!"

Their sole spectator looked pleased with himself.

The visitor's bet had just fired a NOS octane booster in her engine. It wasn't enough for her to compete, or even to win. Ridley wanted to dominate each one of her opponents, and she wanted to elevate each of her teammates to perfection with her.

The last ten minutes played out with the intensity of a classic Celtics-Lakers game, if without the size and skill. When the biggest man on the court, a cheese salesman named Russell, sent Pete sprawling across the paint, the players had to haul each other away for a cooling off.

They cleaned it up, but still played out the final seconds like a ring was on the line. Ridley drove hard into Henri, cutting his angles, pressing her forearm against his back. He kept attacking to her right to beat her.

He kept one hand in front of her face every time she had the ball. She kept pulling up for jumpshots to beat it.

Doesn't matter if I can't see. The net doesn't move.

The game ended seventy-three to sixty-eight for the shirts. It was all a cacophony of trash talking and grudging praise as they went for their stuff on the sidelines. Henri grinned at whatever was hurled his way, but said little.

Ridley made a line for their audience of one.

"A hundred dollars split three ways is sorta messy," she said to him. "One-twenty would have really made a statement."

"What's a hundred bucks to see you all riled up out there playin' like Kobe Bryant?"

She poured the contents of her water bottle down her throat. "You know, I do have a phone?"

"But you know I like to get out of the office," said her boss.

Booker Douglas was a clip over six feet, and thicker in the middle than he'd been in his active operator days. He spoke with expressive richness, his big doe eyes sparkling when he grew excited. He'd grown up with a white father and a black mother in the dregs of St. Louis. He couldn't have had any idea how that ambiguously dusky complexion would gift him with chameleonic adaptability across a dozen countries. As a boy, being too light for some and too dark for others cost him greatly, in playground bruises and furious tears. Later, that same skin would save him in places like Pakistan, Syria, and Lebanon.

"Besides, I wanted to introduce you to your partner," he said, glancing over at the others.

At the Haitian newcomer, tugging a dri-fit shirt over his slick torso.

Ridley chuckled, shaking her head. "You just can't help yourself, O Great Puppetmaster of Boundless Cleverness. Did you tell *him*?"

"Not which one of you it was, but I don't think it'd take him long to guess. Ready for some food? I know you like ice cream after your games out here."

Ridley wiped dribbles of water from her chin. Her broad shoulders and hard limbs made for an imposing appearance, like some collegiate swimmer, or an Amazon. She was undoubt-edly striking. Her hair was like her father's, a thick Greek mahogany that was often pulled back or tied down with a long braid. Her face was not beautiful, but attractive nonetheless. A strong jaw, but not thick. An arrow-straight nose and the slightest overbite behind full lips. The dark brows carved like gull-wings were the Icelandic trait from her mother's side. They framed amber eyes that were almost shockingly soft.

"It's gelato, actually," she said, toweling the sweat off her forehead.

"He's rusty," said a voice from behind her. Faint Haitian accent.

She turned around to see her new partner with a sly, cheerful look on his face.

"I'm Henri Michel," he said, extending a hand.

"And you play like Tracy McGrady," she said, taking it with a firm shake. "I'm Ridley. Has he read you in yet?"

"No. Has he read you in yet?"

"That's what the gelato is about," Booker sighed. "Let's go talk."

"I need a shower first," said Ridley.

Henri swiped a palmful of sweat from his head. "Same for me."

"Good, great. You both stink," said Booker, getting to his feet. "Meet you at Casa Rosada, one hour."

He slapped a hundred dollar bill on the table and headed for the parking lot. Henri turned to follow him.

"Good game, Ridley," he called over his shoulder. "Wicked jumpshot. Really...wicked."

She grinned. Then she picked up the money, called for Nate, and snapped the bill neatly in front of him.

"The winnings. Take our baller boy out for a steak," she said, nodding at Pete.

"Not you?"

"Work trip just came up. Sorry. You know I love social bonding after street balling," she grinned. "Get a filet mignon for me."

He rolled his eyes, but he was amused. "Aright. Go speak all the languages, wherever you're goin'. Don't start any wars by vocabulary accident."

"We all have our own style!"

He took the hundred and bumped her fist. As he left, she grabbed her bag and the motorcycle helmet beside it.

Everyone in Ridley's life believed that she was a diplomatic translator. The cover story worked seamlessly. Anyone who knew as many languages as she did was perfectly suited to such a job. Anyone working as a translator for a mid-level diplomat in the D.C. area was also bound to travel a great deal. Their work would be either drooling levels of boring or confidential, so no one ever asked about it.

The lying really never bothered her. Sometimes that fact itself bothered her, that it flowed so naturally, without reservation. The thing that gnawed quietly at her was not being able to tell anyone what she had seen in her work.

Not that they would ever believe her.

CHAPTER
THREE

———

OLD TOWN WAS UNDENIABLY beautiful in the spring. Cherry blossoms showered their petals along cobblestone streets. The sidewalk cafés brimmed with pedestrians, tourists, and locals. Ridley cut through the rows of colonial houses on her bike, a sleek Indian Scout Bobber.

She was replaying the game in her head, her mistakes, Henri's plays, how disciplined his every move was. Booker had never made a bad choice when it came to pairing operatives, but some were standouts. She worked her face off to be one of the standouts, and she wanted a partner who was as ferociously committed as she was.

Failure had ignited that drive in her.

Ridley had grown up a nomad. Her mother had died when she was only three. It had shattered her father and his dream of what his family would be. He had traveled abroad for his work as a project manager for a construction company doing extensive work in Europe at the time. When their mother died, something wasted away inside of him. He couldn't bear to leave his kids behind, but he hardly knew what to do with them either. So Ridley and her older brother, Alexios, had gone along in tow, across the world.

They'd made their own ways, picking up a new language every year, finding new ways to get into scraps in every city they walked through. Summers they'd spend with their grandmother, Charis, in the Greek islands. She had a business running horseback riding tours, and by the time Ridley was twelve, she was leading tourists around the island on her favorite chestnut mare. When the tourists had gone, she and Alexios galloped bareback along the beach. They raced each other in the salty bright waters of the Aegean until she thought her lungs would burst.

The smell of *loukomades* baking in her grandmother's kitchen nearly made her dizzy with craving. She sneaked extras of the honey-glazed doughnut holes whenever Ya-ya's back was turned.

"Are you starving?" exclaimed Charis once when she found her thieving, laughing as she gave Ridley a kick on the backside. "You eat like a horse!"

"I need enough to fly, Ya-ya. I'm Pegasus!"

GREEK: "Be Bellerophon, slayer of monsters," said her grandmother, "because I need you to find that Chimera rat who is chewing through all the saddle straps."

GREEK: "I'll bring him to you!"

Ridley grabbed a spatula and ran out of the kitchen as Charis hollered about raining down the wrath of the gods if she brought a rat into the house.

That island was the only place that felt like home.

Eventually, Alexios decided he wanted something more conventional. She could hardly believe it when he told her he was going back to the States to get a law degree. How could her brother—who had set off fireworks on the banks of the Seine with her, who had sneaked her into a hard-core club in Berlin so raunchy that it left her shell-shocked, who had stolen a boat from the harbor once so they could joyride from island to island until the sun came up, whom she was always trying to out-race and out-wrestle—choose such a mundane career? But he did leave.

A year later, their grandmother died. Ridley had been in Milan with her father. He had put his fist through a table in an outburst of grief. She'd walked the stone streets until the early hours of the morning, nearly catatonic.

At seventeen, she was adrift. Too old to cling to the wisps of childhood and too lonely to settle anywhere, she set her mind to an apex challenge: she would become the first female Navy SEAL.

No woman had ever gone through that harrowing crucible, that grit-in-your-teeth, blood-in-your-mouth, every-muscle-screaming program that produced some of the finest warriors in the world. She knew she had a rare physical capability. At five feet and eleven inches, with a gas tank that could run for days and the upper body strength that had always rivaled her brother's, she had a solid foundation. Yet it was the mental ferocity that would be the ace card, and her extraordinary swimming prowess that would distinguish her amongst the majority of her peers.

She joined the Navy. She excelled. She applied to join the SEALs and was accepted. She passed the indoctrination training pipeline. When she was accepted into BUD/S: Basic Underwater Demolition/Sea Air Land, it made headlines on every military website in the nation. She was the anonymous exception, a ground-breaking soldier, a frontier-setting woman. None of her two hundred classmates let her forget it, nor did any of the instructors. She ate shit for it every day. Anyone who stood out as a "star" without having earned it was bound to get hammered down.

Ridley endured it all, and discovered that the physical challenges were the least of the difficulties. At its core, the twenty-four-week BUD/S course was about selecting for the best at high-level problem-solving under extreme stress.

She thought she'd finally found her place in the world, her purpose.

Some stories don't go the way they're supposed to.

Astride her Indian Scout, Ridley veered down a narrow alleyway between two townhouses, and kicked her bike into park. She opened the back door of her apartment and set her helmet on the counter. It was a sparse, neat place, exposed brick and hardwood floors. In this area, a complete steal, thanks to a very kind old landlady who said that Ridley reminded her of her goddaughter.

There was a skittering across the hardwood, and a second later a scraggy little mutt with giant brown eyes burst into the kitchen.

"Maddie, I know, I know!"

Ridley knelt to snuggle the softest, sweetest rescue dog she'd ever known. Maddie hardly ever made a sound, but she was eternally watchful. Thankfully she was small enough to fit onboard a flight, and well-behaved enough to take almost anywhere, but in this moment Ridley felt a pang coming on. The joyful little thing had no idea that she was about to leave again, for God only knew how long.

Ridley locked the back door behind her, stripped off her

soggy clothes and tossed them in the washer. As she showered, she knocked the side of her head and stretched out her jaw, as if she still had water in her ear. It was half-subconscious, half-ritualized. The water would never come out. The muffle in that eardrum would never disappear.

She braided her hair into a thick cord, then dressed in jeans, Allbirds, and a purple V-neck. After tugging on a vintage Celtics cap, she tucked her SIG Sauer P365 into her waistband. She always appendix carried unless there was no choice to do so. It kept the draw within a natural movement of the arm, and kept the gun in front of her. Despite the occasional discomfort when sitting, she couldn't have asked for a better combination of magazine capacity, slim frame, and stopping power than the P365. Finally, she slipped a Spyderco Matriarch knife into her back pocket.

Ridley reflexively checked herself in the living room mirror for any sign of the weapons. There was nothing visible.

She never wanted to alert anyone that she was loaded.

As she grabbed Maddie's leash off the hook, the little mutt began hopping in excitement.

"You want some gelato? You want to see Booker? So he can feed you all the bad things? I know he's gonna give you that gelato."

She clipped on and headed out the front. Maddie loved her basso-voiced boss. That man would feed a dog from his own plate before taking a bite himself.

As they walked the seven blocks to the shop, her brain went racing again. It was always the case before a mission, before she had anything to wrap her head around or prepare for. It was pure churn of aimless anxiety.

It always seemed to go back to the water, to the one day that had scrambled her life.

CHAPTER
FOUR

———

IT WAS HER FAULT.

She had known better.

She should not have been so tough and stupid.

She was eleven weeks into BUD/S. She'd made it through the punishing first phase of physical conditioning. She had earned the right to be there, where no woman had ever been before.

It had been an easy dive, a UDT mission at twilight. At depth, they were twenty-seven feet down, carrying Twin 80s, double cylinders of eighty cubic feet of oxygen. All they had to do was rig the explosives onto a horned scully, nothing more than a concrete block with steel rails spiking out of it, designed to gash open the hulls of passing boats.

She'd felt ear congestion that morning, felt the intense pressure as she descended, but did not want to have to re-do the dive. So she went anyway. By this point in the training, pain and discomfort were constant companions anyway.

She had been cranking away to set the explosives when an underwater wave swept into her.

For a second, it had felt like nothing more than an unseen shove, but then there was a sudden, shattering pain in her ear. She felt something warm flowing out of her head, the fluid from her semi-circular canal.

A burst eardrum.

The world spun around her and dissolved into vertigo. She swallowed back her panic as every direction became a blurry mess.

Focus! Find your bearings! Just one fixed point!

The anchor line.

She spotted the rope hanging down from one of the boats and grabbed at it for her life. As she hauled herself up hand over hand, she felt like she was still sinking. Her head broke the surface, lolling in hapless circles.

They pulled her into the boat, her right ear pouring water and blood. The instructor was a medical corpsman who checked her out immediately. The moment he drew back and she saw the expression on his face, she knew.

It was over.

She'd been the freak from day one.

Two hundred and twenty-one men in peak condition had assembled for the hardest ordeal of their lives. When they saw the Amazon standing in their midst, they gawked, chuckled, leered, or mocked. As the surf crashed against that Coronado beach and the echo of instructors roared in the distance, she kept her eyes straight ahead.

The most vivid memory of that day was seeing the infamous brass bell...the bell you rang when you couldn't take it anymore and you had to declare that you were quitting. She made a vow that day to never touch the thing. Yet it was another thing entirely to convince the men in the brown T-shirts of that.

The entire mission of instructors seemed to be to drive the trainees to that bell, but they had a special spike in their arsenals for the only female enrollee in the BUD/S program. She fought, clamored, scrapped, and bled like all the others, though. She'd struggled on the O-course, once crashing off that hellish obstacle line onto the concrete eight feet below. That fall alone had nearly ended her then and there.

One of the instructors had seen it and decided it was the proof he'd been looking for that she didn't belong, that it was time for her to end this farce and quit. So he drove her to misery, doling out extra kicks to her ribs while they lay in the surf and then did endless pushups on the sand.

Then it was Hell Week, and she heard that bell ring, over and over and over...

On the third day, that same especially brutal instructor was hounding her, spewing all of the demeaning and sexist garbage he could imagine. That afternoon, Ridley was plodding out of the mess hall after a chow run. She and her crew had paddled miles out on the ocean, paddled back in, carried the boats on their heads up the beach and kept running laps around the mess hall until they were called in to eat. There, they had ten minutes of rest to shovel down the food before it was back to the boats.

As she was emerging, that instructor descended on her with a verbal mace.

"Where do you think you're goin', fuckin' Cinderella? This beach isn't made for you and I don't give a shit if you're here for dicks or dykes, you're holding these men back! You're failing your boat crew and you're fuckin' embarrassing the Navy. Thanks for giving all us instructors a laugh, it's been a fine goddamn time, but that bell is screaming your fuckin' name now!"

She could barely move her leaden legs, but right then something snapped in her. The silent part of her endurance was gone.

"Sir, the only way you're getting me out of here is in a body bag, sir!"

His glare was so intense that she thought he was actually going to strike her. She met his eyes with titanic resolve. He could see it. The ghost of a smile skimmed his lips.

"Return to your boat!" he barked.

His reign of targeted terror was over. From that day, she was just another soldier. Worthy of raking over the coals, for certain, but with no more distinction than the man beside her. Though for her, that was not good enough. Man or not, she had an insatiable fire in her to be the *best* in her class. She wanted to win every challenge not to show that she could best the men, but simply to be the best.

The men eventually absorbed her into the ranks with respect. She had earned her place there along with every one of them. They would be brothers and sister-in-arms.

Heath Larkin had been by her side for the whole of her BUD/S training. He never scoffed or patronized, but always pushed her as she pushed him, grinding out their boat carries with their lungs burning and sand scratching their eyelids.

Adam Buchmann was the craziest guy she'd ever known, but the ultimate team player who led by fearless example. He always thought up the most efficient ways to clean equipment, even if that meant taking it into the shower with him.

Rob Houston was cool to the bone, a soul man who went

into a strange zen on ruck runs. That white boy from Butte, Montana could also sing like Al Green.

They all went on to pass BUD/S. They all became SEALs.

Where would she be now, if that unseen surge of water hadn't collided with her that day? She had already made it to phase two, where the class had winnowed to only sixty-eight. Everything had gotten harder. Pool competency was the Hell Week of their dive phase, when instructors sabotaged them mid-swim, ripping off fins and masks, tying regulator hoses in knots, trying to induce maximum stress.

Survive and improvise and sort it out.

That was until the instructors hit them with an obstacle designed to be impossible to overcome. It was only there to test a student's limits, to see who persevered for an ungodly amount of time, and who would give up like a puppy failing obedience school.

She nearly passed out from stubbornness during hers, until finally an instructor waved her up to the surface. She had gagged and coughed for a full minute. Heath laughed and clapped her on the back, told her she was a psycho, but a psycho who'd just beaten the rest of her class.

A week later, it would all be for nothing. Unable to ever dive to required depth again, she was discharged from BUD/S on medical grounds.

She would never become the first female Navy SEAL.

It was over.

CHAPTER
FIVE

———

BOOKER SETTLED onto the stone ledge of a planter, holding a cup of chocolate peanut butter gelato. Maddie sat at his feet, her gaze glistening up at him. Ridley stayed standing, spooning dulce de leche into her mouth. Henri stood beside her, somehow looking as elegant as a GQ model as he ate coconut gelato. It looked nothing like a clandestine meeting of some of the most skilled operatives in the nation.

"It's not Ben & Jerry's, but this Italian stuff—" said Booker, jabbing his spoon, "it's got potential."

He dropped a dob of gelato down to Maddie, who snapped it up with delight.

"I got a call the other day from a contact within the French Ministry of Culture," said Booker. "He works in the 'architecture and inheritance' department...told me they'd found something

20

inside Notre Dame while doing the renovations. There was no record of it being there, and it's not like anything they've seen before. It's an iron sarcophagus."

"Iron," repeated Ridley.

"Did they usually bury people directly under churches?" said Henri.

"No, it's unusual. More unusual that the coffin is made of iron. Extremely unusual that it's unnamed, beneath the most famous cathedral in the world. It was in the transept area, close to the choir, which signals somebody of importance. The Ministry has managed to keep it quiet until they could understand more about it, but they won't have much longer before it hits the media. Because come on, that's pretty fascinating."

While fascinating, this was not the kind of thing they'd normally be assigned to investigate. There had to be another angle, something stranger, something more sinister.

"Any markings?" asked Ridley through a mouthful of dulce de leche.

"There were some...*exhortations* carved into the stone that had been placed above the coffin. Curses? Blessings? All in French. Seems they're Bible verses...the promises of the Lord to help protect against the forces of evil."

"They're gonna open it, aren't they," said Henri. "Never open the cursed sarcophagus. No one learns from the movies, do they?"

"Oh, they're going to open it," said Booker, "and you're going to be there for it. Invited by the Ministry of Culture to be off-the-record observers."

"Trip to France? Let's go," said Ridley.

Booker gestured to Henri.

"As you can surely tell, Henri here grew up in Haiti, speaks superb French. And Ridley, you've got at least half—three quarters?—of all the languages in Europe."

Henri gave her an appraising look.

"I moved a lot," she explained, "and listened a lot."

"Talked a lot," said Booker. "The opening is two days from now. You're both booked on a flight out of Dulles tomorrow afternoon, but we have to be *discreet*. You know Chavas is trying to talk the Palestinians into peace talks."

French President Christophe Chavas was confident, dashing, and bore more than a passing resemblance to a young Alain Delon. He had run to the left during national elections, but was soon sobered into centrist positions. He'd bolstered the French economy, cracked down on hives of terrorism within the country, and presented an unflinching posture of integrity and strength with international partners. Now he sought the coveted accomplishment of world affairs: to broker a serious peace deal between the Israelis and Palestinians.

"If the Palestinians sniff out anything about American operatives in Paris on wholly confidential business, they'll bolt. It won't be pretty for Israel, either."

"So I shan't pack my keffiyeh" said Ridley.

They knew what had happened the last time peace talks had collapsed at the eleventh hour. President Clinton had been certain of securing a negotiation between Israeli Prime Minister Ehud Barak and the head of the Palestinian Authority, Yasser Arafat. In the summer of 2000, he'd hosted them at a famous summit at Camp David to hash out a peaceable agreement. It did not go as the American president had dreamt.

Shortly after the talks dissolved, a tidal wave of death engulfed Israel. Suicide bombings ripped through Jerusalem. Israeli reservists were lynched by mobs. Rocket attacks and drive-by shootings and deadly riots brought a clash of Israeli forces down to quell the violence. The Second Intifada had begun.

Years later, a Palestinian Fatah official would admit to the planning of it. Just as the peace talks were starting to derail, Arafat was already giving the green light to begin the bloody attacks back home. A senior Hamas official said that Arafat had armed the terror group just after he left Camp David. It had not been an outburst of spontaneous aggression, but rather a top-down premeditated mass killing. Thousands were left dead.

"The US has nothing to do with these proposed talks, though," said Henri. "We'll stay far under the radar, but what would be the point of Palestinians sabotaging their own peace talks?"

Booker grimaced.

"Reason has so little to do with anything in foreign affairs. It's ego and self-interest with heaps of hatred."

"And messiah complexes," added Ridley.

"Those, too. President Voller..." said Booker, shaking his head grimly, "ugly collection of all those, and deep-soaked in pettiness. When the Palestinians *and* the Israelis refused his tacked-on invitation to hold these talks, be the mediator? Man threw a TV remote at an aide then ranted about it all night on his social media. Great face for the US, huh? Sad state of America when the French president is first choice for peace in the Middle East."

Chavas was positioning himself as the premier voice of the European Union. Even the proud British and the stoic Germans were deferring with respect to his leadership. He was becoming something of a swoon-worthy celebrity abroad, and every mention of him enraged the American president.

"He's just trying to get them to the table, but he couldn't really have picked a touchier time. Passover this year happens to fall on Palm Sunday for the Eastern Orthodox, which is Easter for the Western church, *and that also happens* to coincide with Ramadan this year. First time this has happened in decades. God only knows why Chavas is trying to engage them now."

"Maybe they'll go to France for talks and fall in love with the cheese. It could be peace in our time," said Henri.

"Don't worry," said Ridley, "we won't bother France at all. Unless we have to battle the ghost of Charlemagne or something in front of the Eiffel Tower."

Booker finished his gelato and held it down for Maddie to lick clean.

"Well, the viral videos would be spectacular," he said. "What a way to end our careers that would be."

CHAPTER
SIX

———

WASHINGTON, D.C.

I<small>N THE</small> C<small>ENTRAL</small> I<small>NTELLIGENCE</small> A<small>GENCY</small>, there were divisions within divisions, and divisions within those that were so secretive that only a handful outside of them knew they existed at all. One of the major branches within the agency was the National Clandestine Service. There were plenty of departments that would show up on any diagram available to the public, and then there were the ones that would never be seen, never be officially acknowledged.

Osprey Division was born in the early 1940s under the directive of William J. Donovan. He was a World War I veteran and diplomat to Europe who—years before the creation of the CIA—had lobbied for a centralized, nonmilitary intelligence agency. He was finally appointed to a newly created position by President Roosevelt, with the title of Coordinator of Information. As the battle for Europe intensified against the Nazis, the tales of Heinrich Himmler's obsession with occultism reached the new staff of analysts and intelligence gatherers. It was not enough to just hear the rumors, Donovan insisted to the president. They had to engage, to seek out the mystical objects that the Nazis were pursuing. They had to get them first.

It was a hard sell for Roosevelt, who was not a man of mystic spiritual beliefs. *Just in case...*was the refrain that Donovan employed. It worked, and so Osprey was born in silence, a cadre of committed and discreet operatives who could travel anywhere, investigate anything, spy on anyone, and obtain whatever bizarre and confounding objects of desire that they found.

Eventually, they were folded into the CIA, where they had remained since. There were no more than a dozen operatives within Osprey at any given time. Each was hand-selected and recruited for an exceptional balance of skills, temperament, drive, and openness to possibilities. They would all eventually encounter things that would alter their worldview, that could rock their perception of everything they believed about life. Mission assignments tended to begin with little information. It was essential that they have the adaptability and willingness to engage in anything they came cross.

Booker Douglas was eleventh in the line of Osprey directors.

He'd joined the CIA out of Syracuse, graduating with an absurd GPA and double majors in Middle Eastern Studies and Linguistics. He also had the promise of a vivacious young economics student named Holly, who had made him laugh so hard on their first date at the theater that an usher had escorted them out into the lobby. They got married and settled in Yorktown, but it wasn't long before Booker was sent out into the field.

At first she'd joined him at his posting in Poland, then in

Belgium with their newborn Amelia. By the time he was posted in Morocco, they had twin boys as well, Ty and Steven. It was the last location assignment on which they'd join him. He had grown too valuable to the Middle Eastern initiatives of the US government, and the places where he was needed had become too dangerous. The Douglases moved back to the States, and Booker went dark, into the bowels of some of the most sinister places on earth.

He never told his family what he did, or where he had been. His life was a void to his own children. He struggled to show sympathy for the angst of his teenagers, when his mind still echoed with the ragged death of those who spewed destruction. Holly tolerated and, to her credit, tried to understand. In the end, it was not enough to share a life, a home, a bed. They divorced, and she moved down to the Florida coast. He had failed as a husband, but held onto the pride he had as a father. His kids were good, well-adjusted young adults, kind and honest and striving for their own success in the world.

It was shortly after his divorce that Booker had been approached by a ranking official with the National Clandestine Service of the Agency. She had asked him to join a division so covert that it was nearly invisible to the ranks. What he came to see within the mission field changed his life.

At fifty-four, he'd been on the job as Director of Osprey for the last eight years. He was convinced that he was neither showing nor feeling any signs of burnout. And he was terribly convincing to himself. He lived in a spacious condo in Westmoreland Hills, across the Potomac River from CIA headquarters. He'd always felt that having a body of water between home and office bolstered a healthy boundary.

His grown children urged him to try dating again, knowing their dad's group of darts and trivia buddies was not enough to stave off that seeping middle-aged loneliness. He'd tried going out a few times, but the way he had to lie in wave after wave of conversation felt soul-crippling. He didn't want to be the man who lied, but he also could not be the man who told the truth.

Now, he was sending two of his favorite operatives out on pure speculation. Yet he had seen enough in his career to know, sometimes the sure things turned out to be duds. Sometimes the most innocuous assignments threatened to turn the world upside down. Once upon a time it had been *him* discovering which was which. Tonight he would sit back on his leather couch with his nightly highball of Bulleit, watch the news, and maybe take in another piece of his neighbor's sweet potato pie before putting on a Steve McQueen movie.

Everyone wears out in the end.

CHAPTER
SEVEN

———

WASHINGTON, D.C.

RIDLEY PACKED UP. Only carry-on, go for layers, just the essentials. No weapons, of course. Practical shoes. Anything else she might need for an action, she could buy or pick up at a safehouse in just about any country in the world.

She called her neighbor Ana to take Maddie, as usual. This was the worst part of her job, saying goodbye to that fluffy, yearning little face. Ridley found it crushing every time that she couldn't explain and couldn't promise to be back soon. All dogs knew was the leaving, and the missing.

Ridley kept few friends, but her social circle was broad. Broader than she'd have preferred, really. People seemed to like her, despite her intimidating stature, and her skill with people —which served her extremely well as an operative—led to an aggravating number of people wondering where she went every so often.

She snuggled and pet Maddie goodbye in the kitchen of Ana's apartment.

"Sweetest girl," she murmured, and kissed the top of her dog's head.

"We'll take a walk down to the waterfront. She loves chasing those pigeons," assured Ana, a lithe twenty-something who looked like a dancer and dressed like a boho.

"Thanks, babe. I have no idea how long I'll be. A week? Maybe two? If you have to buy more food, just Venmo me."

"We might get takeout every night," said Ana with a wink. "Have a great time."

Maddie sat in watchful silence as Ridley closed the door behind her.

Ridley took an Uber to Dulles, where she met Henri in the terminal, eating only the yellows from a pack of Starburst. He offered her the rest. She thanked him and pocketed the candy with amusement.

She was somewhat surprised by his manicured appearance. He wore gray herringbone trousers and a black sweater beneath a black jacket. Every item of clothing looked tailored. She'd read his file the night before, just as he'd surely read hers.

When she had played with him, she'd gotten a sense for his calculations, his instincts. He loved puzzles, board games, and logic problems of all sorts. No wonder Booker had paired them together. She had been an analyst in her final years with the Navy, but didn't seek out puzzles just for the thrill of solving them.

They sat at a distance from the other passengers. Their subjects of conversation were not for public consumption. Positioning herself to Henri's right so that she could hear properly out of her left ear, she began with her questions. He laid out the highlights and lowlights. Born in Cap-Haitien, Haiti, abandoned to a missionary's orphanage.

"Do you remember your mother at all?"

"No, but I heard I was one of seven that she gave up. She really should have stopped having sex by the time she gave up the fourth."

The education there at the orphanage was surprisingly good, enabling him to get a visa and a sponsor to travel to the States. He ended up at Philips Andover for high school, and the day he turned eighteen, he applied for citizenship. By that time he was so patriotic for his new country that he hosted a barbecue every 4th of July, where he made his friends listen to a passionate recitation of the Declaration of Independence.

"Do you have it memorized?"

Henri laughed, "The first two paragraphs. Do you want to hear them?"

"If you stand up on the seat for the whole terminal to hear, then yes."

He gave a vigorous shake of his head. "But I think I was meant to be American. You're more hopeful here, more direct. I like that."

After that, he went to Boston University for college, graduating with a degree in criminal justice. Three years in the Drug Enforcement Agency in New York City felt like bailing water out of a sinking ship. He was anxious to move on, to serve his adopted nation on the home soil that had offered him sanctuary. So he applied to one of the most stringent agencies in the country: the Secret Service.

"Don't they admit, like, nobody?"

"One percent."

"You must have included a headshot."

He made his way into the Uniformed Divisions Emergency Response Team. They were responsible for the physical security of the White House grounds, and any diplomatic missions with the D.C. area. He trained to be one of their snipers. Through that rifle scope, the whole world was clarified, heightened, slowed. He became their crack shot, one of the best to ever pass through the Service.

"Married?"

He had been, for eight years, to a raven-haired woman named Mita who'd worked as a sports journalist covering the Nationals. When they split, he spiraled.

"I didn't do well when I got...unmarried. I had been kind of Catholic growing up, but didn't think about it much as an adult. Until I walked into an Anglican church on Christmas Eve. I was drunk and the vicar knew it. He prayed for me right there and then invited me to his home to have Christmas with his family. I didn't have the guts to go the next day, but...I went back the next week, and then I got down on my knees and begged God for a new heart. And he gave me one, and I loved Him for it. It saved everything for me. I would have been kicked out of the Service if I'd gone another month like that."

Ridley was a bit taken aback by his honesty. Operatives like them were so accustomed to faking it, to answering obliquely or downright lying. Maybe he thought that someone else in the same line of work would be someone he could actually be honest with. She was touched, but didn't know what to do with it.

"That's a serious conversion story," she said.

"Yeah. I stayed in the Service for another four years after that. And then Booker Douglas called."

"Yeah, that call," echoed Ridley.

"And you were *the* woman in BUD/S?"

She nodded.

"We heard about you back then. They didn't release your name, but some former SEALs I met knew of you. I read about the medical discharge."

"Just whisper all your secrets in my right ear," she said, tapping the side of her head. "And I'll carry them nowhere."

"Well, Quasimodo was deaf, wasn't he?"

She leaned back and furrowed her brow at him. "Is that your first consolation? A socially awkward hunchback shared my condition?"

"See, it could be worse."

"Yeah, 'C' for effort there."

"Notre Dame!" he protested. "Hunchback. Deafness. I think it makes sense."

Ridley watched a young mother down the row fuss with her toddler, trying to get the child to sit quietly with an iPad.

Could anyone these days raise a kid without the almighty screen?

"So, is your religion okay with digging up a church to mess with a buried body?"

"Who says there's a body?" said Henri.

Touché.

CHAPTER
EIGHT

————

PARIS, FRANCE

RIDLEY AND HENRI landed in De Gaulle airport the following day. Most of the flight had been spent studying the history of Notre Dame's construction and the fire that nearly destroyed it. Research was the part of the job that was wholly unglamorous. For Henri, every scrap of history seemed to light him up with excitement. Ridley just wanted the bullet points.

They checked into a small hotel on Rue Jacob and grabbed a quick meal at a bistro nearby. Henri ate like he was still scraping for food in the orphanage. Ridley had forgotten how damn good the cheese there really was.

Though they strolled by the glittering Eiffel Tower, she was not relaxed for the sightseeing. The smell of baking bread and crushed garlic mingled with wafts of cigarette smoke and an acrid burning from the metro vents. She spotted the bell towers of Notre Dame in the distance, bone-white against the darkness. Victor Hugo had wondered over its majesty and wound tragedy through its most famous tale, yet the cathedral had already been standing for half a millennia by the time he wrote of it.

How many more secrets did that place hold?

The next morning, they walked to the Louvre in the chill spring air. They bypassed the teeming line queued up by the glass pyramid, heading instead to the Porte des Lions. They had just stopped to ask security to notify their contact, when a trim woman wearing a lanyard came striding up to them.

"Madame Samaras? Monsieur Michel? I'm Claudine Gaspar," she said, extending her hand. "Delighted to meet you."

Her English held only the faintest brush of a Parisian accent. She was in her early sixties, lovely, with both an old-fashioned aristocratic bearing, and a sense of wisdom that one could trust. She was one of the head archaeologists at the National Institute for Preventive Archaeological Research, or INRAP.

"We're happy to be here," said Ridley as they shook hands.

"Please come with me," said Claudine.

Security waved them past, and they followed her down the hall, her heels clacking on marble.

"I understand you're here on behalf of Mr. Douglas. Our Minister of Culture has maintained very good friends on the American side. Are you familiar with INRAP?"

Of course. We would never travel for a mission without a thorough briefing.

But it was always best to let them explain.

"Somewhat," said Ridley.

"In this country, we are very careful about our cultural history. It's something to preserve, to cherish. Our Institute conducts diagnostic operations on delicate historical sites, among other things. We are the guardians of the great archaeological heritage of France, but we also work with teams that conduct digs in other parts of the world. We have a marvelous relationship with our Egyptian branch."

Though the spiel was incredibly pompous, Claudine had such a brightness to her that it almost sounded charming.

"You oversee all of this for the Ministry of Culture?" said Henri.

"We were the first call," said Claudine with a grin that was surprisingly cheeky.

As they passed through the Spanish wing, both Americans found it hard to not linger among the masterpieces that surrounded them.

"Have either of you been here before, to the Louvre?"

"No," replied Henri, gazing at the paintings.

FRENCH: *"A few times when I was a teenager,"* said Ridley.

Claudine swiveled her head in surprise.

"You speak French! And I assume you, Monsieur, speak some as well?"

FRENCH: *"I had to learn as a boy in Haiti,"* said Henri.

"Ah, wonderful!"

They turned into the wing that housed French paintings, and Henri's steps slowed as he began to outright gawk.

"I'm sorry for the rush," said Claudine, seeing his sense of awe. "You should stay after for a full tour. I will be very honest, though, I don't understand why the Minister wanted American observers present for this. We know from the burial location that this sarcophagus must have been laid there in the fourteenth century. What could this possibly have to do with a country that did not exist for another four hundred years?"

There's the French snobbery.

She led them to an elevator and pushed the "down" button.

"Whatever the reason, we're honored to witness something like this," said Ridley, hoping the charm worked in return.

"I must insist on discretion, of course. You may take photographs for professional use to take back to your agency, but if they are published or shared anywhere else," she smiled a warning, "there may be a crisis between our allied countries."

The elevator doors opened. They stepped in, and Claudine scanned her lanyard to access one of the exclusive lower levels.

"What is strange to us immediately is the element. The coffin is made of iron, not lead. With the renovation, workers are discovering more iron in Notre Dame than anyone had realized. There were hundreds of big iron staples in the stones of the roof, forming the holy cross above the cathedral."

"That's unusual?" asked Ridley.

"In a Gothic monument of that era, it would be the first of its kind. But that's not the strangest part. We haven't seen a burial space before with these kinds of holy curses scratched into the rock around it. That's very strange."

The elevator opened, and they stepped into the underground Louvre.

Claudine led them into the outer office of a subterranean lab. Though it was brightly lit, there was something suffocating about the thought of working down here all day.

"We have cleaned the exterior thoroughly of any lead dust," said Claudine. "We should no longer need masks."

She pushed through the next door into a spacious, sterile lab. In the center, on a long metal table, lay the sealed sarcophagus. Beside it, an empty table. Around those, an array of odd tools, computers, and scanning technology that looked like medical equipment.

At the computer bay sat a lanky, serious-looking man in his thirties. He glanced up when they entered. Claudine gestured to him.

"This is Nicolas Broussard, our lab technician. He will be recording everything today. Nicolas, these are our American observers, Madame Samaras and Monsieur Michel."

He mumbled hello with a nod.

"We're just waiting for our technicians, one moment," said Claudine, moving off to another room. "Please, don't touch anything, of course."

While Henri wandered over to make chat with Nicolas, Ridley stepped closer to the table. She had not expected it to be so small, almost child-sized. The iron casing was slightly rusted, but in very good shape for its age. The underbelly of Notre Dame had indeed protected it. It looked simple, no decorative touches of any kind carved into the plain surface. She bent over to peer at the seams.

It was welded shut.

That can't be normal.

Claudine re-emerged, now wearing nitrile gloves, with two more techs wearing full white crime-scene suits, hoods and all. They sported masks and booties over their shoes.

"We're going to need these," said Claudine, handing protective glasses to Ridley and Henri.

They both pulled them on as one of the techs tugged on gloves, then picked up a laser cutting tool. It began.

The tech cut a meticulous line around the entire sarcophagus, separating top from bottom. When he set down his equipment, Ridley and Henri exchanged a glance. The technicians braced themselves at the head and the foot of the container. They lifted off the top.

Ridley strained forward to see, until Claudine beckoned her and Henri to approach.

There was no body in this sarcophagus. The inside of it was lined with salt, too much to have simply accumulated. There was nearly a pound of salt scattered along the bottom. All along the inside surface were etchings.

In the center was an urn. Inscribed on the outside of it was a single word in Arabic.

"Do either of you speak Arabic?" asked Claudine.

"It's not one of my languages," said Ridley, "but look at these inscriptions. They're in French as well as Portuguese, Latin, Olde English, Spanish..."

Henri pulled out his camera phone and began snapping photos. "You said this was buried in the fourteenth century?"

Claudine nodded. "But what in God's name is an Arabic urn doing under Notre Dame? There was never any Arab conquest of France."

"There was a lot happening then," he said. "The end of the Templars, the Bubonic plague, the Hundred Years' War..."

The archaeologist gave a faint smile and a quick arch of the eyebrows. She was a little impressed, but not distracted from her examination of it.

"A quarter of the population died from the plague then, and Paris was the biggest city in Europe."

"It's strange to have no name on this though, right?" asked Ridley. "No date?"

"Yes. It's strange. To be buried where it was—in the transept, near the choir, closer to the holy places of the cathedral—means *importance*."

"Who would have had to approve that? Who could have actually buried it there? And wouldn't an Arabic urn be...I dunno, blasphemous? There isn't even a body!"

Claudine gave her a long, serious look, then bent down for closer inspection. "We have never seen something like this before. I think there's something beneath the urn."

She asked in French for one of the techs to pick it up. He obliged, gently lifting the urn with both hands.

Beneath it, set into a molding carved to fit its shape, was the hilt of a saber. The broken base of a golden blade was still attached. On it was a stream of elegant Arabic script.

"That's not—" started Henri, but a yelp of pain interrupted.

The tech holding the urn gasped, and dropped it.

The urn shattered on the floor of the lab.

CHAPTER NINE

———

CLAUDINE CRIED OUT.

Shards of dry clay skittered across the floor.

The tech who had been holding it cradled his hands, groaning. His gloves were steaming as if they'd been seared.

From the smashed pieces of the urn, wisps of smoke spiraled up. At first it seemed like the dissipation of something within the broken vessel, except the darkness grew thicker, into a vortex. They all reeled back, staring, as a ripple of heat scorched through the laboratory.

A shape started to emerge from the smoke, swirling black.

Ridley grabbed for the closest weapon she could see: the laser cutter. Henri hit record and set the camera phone on the table.

The darkness formed in front of them, nearly the shape of a

man, but there was no flesh to it. It was vaporous black. Fire seemed to ooze from its hands. A pair of eyes flamed above the volcanic gash of a mouth. Fiery light blazed from cracks in its ashen torso and arms. Its legs looked like charcoal pillars, and yet they didn't seem to carry any weight, as if this thing was insubstantial.

Broussard shot up out of his desk chair, sheet-white. The techs scrambled backward, garbling French curses behind their masks. Claudine gaped, riveted in place.

The creature of flame and smoke seemed to look around, then contracted inward. Ridley gripped the laser cutter tightly, ready to flip the switch as if it was a lightsaber. She had no idea what it could do against this thing.

Then the thing's flaming eyes snapped wide open, the dark torso swelled, and heat roared from its mouth. The searing blast forced every one of them back again, wincing. The creature looked at the remains of the urn on the ground, then at the sarcophagus. It seemed to hesitate when it saw the broken saber hilt.

Then it turned to one of the techs, and lunged.

They thought he would go up in flames when the creature touched his crêpe-thin suit, but something more terrifying happened. The thing seemed to melt *into* him.

Claudine gasped, "No, Jean-Louis..."

The tech convulsed once, and turned back to the sarcophagus.

Henri followed his eyes. Jean-Louis was staring at the hilt. Henri leapt for it first.

The masked tech was somehow, inexplicably, faster.

He snatched up the hilt and smashed it across the incoming Henri's jaw. The blow sent him stumbling. Ridley swung the laser cutter like a baseball bat. The tech dodged it and front-kicked her. The force was astonishing, hurling her back into a wooden cabinet.

"Jean-Louis!" yelled Broussard, backing into a corner, trembling, but trying to distract his colleague.

The tech seemed unbothered. He clutched the saber hilt tightly, and bolted out of the lab.

"*Oh, mon Dieu, oh mon Dieu,*" mumbled Claudine, shaking as she tried to stand.

Henri staggered, looking concussed.

He can't get away.

It was the only thing that mattered in that moment. Ridley scrambled to her feet and launched down the hall.

A man wearing a full-body white crime scene suit running through the halls of the Louvre would conceivably be stopped by security, just for weirdness alone. As Ridley raced to the Porte des Lions exit, she could see the shocked expressions of visitors, which meant she was surely following in the wake of the fleeing tech.

As she tore past the security entrance line, she heard urgent calls for assistance crackling over the radios. She sprinted out the door.

Outside, she had only to follow the trail of stunned looks across the courtyard, until she spotted a flash of white. It was Jean-Louis, standing by a Volkswagen that had pulled over on the side of the Place du Carrousel. He seemed to be speaking calmly to the driver through the window. Ridley ran full tilt.

She was only a few meters away when the blue Volkswagen pulled off the curb. Jean-Louis straightened up and turned. It was barely in time to see his pursuer before she decked him to the ground. Ridley tore off his mask and goggles.

FRENCH: "*Where is it? Jean-Louis, give it to me!*"

But Jean-Louis looked stunned, dazed, as if he had no idea where he was. She patted him down, nearly ripping at the thin suit. He did not have the saber piece. She looked up to see the blue Volkswagen stalling in traffic.

Well, shit.

"Ridley!"

She turned to see Henri running toward her.

"Keep him!" she yelled back, pointing down at the bewildered tech before leaping off him.

She had no weapon to hijack a car. Traffic was starting to flow. There was no time to wonder. It was much easier to yank a motorcycle rider off their vehicle than it was to drag a driver out of a car. Thankfully, there was no shortage of motorcyclists in Paris.

At that moment, a young man had pulled over to the courtyard curb on his BMW GS bike. Ridley glanced back to be sure that Henri had control of Jean-Louis. She approached the biker acting like a flirty American tourist with a dazzling grin, before hauling him off balance and leaping astride the bike. She sped off from his outraged cries.

The Volkswagen was well ahead, just clearing the sprawling courtyard of the Louvre, turning onto Rue de Rivoli. It had just passed through the intersection when the light went red. Traffic ahead of her slowed.

Whatever just happened, he has to have the saber piece.

Ridley veered up onto the stone walkway, slicing through panicked tourists before jolting back onto the pavement on Rivoli. The Volkswagen was speeding, erratic, drawing all the angry horns. They raced past clothing stores, perfumers, cafés, and art shops along what seemed like the most French assortment of city blocks that could exist. She knew this part of the city, but could only guess at where this accomplice was going.

The car pulled right, down a shady tree-lined avenue. She

cut a tight corner after it, and realized they were about to cross the stately Pont au Change. That bridge was taking them to Île de la Cité, the small isle of Notre Dame. Also on that tiny island was the Palais de Justice, the heart of the country's justice system.

Her mind started ripping through terroristic possibilities. She had not expected the sudden downshift when the Volkswagen pulled over and parked illegally in front of a restaurant. Slowing the bike, she pulled off just past the gilded iron gate of the Justice building.

The driver got out. He was a nondescript Frenchman of average build, in his thirties with dark hair. His sneakers were green and white, and his stride was unusually strong, as though he was being powered forward. He headed straight for the gate to Sainte-Chapelle, and flashed something at the policeman on duty. The guard let him through into the Justice courtyard.

As Ridley rushed to keep him in sight, the officer stepped in front, gripping a FAMAS bullpup rifle.

FRENCH: *"Madame, madame! You cannot enter. You need a pass."*

"A pass? I'm trying to catch up with my boyfriend. He came through a moment ago. He must have thought I was already inside," said Ridley, trying to peer past him.

"I'm sorry, but I can't let you through. You need to buy a ticket."

"A ticket?"

"Yes, for the chapel."

"Can I buy one from you?"

"No, madame. You need to do it online, or on the app."

Ridley whipped out her phone, trying to conceal her fury. She had to search for the app, and as she waited for it to download, nearly twitching with impatience, she texted Henri.

SAINTE-CHAPELLE

The second her digital purchase went through, the guard

waved her past. She ran past the iron gates, through the parking lot, and into the towering Gothic structure.

Ridley hurried through the lower chapel, with its low arches and deep blues and reds. Tourists milled about the postcard stands, but the Volkswagen driver was not among them. She sprinted up the narrow spiraling staircase, and into the upper chapel.

The grandeur of the room was a mosaic of color unlike any other in the world. Intricate glass walls stretched upward into the dark vaulted ceiling. It was the most splendid display of stained glass in the world, the crowning glory of the art that glowed in sunlight.

Ridley had been here before, had gawked at every foot of the famous chapel. Now, she had eyes only for the sightseers. Her eyes raked from face to face, until she saw him. The dark hair, the green and white shoes.

He was standing in the middle of the inlaid stone floor, staring up like every other tourist. She started casually toward him.

Ridley was only ten feet away when she heard him mutter something. Then he stretched his arms wide.

The walls of the chapel imploded.

Every window shattered as if a bomb had detonated outside. Colored glass rained down on the screaming visitors. Ridley dropped to one knee, shielding her face with both arms. The chapel filled with shrieking horror. She lifted her head to see panicked tourists running for the exits, some still filming on their phones.

The Volkswagen driver was trying to mingle into the fleeing crowd. Ridley had no weapon but herself, but she couldn't let him escape. She launched herself, tackling him from behind, into a carpet of crushed glass. He shouted in surprise as she cranked his wrist up behind his back, pinning him to the ground. The man kept yelling indignantly, as though he had no idea why she was detaining him. She frisked him as well as she could without being able to get to his front. There was no sign of the saber hilt.

She cursed under her breath.

Twenty seconds later, Palais de Justice guards burst into the chapel, rifles raised.

CHAPTER
TEN

———

THE WINDOWS of Sainte-Chapelle formed the most glorious array of stained glass in the world. King Louis IX commissioned the chapel to be built in 1242, and only six years later it stood as one of the most magnificent Gothic structures on earth. Each of the windows was fifteen meters high, and across fifteen windows each pane told a story. More than a thousand scenes laid out the biblical history of the world, leading up to the moment that the holy relics were brought to Paris.

On this day, those legendary windows lay in ruins, pulverized across the stone floor of the chapel. A bomb squad with explosive-sniffing dogs was brought in to sweep the lower chapel, the courtyard, and the Palais de Justice next door. The entire block was shut down, though camera crews were camped along the perimeter in droves. The nation watched the coverage, sickened, in utter disbelief. Within only a few years of the burning of Notre Dame, another of their national monuments was destroyed. This one was fully stripped of its splendor, and no one knew the means or motive.

Henri had arrived just moments after the implosion. He'd found Ridley when she was escorted downstairs by the responding officers. Every visitor had been corralled and detained in the parking lot, awaiting questioning. They watched as the Volkswagen man was hauled out in handcuffs and put into a waiting car.

"He looks like Jean-Louis did when we caught up to him," Ridley said to Henri, "like he has no idea what just happened. Almost concussed."

"He had *nothing* on him? No detonator?"

"I couldn't pat him down properly."

"I should have searched his car. It's gone now."

"I mean, I was right behind him. He would have had to climb up and lay explosives along the exterior of every window without being seen—since they exploded inward—imploded? Whatever. There's no possible way that's what happened. He only had about forty seconds on me."

Henri shook his head. "Can we mention the fire demon in the lab?"

"Yeah," said Ridley, "we need to talk about what the hell that was."

"You're about to get questioned," said Henri.

He moved toward her just slightly, intimately, how a loving boyfriend would be keeping close to a woman who'd just witnessed a disaster.

Ridley followed his eyes to a plainclothes man emerging from the chapel, flanked by two Police Nationale officers. He had a smoky complexion and looked of Algerian descent. His face was serious, thick, and weathered.

"Probably DGSI," she murmured.

Direction Générale de la Sécurité Intérieure, or General Directorate for Internal Security. Founded in 2008, the agency was responsible for counter-terrorism and counter-espionage. Unsurprisingly, they were shadowy, and obscure to most elements of the French public. The CIA did not find them nearly so mysterious.

"An attack happening a stone's throw from the Palais de Justice looks really bad for French security."

The man's sharp gaze found Ridley. He walked over.

"Madame, you are the one who stopped the attacker from escaping?"

"Yeah, that was me," she replied, broadening her American speech to sound more disarming.

She didn't want any of them knowing that she spoke or understood French.

Never give up an advantage.

"I'm Guy Zem," he said, shaking her hand. "I'm an officer with the DGSI, the General Directorate for Internal Security."

"I'm Ridley Samaras," she said, "American, obviously. I am so...so sorry about what happened here. This is just..." she trailed off, looking up at the gaping empty sides of the chapel, "horrible."

"Thank you, yes. Yes, it is," he said, then turned to Henri. "Are you together?"

"Yeah, I'm Henri. I wasn't in the chapel, though. We were gonna meet here but I was running behind just a few minutes. Unbelievable few minutes to miss," he said, shaking his head.

"Michel...are you Haitian?"

"Yes. American now, though."

"Ah, do you speak French?"

"Only a little. Creole is similar."

They couldn't tell if Zem believed them. He turned back to Ridley.

"Thank you for what you did today. Would you be willing to answer some questions for me?"

"Sure. I don't know much about what happened, but I'm happy to help if I can."

He pulled out a little notepad and waterproof pen. This was old-school prepared.

"Did you know the man you tackled?"

"No."

"Hmm. The security guard at the gate said that you claimed he was your boyfriend, but I see..." he glanced at Henri, "maybe we have some problem?"

Ridley winced with a small, practiced sigh.

"Shit, that was the same guy? I'm sorry. I lied. I mean, I lied to the security guard. I saw this man going in ahead of me and I didn't know I needed a ticket until I got up there, so I just," she shrugged, "I tried to convince the guard that I could just follow him in. For free. I'm an asshole, I know. It was cheating. I really have never met the guy in my life."

Zem seemed convinced.

Always confess or make up a smaller, embarrassing lie to cover for a bigger one. The investigator will be satisfied that they caught you in a lie and dug out the truth behind it.

"How long did you spend in the lower chapel?"

"Just passed through. I really came for the big show, upstairs."

"Had you ever been to Sainte-Chapelle before?"

"Once, as a teenager. I was too young and dumb to appreciate it then."

"How long was it after you entered the upper chapel that the attack began?"

"Oh, maybe...it was really quick. I don't know. A minute?"

"Could you please describe it to me?"

"He was just standing there. He stretched his arms out wide. It looked like he had something in his hand, but I don't know what. The windows just—" she made an exploding sound."And it seemed like he was the one who did it, the way he acted. Like he didn't even flinch when the glass blew. So I just thought...I had to stop him. I don't know. It was probably dumb, tackling some guy who just blew up a building. He might have had a weapon," she mused, then added with sudden worry, "Did he?"

"No, madame. You were extremely brave to do what you did then. What do you do for a living?"

"I teach jiu-jitsu."

Close enough.

"Oh," he said, surprised but a little impressed. "Now I understand how you were so capable to keep him restrained. And Monsieur Michel, what is your profession?"

"Nothing as fun as that. I'm a computer programmer."

Appropriately dull. No one ever asked any more questions after that answer.

"Will you be staying in Paris for a few more days? In case we need to ask you more questions."

"Yeah," said Ridley. "We're just across the river at a hotel. I'll give you my number."

She reached for his notebook before he could protest in any dignified manner. Jotting down her phone number, she stole the most discreet glance at the notes he'd taken in French.

Accomplice was the only word she could make out in his handwriting. She handed it back.

"I hope we can help. Do you think it was a bomb? Like, on the outside?" she wondered.

"Madame, we will know soon."

"I hope so. Just so crazy..."

She shook her head again.

"You're free to go," he said, gesturing to one of the nearby officers to allow them out.

"Thanks," said Ridley.

"Good luck," added Henri.

Zem tucked his notebook away, not quite satisfied, not quite suspicious, but his brain ticking away at the possibilities.

CHAPTER
ELEVEN

———

PARIS, FRANCE

THE LAB beneath the Louvre was a wreck of disarray. Jean-Louis had been escorted back downstairs by museum security. He was still in a state of shock. He and the other tech had changed out of their white suits and sat in the break room nearby with cans of cola in front of them.

Claudine's elegant visage had crumbled. Broussard had wanted her to call in another official from INRAP, but she refused to compromise her authority over the situation. By the time Ridley and Henri arrived back on the scene, they had already cleaned up the shards of the urn and laid them out on a metal tray.

The operatives gave their account of what had happened with Jean-Louis and then the Volkswagen driver. Then Ridley told them what had happened at Sainte-Chapelle. The color drained from their faces. Claudine had to grasp for a chair so she wouldn't collapse. For a cultural archaeologist, it must have been a sword through the gut. The most priceless and historical display of stained glass in the world was utterly destroyed. And, it seemed, by some power that had been loosed into the world by her own team.

Broussard turned on the news. The images were even more devastating. Claudine cupped a hand over her mouth as she watched. She would murmur under her breath, and a few tears rolled down her cheeks. Some tourist had caught footage on her iPhone of the exact moment that the windows shattered. Every news channel was looping it on play as reporters needlessly narrated it. The man responsible was positioned in the middle of the chapel, barely visible in the corner of their frame, before the entire image dissolved into a jolting, panicked blur.

"I'm so sorry," said Ridley, genuinely moved. "I'm sorry I couldn't stop him. I had no idea."

She felt a flush of furious disappointment, of humiliated failure. She had been the one on the scene. It was her responsibility to avert disaster. It was why this job existed at all, and she had not performed in the moment of crisis. She hadn't shut down the threat.

"Of course not. Of course you could not have known," said Claudine, brushing her face dry with a sleeve. "What *happened?*" she exclaimed quietly, mostly to herself.

"Look, this is the most important thing we can do," said Henri, looking back at the sarcophagus. "What *did* happen here?"

From his spot leaning against the desk, Broussard raised a speculative finger.

"Just speak, Nicolas. What is it?" snapped Claudine.

"My roommate in—" his voice broke and he had to clear his throat, start again. "My roommate in college studied Islamic and Middle Eastern history. I thought it was so interesting. He wrote a paper on jinn, and I think—" he cleared his throat again, "I think that was a jinn. Maybe."

There's a moment of considered silence, each of them staring at the urn, the sarcophagus.

"I believe we need to think with logic," said Claudine. "We released some heat form, something that quickly disappeared. We cannot say we found a fire demon or some nonsense like that."

Ridley exchanged a glance with Henri. Their job was to report to Booker, and the full report he would get. They'd have no part to play in public statements about INRAP's findings, but the nation would eventually demand to know what was in fact buried under Notre Dame.

Broussard shrugged it away, but seemed unsettled by the dismissal. He took a seat at his desk.

"*Alors*, we will find this out. We keep doing the job," said Claudine.

She pulled out two pairs of nitrile gloves, handing them to Ridley and Henri. With the Frenchwoman, they began to closely inspect the pieces of the urn.

"There's something engraved here," said Claudine, pulling over the arm of the magnifier to peer down at it. "Arabic, again!"

Henri lit up. Puzzles were his drug. He tried to look closer without being too invasive. They began sifting again, hunting for more pieces with script on them. Within moments they had pulled out every engraved shard and began trying to fit them together. The fact that none of them could read Arabic was not helpful.

Eventually they pieced it together, and a single word emerged.

"Well," said Henri, looking at it upside down.

Ridley snapped a photo of the script on her phone. She emailed it back to the office on Proton, an end-to-end encryption email service, asking for a translation.

Henri went over to the sarcophagus.

"There are different languages all over the inside," he said, "in different scripts. Like there were multiple people doing the engravings, but then there's just one word on the urn, and that's the only Arabic."

"And Arabic on the broken saber blade," added Ridley, "that's gone. But really, how the hell would anything Arabic get buried under Notre Dame in the era of the Crusades?"

"A jinn is...an interesting theory," said Henri, glancing at Broussard.

"You think we found a genie in a lamp?" said Claudine sharply.

"What do *you* think we found here today?" Ridley challenged, not appreciating the way she had spoken to her partner. "Not what you're going to tell the Minister of Culture, or your colleagues at INRAP, or the public. What do *you really* think?"

One fist propped on her waist, the Frenchwoman looked down at the floor for a moment before answering.

"I think it's clear that it's extraordinary. That thing had capabilities that we cannot explain."

"I'd say."

"I'm here as an archaeologist. This is my job, okay? You are here to observe. I'm happy to have you here as my guests, but I don't think that your opinion on this is going to be enough for me."

Ridley felt the fight rising in her. She was all the angrier now that she'd lost the attacker, and that losing him had meant catastrophe.

Henri had moved toward the sarcophagus, and was too

engrossed in something inside of it to notice his new partner beginning to steam.

"I think Jean-Louis might find your idea of a 'heat form' to be lacking," said Ridley.

Claudine looked appalled, as though this American was violating the sacrosanct manners of hospitality.

"Hey," said Henri, not minding that he was interrupting.

He reached into the sarcophagus and brushed away a layer of salt from the bottom. Beneath the grains was a distinctive symmetrical cross.

"Oh, my God," breathed Claudine. "It's Templar. This is Templar!"

Her face was alight, consumed with wonder. Even Broussard moved in to see.

"Arabic relics in a Templar coffin?" Ridley frowned.

"This is unique, I'm telling you...they must have brought back the urn from the Holy Land."

"Where jinn-fire demons are from," muttered Ridley, still mad that she had shut down Henri.

"And sealed it and buried it in their holiest place," said Henri. "I think we can see why."

Claudine took a brush and gently swept away the remaining grains of salt.

"Notre Dame cast a very dark shadow on the demise of the Templars. The last Grand Master of the Order was Jacques de Molay, and he was burned at the stake on Île de la Cité. He could see the bell towers of the cathedral as they lit the flames."

"1314?" said Henri.

She looked up with an approving nod. "The Grand Master used his last words to curse the king, and the pope, who sat watching him burn. Do you know what happened to them?"

Henri looked soberly back at her, for he did know.

"They were both dead within the year," he said.

CHAPTER
TWELVE

———

PARIS, FRANCE

BACK AT THE hotel that afternoon, they called Booker. Of course, he had seen the news. He had even seen a flash of Ridley in some of the shaky footage taken inside the chapel. He was upset, his bass voice hardening as they debriefed.

There was no way for anyone within the French government to connect them to the disaster unless INRAP or the Minister of Culture wanted to tell the whole outlandish tale. International incident averted, for now.

Booker would have to bring his own boss in on it, the Deputy Director of the NCS. Ben Conway was a surprisingly reasonable person for a bureaucrat. He gave wide latitude to the operatives of Osprey to pursue whatever avenue they found necessary. Yet he could be a fearsome sight when confronting them over their failures.

As Ridley and Henri began to tell of their day, Booker's prickly displeasure faded. They sent him the photos and video footage from the lab. As he watched, his eyes began to shine with stunned fascination. Afterward, he leaned back in his leather office chair and clasped his hands to his head.

"Well, that sure looks like a jinn, doesn't it," he said.

Henri gave Ridley a look of complete humblebrag.

"That's not something the INRAP archaeologist was ready to hear," he said.

"I'm not shocked. I can't imagine what she's writing up in her report this evening. Oh, and that inscription you wanted translated?" said Booker, reaching for a notepad. "*Eabd*. It means slave in Arabic."

"Does this genie not grant wishes? I didn't hear him offer," said Ridley. "He seemed pissed."

"I don't know enough about the jinn legends, lore, truth," said Booker, waving his hands. "Considering what that thing did today, I'm enlisting an expert, and you know I want you to go meet them in person."

While the travel seemed excessive in a time of simple virtual communication, it was true that for recruiting and consulting, initial contact was vital to do in person. The persuasive power of a human being in front of somebody was compelling in ways that digital projection just couldn't achieve.

"We're also on the radar of the DGSI," added Henri. "Do we have connections there?"

"What's your cover story?" Booker asked.

"Easy, uncontroversial interracial relationship between an American jiu-jitsu instructor and a Haitian computer programmer," said Ridley.

"I'll make a call. They're in a constant state of alarm about terrorist attacks these days, especially in Paris, *especially* with their president trying to engage Israel and the Palestinians, everything is a potential threat. They're gonna assume that what happened today was *not* an act of God."

"Heathens," said Henri with a little grin.

"If they go the route of blaming some rogue Americans, they'd have to tell some kind of story about what happened. The minute they pull the States into it, they'd better have the receipts. If they come after you now for what happened at Saint-Chapelle, it will be all quiet pressure, no statements to the media."

"We are motherfuckin' *wraiths*," she said.

"Don't swear. And I'm serious. The Palais de Justice—"

Booker pronunciation of anything French was like a linguistic disembowelment. Ridley cringed every time he went for it.

"—already looks like it's under siege. They were embarrassed today, and you don't want to see the humiliated version of the French."

"We have," said Henri. "It's called Vichy."

Though he did appreciate the country with its culture and history and natural beauty, there was an ambivalence in Henri about France that ran deep. This was the same nation that enslaved his ancestors. Haitians had overthrown the French in a revolution that brought not just liberation for their country, but a blistering cascade of self-destruction, when they put to the torch the infrastructure of their oppressors. If that had not been crippling enough to a people seeking independent success, the new nation had been forced to pay reparations to France for its own freedom. Billions were siphoned off to the land of their former slavemasters.

He bore no resentment toward any French man, woman, or child. No one could be held guilty in the stead of those who came generations before. They had no choice in their ancestry. Yet *France*...he could not quite shake a tinge of bitterness.

What he really loathed was this unforgiving streak within himself.

"I'll make some calls," said Booker, "find out if they're sniffing around. But my God, don't ruin any more historical monuments!"

"We didn't—" started Ridley.

"Don't let anyone else ruin any more historical monuments while you're standing there."

"Copy."

After they hung up, Ridley went into the bathroom to wash her face. She needed a shower, swimming, washing her face, anything with water.

When she reemerged, Henri was eating the kebab he'd picked up on their way back from the Louvre. He tossed Ridley a falafel.

"Do you believe in possession?" he asked.

"It's nine-tenths of the law."

"You must make other people laugh."

She took a bite of falafel and shrugged.

"I don't believe in it like *The Exorcist* possession. *The Exorcism of Emily Rose*, that was a great movie. That actress looked possessed for *sure*. Absolutely freaky."

"So is that a no?"

"I don't know. I had a hell of a day, so I'm gonna need to recalibrate some things. I can't say..." she got serious, "I'm not going to pretzel myself trying to come up with a way to explain how it *couldn't* be possession. I'm gonna guess you do believe it's a real thing?"

"I'm from Haiti, the land of voodoo," he said, wiping his mouth. "We know it is."

She chewed for a moment, looking down at the pita in her hands.

"I'll consider it."

. . .

She went for a run at sunset. The rhythmic thud of her shoes was soothing, the chill of evening air refreshing in her lungs. Since they had not been able to bring weapons into the country, and they'd not stopped at any safehouse on the continent, she was unarmed, and she hated it. France was too volatile these days. Paris was too loaded with radicals to feel secure without a gun on her.

Yet there was also the Paris that had enchanted her as a teenager. It was about the hour that the banks of the Seine filled with young people, friends meeting after work with the most typical of French picnics: wine and cheese and honest-to-God baguettes. Ridley had seen it here before, but not since the age of the ubiquitous cell phone. As she passed by in her long, loping stride, she could hardly believe that all of these twenty-somethings were simply talking to each other. There wasn't an electronic in sight.

Still, there was a discernible dread rippling through these groups. The destruction of Sainte-Chapelle was a horror akin only to the event that had started this whole thing: the burning of Notre Dame. There was a hushed anguish in the air, in their body language, in the tone of their voices. It was everywhere along these streets. She felt that furious guilt once again. She had not been able to stop it.

It was the shattering of the stained glass that replayed in her head. She kept seeing the bewildered expression on the faces of both the Volkswagen driver and Jean-Louis after she'd taken them down in the heat of the moment.

Yet it was the image of the fiery creature that had formed from that broken urn that was fully burned into her.

Osprey was not a division for the faint of heart, for the closed-minded or the stubborn. That had been clear from her first mission, when she'd encountered a shaman in a remote hut in Burma who could read minds. Yet the demonstration of power in that chapel was not like anything she'd witnessed before.

Is that what a jinn can do? It can't be the only one in the world. Why Sainte-Chapelle? Wouldn't it have been blasphemous to bury a fire demon within a cathedral? Why was there so much salt in the sarcophagus?

Her thoughts were interrupted by the buzz of her cell.

Unknown number.

She picked it up.

"Hello?"

"Madame Samaras?"

"Who's calling?"

"This is Agent Guy Zem. Would you come please into my office? I have something that I would like you to see."

CHAPTER
THIRTEEN

PARIS, FRANCE

Two hours later, Ridley and Henri were ushered into the DGSI offices at Place Beauvau. Guy Zem was once again cordial but serious, nearly unreadable in his demeanor toward them.

Maybe he really is a neutral investigator. That would be rare. Everyone has instincts, whether they like it or not, acknowledge them or don't.

He invited them into a dimly lit room that must have been his office, a modest, disheveled place. Both Ridley and Henri gave every scrap of visible material a discreet glance, a few stacks of paper on his desk and a notepad. Nothing in sight looked like it could compromise any investigation. He was still careful and meticulous.

Once they were seated, he picked up a large tablet computer from his desk.

"We collected all of the footage from the people inside Sainte-Chapelle when the incident happened," he said. "I noticed some interesting things. Maybe you could help me understand them. Would you watch this?"

He cued up a video on the tablet and handed it to Ridley. She pressed play.

It was taken from another angle, deeper within the chapel, facing backward. The top of the stairs were in sight.

Oh, no.

Sure enough, within the next two seconds, she came into frame, charging up the stairs, bursting into the chapel. She looked nothing like any other tourist. She was not taking in the awesome sight that rose up around her, but rather she was searching for *someone*, her eyes raking the crowd of tourists.

"It looks to my eyes that you were not there for the sight-seeing," said Zem, intently watching her face for a reaction. "It looks like you were hunting this man."

The video continued, but the camera panned, so that the moment Ridley locked eyes on the Volkswagen driver, she was nearly out of frame.

But then she started walking forward, straight for her target, and directly into frame again.

"Why were you chasing him?"

Quick thinking was the saving grace of any intelligence agency field operative. Every one of them had to be an improv actor. Every lie was a gamble, and the stakes were high.

Ridley handed back the tablet with a sheepish look. Beside her, Henri played his part. He looked at her with a concerned curiosity.

"You're going to think I'm some stupid, arrogant American, okay? Just, please don't..." she sighed, readjusting her seat. "I teach a martial art. I teach my students situational awareness, that no one is coming to save you. You have to be the first line of defense for yourself, and if you're qualified, for others. So maybe I'm always looking for a threat. Maybe I overreact to people who look like...like a problem waiting to happen. Someone looking for trouble."

Henri squeezed her forearm, reassuring his faux girlfriend.

"What an insane day," she muttered. "He looked weird to me, okay? I'm not racist, I'm not...not xenophobic. Obviously, or I probably wouldn't be traveling, right? But I can't turn off this state of mind, this anxiety that there's danger in anyone around me. In everyone."

Zem listened, no change in his gaze so far.

"He didn't look like a tourist. He looked like he was on a mission to do something bad. I saw him go into the chapel—just happened to be the guy I'd seen in front of me at the gate and tried to use to cheat my way through, yeah. I thought I could save the day if there was a day to save." She gave a dark, disbelieving chuckle. "And there was, my God. I had no idea what was coming."

The last part could not have been more true. She raised her hands in full admission. The cop was grave, but he seemed to believe her confession-like tale.

"Madame Samaras, never chase danger. And do not play police in our country. You were next to the Palais de Justice. If you think there is danger, you report it to the courtyard full of officers."

She gave a strained nod.

"You know, Agent Zem," said Henri, "you might be offering a few more thanks. She was right. This time, she was right! You had a courtyard full of guards but none of them saw this man's behavior for what it was. None of them saw what *she* saw. This man—we don't even know who he is—destroyed the most beautiful thing in Paris, and she was the only person who tried to stop him."

"Henri—" Ridley started, touching his hand as if to calm him down.

"No, he should be giving you a commendation, not scolding you!"

"I assure you—" said Zem, deeply uncomfortable with this escalating into a couple's bickering, "we are very, very grateful for what she did today, but you must understand our investigation. How could we not look into something like this?"

"Well, now you have," said Henri, still steaming. "If you think she had anything to do with this—how could you possibly think she was part of this?"

"Monsieur, we do not think that. But," he said, pulling up something on the tablet, "we do believe that there was an accomplice in the chapel today."

He handed it to them again. This time, Henri pressed play.

It was another video from a phone that had continued filming even after the moment of explosion. It was shaky almost to the point of being unwatchable, but Zem had it playing at quarter speed. They could see the Volkswagen driver standing calmly in the hail of glass as people screamed and barreled past him. This was the moment when Ridley had been crouched, shielding her face against the flying shards.

Volkswagen man's arm shot out, grabbing a female tourist trying to flee. He forcibly palmed something off to her. She seemed to stiffen for a second, but took whatever it was from his hand and hurried out of frame.

I missed this. Shit. I missed this!

"Did you notice this woman?" asked Zem.

"No...it looks like he gave her something."

"A detonator," suggested Henri, fully poised to mislead.

"Maybe. We're working to clarify the resolution on this video. But we have identified the woman from the group of people who bought tickets to see the chapel today."

"I don't know her, do I?" said Ridley.

Zem took the tablet back and pulled up an identification photo to show them.

"You tell me."

The woman in the photo was in her forties. She was blonde, fair-skinned, and had a soft prettiness to her. She didn't appear to be the type who would arouse suspicion in any setting.

Henri shook his head, "I don't know her."

"I don't think so..." said Ridley, making a show of peering closely. "What's her name?"

There was a split second pause before Zem answered, as though he was weighing how much to give these American tourists.

"Sofie Hasbo. She is Danish. Appears to be a tourist, just like you."

"How are you gonna find her? Can't she just leave the country?"

"We are on high alert here, as you probably realized. We have measures in place to find anyone trying to cross into or out of our borders. We have also notified INTERPOL. She'll show up in our net," said Zem.

"Damn," muttered Ridley. "Well, okay, good."

Zem did not walk them out. Ridley and Henri waited until they were a block away before breaking their cover.

"That was definitely the saber hilt, wasn't it," said Henri under his breath.

"Yeah. That had to be it," said Ridley, pulling up the collar of her jacket. "If this jinn thing is possessing people, it's...jumping from person to person, but it's like every possessed person has to have that piece of the saber?"

Henri blew out an incredulous breath. "This is new to me.

We can have Booker tune into the INTERPOL alerts for Sofie Hasbo."

"Even if she pings somewhere, she may not even have the saber hilt. If this jinn can just pass from one person to another."

"Maybe it jumps to somebody else only when it has to."

"Like we're threatening it, closing in on it," she said.

His phone dinged with a message. He pulled it out to read.

"Time to pack again," he said. "We're going to England."

"Please be Hogwarts. Because I'll probably believe in boggarts and hippogriffs by the end of the week."

"Try again. Cambridge University. So you might need a new outfit," he sniffed.

"House robes are the great equalizer."

CHAPTER
FOURTEEN

THAT NIGHT, Claudine Gaspar poured herself a glass of Syrah and stepped out on the balcony of her apartment in the 10th arrondissement. Her husband Franck was squawking on the phone in the living room, so she pulled the door shut and leaned onto the wrought-iron railing. In the distance, Canal Saint-Martin glided still and glassy through the city blocks.

She'd forgotten to stop by the boulangerie for the fresh rye she'd promised her twenty-two-year-old daughter, Valerie, home visiting from Brussels this week. Claudine had been in such a haze since leaving the Louvre, she had barely remembered to get off at Gare de l'Est for her short walk home.

Valerie had been sweet about the forgotten rye, but Franck had had one of his very important calls come in that would keep him working into the small hours of the night. Her daughter had invited her out to get dinner at a nearby Indian restaurant, where Valerie was already headed for a reunion with some of her university friends. Claudine had shuffled her out the door with a thank you and a kiss on the cheek, to tell all the friends that she said hello, but she had no intention of chatting with a group of young, carefree ladies tonight. No doubt their table would be buzzing with the shock of the Sainte-Chapelle explosion.

The discovery of the sarcophagus had been no small thing. It had made international headlines, and was of intense personal interest to not only the Minister of Culture, but to millions of French men and women. Even President Chavas himself had asked to be apprised of any findings as soon as they were available. There was no keeping this quiet, though given the catastrophic events of the day, Claudine could delay her report for long enough to fabricate an alternate version.

She swallowed the last of the Syrah and went back inside. Franck made a face of mock anguish at her. She returned a wry smile as she slipped into her study and slid the door shut. Her husband pretended to suffer through these long calls from management, but she knew he was really doing it for her sake. That man had always enjoyed the heat of a crisis.

Claudine took a seat at the desk and pulled up her laptop. She opened an encrypted app for video calls, and dialed.

Today's findings were the kind she had only dreamt of. She had joined INRAP nearly three decades before, but had quickly learned to keep the rogue streak within her quiet. If she wanted to get a foothold in the more prestigious state-sanctioned circles, if she wanted to gain access to the biggest archaeological finds of her nation, she could not question orthodoxy.

With her dignified appearance and masterful intellect, climbing the ranks only required that she not say anything off-kilter. They would always assume that anyone so bright would obviously hold the same right beliefs as they. She just kept her mouth shut at the office.

Yet outside of it, there were people who thought like her, believed as she did.

The call box popped up. On the screen was a handsome man of fifty. His eyes were startling blue under thick black brows, his hair a lush coif of dark curls. He could have been every retiree's dream leading man, almost a scruffier, more intense-looking Pierce Brosnan. He was currently sitting in a room that looked halfway between a library and a greenhouse.

"Good evening, Claudine!" said Tiago Inacio in a faint Portuguese accent. "What kind of day did you have?"

She shook her head, still shell-shocked. "Sainte-Chapelle...I cannot believe it. I just can't believe it. The greatest historical glass-work in the world..."

"I've seen. The shots from inside the chapel are spectacular, I'm sorry to say. But it wasn't a coincidence with what you were doing today, was it?"

Claudine bit her lip. "You will only believe this because you've known it to be true for years. It was the Templars. They found the jinn."

Tiago's eyes glowed. He leaned forward in his chair. "That was it? In Sainte-Chapelle?"

"There was one imprisoned in the sarcophagus, and it escaped—right *into* one of my employees. It just took him over...horrible. He didn't know what had happened."

"How? How did it take him over?" he pressed, enthralled.

"I think it can jump, from person to person. Jean-Louis—I mean this *thing—jinn*—took something from the sarcophagus. It was a broken piece of a saber."

He sat back, brows knit together. "A golden saber?"

"Yes," she said, surprised. "How do you know of it?"

"I never thought it actually existed...Saladin, the great, the

73

founder of the Ayyubid dynasty. He was such a great warrior against the Crusaders that his closest advisors had a saber made for him. They took pieces of gold from all of the places he smashed with an iron fist then ruled over, and forged this weapon. They saw him as the defender of Islam against Christian invaders, and they inscribed it with Arabic verses. That is how they tell it, anyway."

"How did the Templars get his saber? He conquered *them* at Jerusalem."

"The heat of battle, weapons are lost. Some of those weapons are picked up by Templars fighting for their religion and their people."

"This was only a small piece, the hilt, and now it's gone. There was a pair of Americans in the lab today. A man and a woman, they were observing at the invitation of the Ministry of Culture."

He frowned, "Archaeologists?"

"No, no, I'm sure they were not. The Ministry kept very tight lips, but when the jinn got free, they went after it like they were...ready for trouble."

"You think they were government?"

"Without any credentials, but yes, somehow, intelligence. I was only told the day before that they would be on site."

She recounted the opening of the sarcophagus, the blood-chilling appearance of the jinn, and what it did to Jean-Louis. From there, Tiago knew more about the incident at Sainte-Chapelle than Claudine did. In fact, she was almost irritated at how someone sitting in Porto could have the details of an attack inside one of the most secure grounds in Paris. This was her territory, her area of expertise. If she didn't have this to contribute, what was she?

"Do you have someone in the Interior?" she asked.

"*I* have no one. There are Raphaels who serve in many

places, you know, my dear. The Order is anywhere we need to be."

"Then you should have known," said Claudine, prickling. "You can find out about the Americans."

"I saw the American woman on the news. An Amazon. She was in the chapel."

"Yes, she chased after the man who took the saber hilt from the sarcophagus."

"Who has it now?"

"Oh, you don't know?"

He smirked, "The vessel is not really that important. It will always work for the same destination. So it's a good thing that we have you."

Claudine knew it was manipulation, but the sugar was still sweet.

"We're translating the etchings inside the sarcophagus. I'll send them to you as soon as we have them."

"Claudine, do you realize?" said Tiago. "Do you realize what we have? This is in *our* lifetime, the biggest discovery for the Order of Raphael in centuries. It has happened for *us*."

Up until now, she had only seen the events of the day in their immediacy. Their scope and significance were the reason she'd begun this work, but it had taken until now for her to realize what she had seen that morning with her own eyes...

It was she who had found what the Order had been seeking for hundreds of years. It was she who had unleashed the rage of the jinn. It was Tiago who would now have to put it to the chase.

CHAPTER
FIFTEEN

———

PORTO, PORTUGAL

TIAGO ENDED the call and pushed back from his desk. He began pacing the stone floor of his office as if he was a groom waiting for the appearance of a bride. This was it. He nearly skipped to the liquor cabinet to pull from the highest shelf, an unopened bottle of Tears of Llorona Extra Añejo Tequila. He was grinning helplessly as he poured a glass from the four hundred-dollar bottle, then poured another one.

Lifting one in each hand, Tiago bellowed a toast to himself—

"*Saúde!*"

—and swigged from each glass.

He had spent his life in service to the Order of Raphael, with little to show for it but constant studying and eternal vigilance. He'd done his years in the army, trained up in the Cavalry

Reconnaissance, but all that had been only for one reason: to hone his skills for the Order, whenever they may call, *if* ever they would call.

Seven hundred years after its creation, the Order of Raphael was about to rise for the entire world to see.

After the crumbling order of the Knights Templars was ambushed by the French king just after the final Crusades, the scandalous nature of their destruction spawned a thousand tales and treasure hunts. Rumors abounded of their secret stashes of treasure, their cryptic methods of communication, and the ways by which some of them escaped torture and execution to raise the Templars again in a new fashion, under a new name.

It was not altogether a foolish endeavor. By 1312, the Knights Templar were no more. King Philip IV had crushed them for profit and for power, and the pope had eventually given his blessing to the extermination, issuing a papal bull to abolish them entirely.

Yet there were a few faithful who survived, who fled from France back into the land that had been with them from the beginning: Portugal. There, they took refuge under the protection of King Denis, where they rebranded themselves quietly as the Military Order of Christ.

They lobbied under the protection of the Portuguese king to have the new pope recognize their newly named order and restore Templar property to them. They were successful, and by 1319, they had a new papal bull, this time issued in their favor.

The Order looked on the original Templars as fools, of course, begging for scraps from the Catholic Church which had abandoned their comrades to the stake. They were neutered and weak, pathetic in the face of the Church's betrayal of them.

Only a few could see this for what it was. Tiago did not know for certain if his ancestors had been part of the select righteous Raphaels, but he had always felt that wherever his blood *had* come from twenty-eight generations before, they would see it as he did. The Knights Templar had not fought and died for two hundred years in sand and heat to dwindle into a passive, groveling club who went around awarding themselves great medals and badges of honor.

It was time to restore purpose. The Order of Raphael was born in 1324, and they were true believers. It was the pope who had betrayed the Templars to their ultimate end, so the new Order set themselves as the true holy warriors against a corrupted Vatican. The Catholic Church may have had a thousand-year head start on their power base, but the Raphaels would never surrender their struggle. They were about to emerge from the shadows of centuries, and they would prevail in their righteousness.

Tiago set down one of the drinks to turn on the stereo. Music seemed to pour down from the ceiling, the smooth, twanging percussion of Raphael Saadiq, "Love That Girl." Sipping tequila from his glass, he did a soft-shoe around the sofa, and back to his desk.

He dropped back down into the chair, set a drink on each side of the desk, and pulled a cell phone out of the top drawer.

Wheels up tomorrow morning

He sent the text to nine contacts, then placed the phone face down on the desktop. The añejo had never felt so smooth.

CHAPTER
SIXTEEN

CAMBRIDGE, ENGLAND

THE DOWNTOWN SQUARE OF CAMBRIDGE, England was a place of striking juxtaposition. Surrounded by thousand-year-old stone buildings, intricate monuments of monarchic excellence and religious tributes, buzzed a hive of modern life. The stone streets teemed with bicycles, shoppers on their cell phones, students in shorts and tees with bags slung over their shoulders.

The thirty-one colleges that comprised Cambridge University had seen a parade of greatness unlike almost any other schooling system in the world. Henri was more animated than she'd seen him yet, rattling off the names of the notables who'd walked these grounds over the last eight hundred years.

Isaac Newton. Stephen Hawking. Lord Byron. Alan Turing. Charles Darwin. Erasmus. Milton Friedman. Rosalind Franklin.

A.A. Milne. Emma Thompson. Christopher Marlowe. Roger Penrose. John Donne. Francis Crick. William Makepeace Thackeray.

"Rachel Weisz," he said, thumping a hand to his chest.

"This is the kind of homework you were doing?" she said. "Alumni?"

"Knowing where Alan Turing studied doesn't mean I don't have space in my head for the mission."

"Does it make you nostalgic for BU?"

He smiled at her with a genuine delight. It almost made her bashful.

"You remembered my college!" he said. "Maybe it does a little, yeah. I loved school. I loved Boston."

Ridley wouldn't allow herself to think on it very often, but there was a pang of regret in her about college. She had never attended, never properly been a student in any boisterous, curious, intellectual place. She knew she wasn't stupid or *un*educated, but setting foot on a campus made her feel like something of a brute, like everyone would be able to tell that the only things she knew of college was what she'd seen on screen and read in books.

In his academic thrall, Henri didn't seem to notice any of her hesitation. As they approached Trinity College's Great Gate, he threw his arm out against her and pointed at a nearby tree.

"That's Isaac Newton's apple tree!"

"Well shit, is it? Do you think if you sat under it, you'd get a revelation about what to do with a jinn on the loose?"

"The original got blown over by a storm. It's happened a few times since, but every time they graft the tree to a new one and replant it. So it's a descendant of the tree they say he was sitting under when he had his revelation about gravity."

"Ah. So it's a tree-fusion. Do you want a picture with it?"

"I one hundred percent do."

She did not think he would take her up on it, but sure

enough, he thrust his phone into her hand and posed against the trunk. Ridley couldn't help her amusement as she snapped a photo of him grinning in his ivory jeans, black T-shirt, and green-and-white floral jacket.

"I'm sending it to Booker," she said. "Tourist time is over."

"Old man probably has the same picture with himself in it."

They passed through the low stone gate into the Great Court. Magnificent buildings lined a sweeping carpet of close-cut grass. Students milled about in the warm spring sunlight. There was that buzz in the air that signaled that classes would soon be over.

Fortunately, the faculty member they were looking for was still in her office in New Court. They climbed to the third floor and knocked on the ornate wooden door.

A moment later it was pulled open by a young man in jeans and a fashionably frayed T-shirt. The thickness through his arms and shoulders screamed "athlete." He was handsome, with mussed hair, dark brows, and a set of heavy brooding eyes that gave him a distinctly "bad-boy-on-campus" vibe. As soon as he spoke, though, that spell dissolved.

"Hi. Are you the Americans? Here to see Professor White?" he said eagerly in a Welsh accent, stepping back from the doorway.

"Yeah, hi," said Ridley.

"I'm Owen Allchurch, one of her graduate students," he said, shaking their hands as he ushered them in.

The office was neater than they'd expected, a rich library of shelves, stacks of papers, and even a whiteboard with a scribbled outline of something that looked like a timeline.

"I'm Henri, this is Ridley. Thanks for meeting us, Owen. Is Professor White actually here?"

But the woman who popped out from behind a bookshelf was a full-blown counterweight to her surroundings.

Professor White must have been in her fifties, but her movements were flitting, full of little bursts of energy. She wore layers of brown and burgundy, at least one scarf—possibly two—and an array of beautiful gothic jewelry. Her hair was an elaborate mahogany nest atop her head, and there was a sharp, delicate beauty to her features. She set down the textbook she had been holding.

"I'm Lucy White," she said, shaking each of their hands.

They introduced themselves.

"You're looking for some information on the Templars then? What they were up to in their final days?"

"Yeah, but it's a bit more complicated," said Ridley, pulling out a thumb drive from her pocket. "Have you got somewhere we can load this?"

Owen helped set them up on the office desktop computer, where Ridley pulled up the images they'd taken of the saber hilt, of the urn, and of the sarcophagus with its multilingual etchings. The professor was fully aware of the discovery of the pieces beneath Notre Dame, as it had made international news. It was pure catnip for every history professor in Europe. They did not tell her about the appearance of the fire demon from the broken urn.

Best left on a need-to-know basis.

Professor White flipped intently through the photos, zooming in, murmuring into the hand she'd propped her chin on.

"This is incredible. Nothing like this has been discovered in decades. But under Notre Dame? Unthinkable."

As professor of medieval history at Trinity College, she had built a reputation as the world's premiere scholar on military religious orders and the Crusades. In all her career, no one had ever brought her such an extraordinary artifact finding. It was the sort of thing an academic could wish for her entire life and never be so lucky as to encounter.

When she got to the photo of the Templar cross engraved in the sarcophagus, she gasped.

"It is. My God, look at it."

"That's iron proof," said Owen. "Oh, I mean literally, I guess. Isn't this iron?"

Henri nodded. "The whole sarcophagus."

"Carbon dating could place it within a window of a few decades, but actually the construction period of Notre Dame overlaps beautifully with the life of the Knights Templar," said Professor White.

"Have you ever seen anything like this?" asked Ridley.

"No one's ever found anything like this."

The professor may have come across as scattered due to her appearance, but the woman had the focus of a peregrine falcon on a hunt.

"The Knights Templar were extraordinary, really extraordinary. They weren't just soldiers—I mean—they were bankers! So effective that it actually brought about their destruction. Never loan to a monarch! When it's time for repayment, they may just decide to execute you instead of making good on their debts."

"So why all of these languages?" asked Ridley, pointing to the inscriptions. "I don't have translations for everything yet, but at least some of them are curses, and then some blessings of spiritual fortification, something-something."

"Templars drew from all across Europe. They had fortresses in every country, and then some in the Middle East. But still, I've...I've never seen Arabic in any of their works."

"And what about the saber piece?" asked Henri. "Arabic on that, too."

Owen spoke up, "And the urn."

Ridley pointed at him, affirming. "And the urn."

"They were incredibly cryptic," said Professor White. "You have to suppose it's one of the reasons they've been so romanticized. They literally built tunnels beneath half their strongholds, to be able to escape in a moment without being noticed. Turns out they needed them more than a few times, especially there at the end."

"King Philip's ambush, right?" said Henri.

"That was a truly remarkable moment. He ambushed the Templars. They were renowned for their ability to communicate messages at nearly the speed of flight, so he knew that when he came for them, he'd have to get them *all,* all at once. Friday the thirteenth," she said, pausing for delicious effect, "he deployed soldiers to every known Templar House across France. They struck within minutes of each other—and this was before pocketwatches! Extraordinary coordination, almost like the Templars themselves."

"How does this help us right now?" said Ridley, somewhat fascinated by the history lesson but also somewhat impatient to get to the point.

"I should hope you'd like to know the full picture, and then *you* can determine what's helpful to you as you investigate further."

It was a clear scold, but not so sharp as to embarrass Ridley. This woman was a bit fiercer than she seemed.

"You might also like to know that the Templars were tortured for years into giving confessions. Outrageous things, complete rubbish. Many of them recanted, but then the pope was persuaded to disown them, so they were done anyhow! The last Grand Master, burned at the stake..." she trailed off, shaking her head. "Wonder if they knew we'd be talking about them all these hundreds of years later."

"No doubt they did," said Owen, "but they'd have thought we'd be regaling the tales of their bravery in battle."

"Mmm," agreed Professor White. "Debts and demise don't have quite the same chivalric glamour, do they? Now, let's get you what you need."

CHAPTER
SEVENTEEN

———

Ridley was relieved to hear the professor correct course back to the matters at hand.

"So, the Arabic is new to you. There's no Templar precedent. Is there any example anywhere that you know of them burying a sarcophagus that has nothing in it but salt?" asked Henri, scrubbing at his short hair with both hands.

"And what might any of this have to do with the legend of the jinn?" added Ridley.

It was time to go there.

"Legend of the jinn?" said Professor White in surprise.

Owen took a step forward. "I might be able to help with this, Professor!"

"Oh, yes, please. Owen's the brightest graduate studying here, in my opinion," she said, then added with a not-so-confidential whisper, "and he's got the most *gorgeous singing voice I've ever heard.*"

"I just sang as a boy—"

"King's College Choir," she said. "Right here."

He tried to shake it off, but grinned at her delight. "I've been studying the Templars in relation to their true origins, where they took their name from, all that. They called themselves the Poor Fellow-Soldiers of Christ and of the Temple of Solomon, which is pretty interesting because they were Christian and the Temple was Jewish—obviously—so they had no use for Solomon's building anymore. It was supposed to be obsolete at Jesus' crucifixion, yeah?"

Henri nodded. "The veil of the temple was torn from top to bottom. Then anyone who entered could see into the Holy of Holies. It did away with the separation between God and man."

"Exactly, yeah," Owen continued. "So why...devote themselves to a Jewish temple? Why make their headquarters the Temple Mount for nearly seventy years, until they were conquered by Saladin?"

His manner of speaking was odd, as if he was wandering into his own sentences. He spoke with graceful gestures, as if drawing out his thoughts in front of him. All of that with his Welsh lilt, and the effect was a bit entrancing.

"And they were excavating there almost the entire time! There's no evidence they found any artifacts worth anything, really, but the stories of Solomon's treasure were..." he exploded his hands beside his head for effect. "All these legends about the Holy Grail: that rubbish was invented in the Medieval Age. Who would have kept a basic cup from a dinner? They had a lot more important things to worry about, right? And the Spear of Destiny that people thought pierced Jesus' side: I really don't think the Roman soldier gave up his weapon for posterity.

"The Ark of the Covenant...*that* one...that one existed, only it hasn't shown up with face-melting angels the way we dreamed about."

Ridley glanced at Henri, impressed by the young man's passion. This was clearly his element. Professor White had sat back and was listening contentedly, a proud teacher.

"But this—" he said, running to grab a book off one of the far shelves and flipping madly through its pages, "this is what I believe they were really, *really* looking for. Aside from the Ark."

They leaned in to see an image of a faded vertical paper. Above a block of angular kufic script was a six-pointed star surrounded by an ornate circle.

"This is in the Met," said Owen. "It's an Islamic scroll, probably kept in an amulet box, a lot of incantations and verses on it. And that up there," he pointed to the star, "is the Seal of Solomon."

"So it's been found," said Ridley. "Now sitting in our country's top museum."

"No! This is just a drawing. It's probably the precursor to the Star of David, if you look at it, makes sense. The real thing was a *ring* that King Solomon wore! Allegedly," he added, glancing at his professor. "The first mention of it was from Josephus himself—first-century historian, so, that's a pretty good start."

"So, there's something about it...?" said Henri.

"Yeah," he nodded enthusiastically. "It was made of iron, and they said it controlled jinn."

Ridley let out a barely audible, "Huh."

There was a moment's pause. Henri lifted his brows. "So, the Templars wanted this, which meant they wanted control of the jinn, which means—"

"They must have been trying to imprison them," she said. "What else would the sarcophagus be for? Welded shut?"

"Why the iron? All of the salt?" asked Henri.

Owen seemed a bit lost in the back-and-forth between partners, but offered up a hand.

"There's no textbook, but iron and salt are supposed to be to jinn what—like—garlic and crosses are to vampires."

"Is there something equivalent to sunlight?" asked Ridley. "The all-destroying weapon?"

"Maybe the Seal, if jinn were real. Anyhow, that's what the Templars believed. They really spent their lives and fortunes hunting down these things, they believed in it so much."

She looked at Henri. It was time to tell.

"Funny enough," she started, and launched into the full account of what had occurred that day in the lab, and the truth about what happened in Sainte-Chapelle.

The professor and Owen both listened, rapt. They asked a few questions along the way, but were mostly so stunned that they just stared. At the end, Professor White stood up and went to a cupboard.

"What's the least judgmental alcohol you can drink before noon? Oh, I don't even care about judgment," she said, pulling down a bottle of port. "You're the ones who've come into my office telling me that a fire demon blew up the most famous stained glass in the world in the middle of Paris yesterday. Care for one?" She hovered the bottle over a glass.

"No, thanks," said Ridley.

Henri lifted his hand to pass.

"Owen?"

"No, thank you, professor."

She shrugged, then thought twice about the glass, and returned to her seat with just the bottle.

"It sounds like—this thing is really powerful—it sounds like an ifrit. Like, really malevolent," said Owen. "I don't know what the saber is, I'm sorry."

"Some talisman of power, don't you think?" suggested Henri. "The way they're passing it. Like *it* possesses *them*."

Professor White looked at Owen. "You've done an awful lot of research on the jinn, then. Is this really all for your graduate work?"

"I'm trying to understand what the Templars believed, and I can't do that without knowing what it is they believed about their quarry," he explained, almost sheepish. " I didn't—I didn't believe it was real."

Henri gave a wry smile. "Surprise."

"What a difference a day makes," said Ridley. "So what would an ifrit want? Just to start chaos? Destroy sacred buildings? And why just stop with Sainte-Chapelle? Why not move right next door and take down Notre Dame. Can't imagine it was happy about being buried under a church."

Professor White spoke up from behind her port. "You know they discovered iron staples in the roof when they were renovating it. In the shape of a cross, of course. Giant iron staples. They'd never been used in a Gothic structure before that. Makes you think. Well, it makes *me* think, now."

"Iron kept it in," said Henri.

"Until Jean-Louis had to go and burn his hands on that genie lamp," said Ridley.

"Alerts are out all over Europe for this Danish woman, just a tourist who happened to pass by the Volkswagen man at the wrong second. We don't have anything else to go on yet, but it appears he handed off the broken saber hilt to her."

Owen grimaced slightly. He rubbed at his forehead in frustrated thought.

"I honestly don't know what it's doing. A lot of the lesser jinn are just out for chaos, but the more powerful ones, ifrits...I think they're more intentional. And then there are marids, which are..." he shuddered. "They're pretty unhappy monsters, usually just found in water. And then there are the Seven Kings of the Jinn..."

"Say what?" Ridley interrupted.

"They're, um...well, they're myths, obviously." He looked between them. "Well, I guess not obviously anymore. That's... wow, what a day."

He looked like he didn't even know where to put his own hands, he was so amped.

"Hey, you're helping us already," said Ridley with a relaxing smile.

"None of my books are here, I'm sorry. Professor didn't really know—" said Owen, glancing over at her, "—that I've been studying this on the side, as part of my Templar work. But I do have something I can show you!"

Henri loosened up his own body language in an effort to put the young man at ease.

"You know, it's a beautiful day. Why don't you grab whatever you've got on the jinn and we meet somewhere outside?"

Owen grinned in relief. "I've got the book and I've got the place!"

Thirty minutes later, Ridley, Henri, and Owen were camped out on the lush green of the Backs, the sprawling lawns that lay behind the imperious colleges. Flat gondolas drifted past them on the narrow river Cam. A breeze riffled through banks of daffodils and crocuses. It couldn't have been a more idyllic day if someone had cast an enchantment spell on it.

As the three of them sat over a ghoulish book of dark Middle Eastern lore.

"They can all shapeshift, or become invisible," said Owen, "but I think it's more that they can take on substance or vanish into some—some immaterial, spiritual realm, yeah? Hard to say."

Henri frowned. "All of these references are pretty late. Nothing from the B.C. Period?"

"Oh, yeah! I mean, not exact, but some..." he said, rifling through the pages. "There are some Mesopotamian writings from 3000 B.C. *Ancient* scholars in the Middle East thought they were fallen deities from the Babylonian civilization. Or even Sumerian! About 2300 B.C. Their demons—jinn—were said to be *legion*, and really, really evil."

"That's so out of character for demons," said Henri.

Owen cracked a laugh.

Ridley was staring down at the open pages, at grisly depictions on stone, and illustrations on scrolls of these malevolent spirit creatures. None of them did justice to the devil she'd seen take shape in the basement of the Louvre.

"And these things can possess people like regular demons," she said.

"Yeah, they say," he replied quietly. "Call them *masru'*. That's what they call a possessed person, I mean."

"And they're ruled by kings?"

He gave a dramatically grave look. "Yeah. Seven."

Owen flipped to another chapter and leaned down into the book.

"They all have names. They even all have *titles*, except for one. His—*its*—name is Shamhuresh."

He held up the book for them. On the page was a gruesome illustration, a dark mass of burnt feathers that seemed to have white sparks strewn across it. A thick pair of ram's horns curled over a wrinkled face that looked half-human, half-goat.

"Is he supposed to be the king of the kings of the jinn?" asked Henri.

"No reference to that anywhere, but Shamhuresh was said to be the companion of Muhammad."

"So he must like the whole blood and conquest thing," said Ridley. "What are the other ones?"

"There aren't any depictions that I can find...but the White One, the Golden One, The Red One, Cyclone, Two Thunders, and Prosperous."

Henri and Ridley exchanged a glance. That was a lot.

"What happened to all of these creatures?" asked Henri.

Owen shrugged, looking almost thrilled by the fantasy. "I dunno. Maybe they're still out there somewhere. Why would you think this ifrit is going to find them?!"

"The word on the urn was *eabd*," said Ridley. "Slave."

"Every slave serves *somebody*," said Henri.

Her gaze roamed over the happy scene before her, of picnickers and boaters and pedestrians walking their dogs along the river banks. If they did their job, these people would remain blissfully ignorant of whatever mangled darkness they were pursuing.

"Who said that bit about powers and principalities of darkness?" she asked.

"Paul," replied Henri.

"Yeah. Is it better to see them or to just wander around every day like there's nothing else out there?"

He squinted out at the passersby. "One day those worlds will cross over. You always want to see them first."

CHAPTER
EIGHTEEN

———

LONDON, ENGLAND

RIDLEY AND HENRI took the train back to London that evening and checked into a hotel near Oxford Circus. On the way up to their separate rooms, Henri rubbed a hand along the top of his head in irritation.

"I'm gonna need a drink to think clearly tonight."

She raised her hand for participation.

Ridley knew by this point that he would want to change clothes. She could not understand how he fit so many outfits into his carry-on luggage, but the man wore them well. She dressed in an outfit dark enough to be acceptable in most dimly lit bars.

They each rigged their doors with a simplistic paper wedge to detect for intrusion, then took a cab to The Connaught Bar.

"Oh, God, you have delivered me here," she murmured as they walked in.

It was all gleaming leather, black and white and gold art deco. The bartenders in the back were immaculately dressed. One of the servers mixed martinis from a trolley cart.

"This is the best bar in the world," said Henri. "Capital 'B.' I don't waste my travel opportunities. And I always tip the concierge for the hookup."

"Are we making commission if we find Solomon's treasure?"

"It's only money."

"Will that line work on the IRS, my landlord, my electric company, my coffeeshop, my internet provider, my—"

She cut herself off to level him with a look of annoyance.

"You learn a lot more about the value of money when you don't have it," he said. "I got advanced degrees in that when I was a boy."

Oh, shit, of course, what was I thinking...

She was relieved that just then a maître'd showed them to a private table.

After they'd gotten some cocktails, while they were waiting on a black truffle pizza, the two settled down into their tufted leather seats. They enjoyed a brief moment of feeling like the high-class cosmopolitans who surrounded them, while the din of voices and faint string music concealed their conversation well.

"What do you believe, Ridley?" asked Henri with surprising directness.

"About what?"

"You know, we all have these ways of seeing the world, understanding things, putting the stuff we really can't under-stand into different categories. I see a God. I see a universe beyond all human understanding. I see forces arrayed against God and anyone who wants to go with Him.

"So, what I see when I look at that jinn," he pointed to an imaginary figure across the room, "is some evil thing that crawled out of the wrong side of creation. That's what I believe."

Ridley had to take a real gulp of her rum and rye and vermouth drink.

"Shit, was that our homework? You sound like you had that written down. Um, okay. God? Yeah, of course. It's the only thing that makes sense. But demons? Jinn?" she said, tapping anxiously on the arm of her chair. "Can't say I really get that one. Although yesterday I would have said *bullshit*. Maybe that's what they call character growth."

"No, I don't think that's what they call character growth."

"Agree to disagree. But let's go the whole hog. Come on. Barbecue's not over. What do you say about angels?"

"Yes. Exist."

"I guess that goes with the 'demons exist' package. What about ghosts?"

"Mmm, no."

"That's not fun. Aliens?"

"Hard to look out at that universe and think we're the only things God created to take glory in Him."

"Mm, *preacher!* So then, is a jinn just another name for a demon?"

"I think like a class of demon, a type, yeah."

"So, think you can pray this thing away?" she asked, flashing a sarcastic smile.

He didn't take the bait. "I pray all day and straight up beg for help in danger. This is a material world but it has a real spiritual dimension. You can't get rid of the physical just because you pray in the spiritual."

Ridley's wry expression went serious.

That's the best answer I've ever heard.

But instead, she only said, "Well, don't let me stop you doing any of that."

One of the men across the room in a Savile Row suit was trying to catch her glance. She finally locked eyes with him, though did not return anything but a leaden gaze to his flattering smile.

"So then, it's to be iron and salt!" she said, looking back at Henri.

They lifted their cocktails to it.

A server dropped the truffle pizza at their table. Ridley felt a knot twist in her stomach as if she hadn't eaten in days. She was just digging into a slice when Henri pulled out his buzzing cell phone.

"Hold on," he said to her, answering the phone as he stepped away into the hotel hall.

She didn't mind being left with the pizza, even as Savile Row thought he saw an opening. He tried to toast her across the room, but she only called over the server for a new cocktail.

A moment later, Henri returned.

"That was Nicolas Broussard," he said under his breath, sliding back into his chair.

"The INRAP lab tech? Has your number?"

"Don't you know where I grew up? Bribes. They make wheels turn, people talk."

The man of faith has unexpected wiles.

"What did he have to talk about?"

"I wanted all of the inscription translations before Claudine Gaspar's office filtered and delayed them."

"You think she's purposefully cutting us out of discovery?"

"Why wouldn't she?"

Touché. Ridley did not like that she hadn't thought of this. "What does he have for us?"

Henri opened up Proton Mail on his phone and downloaded an email attachment.

"This was the one written in stylized old French. *The last hold of treasure, beneath the earth of the northmen.*"

"You must be joking," said Ridley. "Is this a game?"

He burst into a grin. "It's a riddle."

Back in Henri's hotel room, they settled into the puzzle. He began searching online for any medieval references to "earth of the northmen." The internet returned too many options to intelligently narrow it down.

Ridley pulled out her phone and dialed Professor White on speaker, who was giddy with the news. From the sounds, it was apparent that she was making dinner, and not delicately.

"We were thinking that 'earth of the northmen' is Scandinavian," said Ridley. "Did the Templars have any strongholds there?"

"There's no written evidence of them ever going that far north. The Hospitallers did venture there, and the Teutonic Knights held land in Sweden. They really had no reason to go to the darkest and coldest regions of the north. It was the Holy Land that obsessed them, and making their seat of power in Europe."

"What were their most northern strongholds then?" asked Henri.

"Scotland. I can't imagine those were very desirable postings."

"Were Scots ever referred to as 'northmen'?"

"Not in Templar writings, and not in any medieval literature, no."

Ridley clasped her hands over her head. "These ancient treasure hunts, man..."

"Wait," said Professor White sharply.

They heard the sound of her clanging a pan down on the stove.

"*Northmen*...you're not wrong about Scandinavia! Well, no, partly wrong, but *Normant* was the Scandinavian word for *northmen*. That became *Normanz* in Old French. That was the word, right? *Normanz?*"

Henri re-checked the photo attachment that Broussard had sent. "That's it."

"It's Normandy!"

"Oh, shit," said Ridley, a smile creeping out.

"Okay, what were the Templar locations in Normandy? We're looking for something buried under the earth," said Henri.

"There were a few," said Professor White, "but the most famous is Château de Gisors. Still standing. A foreboding tower, really. Years back there was much ado about it when some groundskeeper claimed he'd found treasure in the tunnels beneath. The French excavated it to death but found nothing. Can't imagine there'd be anything there for treasure now, or they'd have found it already."

"You know how much work it took to chisel those words into iron?" said Henri. "It had to be significant to go to all that work, to point the way."

"I think it's time to pick up some gear," said Ridley.

CHAPTER
NINETEEN

TIAGO INACIO STROLLED into the Louvre at precisely one hour before closing. He wore a black cashmere sweater and gleaming Ferragamo Oxfords. A pair of associates who looked like former special ops flanked him. He looked like one of the ultra-wealthy donors who were given discreet access to works before they went public.

He did adore this place, the most legendary museum in the world. The half dozen times he had walked its halls, he'd marveled at the extent of human creativity. Though there was no wing he wouldn't visit, no exhibit he wouldn't bask in, it was the sunlit gallery housing the Italian paintings that always pulled him back.

It was there that his uncle had first introduced him to Caravaggio's *Death of the Virgin*. It was sensuous and anguished, a sublime piece of grief. The Vatican had commissioned its creation, but upon seeing it, rejected the masterpiece. It was too realistic, too vivid, too devastating. It was ghastly and heretical to portray their vaunted Virgin as so human. They thought the woman used as a model was a prostitute known by the artist. Caravaggio, himself a brutal and volatile man, was furious with the rejection, but he was paid for it. His patron sold the painting almost immediately. To the benefit of the world, it had ended up in a museum rather than a church.

Here, thought Tiago, it was properly appreciated.

The clacking of his own shoes against the marble was soon joined by the echo of another pair, as Claudine Gaspar came striding down the corridor to meet them.

"Senhor Inacio! Welcome to the Louvre."

Though she greeted him with a formal handshake and a steady voice, she was fluttering with nerves. She had only met this man twice before, and both times they had been within a group. Now the need to impress him—or rather to not fail him —was making her anxious.

"Thank you, madame. It's one of my favorite places in the world," he said, gazing around.

He appeared so full of wonder that she believed him entirely. It wasn't an act of elitism or feigned patronage.

"I understand," she said with a smile, feeling more at ease. "I'm fortunate to walk through the finest halls in the world every day."

"These are my associates, Bruno—"

He gestured to the tall man beside him with dark designer stubble and a widow's peak.

"—and João."

On his other side nodded a thick-jawed man with bright green eyes.

Claudine gave them a polite smile. "Please, come with me."

They followed her to the nearby elevator, where she scanned her key card for access to the lower floors.

The lab was empty tonight except for Broussard, who was nursing a Coke and looking like he wanted to be anywhere else right now. He was fast to his feet when they entered the lab, though.

"This is my assistant technician, Nicolas."

Tiago shook his hand. "Hello. Thank you for being here."

Broussard was disarmed by the politesse of a man who was so clearly a VIP.

"Sure, of course."

Tiago turned to Claudine. "Where is it?"

She led him around the bend to the center of the lab. The sarcophagus lay on a steel table. The broken pieces of the urn were arranged on another.

"We've left everything as it was since I called you. I've spoken with the Minister and he's agreed to delay the announcement of our findings for now, especially in light of the tragedy that all of France has just endured."

She began the demonstration, going meticulously over each piece, with the broken urn, the Templar cross, the salt...Tiago followed along with intense focus. Of course he knew of the Templars' quests, their search across the earth for the most sacred items of their faith. The Seal of Solomon was lesser known among these, but for the Order of Raphael, it was the greatest treasure of them all.

Let the Catholic Church have the Holy Grail, which could only offer healing to one who drank from it. They could have the Ark of the Covenant, which was only deadly to those who disrespected the Lord by disrespecting it. Those were not weapons, not instruments to wield but only tokens of the supernatural.

The Seal of Solomon was pure power. The Church had spent

thousands of years trying to expel and keep at bay the darkest spirits of the universe. Always on the back foot, always reactive. The Church could keep playing defense. The Raphaels were there to play offense.

Claudine's confidence grew with every passing moment. Tiago was in her arena, after all, and she exuded the expertise that he sought. When she got to the indentation where the saber hilt had been embedded, he moved closer to inspect.

"The broken part of the blade did have Arabic inscriptions on it," said Claudine. "I wish we'd been able to record or translate them, but they were lost quite quickly. Taken."

"A great loss, but it was only the beginning. Where is the rest of the sword, I wonder?"

"We have no direct information on that, but we have translated all of the engravings inside the sarcophagus."

She beckoned to Broussard, who handed Tiago a sheaf of papers. He browsed through them.

"Most of them are verses from the Bible or parts of the Catholic creed. Then there's this strange bit here," she said, pointing to a small, faint line in Old French script. *"The last hold of treasure, beneath the earth of the northmen."*

He looked at the printed paper, then peered closely at the inscription.

"The *'northmen'* is Normandy," Tiago said quietly, "but there's no treasure left now, is there? There is only a jinn called 'slave' looking for...something."

Tiago straightened up and looked at her.

"There will be no announcement for now. We have a member within the Interior who will make sure that the Ministry understands. But you," he said, brightening with a real charm, "you have presided over something magnificent, Claudine. I think—I believe that soon everyone will know. They'll see and believe and bow the knee. It began here, with you."

His expression was so warm that she nearly blushed. Here she was, a world-class professional in her sixties, and she still felt radiant under this man's compliments.

"Now, where in Paris might one get a salt block and some iron knives?" he asked.

CHAPTER
TWENTY

———

AFTER THE SHATTERING of Sainte-Chapelle and the sheer display of destructive force from the jinn-possessed, Ridley was adamant that they go to Gisors armed. Booker had the office arrange for a rental car out of a nondescript lot near Charles de Gaulle airport.

The worker who handed them the keys over the desk was a deadpan Swiss with stringy hair. He had loaded the car himself with their agency-approved wish list. A SIG Sauer P320 AXG Legion. A Walther PDP. Two fitted suppressors. A stack of extra magazines loaded with hollow-tip rounds. A CRKT M16 tactical folding knife. And at Ridley's request, a Black Emerson Wave karambit.

As soon as she took it out from the hidden compartment beneath the floorboard, she twirled it, hefting the weight and balance of the thing. It was practically a velociraptor's claw in blade form. She had to admit that even holding one made her itch to be able to use it.

Wait for the right time. There's always one deadly moment.

She folded it into the handle and slipped it into her belt.

By late morning, Ridley and Henri were winding through the Norman countryside in a gray BMW 3 Series. A faint drizzle shrouded the pastures around them. In the back of the vehicle was a cache of hardware, just in case they might need to dig into that part *beneath the earth.* They had a shovel, pickaxes of various sizes, gloves, a small trowel, crowbar, bolt-cutters, flashlights, headlamps, and even a measure of rope.

When they reached the historic site, they parked outside the walls. Thanks to the dismal weather, there were only three other cars in the lot. Ridley and Henri left the tools behind to take a look around.

Château de Gisors had been the creation of the English King William II, nearly a thousand years ago. In an attempt to defend the Anglo-Saxon territories of the north, he had built a number of castles throughout Normandy. When France conquered the English lands not long after, the French king granted the holding to the Templars.

For almost two hundred years, the knightly Order occupied the castle. Yet it would eventually become a jail for them, when King Philip IV ordered them slaughtered, disbanded, and thrown into dungeons. It was the final prison of the last Grand Master, Jacques de Molay, before he was burned at the stake.

Gravel crunched under Ridley and Henri's feet as they entered the walled bailey yard. Before them, high up on a motte, loomed the circular stone walls of the tower. There was no one else in sight.

"Tunnels, tunnels," said Henri, looking around.

When Ridley found the gated entrance, she saw that the padlock was crushed. The chain lay on the ground. She gave a quick scan, but there was no sign of anyone. She beckoned Henri sharply.

Pulling open the rusted iron gate, she padded through across soggy grass, toward the stone steps leading down into the earth.

As she angled around, she saw a spatter of red across the rock walls of the stairwell...then spotted the body lying crumpled at the bottom. She drew the SIG from her waistband. Henri drew his Walther.

There was no movement, no sound other than the faint patter of rain. He scanned the rest of the grounds as Ridley descended the steps.

The iron gate at the bottom of the short staircase was broken open as well. She knelt down to check the body, keeping her gun trained on the entryway. Confirmed dead. It was an older man, who had bled out through a ragged gash in his neck.

Ridley rose up and swept into the tunnel. Henri brought up the rear.

The tunnels were brightly lit for tourists, a winding, low-ceilinged labyrinth of arched stones. They moved through the maze like a seasoned team, covering and clearing for each other in silence.

They rounded one corner and stopped.

In an alcove ahead was a scene of wreckage. The wall looked torn open, revealing a secret chamber behind it. They both moved closer. Henri pulled out a tactical flashlight and beamed it into the dark space.

"Oh, hell," he murmured.

Across the back wall was a mural streaked with dirt. A Latin engraving below was barely visible. In the middle was what seemed to be an indentation. Ridley peered closer, and reached out to feel the edges.

"Henri," she said quietly, "doesn't this look like that same shape in the sarcophagus? Where it was cut away, where the saber hilt was embedded?"

There was no shape of a hilt to this, though. It was a neatly cut rectangle.

"It's about the same width as the blade," he said.

"Is this some damn sword-in-the-stone game?"

"I'm going to get some footage," he said, holstering his gun. "Cover."

Ridley kept her SIG at low ready, scanning the tunnel halls as Henri leaned in to document the markings on his phone camera. Then he spotted more wall writings on the inside of the chamber wall, just above the ground. There was a rock blocking one section of it.

He reached in to remove it.

And realized too late that it was not a rock, but a clay urn. Ridley saw it, and a surge of alarm tore through her.

"Put it down!"

It was too late. Henri hissed sharply in pain and dropped the scalding hot urn.

It crashed to the ground.

From the broken vessel, a tendril of smoke began to rise. It grew and grew. They reeled back, guns trained on the swirling pillar as it thickened into a true shape.

"If either of us gets possessed by this thing—" started Ridley.

"Don't let them leave," he finished.

What emerged from the oily shadow was wiry and hunched. It looked more goblin than human, smoke wisping from its skin. A pair of eyes opened like burning coals, and a rattling, shrieking hiss raked their ears.

This was not the same malignant creature that had emerged in the laboratory under the Louvre. What stood before them was not the powerful ifrit, but a lesser jinn.

It lurched forward.

Ridley loosed a torrent of shots. Every one of the rounds was absorbed into the blackness of the creature. It did not even flinch. Henri hit a headshot, but it didn't matter. The round had no effect.

"Blades?" she shouted above the rattling hiss.

She snatched the karambit from her belt with her right hand. As she backed down the tunnel toward the exit, drawing the creature after her, Henri used the distraction to shiv the thing in the back with his M16 blade, a flurry of quick stabs into its torso.

The jinn whirled around, lashing at Henri with blow after blow, hurling him back against the stone walls. It turned around to face Ridley, who emptied her magazine into its face.

Nothing. It burst forward in a wave of scorching heat.

She dodged. As the jinn lunged past her, she slashed at it with the karambit. The blade tore along its midsection, but there was no blood. It looked like flames within the gash.

The thing shrieked and flew up the stone stairs. Henri scrambled to his feet, following Ridley as she sprinted up after it. They both burst out into the open, but the jinn was gone. The bailey was quiet, and rain pelted down on their stunned faces.

"I should have known," said Henri, furious. "I shouldn't have picked it up. I thought I was just moving a stupid rock."

"At least it didn't possess you, but shit." She nodded to the village only a hundred yards beyond the walls. "Somebody will have heard those shots. Time to go."

. . .

Henri drove as they argued over who to call. He wanted to consult with Professor White about the wall markings. Ridley was adamant that due to the involvement and appearance of the jinn, Owen Allchurch would be a better first resource. They had taken his contact info the day before.

The debate was cut short when she simply dialed Owen on speaker. The excitement in his voice was evident the moment he realized who was calling him. At first Ridley said as little as possible, simply asking him to interpret the photos she was sending him from Henri's phone.

He reviewed them, talking through every marking, stringing together his ideas in almost incoherent fashion.

Until finally, he exclaimed, "Yes! I know where this points to. You *cannot* believe this, though."

"Try me."

"This fourth image has a book in it, that small thing on the right, mid-height. Books were rare back then. Only the rich had them. Of course, the Templars *were* rich, incredibly rich. They wrote below this depiction, *the final grail of knowledge*."

"Oh no. That's not the Holy Grail, is it?"

"No, no. The first use of the word 'grail' was right around 1300. It was a chalice, a drinking cup, but it was also to refer to… as like…an ideal, something sought-after."

"So a book that's sought after," said Henri.

"Yeah! I'm fairly certain."

"That's good work," said Ridley. "So where does this point to? What's our destination for finding whatever's next?"

"Oh, I—I'll meet you in La Rochelle. You're about five-and-a-half hours away."

"No, no, just tell us where to look. We've got it."

"I'm already booking a flight there. I'll meet you first thing in the morning. I'll call you."

"Owen, we're not having you on site. It's unnecessary and dangerous."

"You don't know if it's unnecessary."

He paused, letting the thought simply hang in the silence.

There was little she could do to wring the information out of him over the phone, and they all knew it. She shook her head with a scowl.

"We'll call you. You will do what we say, the second we say it, nothing less. Don't bring anything more than a backpack."

"This is brilliant. I'll be there. Everything you said, don't worry."

They hung up, and Henri glanced over at her.

"You didn't want to warn him about the other jinn?"

"Can you think of anything that would make him more determined to insert himself into all of this? This shit is dangerous now. That old man..."

She flexed a hand out in frustration. It was likely they'd never learn the name of the man that had been slain on the steps of Gisors.

A tourist? A local? A groundskeeper?

What they knew was that this ifrit had made Sofie Hasbo's hands those of a killer.

"God be with that man's family," said Henri quietly.

Anger scorched in Ridley's stomach. She had to battle it back and refocus.

"I'll look up La Rochelle. We can try to find out where we're really headed."

CHAPTER
TWENTY-ONE

———

LA ROCHELLE, FRANCE

Six hours after leaving the blood-stained tunnels of Gisors, Ridley and Henri arrived on the cobblestone streets of La Rochelle. The sun was disappearing into the ocean in streaks of fuchsia. The water of Old Harbour below gleamed a soft pink. Rows of sailboats bobbed gently along their moorings.

The town lay on the west coast of France, a prime location in the Bay of Biscay. It was the only deep water port on the nation's Atlantic coastline, and as such had become a hub of commercial trade. It was in such a prime location that the Germans had used it as their submarine base during the Occupation. At the mouth of the harbor, two stone towers flanked a narrow channel. Long ago, the city's defenders would hoist a massive chain across the water between them, to block or destroy invading ships.

Today, at this hour, it was a mellow place. The shops and restaurants along the harbor were just beginning to glow. The din of evening traffic carried across the harbor.

They parked the BMW by the marina and got out to look around. Owen had only agreed to meet them here, without any further detail.

Ridley checked the time on her Tactix Delta watch, then scoured the waterfront.

"Think it's the towers?" she asked.

"That's what I would think too, except they weren't built until seventy years *after* the Templars fled this place. Some say they took all their treasure out of here with their fleet."

She shrugged dismissively. "So I drive, you read. You think the kid really made it here in time?"

At that moment, she spotted Owen Allchurch walking along the bulkhead. He hadn't seen them yet. The young grad student was wearing pale distressed jeans, a white T-shirt with a huge silver skull on the front, and a denim jacket. There was a small street bag slung over one shoulder. He looked like a young footballer who'd just signed his first big contract with a Premier League club.

"Oh, man," chuckled Ridley. "I should have said something about attire."

They started walking. The moment he saw them, an unguarded grin burst out.

"I can't believe all this," he said. "This is really crazy, yeah?"

"You haven't been wrong yet," said Henri.

"Do you guys do this often? Like, is this your job, goin' about—finding mad shit around the world?"

"Owen," said Ridley in a firm address, "We agreed to let you join us *only here*. Because honestly, it's just that you were being a bit of an asshole about it and we don't have time to waste."

He tried to look scolded but he was still too thrilled by the whole thing.

"So, where are we going already?" she said.

Owen gestured across the harbor, beyond the towers, to a single ornate spire rising up in the twilight.

"The Lantern Tower. The lighthouse. Also a prison for priests, sometimes. Also, it's closed, so, we're gonna need to give it a—" He made a cracking sound. "I've done a few in my days. Nearly got kicked out of the choir, actually."

Henri just stared at him.

"Yeah, we've got this," said Ridley, already cringing with regret.

They grabbed their tactical flashlights, gloves, the small pickaxe, the bolt-cutters, and a crowbar from the BMW. As they made their way down the cobblestone, past outdoor cafés and strolling pedestrians, Owen was briefing them on the history of the Templars in La Rochelle. Much of it had been rebuilt, but the base was untouched. It was also six feet thick.

"I went over everything again and again on my flight," he told them as they reached the tower. "It's still here, I'm *certain* of it."

They waited until they were clear of the foot traffic for a moment, and vaulted over the low thick wall into the little courtyard full of scrub brush. Henri used the bolt-cutter to take off the padlock chain on the small red door of the lighthouse. The next door beyond it was a heavy metal thing that had to be cut and pried open.

Once they were inside the circular lower level, Ridley scoped the arched ceiling with her flashlight. It was no wider than twenty feet.

"Okay," said Owen. "Which way is west?"

Ridley checked her watch compass and pointed in the direction. He went to the alcove situated at due west. It had been carved as an opening for a cannon, and a low, covered window was just barely large enough to slot through an iron barrel for firing outward. He reached up to the arched ceiling of the alcove, tracing along it with his fingers.

"Here, yeah, it's here! I need the little pickaxe."

Henri handed it to him, and the young Welshman began carving away at the mortar.

"It's not sealed up as well as the others, which is a bit of a miracle, really, that it didn't come loose. I guess they didn't fire a cannon through this port very often."

A moment later, he pulled out the loose stone and reached up into the niche.

"Wait!" said Henri. He tossed the gloves at Owen. "Don't touch anything without those."

Owen pulled them on and reached back up. "Buzzin'," he whispered to himself.

Seconds later, he pulled out a small clay urn.

"Put it down," said Henri. "Gently, right now. Don't hold it."

Owen set it on the floor. Ridley crouched and shined a light on it. There was one Arabic word inscribed on the outside. Henri snapped a photo of it.

"Do we know what's in here," she said.

"Is that a jinn? Is that like the genie lamp?" said Owen, his eyes shining.

"Shit genies. They grant no wishes to the person who breaks them out. Unless you want to be burnt up or possessed."

"There's more up here," he said, reaching back up into the dark compartment. "Something stuck..."

He tugged, then yanked. When he pulled his hand back out, he was holding the gleaming shard of a saber blade.

"It *is* collecting the pieces of the saber," said Ridley. "There *was* one at Gisors, too!"

The Arabic script was faint under a layer of grime, but bits of the golden finish glinted through. Henri snapped photos from every angle.

"Isn't there anything else up there?" he asked. "This isn't the end of the saber. There has to be more to find."

Owen craned his neck to peer into the crevice.

"Yeah, yeah, there's something here. Phone?"

Henri handed it to him, and he took some flash photos.

"This is completely amazing," he said to himself, stepping out of the alcove. "They really left treasure. The Templars really did it."

"*Treasure* is a funny word," said Ridley, looking down at the urn. "We're gonna need to chuck this in the ocean."

"Put it in a weighted box," said Henri. "You don't want that washing up on shore."

"Like Jumanji," said Owen, and they both looked at him. "Because it didn't go well."

Each of their flashlights dimmed for a moment. Ridley shook hers.

"What is—"

The darkness around them suddenly thickened, almost *growing* as if it was a living thing. It seemed to swallow the light. They looked to the urn on the floor, but it was quiet, intact.

"I don't think—" Henri started.

A glimpse of color by the door snapped Ridley's head up. In an instant, she'd drawn her gun and braced her wrists together against the weak beam of the flashlight. Henri pulled his Walther from its holster as he stepped back.

There in the doorway stood a blonde woman, her head cranked forward at a strange angle, every muscle in her body taut. In one hand she held the golden saber with the broken blade.

Sofie Hasbo.

CHAPTER
TWENTY-TWO

————

LA ROCHELLE, FRANCE

Owen had no idea who this woman was, but there was something terrifying in the way she stood and the way she held her head, the way she was staring at them through the oily darkness. Taking a cue from Ridley and Henri's reactions, he scrambled backward.

"Hands! Show me your hands!" yelled Henri.

DUTCH: *"Raise your hands!"* said Ridley.

It wasn't Danish, but it was the best she could do. It didn't matter. Sofie Hasbo did not raise her hands.

The movement was hardly more than a flash. She bolted across the room at a speed that was inhuman, hurling Owen into a wall as she snatched the piece of the saber they'd just recovered.

With the way she just moved, Ridley and Henri couldn't

afford to fire inside. The circular stone structure would mean a hail of ricocheted bullets if they missed. They could only train their guns on her, trigger fingers ready.

They watched as she fit the shard to the golden saber. It affixed somehow, sticking to the broken place, but there was a dark jagged line across it. She turned to face them with the blade raised, when a sound at the entrance distracted her.

They all looked to the door.

Emerging around the corner was a man wearing black tactical gear, gripping a Glock in front of his face.

When Sofie Hasbo saw him, she opened her mouth, and howled a scorching wave of heat. He keeled back with a cry of pain. In another flash, she lurched forward and stabbed him through the chest.

The ragged blade went clean through his lungs. The force of strength behind it was astonishing.

Multiple shots ripped through the entryway. The bullets struck her torso, but she hardly flinched. She looked straight down the dark hall and spoke for the first time. Shockingly, her voice was normal.

"You knew that wouldn't work."

She bolted down the small hallway toward the door, and they heard another muffled yelp.

"Stay in here!" Henri told Owen.

He and Ridley started after Sofie Hasbo, having to step over the intruder's body, and then the body of a second man in the hallway, similarly dressed. They heard a series of low shouts outside, then gunshots.

"Who are these guys?" Ridley hissed.

They flanked the doorway, guns at the low ready. Henri shot her a look. There were two SUVs parked along the street. Around the vehicles, a handful of combatants were taking cover, bristling with rifles, engaged with the fleeing Sofie Hasbo.

"No markings," she said.

More shots rang out across the waterfront, followed by screams of alarm from civilians nearby. Police would be here within minutes.

"Move," said Henri.

They swept out into the little courtyard and took cover behind the thick wall. Ridley could spot three men and one woman, all wearing the same black tactical gear. Through a break in the live fire, they heard shouting in a foreign language.

Portuguese?

One who sounded in command rallied for the others to regroup. Then, to Ridley and Henri's surprise, he called out in English.

"Americans! I know you have weapons. I know you are professionals, but you need to put them down now if you want to leave La Rochelle alive. Put them down and walk down the street."

The two exchanged a look. This was unexpected.

"Thanks for the suggestion!" Ridley called back, "but we'd like you to go first."

"You'll be very uncomfortable when the police arrive."

She couldn't tell if he was bluffing or boasting. If he had some arrangement with the cops, then she and Henri really would be in trouble. If the French found armed foreign operatives with two dead men in their wake, there would be some kind of diplomatic hell to pay.

"We have everything we need. Get Owen," whispered Henri. "I'll cover."

He was the sniper. It was only fair. As he let off a round of shots at the SUVs, she ran back inside the tower, hauled the bewildered Owen out into the courtyard, and shoved him into cover near Henri.

The Portuguese returned fire, bullets biting into the ancient stone all around them.

"We can't wait them out, if they're in with the cops," Ridley said to Henri. "Can't trust them an inch, either."

She scanned the surroundings, pulling out her focus to take in everything around her. Detaching. The tower was set against the bulkhead, the huge wall that lined the beach parking lot and rose up high to shield the shore against massive waves. If they could circle around toward the water and keep tight against the huge wall of the bulkhead, they'd have a chance.

"The beach," she said to Henri, and grabbed Owen's jacket. "Move. Stay low."

The Portuguese leader called again, "Don't be stupid and brave. Be wise and brave and take the loss."

Henri strafed along the wall as they backed away, their cover diminishing with the curve of the stones. He loosed a few shots to keep heads down by the SUVs. Ridley kept herself between their line of sight and Owen. They vaulted over the wall and landed in the soft grass below.

Ridley bounded back to her feet, gripping her SIG, watching above. Seconds later, Henri leapt over. She kept her gun trained upward as they headed for the parking lot, scanning the overhead walk that bordered the street.

That was unexpected.

Tiago had no interest in following the Americans. They didn't have the saber, which was in the hands of a possessed woman with supernatural strength and speed. Even then, the murderous jinn had a long way to go to obtain every piece and make the blade complete.

Unfortunately, it required blood to seal each broken shard back to the whole. As Tiago stepped over the bodies of his two blood-soaked men in the tower, he was grieved. He knew their families, the sports that their children played, their holiday traditions. Yet, this was the final play. Like him, like the rest of his assembled squad, they were prepared to give up everything to achieve what the Order had never before been able to.

He had been bluffing about the police. There were Raphaels within the French ranks, but none in La Rochelle. Calling down their help would take time, and this was a race they could not afford to fall behind in.

They documented the entire scene, including the markings in the crevice. Then they loaded the bodies of their fallen into the SUVs and sped off into the night.

The wail of sirens rang in Tiago's ears as they drove away. He looked through the digital photos they'd taken of the crevice markings. He knew where they were going next.

This one would not be easy.

CHAPTER
TWENTY-THREE

_____

NANTES, FRANCE

THEY DROVE NORTH, with Ridley behind the wheel.

"Who the hell are they?" she said.

"You're sure they were speaking Portuguese?" asked Henri.

"Yeah, I'm sure," she shot back.

Owen piped up from the back. "After they were driven out of France, the Templars went to Portugal."

"I thought they were destroyed," said Ridley.

"Yeah, but a few of them made it out. There's some—I mean, I tried to follow the trail of their evolution as far as I could. The survivors were given refuge by the king of Portugal as long as they took a new name—didn't want to piss anybody off—so they turned themselves into the Military Order of Christ. Everyone kind of lost interest because they'd lost all their power and most of their money. That Military Order still exists, actually, but now they just give themselves badges and medals and hold mayorships. Would anyone like some crisps?" he asked, pulling a snack bag out of his backpack.

He always got voraciously hungry after a surge of adrenaline. In his rugby days, he was known to pound down a double order of fish and chips at the local pub. He knew that eventually, the athlete's appetite combined with the graduate student's life would make him fluffy around the middle. He'd considered joining a rec league or taking up rowing, but right now, he simply needed to clear the hunger in order to think.

"No, thanks. Okay, so they're Templar-lite?" said Ridley.

"Yeah, but there's some stuff out there that talks about another group, some sect that split off really soon after they made it to Portugal. This one thought the remaining Templars had gone soft, and their new Military Order wasn't really military enough. So they called themselves the Order of Raphael, and went dark."

"Could you define *dark?*" said Henri.

Owen made a sound of frustration at his own lack of answers. "There aren't many records. They haven't left many writings, but in the early days they pretty much declared war on the Catholic Church. They took it personally that the pope had signed off on their torture and execution just to go along with a French king's power grab."

"Did they die out?" asked Ridley.

He shrugged.

Henri frowned. "How did they know about any of this? That's what I can't get. How did they know what we were looking for? How did they know where *we* were?"

"That's a damn good question," said Ridley. "However they found out, they're probably going to know where we're heading next. Which is where, our learned friend?" She glanced in the rearview mirror.

Owen, chomping on crisps, was going through the photos they'd taken. He talked half to them, half to himself.

"I'm lookin' here. The Arabic is so incredible...no record of the Templars using it anywhere else, ever. I wonder who they got to write it."

"Can you read it?" asked Henri.

"No, sorry, not a word, but this writing on the urn...was there an urn in Gisors?"

Ridley replied slowly, "Yes."

"Was there writing on it?"

From the passenger seat, Henri spoke up. "We didn't get a photo. It broke."

Owen stared between them. "Another one?"

"That's why I told you to wear gloves. It heats up and you drop it, and then a fire demon comes out and things get..."

"Wait, what happened? Again?"

They hadn't told him about the jinn when they phoned him at Cambridge, but there was little to lose at this point by reading him in. The fuller the picture he had of the situation, the better an asset he would be. So they relayed, in short, what had happened in the tunnels below Gisors.

Ridley left out the part about the man crumpled in death at the bottom of the stairs.

Once Owen had processed the wild story of their close call, he dug back into the photos from La Rochelle.

"It's good for us that these markings are in Latin, not Arabic. I took that as a boy. Hated it, but part of a classical King's education. It's been more useful than I'd have thought, really."

"So what does it say?" pressed Ridley.

"*Not Augustine, Franciscan, or Dominican, but west of the gates. Beyond the River of Wells. Wm watched and died in his disobedience.*"

She gave a hard-edged laugh. "So we don't even know what country."

He was already frustrated by his own confusion.

"Those are all friaries," said Henri, coming alive in the puzzle. "Augustine. Franciscan. Dominican. Where would they all be together?"

"Italy?" suggested Ridley.

"Augustine wasn't Italian. He was a Berber. African," said Henri.

"No way!" said Owen. "We didn't learn that in school."

"Not surprising," he said dryly. "But Saint Francis of Assisi was Italian. The Dominicans were French."

"Meet in the Mediterranean," said Ridley. "On a yacht."

Henri pulled out his cell phone and drew up an encrypted browser. "Well, then we have the River of Wells, and search results say...that's the River Fleet, ladies and gentlemen. Called the River of Wells in the thirteenth century."

"Okay. Okay!" exclaimed Owen. "So we have London, and it *was* walled in that time, so it had gates."

"All of those friaries must have existed within the city proper then."

As much as she enjoyed the historical nerds weaponizing their knowledge, Ridley needed to cut straight. "What's the biggest Templar site in London?"

"It's...Temple Church. Yeah," said Owen, "it's west of old London. It's west of Fleet River. That's it!"

"*Wm?*" wondered Henri. "Short for William?"

"Sir William Marshall is buried there. He's famous for being the greatest knight who ever lived."

"Did he die there in disobedience?" asked Ridley.

"No, not that guy."

"Well, you have time, Sherlock...and Watson. At least we know where we're going."

"Can you guys—would you help me get back to England?"

"There's no room on the jet," said Henri, deadpan.

Owen looked at him, trying to gauge if he was joking.

"We'll get you a ticket," Ridley said, then she looked at her partner.

Henri, who had been scrolling on his phone, spoke. "The Temple Church is closed tomorrow for a special concert performance. The Royals will be there. Of course."

"We have to beat this Portuguese death squad to the spot. Then again, if this ifrit version of Sofie Hasbo gets there first—"

"She might Sainte-Chapelle the place."

Owen was crunching loudly in the back, hanging on their every word.

"We're going to need someone in London, someone official," said Henri.

Ridley hesitated for a moment, then said finally, "Will the Superintendent of the Metro Police do?"

Henri gave an enthusiastic nod. "Yeah, that should do."

"I can't promise she'll be happy to hear from me, but I'm sure she'll get over it when she understands the situation."

He gave her a side-eye. "Was it a personal or professional screwup? What are we walking into?"

"It was a nearly-there. Too many glasses of wine at a hotel bar after a mission success. Nothing really happened. I'm just saying she may be a bit sore about it—the fact that nothing really happened."

Henri raised a brow.

Part of their work was accumulating contacts, building trust and good will with people in positions that could be advantageous to their achieving their objectives. She was good at keeping lines open, but sometimes the best of intentions ended up misunderstood. Sometimes the lead ended up feeling strung along, and resentful for it.

The Superintendent of the London Police, through half a bottle of wine, made half a pass at Ridley, who suddenly felt that the cocktail table separating them was too small. Declining her out of professional decorum would have been easier if Ridley hadn't drunk the *other* half of that wine bottle herself. For someone as composed as this high-ranking woman, though, the rejection was embarrassing. She was notably cooler the next day in her office. It was the last time they'd spoken.

Ridley never meant to burn any good bridge, but sometimes the underside still ended up charred.

"*Nearly!*" She looked in the rearview. "Owen, never mix the two, all right? Remember how many Bond girls ended up dead. It's not worth it."

Owen grinned.

Henri put a hand over his face.

CHAPTER
TWENTY-FOUR

———

LONDON, ENGLAND

IT PAINED Renu Darji that the best coffeeshop in London did not open until 8:30 in the morning. She had discovered in her thirties that New York City shops opened at the crack of summer dawn, a very considerate 5:30 a.m.

In her own city, she woke up every day of the week at 5, went for a run in Regent's Park, showered, and made herself a protein smoothie. She would leave her flat in Marylebone at 8:15 for the short walk down to Workshop Coffee, arrive promptly a minute before they opened the door, pick up her favorite Rwandan blend, a slice of lemon loaf, and make it down to Bond Street Station in time to catch the metro.

From there, it was a ten minute ride to Embankment Station, and only a six-minute walk to Scotland Yard. She arrived each morning at 8:55, her lanyard ID around her neck, the lemon loaf already gone. The coffee cup hit her desk by 9:00.

As long as her mornings were ordered, she felt she could handle any crisis that might come in a day in one of the biggest cities in the world. The first item on today's agenda was a meeting with the Deputy Assistant Commissioner of the Metropolitan Police, the head of Royalty and Specialist Protection (RaSP) and the director of the Special Escort Group (SEG).

The four gathered in a conference room with their assistants, where the SEG director Jamie Clarke, a jowly man with a thick Scouse accent, laid out the plan of action. Experience could make some complacent, but it had only made Clarke more thorough. He ran a department for high-risk protection work that was world class. It was small, filled with elite motorcyclists and drivers, all of whom were quick thinkers.

The assignment for that afternoon would be cooperative. The Temple Church would be secured by RaSP at T-minus four hours. There was no need to shut anything down, except to secure the building itself. The choir and all staff had a special entrance and every name had been added to a master list. At T-minus one hour, the small fleet of SEG officers would arrive at Buckingham Palace to pick up the Prince and Countess of Wessex and Forfar, who were visiting London from their home in Bagshot.

The SEG motorcycles were low-key in appearance with little equipment, but their drivers were armed. They used whistles instead of sirens to communicate, as the latter seemed ever-present in the cacophony of the city. Whistles could be more communicative, and tended to get a better response from other motorists and pedestrians. Unlike in some major cities that blocked off city streets and tried to control every element, the Metro Police preferred fluidity. Keep general traffic moving.

Momentarily pause a street only long enough to flow through it.

"Who's the lead driver on this?" asked Renu as Clarke finished laying out the timeline of the royal escort return.

"Sergeant Loveless. He's competent, got his head on a swivel."

The lead motorcyclist was the only one who knew the route, because they made it up as they went. The lead would radio back to the other drivers with instructions on what turns to take. They had to be adaptable to the second when traffic morphed or when signals of danger popped up. Whatever happened, the escort must never, ever stop.

"Always choirs, innit?" the DAC remarked to her. "Royals never want to go to a Radiohead show?"

"I saw Elton John once with the princess."

"Which one?"

"Rocketman."

"I meant which prince—" he rolled his eyes but gave it up.

"It was all very sparkly. The man can really play."

They wrapped up, and Renu was back in her office before 10 a.m. Her assistant, Phil, who looked like a tall Harry Potter with his shaggy dark hair and spectacles, confirmed her travel time. She would be the one on site today at the Temple Church.

"I'll have the car 'round for you at half past two."

She was distracted by the phone buzzing in her pocket. When she saw the ID of the caller, she stared in disbelief.

"Or," said Phil, "I could have one standing by if you'd prefer to drive yourself?"

"Yes, thanks, have one standing by. Excuse me, Phil..."

He took his cue and shut the office door behind himself. Renu picked up the call.

"Ridley Samaras. I always knew that one day you'd come calling on my mobile."

. . .

Ridley and Henri had agreed to let Owen come with them to the meeting, but he had to sit at a distance unless they needed his input. Meeting with the Superintendent of Police about an imminent threat to the city was just a bit above him at this point. They couldn't risk making Renu uncomfortable with the presence of a civilian.

The three of them took the metro to Trafalgar Square, found the majestic church of St. Martin-in-the-Fields, and took a set of stairs from the street down into the crypt below.

It had all been outfitted for the modern diner and shopper. As they walked into a huge room with stone vaulted ceilings and dining tables, Henri shook his head in surprise.

"I really thought we were meeting in a crypt," he said.

"Look down," said Ridley.

He glanced at his feet, and realized he was standing on an engraved headstone. He cursed in Creole and hopped off, only to land on another.

Owen read the inscription. "Miss Martha Oliphant, rest in peace."

The Café in the Crypt was lined with steel serving counters that housed enticing arrays of pastries and hot dishes. Casual visitors were spread out among the tables. The place was only about half full.

"Can I buy you lunch?" said Owen.

Ridley found this pleasantly unexpected. She kept thinking of him as a kid, but in reality, he was only five years her junior. He had a rough charm that was in no way self-conscious, and had shown himself to be quite thoughtful of others. She was so mission-focused that sometimes she forgot to notice things like this. He surprised her.

"We'll skip it for now," said Ridley, "but thanks."

"Go get some food for yourself," said Henri. "Sit somewhere nearby, but *don't* look our way, okay? Be discreet."

Owen nodded heartily and went off to the cafeteria line. Ridley checked her watch.

"She's chronically on time."

As if on cue, Renu Darji walked into the café.

The Indian woman was no taller than five-foot-three, in her late forties. She wore a trim leather jacket, a purple button-up, and black trousers over a pair of low block heels. Her hair was swept back, strands coming loose in the front. Ridley had forgotten how jet black it was. Her gaze quickly found the two of them.

"Hello, Yankees."

Ridley felt awkward. A handshake would be inappropriately formal, but a hug was out of the question. So she brandished her warmest, most thrilling smile instead.

"Renu. Thank you for coming. This is my partner, Henri."

"Pleasure to meet you," he said, reaching to shake her hand.

On hearing his accent, Renu apologized. "Oh, I'm sorry— Yankee was presumptuous."

"Yankee by choice. Very proud of it. I don't even mind the song."

"It is a catchy one—" said Ridley.

"Don't sing it, Ridley," he said dryly.

This got a small grin from Renu as they headed into a deep alcove, and took up seats at a cushioned booth.

"You've got thirty minutes of my time," said Renu, taking off her jacket.

Ridley and Henri had rehearsed what to say, what to leave out, and what could be added in when she began questioning. Of course Renu and every other European had seen the images of Sainte-Chapelle on the news. The Metro Police had received the red notice from INTERPOL on Sofie Hasbo. To say anything about the jinn to Renu would be calamitous. What they unfolded to her was a story about the bizarre, violent international hunt for some ancient relics.

"We have very credible reasons to believe that Sofie Hasbo or an unidentified accomplice will attempt to gain access to the Temple Church today," concluded Henri.

Renu surveyed them with eyes that were impossibly dark and implacable.

"I understand the French took the first offender into custody, identified him as Thomas Declerq, a Belgian immigrant who worked as a colorist for comic books. He had no known communications with Hasbo, and even denied any knowledge of what happened in the chapel. So," she said, crossing one leg over the other and draping her forearms over her knees, "what information do you have that indicates a second, unknown accomplice?"

Ridley wanted to grin. The woman had risen to superintendent not for any nepotism, quotas, or favoritism. Renu Darji was a perceptive pragmatist. She had once likened her own career path to the trek of a mountain goat. The mountain would never be fair or safe or predictable. She would have to set her own pace, judge her own footholds, and never hesitate.

It helped that she had a savvy, disarming way of using posture and body language and wits.

"You know there are sources of intelligence we can't give up," said Ridley.

"HUMINT or SIGINT?"

Human intelligence or signal intelligence.

"HUMINT."

"Who else knows about this?"

Ridley looked at her soberly for a long moment, then glanced quickly at Henri. He gave a look, *I guess we have to tell her.*

"There's another set of hostiles out there. They're not connected to Sofie Hasbo or Declerq, but they're after the same thing. They know where it is, and given the well-armed squad we ran into last night at another location of interest, we'd say they're pretty serious about beating us to the target. And they like their weapons."

"Connections to any known organization?"

"Well...not sure they're *known*," said Ridley, "but they allegedly call themselves the Order of Raphael."

Renu stared at her.

"Yes, I know them."

CHAPTER
TWENTY-FIVE

LONDON, ENGLAND

"How do you know about the Order? They're so obscure that our resident scholar wasn't even sure they existed," said Henri, sitting forward with a new intensity.

"I don't know much, but there was a case I worked on years ago," said Renu, "when I was a D.C.I. There was a kidnapping in Westminster of a young boy, a choir member at the Abbey. As kidnapping cases go with young children, nothing seemed strange or bizarre. We went about following these wafer-thin leads.

"Of course, there was always the whiff of suspicion because James—the boy—had been an altar boy at the Church. At first there was nothing linking anyone at the Abbey to his disappearance, but eventually there were some smoke signals."

She glanced up at a few diners walking past the alcove. Her voice grew softer.

"There was a rising young star in their midst, an auxiliary bishop who was being groomed to succeed the Archbishop of Westminster one day. I don't know how familiar you are with the Catholic Church in England, but that's the highest-ranking member in the U.K. His protegé held a lot of influence just by association, but this man, Bishop Barella, had one of those typically scandalous histories, rumors of boy victims following in his wake. But he'd been abusing one *specifically* in the diocese since he was six years old. James, the boy who vanished."

Ridley's jaw flexed so tightly that the muscles along her cheek rippled. She could sense a surge of anger in Henri, ever so slight, though the man had a poker face you couldn't beat.

"Why would he kidnap the kid? Jeopardize everything when he was already getting away with that fucked-up shit?" she said through grinding teeth.

Renu lifted a hand. "He felt he had no choice but to make James disappear. Another bishop had discovered the abuse and decided to use it as blackmail."

"For money?" asked Henri.

"For promotion. The blackmailer threatened the bishop with taking evidence to the authorities, and he had it. Most Catholic clergy wouldn't dream of reporting it to the police before taking it to their superiors, but this one did."

"Smart man," muttered Ridley.

"Smart, but weird, no? The young bishop panicked. If the blackmailer reported internally, Barella knew he would just be moved on, quietly, efficiently, maybe even taken to the Vatican for protection. We know how that works. If he ended up in the hands of the police, the consequences would be quite a bit more serious. One would hope.

"The good news is we recovered James. Bishop Barella had

planned to use his connections to smuggle him out of the country to some diocese in Romania. The bastard had told the boy that his family would be struck down by God if he ever told a soul or tried to get home."

Ridley tried to calm her breathing, to not grind her teeth flat in anger.

"Did you find out why the blackmailer preferred the law to the Church?" asked Henri.

Renu gave him a sly smile, impressed with his line of questioning. "There you go. He wasn't a true Catholic. Not in the believing sense of the word. Not even in allegiance. We got warrants and found his digital trail. It's a hard thing to erase. Even spies are terribly sloppy these days."

She eyed Ridley, who arched a brow back at her.

Not me you're referring to.

"Wait, he was a spy?" said Ridley, then quickly realized. "For the Order."

"America," Renu sighed with a smile, "still sending their best and brightest. Yeah, he was. He only joined the Catholic Church as a plant, twenty-four years earlier."

Henri puffed out his cheeks in astonishment. "That's a Soviet-level long game."

"What happened to him? Blackmail's a crime, right?" said Ridley.

"Frankly, he got away with it. Some of the dodgiest police work I've seen in my career," said Renu, shaking her head. "Someone higher up in the chain got the word that we were to lay off. We had an airtight, flawless case against him. All I could think is that he was some sort of intelligence asset, but there was no evidence at all of that. He disappeared. Vanished completely from our every radar. To this day, I have no idea what became of him.

"The abuser, Barella, *was* in fact moved out of the country before we could nab him, as expected. The official Church of England may not be Catholic, but the Roman Catholic organization still wields enormous power in this country. The young bishop found his way to Vatican City, the perfect shelter, a law unto itself."

Her voice was laced with acid.

"How did the cops explain the boy's kidnapping?" asked Ridley.

"Blamed it on the smugglers. They were Pakistani, and after the abomination that was the Rotherham scandal...it was entirely believable."

"So the abuser got away with it, too. Gets to live out his days under the Sistine Chapel."

Renu sat back. "Oh, no. Bishop Barella was found floating in the Tiber. There was a picture tucked into his pocket. A copy of a painting by Bartolomé Murillo, *Saint Raphael the Archangel*. They took him right out from under the nose of the Vatican."

Ridley dipped her head forward in shock.

"If they're coming to London," said Renu, "I'll do everything I can—within my power—to stop them. If they're coming after you, though? I'm afraid I won't be able to do enough."

After Renu left, Ridley and Henri collected Owen, who was full of fried chicken and questions. As they made their way back up to Trafalgar Square, they recapped the conversation in low voices. When they told him about the modern iteration of the Order of Raphael, he put a hand on his head.

"Bloody *madness*," he said under his breath. "What does this goddamn saber do?"

Ridley caught a glance of Henri's wince. She nudged Owen's arm and whispered, "Language."

He mouthed back in surprise, "*Sorry*."

Renu had told them she would put out an alert for Sofie Hasbo as a Potentially Dangerous Person, but there was no way to identify the Raphaels. She would expand the perimeter around the Temple Church and add more security personnel. The entire thing would be surveilled as usual by CCTV cameras on every block.

The three of them, however, would not be allowed anywhere on the premises. She trusted them, but this was about the sovereignty of an allied nation. For the sake of avoiding international scandal and endangering her entire career, Renu had barred the CIA operatives from the Church.

"You're welcome to find your own vantage point. I know you will anyway," she'd said to them, "but this is my jurisdiction, and my country. You'll stand down."

As they walked across the Square, Ridley took out her phone and began searching for something.

"We're grabbing the train here?" said Henri.

"The metro," she said. "Yeah. I'm just looking up the nearest pub to Temple Church. Renu banned us from the playground today? We're gonna look right over her shoulder."

CHAPTER
TWENTY-SIX

———

HALF AN HOUR LATER, Ridley, Henri, and Owen walked into the Old English Bank Pub on the corner of Fleet Street and Chancery Lane. It was barely more than a sprint past Barclay's Bank and a barrister's office, across the street to Temple Church.

The pub had high ceilings, paneled wood, chandeliers, and heavy drapes. There was gilding and wrought iron and an ornate coffered ceiling. It looked like some Victorian social spot for high class bankers.

The Americans ordered some virgin cocktails. There would be no alcohol on a day like this, lying in wait for potential trouble, but Owen insisted he needed some real liquor after the revelations of the day so far. He ordered a pint while they grabbed some hummus and focaccia and took it all upstairs. They sat at a table on the small balcony above the bar.

Henri, ever the sniper, looked like a tiger in the grass with his scanning gaze. Ridley grazed on their appetizers while her eyes darted at every bit of motion down below.

The concert was still hours away. It was going to be recorded but not televised, so there was no way to get an inside look at the security layout or the guest configuration in real time. The lead performer of the evening was Diane Bellingsworth, a towering platinum-haired soprano.

"I'm a bit in love with her," said Owen. "She is *fit*."

"She could be your mother," said Ridley.

"Are you sayin' you wouldn't?" The Welsh emphasis on his *t*'s gave the question something extra.

She looked at the red carpet photo on Owen's phone, and cocked her head. "Mm, my bad."

He held it up for Henri, who gave an approving look.

"And you should hear her voice," he said. "Achh...I'd sing with her."

"Maybe the ifrit has some appreciation for solos," said Ridley. "Just sit and enjoy the music, you demonic genie."

The front door swung open then and three men walked in. Both Ridley and Henri eyed the newcomers. By their body language, it was clear that one was the alpha. They were dressed similarly, in an assortment of jeans and dark trousers, crew neck shirts and lightweight jackets. They looked like a unit. It was their shoes that sealed it, though. They were lightweight black Salomons. Tactical footwear with low-key but vicious treads.

Ridley gave Henri a quick look of alarm. He had noticed the same.

The men walked up to the bar. One of the associates was tall, with a widow's peak. The other had a thick jaw. The alpha himself was a handsome man, old enough to be a silver fox though his hair was a thick, curling black.

His eyes drifted up, and settled on the Americans. He muttered something to his companions, and together they strolled to the bottom of the stairs.

Ridley's hand went immediately to the karambit that was sheathed along her waist. Henri drew out his M16 knife, flipped it open, and lay it flat beside his leg. Seeing their reaction, Owen's eyes went wide with alarm.

The black-haired man appeared at the top of the steps, alone. The other two loitered at the bottom of the stairway.

"I think we've met," said the man in a faint Portuguese accent, "but we were all shouting. I'm Tiago. No need to shake hands. I assume yours are otherwise occupied anyhow."

He pulled up a chair to face them, though keeping a respectable distance.

Ridley gave him a dead-eyed stare. "You can call us Lucy and Ricky. And Ricky junior over there."

Tiago laughed with real enjoyment.

"If I'd known we were doing that, I'd be John Wayne instead of Tiago. Interesting how we think alike, all of us ending up in the same pub at the same time for the same reason."

"Of all the gin joints in all the towns in all the world," said Ridley.

Tiago held up his hands like it was truly amazing.

"What's your plan today?" asked Henri. "Just wait for a disaster to unfold?"

For the first time, Tiago's blue gaze stilled into something quiet and sinister.

"We're waiting for the ifrit, aren't we? How else can we find it but anticipate what it wants, and where to find it?"

Ridley had to sit forward, angling her left side toward Tiago. *Damn this shitty ear. Forever.*

"What do *you* think it wants?" said Owen, almost overly bold.

Tiago shook his head. "We are here for our own reasons. I assume you're just being good guy American G.I. Joes running around, trying to save the world?"

"Is that what we're supposed to be doing?" Ridley shot back. "Saving the world?"

"You don't even know what the stakes are, do you? You're ignorant. You just got a mission from somebody sitting behind a desk in Washington and now you've stepped into something you're *struggling* to understand, barely keeping up, trying to learn 'on the fly,' as you say it."

"You're the Order of Raphael," said Henri in a steely voice. "We know where you came from. A seven hundred-year-old organization of rebels. You must be very accomplished to survive this long."

Tiago was clearly offended. "We are the true Templars. A thousand years of faithfulness you could never dream of."

"Faithfulness to what? The Temple of Solomon or to Christ?"

Tiago thought for a moment of where to begin. "Do you know the story of the Watchers?"

"From the Book of Enoch, those Watchers?"

"Yes. Good for you, to know that. The apocryphal book, never accepted as part of the Bible, but a contemporary."

"Are Watchers like the Nephilim things?" asked Owen.

"They're related."

Ridley interjected with a bit of bite. "Enlighten the heathens."

"In the Book of Enoch, it says they were celestial beings that God created to lead humanity," said Henri, "like governors for different areas of the earth. They were corrupted by their own pride when the people started to worship them like gods. They led the humans away from Yahweh and started teaching them things like weapons-making and spells, cosmetics, astrology..." he waved a hand. "So God punished the Watchers. Chained them up for a million years in darkness, until he judges them at the end of times."

"You believe," said Tiago quietly, reverently.

"Not the same way you do."

"The angels heard the cries of mankind. They saw the bloodshed on earth and they beseeched the Lord. And Yahweh sent Michael, and Gabriel, and Uriel to them, to punish them for their evils. And he sent Raphael to bind Azazel, the one to whom all sin belongs. Raphael threw him into the earth and covered him with darkness to let him live there forever, that he may not see the light."

The solemn ring of Tiago's voice was almost mesmerizing.

"Jude six," Henri murmured, understanding in his voice. *"And the angels who did not keep their positions of authority but abandoned their proper dwelling—those he put and has kept in gloomy darkness...in eternal chains until the judgment of the great day."*

"Of the holy angels who watch over humanity now," said Tiago, his eyes shining, "it is Raphael who is over the spirits of men. He is faithful. *We* are faithful, and we are the only ones who continued the true work of the Templars."

"Getting the Seal of Solomon, to control the Watchers?" said Owen, sitting rapt at the tale. "Does this mean you're the new Grand Master, then? Like the Templars?"

Tiago's chuckle sent a ripple of foreboding through Ridley.

"Oh, no. I'm not. Our Grand Master is the greatest of them all, and will get to see the greatest treasure that the Order has ever dreamed of. The pope knows nothing of spiritual power."

"How is that?" asked Henri.

"The Catholic Church has claimed spiritual authority in this world, but they have no true power," he replied with clear disgust. "With their silly exorcisms and all of their corruption. *We* will put the destroying spirits in their place. We're the only ones who can do it."

"And what does this saber have to do with it?"

He cocked his head. "You act like we're here to help you. You're like, uh—baby frogs," he fished for the English word, "tadpoles. You don't even know how big the pond is and you think we'll guide you around?"

Grandiose talk irritated Ridley. "So you're just following this one ifrit hoping it will be the key to you toppling the Catholic Church? Really?"

"Maybe you'll stay alive long enough to see it." His voice had chilled.

"And what about the saber? What is it to you?" said Henri.

Tiago scoffed, rising from his chair. "Enjoy your afternoon."

He trotted down the stairs to rejoin his men. They left the pub.

"They'll be watching us," said Henri. "Maybe they have a roof spotter in position."

"I'm glad he came to talk to us," said Ridley, still staring at the door.

"You think that helped?" asked Owen.

"Well, we have a read on the opposition now, don't we? And faces. And we know their objective. Sort of."

Ridley re-sheathed her karambit. Henri tucked away his knife. He pulled up an app on his phone and cued into the radio frequency of the police.

"Time to listen," he said.

CHAPTER
TWENTY-SEVEN

———

LONDON, ENGLAND

THE ROYALS WOULD ARRIVE in less than half an hour. As the ranking officer on site, Renu Darji had spent the last hour walking the perimeter they'd set, checking in with every officer at their position. One of the officers was on comms back at the station, monitoring the CCTV for the area.

Renu was efficient and respectful in all her interactions. Her reputation within the force reflected it. It was the only way to get the best out of people, she believed. That, and firm confidence.

The lead driver for the SEG called through their estimated arrival time. They'd come through Tudor Street on the east side, cross the wide open King's Bench Walk, and deliver their charges outside the Inner Temple Library. There, a pair of guards would greet the entourage. Members of the Royalty

146

Protection Group who had traveled with the Wessex family would escort them from there through the Church Court and into Temple Church.

There was an unexpected addition, however. The royal couple's fourteen-year-old daughter had decided at the last minute to accompany them.

Renu had circled through the quiet courtyard, back to the entrance. She was just greeting the officers at the door when her radio squawked:

"PDP on the west side of the perimeter!"

Potentially Dangerous Person.

She grabbed at the receiver.

"Sergeant, can you identify?"

"Ma'am, it looks like our person of interest."

Renu was already moving, running for the west end of the courtyard. "What's your location?"

"Middle Temple Lane at the end of Pump Court, ma'am!"

"Do not approach unless necessary, officer. Use extreme caution."

As she sprinted through the cloisters, she could already hear the shouting ahead. If this thing could do to London what it did to Paris...she hurtled through the court and out onto the lane.

There, three officers were bristling with their guns drawn, barking orders at a blonde woman who was lowering herself to the ground. Renu caught her breath as she watched the woman, slow and compliant.

Too compliant.

She felt a sharp pang of alarm.

Sergeant Atwood, who had radioed the sighting, snapped a pair of cuffs on the woman behind her back. One officer pulled on her gloves and began to frisk the intruder.

"Did she have anything in her hands?" Renu asked the sergeant.

"Nothing, ma'am. She said nothin', obeyed my orders right away."

Renu had studied the INTERPOL photo of Sofie Hasbo for nearly twenty minutes to be able to pick her face out of any crowd, but still she pulled up her mobile for reference.

"She's clean," announced the search officer.

"Stand her up," Renu said.

They hauled the woman to her feet. The profile photo matched beyond doubt.

"Are you Sofie Hasbo?"

"I'm—yes," she replied in a thick Danish accent. "English is not good. I'm sorry."

"What are you doing here, ma'am?"

"Where is I?"

"London."

Sofie Hasbo stared at Renu as if in total shock.

She was wearing the same clothes seen in the footage of the Sainte-Chapelle attack. They were dirtied and wrinkled, as though she hadn't washed them in days. Her expression was haggard, as though she had not slept. But the strangest bit was the look of desperate confusion on her face.

Renu had apprehended all types of suspects in her years on the force. All ages, all crimes, in hygiene or filth, showing sociopathy or remorse, hardened killer or accidental offender, she'd seen them up close at the moment they were caught. The expression on this woman's face looked as genuine as any she'd ever seen.

As though Sofie Hasbo had no idea what was going on.

"Take her in. Clear the area. Reestablish the perimeter," said Renu.

One of the officers radioed for the van that had been parked down the block. As Renu turned to head back through the courtyard, she addressed the responding officer, Sergeant Atwood.

"Good work. Good eye. Carry on."

He gave a nod. "Ma'am."

She headed back to Temple Church.

Atwood adjusted his Kevlar vest, rearranging the golden blade of a broken saber tucked beneath it.

Renu had not even made it five yards before she felt her mobile buzz with a text. It was from Ridley.

Was it her?

Of course, she realized, Ridley must have been listening on some scanner. It annoyed Renu, but she couldn't help but admire the woman.

She messaged back.

Yes. Unarmed. Barely speaks English. Taking her to the station.

She tucked the mobile away and returned her attention to Temple Church. Fifteen minutes to arrival.

On the curb outside Old English Bank Pub, Ridley looked down at her phone, reading aloud Renu's message.

"*Barely speaks English* is convenient."

"Wherever they're taking her, that station could be in trouble," said Henri.

"But why would she allow anyone to take her into custody like that? I mean, why would the ifrit allow."

Owen spoke up from over their shoulders. "It doesn't need her anymore."

Shit. Worst case scenario.

"It's jumped possession again," said Ridley. "Someone else has the saber."

She had never texted so quickly in her life as what she sent back to Renu.

Renu heard her mobile buzz again, but she had no time for another inquiring Ridley text. The SEG unit was just turning off Tudor Street, its lead motorcyclist leading a small procession. The Bentley in the middle swung around to the edge of the courtyard, and from it emerged the stately royal couple.

The Duke of Wessex was the youngest brother of the reigning king. He was the quietest royal, the one most people forgot about. For that, Renu had always liked him the best. His wife was a regal brunette, the most committed patron of charity work in the royal family since Princess Diana. Few knew it, however, as she lived her life as quietly as her husband. One of the aristocratic luxuries that they were always up for, however, was a classical concert.

Their bodyguards escorted them into the chapel and to their designated seats. Only then did the doors open to the rest of the concertgoers. Every name was on an ID list, and every attendee had to come through the same Tudor Street entrance.

There were three entrances into Temple Church, two into the chancel and one at the very end leading into the round. All were guarded, but today, guests were entering only through the side, into the chancel.

Renu watched as they began to meander through the courtyard. She should have been feeling a sense of relief, having apprehended the suspect peacefully before the event even began. Yet something felt too easy about it. The warning from the Americans echoed in her head: *or an unidentified accomplice.*

But there was nothing to do now except remain vigilant.

She positioned herself in the courtyard with a full view of everyone's faces as they funneled through the same church door. Body language, facial expressions, and attire were her only methods of evaluation now.

Sergeant Atwood strode toward the West Porch entrance, the iron-gated door of the round. He greeted the officer posted there, and walked into Temple Church, the saber tucked into his vest, well out of sight.

CHAPTER
TWENTY-EIGHT

LONDON, ENGLAND

THE MAJESTIC CHORDS of the organ filled the church, ringing off vaulted stone ceilings. Guests filed into the pews. The royals were already seated, flanked by a small unit of protective agents. A few police officers were posted discreetly around the edges of the chancel.

Sergeant Atwood made his way past the effigies of great ancient knights laid prone along the floor. He opened a wooden door along one of the walls and slipped inside, shutting it tightly behind him. Climbing the circular stairwell, he stopped at a large wooden cupboard that was set in the stone wall. He pulled it open.

The compartment was hardly more than four feet long by three feet wide, a cruelly cramped penitentiary cell. Narrow slits overlooked the church below. Atwood pulled out the broken saber and climbed into the cell. The thundering of the organ drowned out the sound of him chipping away at the mortar.

Ridley had told Owen that he couldn't come with them, but it was Henri's stern look that put him back in his seat.

You can leave here if you like, but you will not come to Temple Church.

Then he and Ridley crossed the street to Inner Temple Lane, a narrow passage that led straight down to the church court. An officer was posted at the entrance. They knew that would be as far as they could go, but at least it offered them a sightline to one of the church entrances: West Porch.

"This would be a lot easier if a possessed person had smoking skin or glowing eyes," muttered Ridley.

"A puzzle with no clues," Henri muttered.

She thought for a moment, looking around. "If she didn't have the saber on her when they caught her, why did she come here?"

The question gave them both pause.

"Only the ifrit would have directed her here," he said. "Sofie Hasbo must have had it right up to the last minute, then given it to someone nearby."

Her gaze settled on an officer who was now eyeing them from a distance with suspicion.

"Someone who could pass through the perimeter."

Henri glanced at the officer. "Oh, dear God."

Ridley yanked out her phone to text,

Accomplice may be an officer! Don't touch the saber

Strains of music floated through the church courtyard. The concert was beginning, and the faint but soaring voice of Diane

Bellingsworth rang into the spring afternoon. Renu was debriefing two officers on their suspect capture at the perimeter when she felt her phone buzz again in her pocket. Annoyed, she excused herself and pulled it out to read.

Her head snapped up in alarm.

Sergeant Atwood descended the stone steps. The hilt of the saber was barely visible beneath his vest. He stepped out of the stairwell and shut the door quietly behind him.

At the front of the church, the soloist stood like a blonde Amazon in front of a small orchestra. Her emerald gown cascaded down the platform.

On the side, very close to her, sat the Earl and Countess of Wessex beside their teenage daughter. Their expressions were staid but attentive. Members of the Royalty Protection Group stood at a respectful distance behind them, always watching. Yet they would not be on high alert for a threat in uniform.

Sergeant Atwood moved slowly along the wall, scanning the church like any watchful cop. As he reached the front section, his eyes fell on the royals.

His hand went to the hilt of the saber.

One of the bodyguards standing by the pews spotted him. As Atwood took a step toward the royals, the agent burst forward and collided with him. They both crashed to the ground.

The rest of the bodyguards launched. Two of them moved instantly to cover the royals. The other dropped down to help restrain Atwood.

By now, the rest of the audience had realized the commotion. Diane Bellingsworth and the orchestra had gone quiet. Officers from every corner of the church descended on the scuffle.

Perhaps the ifrit sought chaos. Perhaps it sought royal blood. What happened next could not be explained, could not be dismissed, and could hardly be believed. Only one blurry video would emerge later, taken from the back of the church on a phone.

As if they had landed on a grenade, the two protective agents pinning Sergeant Atwood to the ground were blown backward. A stunning force hurled them against the stone walls. They landed in heaps.

Atwood rose up from the floor like a leviathan, yanking the broken saber from under his Kevlar vest. Screams split the air as people stampeded for the exits.

Just as a crowd was trying to barrel out of the door, Renu Darji and a handful of other officers were charging in. She gripped a Glock 17, while the two behind her braced their HK MP5 rifles.

The other bodyguards had begun to rush the royals off the premises, but they hadn't even reached the door when Sergeant Atwood bolted across the floor. With one hand, he seized a bodyguard and tossed him over a pew. The last one standing drew his pistol to fire, but the possessed sergeant leapt forward. He knocked the agent back and stood triumphantly on his chest.

The royals' teenage daughter was screaming. The Earl and the Countess huddled over her like human shields. Every cop on site had formed a half-circle around the attacker, their Glocks pointed at their colleague as they hollered and pleaded with him to drop his weapon.

Renu plunged into the fray, commanding the sergeant with a voice that belonged to someone twice her size.

But Atwood could not stop himself. He raised the saber and slashed downward.

The sound of two dozen gunshots blasted off the vaulted

ceilings. The sergeant's body spasmed, bursts of blood ripping across his torso, his arms, his scalp. He collapsed to the stone.

But the cacophony of shots had also mingled with the scream of the Countess. She was clutching at her face in agony, blood streaming through her fingers and down her neck.

Renu barked orders into the radio for an ambulance. As some officers attended the wounded royal, she went to secure Sergeant Atwood.

He was splayed out on the stone. His eyes were open, glassy, lifeless. Scarlet pools seeped across the gray floor. A dingy gold saber lay beside him. Its broken blade was coated in blood.

Renu gave a quick, anguished shake of her head. Atwood had been talking to her only half an hour ago, as sharp and focused and normal as he could be.

"Constable," she said to the nearest officer, "retrieve the weapon. Tag it. Put it in evidence."

Constable Tom Slade-Lawes nodded. "Ma'am."

He holstered his weapon and pulled on a pair of gloves.

CHAPTER
TWENTY-NINE

AT THE FIRST screams from Temple Church, half the officers on the perimeter had turned their attention inward. The radio call seconds later sent them scrambling into action, sprinting for the ancient building.

"Renu didn't respond," said Ridley. "She has no idea what the saber does because we didn't fucking tell her!"

"Hey, steady," said Henri. "There are three walking exits from the church courtyard, yes?"

"Middle Temple Lane, Inner Temple Lane, and Tudor Street."

She obsessively studied maps for every known location, for every mission. Her mid-flight reading on the plane from Nantes to London had been a series of detailed maps of Fleet Street, from metro stops to sewer lines.

Never get lost on foreign streets.

"We have to follow the saber," he said. "Go get eyes on Tudor Street."

She took off around the block, able to run without suspicion due to the chaos in the streets. Everyone else was running, too, having heard the sounds of gunshots and screaming.

Ridley cut down an alleyway, but a jittery officer, unaccustomed to holding a gun, barked at her to back away from the perimeter. She headed down another lane, but by the time she found a way to sneak around to the Tudor Street entrance, emergency vehicles were wailing their way in. Nothing would happen outside of the church court. Everything would go down inside the perimeter, out of sight.

She texted Renu again, though she knew that a superintendent on the scene here wouldn't be taking text messages at a time like this.

URGENT: leave the saber where it lies

She paced a groove in the sidewalk, watching the flashing cop cars, ambulances, and police vans pour in.

Where's that Portuguese angel-worshipping militia in all this?

The Countess of Wessex had suffered a deep gash across her cheek, the blade having missed her eye by only millimeters. She and her family were rushed to hospital under heavy protection. The fleeing concert guests had been contained within the court perimeter. They were checked for any and all medical needs, while some were detained for questioning.

When the Commissioner of Metro Police arrived on the scene, Renu briefed him, and promptly took an earful for the disaster that had unfolded on her watch.

He was pleased to hear of their apprehension of Sofie

Hasbo, but he also demanded to know why Renu had increased security at Temple Church in the first place. She told him that she had been delivered an anonymous tip. Given the tipster's knowledge of the INTERPOL red notice, combined with the catastrophe at Sainte-Chapelle that very week, she thought it prudent to take it seriously.

The lie was grave. It fairly burned at the back of her tongue as she told it.

The crisis in that moment, however, was something much more immediate. An officer under her command had attacked a royal under her protection. She had wanted this position of leadership, and it was time to own the mantle fully. This was her fault. An inquest would be opened that very evening.

There in Church Court, the shock within the officer ranks was palpable. Back at Scotland Yard, analysts were already poring through the personal data, virtual activity, and electronic tracking of Sergeant Atwood. There had been no warning signs from his behavior, the Commissioner told Renu. So far, the team had turned up no red flags in his history.

She was properly attentive and deferential, but she just wanted him to leave the scene already. A legion of cameras and microphones awaited him somewhere, and she had some Americans she urgently needed to talk to.

When he finally moved on to begin the press conference, Renu pulled out her phone.

Only then did she see Ridley's message about the saber. Instead of texting, she dialed directly. It hardly finished a full ring.

"The saber's in evidence, Ridley. It was a weapon used in the commission of a crime."

"No, it's not in evidence," came her response. "I'll bet you a hundred quid it's gone missing."

"What the fuck are you talking about?"

Constable Tom Slade-Lawes had gone missing, and true to Ridley's prediction, the saber had never been tagged into evidence. A series of frenzied calls followed. The entire Metro PD, already on edge from the news of Sergeant Atwood, went into search mode.

It was not for another hour that Renu was able to wave Ridley, Henri, and Owen through the perimeter. At the front of the church, a forensics crew in their white crepe suits were attending to the bloody floor. Two Detective Chief Inspectors hovered about, conferring.

Renu took them to sit in the back pews. She was usually the embodiment of dignified cool. Ridley had never before seen those dark eyes set in a thousand-yard stare.

"You walked into my city this morning with a story about a Danish terrorist," she said in a low, tight voice, "and I believed your intelligence because I believed in your credibility."

When her eyes hit on Ridley, the American felt a heat rise in her cheeks.

We failed. I fucked up. I should have done better.

"Your suspicions was accurate, and your update was accurate. And then your next update was accurate, which means you were either withholding intelligence from me at the start, or you were receiving real time information *somehow*. How did you know it was an officer? And how the *hell* did you know that saber had gone missing?"

Henri glanced at Ridley. She drew a deep breath and leaned forward. She was under no obligation to share their full spectrum of intel, but this was her responsibility. Renu was her contact, and now the woman's job was at risk.

"I'm sorry for what happened today. I'll answer those questions. I'll tell you what's happening, but it's not something you would have believed this morning. And Owen here can help fill in any of the gaps I leave."

For the next ten minutes, they gave Renu the full story: what had emerged when they opened that sarcophagus, the possessing ifrit that seemed to use the broken saber as a vehicle between people, the disaster at Sainte-Chapelle, finding the body of a tourist at Nantes, the clues they'd been following from one Templar site to another, the showdown at La Rochelle with the Order of Raphael, meeting Tiago face to face across the street from Temple Church, and what they had realized today for certain when Sofie Hasbo was apprehended without the saber on her.

Renu sat in total silence as they spoke, her eyes going from one to another. "So you didn't come to London to stop a terrorist. You came here on a treasure hunt."

Ridley squinted. "More like a scavenger hunt."

"It's a treasure hunt," said Owen eagerly.

"And how are you gonna stop this thing?" asked Renu. "Are you going to kill Constable Slade-Lawes?"

"It may not even be him," said Ridley, her voice gentle. "The saber passes, the ifrit passes...like the lab tech passed it to Volkswagen—the man named Declerq—who passed it to Sofie Hasbo, who passed it to the sergeant. We don't want to hurt any of them—"

"Sergeant Atwood is *dead!*" she snapped.

Renu pressed her fingers to her forehead, trying to keep calm. The others went quiet for a moment, until she spoke again.

"What happens if *you* retrieve the saber?"

"We won't touch it," said Henri. "This ifrit is using people to find the other pieces of the saber that have been hidden away for almost a thousand years. It's putting the blade back together."

Ridley leaned closer to Renu. "I'm sorry this came to your doorstep. We'll do everything to bring the constable back safely. And we won't stop chasing this thing."

The police superintendent closed her eyes and drew in a deep, slow breath. "What do you want from me?"

"Uh, ma'am?" said Owen. "Would you let me up there, please?"

She opened her eyes to see him nod to a wooden door.

"Your officer must have already been up there. See, that's the only way he could have gotten the saber piece. They're all hidden away—sealed up with clues and maps, and we need to know where he's going, right now. The only clues are in that stairwell...ma'am."

She looked at him for a long moment, then said, "I'll go up with you."

Tiago quickly realized that the police presence at Temple Church following the incident crushed his plans. If they waited until it reopened to find the hidden clue, the Americans would be well on their way to the next location. They'd somehow gained access to the building through one of the ranking officers on scene. Despite the shortlist of numbers Tiago might normally call to smooth the way here in London, he had no time to waste going through any chain of command.

That saber would have to leave the premises, and whoever had it would be on their way to the next breadcrumb of the Templar trail. Tiago posted a man at each of the exit points, and waited for the evidence vans to arrive.

Yet when Constable Tom Slade-Lawes slipped past the perimeter with a trash bag the size of a short sword, it was

Bruno who phoned his boss instantly. He never took his eyes off the cop, as Slade-Lawes proceeded down Middle Temple Lane toward the Thames. By the time the officer reached the main thoroughfare, a black Mercedes was swinging around the block to pick up Bruno.

The officer called for a taxi. Tiago and his compatriots followed close behind.

CHAPTER
THIRTY

———

ENGLAND

By nine o'clock that night, Ridley, Henri, and Owen were back in the BMW, driving west. Moments before they finally left Temple Church, they'd gotten a message from Booker.

CALL

The hour was of no consequence. So they rang him at midnight and gave him the debrief of the attack that he'd seen on the news that day. They also told him about meeting their Portuguese adversary face to face.

"Tiago's not a common name in Portugal, is it?" said Henri dryly. "We can find him."

"You'll find him again," said Booker. "Or he'll find you. Did you run SDRs getting out of there?"

Surveillance Detection Routes, the most basic tactic of spy

training. An operative would employ a sequence of misdirections using time, distance, and change of direction to expose anyone who might be surveilling them. Flush out, confuse, and when possible, leave the following party in the dust.

"Yeah. No one's on us," Ridley replied.

"Where are you headed now?"

"Cornwall. We're storming a castle."

"Do you need arrows? Catapults? I miss the old battles," said Booker.

"I can see you with a battle axe. It's very fetching with your Viking beard."

"I think 'the Black Viking' would be very scary," added Henri.

"Tell me what you need, you idiots," said Booker, but she could hear him smile.

Henri gave him the shopping list. Booker gave him an address along their route for a dead drop pickup. He told Henri to get some food, and Ridley to get some sleep. The man really knew them.

It would be a six-hour trip through the night with no time to waste. They stopped at a late-night corner shop to fuel up on some stale sandwiches. They bought water for the car, lighters, and a roll of duct tape, just in case. Back on the road, Henri lay down in the back seat to doze off. Owen took the wheel. Ridley couldn't sleep for the ritual churn that her brain decided to dive into at night.

She hadn't always been this way. Back in BUD/S she could sleep like a puppy after playtime. Though that was probably the case with every cadet, worn to the bone after every day's training.

It had only been since joining Osprey that anxiety began to pile in the corners of her mind. On mission, in action, she was a force of discipline, focus, and cool. The strangeness of her encounters hardly affected her in the moment. She was loathe to admit that afterward, vapors of doubt kept seeping into her thoughts. Disbelief grappled with belief. Worry about the next day threw her back into memories of failure in the past.

"Henri said you were in the SEALs," said Owen, breaking into her spiral.

"Oh, no. Nope. I never made it. I had an accident underwater, lost most of the hearing in my right ear."

"Oh, bloody hell...you can't hear out the right? You can't even tell." After a considered moment, he asked, "Bet that was hard, eh? Not failing but still losin' out."

She glanced at him. "That's exactly what it was like."

"What did your family think?"

How can anyone summarize something like that?

"My mother died when I was young, so it's just my dad and brother."

He didn't interrupt to say how sorry he was, like most people did when they heard. She appreciated that.

"My dad is a proud American but *also* a prideful Greek. He actually had us read Socrates and Plato. He was probably a little impressed when I got into BUD/S but he didn't make a big deal out of it. He'd rather have me be an Athenian than a Spartan."

"What does he do for work?"

"Project manager for an international construction company. Hence my gypsy upbringing."

It had not been easy for her, and in turn she made sure it wouldn't be easy for her father. Ridley felt like he was running from grief, always moving, a shark who could not bear to stay still. She just wanted an anchor. She wanted a home.

For many years, the only place she had was the island, her grandmother Charis' horse farm. She was the closest thing that she and her brother had to a mother after their own died.

Charis taught her grandkids to ride like Greek warriors, to play a sharp game of cards, and to make the world's best *bougatsa*.

Ridley had not been back to the island since her grandmother died. It just seemed like the shimmer of magic there had gone with her.

"All that travel then—that's why you know so many languages?"

"Yeah. I took to it more than my brother, Alexios. Alex. He's an intellectual property attorney now in Chicago."

"That sounds rich."

"And boring, but he's got a sweet wife. Someday I'm sure he'll have some sweet kids."

"How did your mum die?"

Ridley drew in a deep breath. "She drowned. Saving me. It wasn't...I don't remember that much. I don't even remember her that much."

Suddenly she didn't want to talk about it anymore. She didn't want to go there.

"So what happened with you? How'd you end up wanting a degree in history?"

"Honestly, I was a singer when I was young so everyone celebrated me...had me perform at family events and the adults just loved it. So that's who I was, the singer, but then I aged out of King's Choir and I didn't know what to call myself anymore. I wasn't gonna sing at Covent Garden. I found rugby, though, played half-scrum up through uni, but knew I wasn't really good enough at that either, to play professionally. I think I lost myself again."

"You've done all that and you're already an expert in this other stuff?"

She was surprised at how bashful his grin was, even in the darkness.

"Not an expert, I'm just learning these arcane things and... honestly, I really love it."

"So that's who you are now? You see yourself?"

He considered it. "Yeah. I still play rugby on Sundays, though. I'm not gonna lose my figure over a stack of books."

"That stack of books may have gotten you here, but it's all the rugby practice that will help you keep up. You know what a team's like. We're not taking deadweight."

"Yeah, of course," he said with a vigorous nod. "D'you think we can beat it? I mean...if we just keep following the ifrit, eventually it's going to win, unless...we stop it. I've no idea how the Templars got them all into those tiny bottles. But what do we do without a way to control this absolute knob of a jinn..."

Ridley thought for a moment. "I don't understand what the saber is for. It can't be anything good, but why did the Templars bury it in their own strongholds?" Then she added, "And why did they break it apart?"

Owen shrugged helplessly, holding up a hand. "Honestly, I haven't seen anything in their records about a saber. Maybe it was too dangerous a secret to even write down!"

He gave her a long look.

"Is everything you do like this? Are you CIA? Officially."

She laughed. "Owen, you're an idiot for waiting so long to ask that, but no, every job is different. This one is much too public for my liking. We try to keep things low-key. Discreet."

"Why? Why not let it out, let the people see what's going on?"

"A person is smart. People are stupid. Dumb, panicky animals—"

"Agent K," he grinned, catching on. He'd seen *Men in Black*.

She pointed a finger his way and winked. "He was right."

. . .

The dead-drop pickup was everything they'd requested. They walked away with a duffel of deadly efficient goods.

They reached Cornwall in the early hours of the morning.

When they pulled up along the coast of Marazion Beach, they stepped out of the BMW and shook off their grogginess.

In the distance, across the water, the silhouette of a castle rose up along the horizon: Saint Michael's Mount.

"There wasn't actually any record of this being a Templar site," said Owen.

They both stared at him.

"No, but I'm sure this is the place. I really am."

"Is this high tide coming in or low tide going out?" wondered Ridley.

Saint Michael's Mount sat atop a small tidal island. The causeway was underwater by a few feet, but that would soon be changing.

"We're about to see low tide," said Henri, "and the island doesn't open for tourists for another six hours."

The town around them was still shrouded and drowsy. They couldn't see anyone about, and lights were scant.

"Let's load up," said Ridley.

This was no longer just a race against a violent creature of the supernatural, but a fanatical Portuguese religious order. Now they knew who they were up against. And they had firepower to spare.

Owen insisted on carrying the duffel. It was no small bag, but they allowed him the job. Ridley and Henri threaded suppressors onto their pistols and slid extra mags into their pockets.

Ridley looked at Owen. "Here's the part where I ask, 'do you know how to use this thing?'" she said, pulling out a Glock 19.

"I've shot some pellet guns."

"Brits," she sighed. "It's that, with a lot more kick. Brace and squeeze, don't pull. Safety is off. You don't join in any firefights, please. Shoot only if absolutely necessary."

"Copy that."

She looked toward the island, the castle ramparts looming majestically against the blue-gray dawn.

Ready to meet again.

CHAPTER
THIRTY-ONE

———

CORNWALL, ENGLAND

CONSTABLE TOM SLADE-LAWES clambered up the steep wall of rock on the back side of the island. Dark rings had formed beneath his eyes. He no longer wore the conspicuous uniform of a London police officer, but an ill-fitting pair of trousers and cable-knit sweater that he'd nicked from the luggage of a distracted couple. The saber was tucked into the back of his belt, glinting gold, its jagged point swinging with every step.

It was sending him to the next shard of its blade.

A monastery had once sat atop Saint Michael's Mount, as far back as the eighth century. Nearly four hundred years later, a castle was built on the highest ground. It had changed hands over the centuries, been conquered and captured and recaptured and even sold. Eventually it became a seaport with a scattering of cottages, schools, and chapels. It had been fortified against the Nazi threat in World War II, and then finally given to the National Trust.

Today, tourists crossed the causeway at low tide and bought tickets to enter the island grounds. A small ferry shuttled across those who did not want to be slave to the tides. The mini port was encircled by thick stone walls, where no more than a dozen boats bobbed on the aquamarine waters of the Cornish coast. Ancient-looking cottages lined the quayside.

Alan Turner was in his late fifties, his hands weathered and his belly grown thick. He'd worked on this little island for thirty-seven years, first bussing for, then managing, and then owning the Sail Loft, one of only a few places for tourists to eat lunch on St. Michael's. While his tenure of nearly four decades was nothing in the grand sweep of the island's history, he felt as much a part of it as the kings and earls and friars who had laid claim to it over hundreds of years.

This morning, like every morning but Sunday, he was first to reach the port. Though the horizon was still heavy with pre-dawn gloom, Turner knew it would soon dissolve into pure sunshine. He loved being the first one awake.

As he unloaded some of the day's supplies from his vessel onto the quay, he caught sight of a boat approaching. It was small, fast, and sleeker than most that found their way into this tiny port. He squinted as they pulled in past the stone walls. They didn't dock in the harbor, but pulled up to the boat launch as expertly as he had ever seen.

He was about to call out to the helmsman, wanting a declaration of any strange visitors to *his* island, but then a handful of men poured out from the cabin. These were not visitors; they were intruders.

His voice died in his throat. Turner readjusted the crate in his arms and slipped back into the weather-worn stone building.

Ridley and Henri crossed the causeway with Owen at a fast jog. It took them only a few minutes to reach the sloping cobblestone entryway. Early morning light was just beginning to seep through the fog. The island was eerily quiet.

The Americans drew their weapons, holding at low ready. Threats could present anywhere among the stone walls and crumbling chapels. As they made their way across the harbor front, keeping close to the row of buildings, Ridley spotted a vehicle that was pulled up to the boat launch. It looked too expensive and too fast for a tourist to bother using for the short jaunt from shore to island. Henri noted it, too.

As they were about to sweep the next corner, they saw a flash of movement ahead. Their weapon hands flinched, but it was only what looked like a shopkeeper. He appeared as weatherbeaten and salt-sprayed as anyone who'd spent decades on the shore. And he looked startled as hell to see the guns in their hands.

"What's on here?" he exclaimed in a burly West Country accent.

Ridley and Henri relaxed. Owen held up his hands in apology.

"Sorry to disturb you," said Henri, "Mister...?"

"Turner. My name's Alan. Who are you? What's goin' on this mornin'?" he said, glancing out at the seaport, at the sleek boat.

"Mr. Turner, have you seen others this morning?" asked Ridley.

"Some men came on here earlier, ridin' that boat there. In forty years, never seen any tourists like them."

"Did they see you? Did you talk to them?"

He shook his head. "No, no. I want nothin' to do with trouble, and they looked it. There's nothin' valuable on this island that would be easy to make off with. Can't think o' what they'd be wantin'. So I thought I'd wait for some o' the other islanders to arrive before I go lookin' for them."

"How many people are on the island?" she asked.

"The family lives up there. Six o' them. They lease the land back to the National Trust, and they get to live in the castle. They 'andle all the tourist business."

"Kids?"

"Four of 'em."

"Mr. Turner," said Henri, "Please don't go looking for these visitors, at all. Don't say anything yet to anyone else. We don't want this to get more complicated with people getting curious and trying to find them."

"Okay then," he said, bewildered. "I won't even ask why a bunch of Americans are carryin' guns in Cornwall, then."

"They're with me," said Owen, his voice Welsh all the way down. He spoke as if that held a lot of weight.

"Is this your shop?" asked Ridley, pointing to the stone building behind him.

"A restaurant," said the man.

"Go inside, stay quiet. Don't come out if you hear anything crazy, okay?" she said. "Please."

"You won't be destroyin' my island," he said, shaking a finger at them even as he retreated. "Get those tossers off this place and get yourselves gone before anyone else sees you!"

He went inside and shut the door behind him.

"They beat us here?" exclaimed Owen.

Ridley looked at Henri. "How the hell..."

He shook his head, and signaled to move. They had to reach that castle.

CHAPTER
THIRTY-TWO

———

CORNWALL, ENGLAND

RIDLEY'S WARNING to Owen about keeping up with them physically was accurate. As he barreled up the steep hill alongside them, he thanked God that he hadn't lost too much of his wind since his rugby days. The Americans kept a brutal pace along the winding stone pathway. Trees obscured any view of the castle as they went, but also offered them concealment in their approach.

Ridley had studied the map during the long drive, and planned their approach with Henri. The stone steps to the main entrance opened up completely from the trees. If they went that way, it would grant full visibility to anyone inside the castle.

They wanted to stay within cover. When a small pathway broke off from the main, they took it up to the left side of the keep.

Owen dropped the duffel. They pulled out the gear. Three REBS Compact Launchers. They suited up with rappelling gear, shot the grappling hooks over the wall, and began their ascent.

Owen struggled to get the rhythm, cursing under his breath. Henri patiently offered him some tips, and finally the three of them pulled themselves over the battlements.

They unsnapped their leads and scanned the large terrace on which they'd landed. Ahead of them was a small chapel, as if it had been plucked from church grounds and set atop this castle. A set of stairs led up to its entrance.

"That's it," said Owen under his breath.

Ridley and Henri had just started a quiet sweep across toward the door, Owen close behind, when a hail of gunshots exploded across the castle.

Henri shoved Owen down as they dove for cover. Bullets bit into the stone around them.

Ridley glanced out.

One hostile behind cover in the narrow passageway between the chapel and the tower.

She motioned to Henri, *cover me.*

He lay down a line of fire as she burst forward, strafing to get out of the gunman's sightline as fast as she could. She slammed up against the tower wall.

Knowing she was there and that her approach would be blind, he had to reposition. Ridley crept forward in a low crouch, holding her aim...until the enemy's torso appeared along the wall, loosing a volley toward her at head height.

With just enough time to see his surprise, she shot upward. He spasmed backward, and fell. His HK MP7 clattered to the ground.

Ridley picked it up, checked the round count, and grabbed his extra mags. She holstered her SIG handgun and motioned for Henri and Owen to make the dash.

They slid behind her.

"He's a Raphael," said Henri. "Didn't happen to have a Mod 7 on him?"

He missed the quiet, steady precision of a sniper rifle. To have that .300 Winchester Magnum caliber on the roof of a castle would have been a dream.

"Think they're in the chapel?" she asked.

"With the racket he just made, we're about to find out."

Owen was staring down at the man. He had never seen someone gunned down in real life. He'd never stood over a dead body with oozing bullet wounds.

"Hey," said Ridley, touching his chin to redirect his eyes at her. "You're good. Draw your weapon, keep your finger off the trigger until you're about to shoot, okay? Let's go."

They moved, heading for the outer wall of the chapel. They were halfway across the terrace when a man dodged out from the front of the chapel, firing a burst.

Ridley and Henri unleashed at him. The MP7 was a glory of firepower in her hands, but the enemy had slipped back behind cover already.

She and Owen rushed for the chapel wall. She could hear loud voices inside, but couldn't make out anything through the thick stained glass windows.

Henri spread the field, dropping below a corner of the battlements. The enemy dipped out again, loosing a barrage. This time, he was in Henri's sightline. The retired sniper dropped him with a double.

He motioned to Ridley, *I'm moving, cover me.*

He went. She and Owen followed.

They swept forward, up the stairs to the entrance. The door was open. Someone inside shouted commands.

Henri stole a glance. The place was small, no more than sixty feet long. A massive organ loomed at the back, to Henri's right. Down the left, the body of the chapel was lined with wooden chairs, filled with ornate iron statues, and glowing with stained glass. Thick pillars jutted out from the narrow walls, plenty of alcoves for cover.

A handful of the Order was scattered within, armed with rifles and high-end tactical gear. Someone was standing at the front of the chapel, in front of the altar, his back to the room.

Henri's surveillance was short-lived, as a volley of bullets ripped against the doorframe. Calls in Portuguese rang out.

"Five or six," he told Ridley with a shake of his head.

They weren't going to be making entry while the Portuguese held the position.

From inside, they heard the smashing of stone. This time Ridley dodged a look in.

The altar had been torn apart and tossed across the room. A man was crouching over the hole where it used to be, reaching down. Then he stood up and turned to face the chapel. Constable Tom Slade-Lawes. He held the broken saber in one hand, a golden shard of it in the other. His face contorted as a flash of heat tore down the rows.

Every one of the Raphaels was distracted momentarily by the scene. Ridley raised the MP7 and shot down the one closest to the door, the one who had been firing at them.

Things go to chaos pretty fast when you're trapped between two dangers.

The Raphaels retreated into cover.

"Constable!" shouted Henri from the doorway. "Don't let it control you!"

But Slade-Lawes did not have a choice. He gave that low, bone-cracking shriek that they'd first heard in the lab beneath the Louvre. Then he turned and launched himself through the huge stained glass window behind the altar. The colored glass shattered to pieces on the stone floor.

"Does it hate stained glass windows?" exclaimed Ridley.

The Raphaels turned their attention back to the Americans outside the door. They had bunkered down though, and didn't seem to be advancing.

Owen stepped away unseen to the outer wall, raised the Glock, and shot out one of the narrow windows. Now there was another angle of threat. When Ridley and Henri realized who was shooting out the glass, they exchanged an impressed glance.

When Owen had shot them all to pieces, he peeked quickly over one of the sills.

One man was crouching over the altar space, taking photos on a cell phone. Every other was giving him cover, their aim flitting between the windows and the doorway, rattling off volleys to keep the threat at bay.

Tiago was among them, rifle at the ready, calling out commands in Portuguese.

The designated photographer finished his work and dove for cover with the others. Laying down suppressive fire, they all began moving to the front of the chapel.

"They're going out the window!" said Ridley.

"Let them go," said Henri. "All we need is the next clue."

A fury scorched through her. They could pursue, they could finish off these militants. She knew it. But she swallowed the fire of her temper. He was right.

Don't be stupid. Don't be rash. You're not losing. You're being strategic.

The last of the Raphaels slipped out of the chapel.

Owen came back around to rejoin them, slightly spooked to have lost sight of the enemy.

"Come on," she said.

They swept into the chapel, guns raised. Owen ran to the

179

front and snapped flash photos of the hidden compartment from every angle he could get.

"Got it!"

"Let's go," she called.

They ran out, back across the terrace, and rappelled down the battlements. Leaving all the gear, they rushed down the hill.

Dawn had crept over the horizon, and the world would soon be awake.

The family in that castle certainly is now...

The three of them reached the village on high alert. They took cover behind the first building they could get to, slipping through the alleys and cobblestone streets.

Just as they stepped around the last row of cottages to the waterfront, Henri, in the lead, pulled up short.

There on the quay, Alan Turner stood frozen in place. The Order had formed a semi-circle around him at a distance, every weapon aimed properly at his torso. But Turner's eyes were fixed on something else.

Approaching him from the other side was Constable Slade-Lawes. He lifted the saber and slashed it against the old man's throat.

CHAPTER
THIRTY-THREE

CORNWALL, ENGLAND

Blood spurted and flowed from Turner's neck. He collapsed to his knees, gagging, reaching for his throat.

The golden saber seemed to shimmer, and the break line of the newest shard vanished. It had sealed perfectly against the golden blade.

Like new.

Ridley swung the barrel of the MP7 around the corner and let off a volley of shots at the possessed constable. Her aim was on, but he was gone before her trigger finger could react.

One of the Raphaels cried out in pain as the crossfire struck him in the arm.

But Slade-Lawes had leapt off the quay like a jumping spider. He landed in a small motorboat at least a dozen feet off the wall. Everyone else was stricken with shock, their reactions delayed by a costly two seconds. The constable fired up the engine.

Ridley and Henri couldn't break cover to get an angle on the boat. The Raphaels had kept their weapons fully trained on the position of the Americans. Not one even considered shooting at Slade-Lawes as the boat tore out of the small harbor.

Standing on the edge of the quay, Tiago watched the boat go. Then he beckoned his men, calling for their exit. Ridley and Henri exchanged fire with the Portuguese as they backed down the boat launch, boarded their vessel, and gunned the engine.

Their boat was fast, and high tide made it even easier to jet out within seconds. As they plowed through the water toward the open ocean, Ridley and Henri lowered their guns. Owen gingerly tucked the Glock into the back of his waistband.

They went over to Alan Turner. Ridley and Henri knelt down, trying to avoid the blood that was draining across the cobblestone. There was no carotid artery left for him to check. She trembled, angry tears beginning to prickle in her eyes.

Ridley kept remarkably calm in combat. Dreams about the enemies she'd killed never haunted her sleep, but memories of the innocent burned deep within her.

We couldn't get there before the tourist died at La Rochelle. We couldn't prevent Atwood's death. We couldn't stop Turner's murder.

The fury swelled. She pawed at her eyes in frustration, stood, and looked out at the Cornish waters.

I'll destroy you.

They couldn't stay on the island a moment more. Ridley swam out to one of the small boats, started up the engine, and steered it close enough to the boat launch for Henri and Owen to jump in. They sped out of the harbor.

The boat was back at Marazion Beach in minutes. They

trekked to where they'd parked the BMW and stashed the MP7 in the trunk.

Ridley was still soaking wet from her retrieval of the boat. Her shirt clung to her, her jeans dripped off her ankles. Henri dug out a small quick-dry towel from his luggage for her, then he got behind the wheel. They drove northeast.

In the backseat, Owen's face was pale and blank.

"We need some food," said Henri, glancing back at the young grad student. "First place we find."

Their traveling companion needed a reset more than Henri actually needed food. When they finally pulled off the road into a little village, they found a café with an outdoor patio that was just opening its doors.

Ridley stayed out on the patio and pulled off her soaking shoes and socks. Owen and Henri went inside. The owner greeted her first customers with an exceptional amount of cheer. She was without a doubt a morning person.

As they stood back looking over the breakfast menu, Henri murmured softly to Owen.

"You're all right. We're just gonna get a cup of coffee now. What kind do you drink?"

Owen was clearly still shell-shocked. "I'll get a mocha."

"Mocha, okay. You know what Ridley likes?"

This question seemed to clear some of his daze. Henri could see that he really wanted to know the answer.

"A flat white," said Henri. "I had to learn that the first day we worked together. A flat white early in the morning. Any other time, she needs that foam. We go latte."

"Have you worked together for long?"

"A week," said Henri with a smile, "but you have to learn your partner's coffee order right away. That's an important building block. Oh, and we'll get some food, okay?"

When they got back to the patio with their food and drink,

Ridley had unwound her braids and was wringing out locks of her thick hair. Henri noted Owen's reaction, just the slightest shift in posture, a softer expression, a spring of bashful energy.

This was not going to work out well.

Ridley had no cares but the English muffin breakfast sandwich in her hands. She swigged the coffee as they began to talk.

"The blade," said Henri, sober over his cappuccino. "It seals back together with blood."

"The tourist at Gisors..." she said.

"The countess."

"The Order," she said, shaking her head, "they just stood there. They weren't trying to stop the constable—the ifrit—from killing that man Turner. They weren't even trying to stop this thing in the chapel."

Owen had been chewing quietly. "Maybe they know they can't. I mean, God's honest truth, can *we* stop it?"

"Or we're facing something worse," she ventured. "They want the ifrit to piece the saber back together."

Owen sat up. "No, no, the Templars were set against the jinn. It was the work of their lives. They can't be working with it."

"Then why are they following it and not even trying to stop it?" she asked. "It's like they're fucking escorts."

"It's only the Seal of Solomon that can stop the jinn. It's the only absolute," he insisted.

"If it exists," said Henri.

"Yeah, but they have to *believe* it exists or they wouldn't be out here!"

Ridley thought for a moment, feeling her mind grow clearer with every sip of the coffee. "What if the clues don't just take us to the next piece of the saber, then? You think they lead to the Seal?"

Owen sat back, deflated. He scrubbed a hand over his hair.

"No, the Templars never found the Seal...even that bloke from the Order said that that's what they're after, the Seal. They've been around for eight hundred years..."

"And now they're going after this jinn as if it's the Holy Grail," said Henri.

"There's no Holy Grail."

"It's a saying."

"Owen, can you just figure out where we're going next?" said Ridley.

He obediently began studying the photos he'd taken. He borrowed a pen from the café, sketched on a napkin, and occasionally mumbled to himself.

She and Henri left him alone to his work, watching him grow frustrated at times. Finally, he sat back with a sigh.

"Richard the Lionheart took Cyprus from the Byzantines— it was really a whole mess, he was on his way to the Holy Land but then his emissary who was a princess got kidnapped there —and then *he* sold it to the Templars. He needed the money to keep crusading and the Templars needed a launching point for more crusades.

"They built all over the island. There are loads of castles still standin'." His eyes were starting to shine, his hands gesturing gracefully through the air as if telling a story for himself. "*These* engravings are sendin' us there, but I think—I think it's sneaky-like. See, this is a literary trick."

He showed them the photos on his phone, pointing in excitement.

"You read it straight through and it makes you believe one thing, but it's meant to be that every other line corresponds, so it's really in two parts. The second part revises—it...it abrogates the first part. So at first it looks like we're going to Limassol Castle on the southern coast, but if you go back..." he flipped photos. "It's actually on the northern, and it's high up. It's got to be Saint Hilarion."

"Saint Hilarion is the name of a castle?"

"Yeah. We're gonna need some hiking shoes."

Henri pulled some euros from his pocket. "Owen, would you grab me a a piece of banana bread?"

Owen looked at the money, then looked at Henri. He knew he was being momentarily gotten rid of, but he took it anyway.

"Yeah, all right."

After he'd disappeared into the café, Henri cleared his throat. "We can't take him to Cyprus."

Ridley raised a brow. "What's your argument?"

"The kid is nearly in shock. He's not trained for this."

She considered it. "Look what he did in the heat of battle. He made a tactical decision to shoot out those windows, distract the enemy. He made a good call. We keep him safe."

"He just saw two people die in front of him. It's not normal. He's not okay with it."

"You don't train to see someone die in front of you. It just happens, and then you've seen it. Forever. He didn't fuck up, Henri, and we need his eyes on this."

"So we send him photos, we call him, but we keep him at a safe location, at a distance, out of danger."

"He's able. I think he earned his place back there, and he wants to be here."

"That's another thing. He may want to be here for other reasons, too." He gave a knowing arch of his brow.

"You're saying *me*?" she exclaimed. "Come on, this is like his historical dream come true, some Indiana Jones fantasy he's probably had for years."

"Yeah, and you're his Marion."

"She could really run, that woman. Amazing sprint form."

"Ridley. I want to be together on this."

She sat forward, frustrated that all of her clothes were still wet against her skin, frustrated that they were still chasing.

"Cyprus is neutral. Let's give him this one more, then we send him packing. I think he's proven himself for that...?"

"Okay," said Henri with a reluctant nod. "One more location."

CHAPTER
THIRTY-FOUR

―――――

CYPRUS

It was a warm, windy morning when the Embraer Phenom 100EV touched down on the western coast of Cyprus.

Ridley, Henri, and Owen stepped off the small charter jet onto the tarmac. A salty breeze ruffled through towering palm trees. Ridley turned her face up to the sun. The Mediterranean warmth on her skin felt like home.

They were met there in the open by a very tall, rumpled operative named Rafael Russo. Ridley couldn't believe the irony of his name, but kept her mouth shut for the sake of not having to explain it all.

Rafael tossed away the butt of a cigarette before greeting them. He wore his hair short on the sides, sported a dark beard, and had the kind of flinty, broken face that might belong to a bare-knuckle boxer.

"Ospreys, huh?" he said as they loaded their bags into the Land Rover. "Your people are always up to some interesting shit. Don't worry, I won't ask. We've got weapons in the back, coffee in the front, if you can handle it."

"Turkish or Cypriot?" asked Ridley, climbing into the front seat as Henri deferred it to her.

"They'd both shoot me for saying it, but I've been here twenty months and still can't taste the difference," he said, getting behind the wheel. "Only difference is what side of the island you're on."

Israel and Palestine were not the only international bodies trying to negotiate a two-state solution. Cyprus was a divided land. The western half of the island was Greek, the eastern side Turkish, and there was little agreement on anything regarding Cypriot life, governance, or economy.

Recently, the Republic of Cyprus had made an agreement with Greece and Israel to build the EastMed pipeline, forming the world's longest power cable. This incensed Ankara, since a section of the pipe would run through Turkish waters. Britain had been trying to bring together Greek and Turkish leadership at U.N. gatherings to work it out sensibly, but it had all come to nothing.

As Israel had become economically allied with western Cyprus, Turkey had been growing more entangled with Palestinian leadership. With the prospect of peace talks between President Badr of the PA and the Israeli Prime Minister Shalmi, tensions on the divided island were rippling.

In the northeast, the influence of more radically religious Turks was growing evident. More mosques were being built, more local politicians who were faithful Muslims were being financed. This trend was unnerving even some of the more moderate Turkish-Cypriots.

They were heading into the simmering tension of that very northeast.

"Two and a half hours," Rafael told them, plugging in the coordinates on his phone. "I hope you all are hard of hearing, because I'm a karaoke man."

"My kind of Uber," said Henri with a little smile.

It somehow fit completely when Redbone's "Come and Get Your Love" began twanging through the speakers. They pulled off the tarmac.

"*Malaka*," murmured Ridley as Rafael began to sing.

On the southeastern coast of Cyprus, along the harbor of Limassol, Tiago emerged from the back of a Mercedes. He slid on a pair of shades and tugged at the collar of his sky blue polo. Bruno and João climbed out with him. The three of them did their best to blend in as they crossed the old town square.

They made their way to the square fortress just across from it. The ancient stones were sun-bleached, and neatly cut. A banner flapped in the wind by the stairway entrance. Limassol Castle, nearly a thousand years old, where Richard the Lionheart married a princess of Navarre to make her Queen of England, was now a tourist destination.

This was very, very inconvenient for a treasure hunt. Unlike their arrival at Saint Michael's Mount, which had been perfectly timed to avoid any civilians, their timing here was less than ideal, yet unavoidable. It was more important to beat the Americans to the site rather than to bypass tourists.

The trio dutifully purchased tickets at the entryway. Once inside, they muttered to themselves in relief. The place was nearly empty.

Tiago led them down into the cavernous vaulted hall, which

had been practically turned into a museum with its plexiglass displays.

Disgusting look, he thought, *a desecration.*

There were so many engravings on the walls, carvings that jutted out, stones that were oddly placed, alcoves that were sealed off with iron gates, that their search felt almost blind at the start.

"*Look to the sea*
The highest door
North
Above"

João, who had been following the compass on his watch, finally tossed up his hands. "This one doesn't make sense. It doesn't."

Tiago repeated the lines again. He turned down one narrow stone hallway, then into a cramped cell. Mumbling to himself, looking around.

Something struck him.

He pulled up the photo they'd taken of the engraving in the Welsh castle. A moment later, his bitter laughter filled the cell. His companions appeared at the door.

"*Look—to the sea*
The highest window—
North
Of the queen"

He turned the photo for them to see. They peered at it, but nothing seemed to register.

"*Look NORTH to the sea*
The highest window OF THE QUEEN"

He stormed out of the cell, blowing past João and Bruno.

"We're in the wrong fucking castle."

CHAPTER
THIRTY-FIVE

———

NEARLY THREE HOURS after leaving Paphos on the west coast, Rafael pulled the Land Rover into the parking lot at the base of a rocky, ragged hillside. It was strangely empty of other cars.

Ridley and Henri pulled out their new gear from the back: tools for digging and tools for killing, all loaded neatly into 5.11 Tactical RUSH backpacks.

"Are you giving me something this time...?" Owen asked Ridley.

"No," she said, pulling her bag over her shoulders. "Just stay close."

Rafael would stay in the lot and alert them if anyone showed up fitting the description of the Raphaels.

The three of them began to hike.

Saint Hilarion Castle sat atop the Kyrenia Mountains as a

crumbling sentinel of a bygone era. It was once part of a triad of fortresses along the coast which guarded against Arab raiders. The structure was in remarkably good shape for its thousand years.

As they passed through the lower ward which housed the stables and the barracks, Henri and Owen had to keep their wonder in check. This was not the time for appreciating the masonry of the Byzantines.

They reached the upper ward within minutes. Climbing under arches and up through broken towers, they scanned for any sign of their target.

"*Look north to the sea*
The highest window of the queen"

Ridley repeated it under her breath, again and again. She couldn't say why, but she simply *knew* they had gotten here before Tiago and his bruisers.

"There's a window intact, somewhere up high," said Owen, his breath coming faster as he kept up their pace. "It's an ocean view. It's called the Queen's Window—Queen Eleanor it must have been. She was from Aragon—Barcelona."

There were metal rails everywhere trying to keep tourists safe at these heights. They climbed another set of steps dug into the rock, then passed through a broken wall.

There it was. Overlooking the sprawling turquoise waters in the distance was a majestic, Gothic double window. It was more ornate than anything else in the castle.

But there was a section of stone missing from the windowsill. As they got closer, they saw a small cache within. It was lined with salt, and little chips of iron. In the middle was an empty niche where the shard of a blade might fit.

Beside it lay the pieces of a broken urn.

"Oh, shit," said Ridley.

She pulled the HK USP from her waistband into low ready,

wheeling about for any sight of the ifrit-possessed constable. Henri pulled his Glock 19, but didn't take his eyes off the urn.

"There's another word on it," he said. "A name?"

Owen took a tentative step, his camera phone braced.

"Careful!" said Henri.

He obeyed, sliding his foot forward ever so slowly, and snapped a photo.

From the broken urn, a tendril of smoke emerged.

"Oh, here we go again," said Henri.

He yanked Owen back as the tendril became a thick funnel, rising up past the windowframe, growing darker and darker. They stared as it began to take shape. A familiar hunched figure was forming, an ink-black goblin with smoking skin. Then the eyes appeared, those burning embers.

A rattling cough echoed from its chest. Then they realized it was not coughing but laughing, the most wicked sound that had ever scraped into Ridley's ears.

They backed away, guns trained squarely on its torso.

Ridley glanced down at its 'feet.'

"Henri, look at the boundary!"

He saw it, too. The jinn seemed rooted to the small chamber within the windowsill.

"That salt and iron shit works?" she exclaimed.

From the jinn came a deep hissing voice. *"You do not serve Maymun, the Prosperous. You cannot free my master. You have no saber."*

"You serve Maymun?" asked Owen, then aside to the others, "That's one of the kings."

The jinn smiled. It was like looking into the mouth of a smoldering volcano.

"The saber will free your master, the king?" he pressed again.

"You think that I will give you the answer, but you have brought nothing to give me."

"What do you want?" said Ridley.

She still clutched her HK, though she was fairly certain it would do nothing against this fiery shadow-creature.

"Prove yourselves worthy of knowledge."

"Okay, sure, yeah. How?"

"Give me an answer and I will give you an answer."

The three of them exchanged glances. Playing games with demons felt like a very bad idea, but there was really no choice.

"You guys love puzzles," said Ridley. "Get ready to shine."

Owen looked at the jinn. "Give us the riddle."

"I have cities but no houses. I have mountains but no trees. I have water but no fish. What...am...I?"

He and Henri immediately started mumbling to themselves. Headshakes and sounds of frustration, and swapping ideas that the other would smack down.

"A map?" said Henri finally to Owen, who nodded his head vigorously. "A map!"

The jinn curled its long fingers, and gave a nod.

"Now your answer. Will the saber free the jinn king?" asked Ridley.

"Yes."

"From where?"

"One answer for one answer."

She scoffed in irritation.

"I disappear when you speak my name."

"I wish you would," she muttered under her breath.

This one Henri pondered without saying anything, then exclaimed, "Silence."

The jinn nodded. *"From their chains in the eternal darkness. And now, you have one question left."*

Ridley was done messing around with these supernatural prophecies. "There's an engraving below you that tells us where the next piece of the saber is hidden. Where does it tell us to go?"

The jinn stared at her for a moment. Its eyes smoldered like coals, light warping and flickering in an eerie dance.

"What can run but never walk, has a mouth but never talks, has a head that never weeps, and a bed that never sleeps?"

"Have at it," she said to Henri and Owen, who powwowed again, furiously brainstorming.

"A river," Owen suggested to them. "It runs, has a mouth and a head and a bed!"

Henri hesitated, but nodded.

"A river," he said to the jinn.

"I will give you the answer when I move aside."

Owen looked down at the place where the jinn was rooted. "Can you?"

"No," said Ridley, "he can't. He's screwing with us. Trying to get us to release him from his prison of iron and salt." She pointed at the jinn. "You're a tricky piece of shit."

The jinn snickered again.

Henri sighed. "You just can't trust a demon these days."

She beckoned for the three of them to back far away from the jinn. They moved in close, lowering their voices to near whispers.

"We can't let him go," she said.

"I don't see another way," Henri replied.

"Can we just move the iron and salt?" asked Owen.

She looked back at the hovering creature. "I think he'd be pretty mad about that, and then we'd be within reach of an angry jinn."

"There's no way the Templars imprisoned all the jinn in the world," said Henri. "There must already be others out there, including the one that got free from Gisors."

"They're disaster demons! We're here to prevent all this, not give up yardage."

"So what's the alternative? We stop here? The ifrit goes on and frees this jinn king it's looking for?"

She squinted her eyes shut, thinking. "It didn't just appear when the urn broke. It was already broken when we got here."

Owen followed along with her. "It formed when it wanted to."

"Can we get it to vanish again?"

Henri gave a wry, approving smile. "Iron and salt. It will let us close if it thinks we're setting it free."

They went back to face the jinn.

"Okay," said Ridley. "We'll move the boundary."

"Free me and you will see."

She stepped forward. Henri stood by Owen, still holding his Glock. As she knelt down to brush away the circle of chips, Ridley could feel the heat rolling off the jinn. Strangely, there was no scent of smoke.

She put her hands out and reached for the line...but instead of brushing the chips away, she brushed them in. They fell like ash over the urn.

The jinn reeled, shrieking. Ridley stumbled and fell backward as it recoiled, shrank, and disappeared into a funnel of smoke once again.

Her heart was thudding, but she crawled forward and peered into the small cache.

"Step right on up, Owen."

They photographed it, holstered their weapons, packed up their tools, and scampered back down through the castle as quickly as they could. A few other tourists had just started their hike up.

How were we that lucky?

Looking down on the parking lot, they spotted Rafael leaning against the Land Rover, smoking a cigarette.

Then they saw another figure, their back to the mountain, approaching him across the pavement.

"No," said Henri in devastated protest.

It was Constable Tom Slade-Lawes.

CHAPTER
THIRTY-SIX

KYRENIA, CYPRUS

"ARE YOU AMERICAN?" called a voice across the parking lot.

Rafael looked up to see a man approaching. He bore a faint smile. His hands were empty. Instinctively, Rafael straightened up, holding his cigarette ready to toss. He didn't like how fast this guy was walking.

"I can't seem to find anyone out here who speaks English," said the man in his London accent.

Then Rafael heard a yell from the mountainside. It was Ridley. He couldn't make out what she was yelling, but the alarm in her voice was enough.

The stranger was just closing within six feet when Rafael flicked the lit cigarette at his eyes. The man winced backward, offering a split second for Rafael to draw his HK VP9.

"Don't move!" he shouted.

But he was holding something in his fingers now. Rafael realized it was his burning cigarette. Somehow, this man had caught it.

Rafael could see Ridley, Henri, and Owen out of the corner of his eye. They were tearing down the hill toward him.

The man whispered, "Don't move."

He put the cigarette to his mouth.

Rafael's arm tightened into a steely cord, ready to fire on anything that this friendly menace did next. The Englishman dragged deeply on the cigarette, and blew out a stream of smoke that was impossibly thick. It billowed into Rafael's face in a choking cloud of gray.

He coughed and squinted, eyes burning. He tried to back out of it, to locate the man with the barrel of his gun.

When a flash of gold came slicing through the smoke.

Henri reached the parking lot a step ahead of Ridley, both their weapons drawn. Rafael and Constable Slade-Lawes had disappeared into a veil of gray.

They each angled out, guns trained on the smoke.

"Rafael!" called Henri.

The cloud began to dissipate. Only Slade-Lawes was standing, holding the broken saber. Blood dripped from the end of it. Rafael lay on the ground, clutching at his abdomen, his shirt stained scarlet.

"Drop it!" yelled Henri.

"Tom! Put down the saber!" Ridley said.

He began to turn toward them, his hand lifting up the blade. Ridley shot. Henri shot.

Half a dozen bullets ripped into Slade-Lawes' torso. He collapsed to the ground. The saber clattered to the pavement, skidding beneath the Land Rover.

They went up to confirm the kill. The English constable was dead.

Damnit. It didn't have to end like this!

They put away their guns. Henri pulled off his own shirt and pressed it against Rafael's stomach. The gash was deep, but didn't appear to have reached his organs.

"There's a hospital in Nicosia," said Ridley. "It's almost an hour."

"Rafael," said Henri, holding up his head, "is there first aid in the car?"

"Glove compartment," he groaned.

Owen, who had appeared beside them, grabbed it and handed it off. Ridley pulled it open and began rifling through it.

Then Owen spotted the saber lying beneath the car. Pulling down his jacket sleeve to cover his hand like a glove, he lay down on his stomach, and reached for it.

Ridley was handing over bandages and antiseptic, when out of the corner of her eye she saw Owen rise to his feet.

What had he been doing on the ground?

Then she saw the saber in his hand.

"Owen, don't—"

"I'm not touching it! See?" he showed her the way he'd tucked his jacket over his hand.

"Just put it down," she said.

Owen looked down at the blade.

His eyes lingered too long, and she knew they had lost him.

"Owen!"

She drew her HK, agonized, and aimed it at him. Henri looked up in time to see Owen lift his face. Something had gone dark. His brooding blue eyes fixed on Ridley.

"No! Put it down, Owen, please," she cried.

"Shoot me and you kill him."

The voice was his but the words were not. Still, they were true, and she knew it.

"Owen, you can give it up," said Henri, standing up slowly. "Give up the saber and the ifrit has no home."

They had no idea if it was true, but it was all they could do to hope.

He laughed at them. That boyish grin looked suddenly eerie as he pulled open the driver's side door.

"Ridley..." said Henri.

"I can't! And you can't either!" she called back.

Owen slid behind the wheel of the Land Rover.

"We'll see you soon," she said, and spat on the ground.

He flashed a horrible smile, and peeled out of the parking lot.

CHAPTER
THIRTY-SEVEN

———

NICOSIA, CYPRUS

They reached Nicosia in an old Mercedes-Benz that Ridley had jacked from the parking lot. She hadn't hot-wired a car in years, but Henri was tending to the their colleague's slashed belly, his hands slick with blood. Her fingers fumbled with the wires as she listened to Rafael's groans only yards away.

By the time they reached the city hospital, the backseat leather was streaked with blood, but Rafael was in stable condition. He told Ridley and Henri to leave before he even made it onto a gurney. This was his domain. He'd take it from here.

They wandered off into city, as they could not get caught up in any criminal investigation should the cops take an interest in his wounds.

Nicosia was a divided capital, half Orthodox Greek and half Turkish Muslim with a U.N. Buffer Zone in the midst. The

Americans would not be able to cross back into the Greek side with the rest of the foot traffic, as their manufactured passports had been in the Land Rover along with the rest of their belongings. It was utterly foreign to both of them, a strange mix of cultures.

They stopped to buy new clothes with some euros that Ridley had stashed in a back pocket. Blood-smeared outfits just would not do in a foreign city.

As twilight set in, they made their way to a sprawling city park. There was a phone call they had to make that neither of them wanted to. Henri reluctantly dialed Professor Lucy White.

She was at an end-of-year faculty dinner, and had to excuse herself to somewhere quiet just to hear them. They fed her the lies they'd become so accustomed to using in their work.

Owen has been such a help, but we had to travel to this last location alone...He's probably traveling back to Cambridge this moment and isn't picking up...could you help us decipher this latest rune and riddle?

She was flustered by the news about Owen. It wasn't like him, she said. He was an over-communicator, if anything. If he was heading back to Cambridge, wouldn't he have told her?

Yet if she truly doubted them, it didn't prevent her from lending them her expertise.

Thankfully, the photos they had taken that day were on Ridley's phone. She sent them to Professor White, who went off to work on them. When she called back a few minutes later, she was decisive.

"Arwad. It's a tiny—really tiny—little island off the coast of Syria. It was the last of the Templars fortresses standing in the Holy Land. Not a very pleasant place to be nowadays, I'd imagine."

"Do you have an exact location within the fortress?" asked Henri.

"No, I don't. That'll take some time, won't it? But I'll work on it tonight and send you all I can."

It was the best they would get. They thanked her, and then called Booker. As it rang, Henri sat back and covered his face with one hand. Ridley stood, arms folded, not wanting to admit what had happened at Saint Hilarion that day.

The boss was home, feeding his cat.

Is home the best or worst place to get bad news?

"Team," he said, "tell me where you're at."

They debriefed him on all of it. When they got to the part about losing Owen to the saber, it was Ridley who spoke.

"I was the one who wanted him here. I made the call. This is on me."

There was a moment's pause. It seemed infinite to her.

"You're not a unit, and you're not a commander. You *are* a team," he said.

"I was in agreement," said Henri, shooting Ridley a look. "I thought he had the capabilities, so I also thought he should come."

She shook her head at him.

Don't do this.

"How do you get him back then? Because we're not leaving that kid to die in Syria."

"No, we are not," she said, jaw clenched, furious at herself. "We have to get the saber into someone else's hands."

"How many more pieces does this damn saber have?"

"Hard to estimate," said Henri. "But this jinn said something about freeing a king with it. Maybe freeing all of them. There are allegedly seven jinn kings, we've been told. We've seen it grab...what, five?"

Ridley nodded at him. "Five saber shards."

"You're running behind this thing," Booker said, "and you're going into real enemy territory here."

"We need transpo, sir," said Ridley. "A Ground Branch unit."

"I'll arrange it, put you in touch. You're going by water. This Arwad place is only a mile off the Syrian coast, and what we absolutely don't need is an incident in the Middle East. The alphabets are on a real edge right now with the heat between Israel and the Palestinians."

The 'alphabets' in question were every federal agency that went by an acronym.

"How fast do you think this kid can get himself there? Jinn aren't magical swimmers, are they?"

"I don't think so. Not the ocean, anyway. They hate salt," said Ridley. "Really hate salt."

"I know you want to save this boy, but if that fails," said Booker, with a grave pause, "you know it's your responsibility to stop him."

They could hear the dread in his voice. They didn't know much about his service with the agency before Osprey, but they knew enough. Death may have left its stain on him, but he was not afraid of it...to call for it, or to meet with it himself.

"Yes, sir," said Henri.

"Get to the southeastern coast. I'll be in touch about your launch point."

Henri hot-wired a Kia for them. Stealing always burned his conscience, but they had no other option if they wanted to get down to the rescue point. Certain skills of his were unfortunately suited for law-breaking and theft.

They drove south to the coast in their stolen vehicle, and then east into the darkness. They hardly spoke.

By the time they were twenty minutes out from the farthest edge of Cyprus, Booker sent them an encrypted text.

Protaras. Green Bay, 0400 hours.

Cavo Maris Beach Hotel, reservation 'Hutton.'

They got to the hotel and checked in, realizing it would be suspicious that they didn't have bags, but there was still enough time to get some shut-eye before their early departure the next day.

Henri, desperate to rinse off the stains of Rafael's blood, took a shower. Ridley went to the beach.

In the dark, it was nearly empty. The hotel glowed in the distance and lights twinkled along the coast, but the rhythmic sloshing of the waves made her feel alone. It was exactly what she was looking for.

She took off her shoes and sprinted. Did pushups. Did burpees until she was exhausted, finally collapsing in the surf. She welcomed the burning, the taste of the salty air as she sucked wind, the grit of the sand between her fingers, caking her face. It felt like another lifetime. She could almost hear the ferocious barks of the SEAL instructors echoing across the beach.

Yet the physical drain had not slowed the spiral of trouble in her brain.

Where will Owen be when the sun rises here?

She spotted a dark figure padding across the sand toward her. Henri.

"Hey," he said when he reached her, folding himself cross-legged onto the ground.

Ridley nodded hello. For a moment they sat in silence.

"I vouched for him," said Ridley. "I know this is on me."

He didn't dispute or attempt to reassure.

"So it's on me to not let it end like Atwood, or Slade-Lawes," she said.

"You think you can control that..." he said, shaking his head, "but that's not gonna be on you because you can't control that."

"I'm the one who shot that constable."

"And you'll do the same with Owen if you have to."

She snatched up a small rock and hurled it into the surf. "If he hadn't picked up that fucking saber...what was he thinking? A layer of cotton would stop this supernatural beast? *Shit!*"

"You mistook his enthusiasm for capability, but...we don't take civilian volunteers. For a reason."

Her anger drove her to silence.

Finally, Henri spoke again, this time more softly. "Your mother saved you, didn't she?"

Her gaze snapped to him.

Did he hear me telling Owen?

She knew that he had gotten the broad strokes, that her mother had died when Ridley was only three years old. He'd read into her file, of course, the basic primer, as she had also had access to some of his biography and record of service. Booker had always had partners swap files to help them get up to speed on the professional essentials. But there was no mention in that file about the particular devastation of the circumstances.

"Yeah," she replied after a moment. "Yeah, she did. How did you know that?"

"I've pieced some things together."

Ridley squinted out at the water, her gaze roaming the dark horizon.

"She loved swimming. She took me out on a lake one day, in some—some pontoon thing. I was in water wings, even though I hated them and could already swim on my own, but she...she insisted. It was just a lake, but there was some current thing in one of the deepest parts that made it dangerous for swimmers. I guess she didn't know that."

She fidgeted with her hands, rubbing her thumb along her middle finger. She could feel his gaze on her, solid, patient.

"I was only three, okay? I don't remember all of it. I *do*

remember...her shoving me up onto the boat. I think she was trying to keep really calm to not upset me, but she was...she was panicking."

Ridley's voice tightened.

Her eyes. Pure terror in her eyes.

"She got me to safety. I reached for her. She tried to get up on the boat, but I couldn't pull her up. I was three...and there was a piece of seaweed on me, I remember. I don't know—I don't understand what happened, what *actually* happened, but she went under. And she never came up."

They were details that Ridley had shared only half a dozen times in her life. Two lovers, two friends, Booker, and now Henri. Each time, she thought she never wanted to tell the story again. She'd closed the account, enough investors in this part of her life. Somehow, here she was again. She could feel that surge, that kind of tidal wave that could engulf a three-year-old in fear and confusion.

"They found me a few hours later. It took them five days to recover her body, out of a *lake*. That's how treacherous it was down there."

He was quiet with her for a moment.

"Do you remember her much from before?"

She hated this part, and felt her throat growing thick.

"Yeah. Not as much as I wish, but I didn't get much of what I wished for as a little kid."

She shook her head, cleared her throat, and looked at him.

"You know that life better than me," she said. "Orphanage, right?"

He nodded. "Like half the kids in Haiti. My father...who knows. My mother had six more kids after me...abandoned all of us. They split us up, so I only know two of my brothers," he said, leaning back. "I wish I'd been able to take care of them, to look out for them like a big brother wants to."

The silence sat between them, worn and heavy. This was okay.

"And then you made your career in the Secret Service, looking out for people," said Ridley.

He gave a short laugh, nodding in realization.

"I did that. And then you were the best swimmer in your BUD/S class," he said.

She sniffed with the faintest etch of a smile. "Damn right."

Her toes scuffed the sand. Then Ridley grew somber.

"We push the saber onto someone else," she said, "and if we can't get it out of Owen's hands, I'll take the shot."

CHAPTER
THIRTY-EIGHT

FAINT LAVENDER STREAKED the horizon the next morning as Ridley and Henri made their way down to the beach. There, on the rocky end that jutted out like a peninsula, stood two silhouettes in the pre-dawn light. As they approached, the one closest to them called out.

"Morning! Where are y'all headed this early?"

"Arwad," said Ridley.

"Ridley Samaras?"

"Yeah. This is Henri Michel."

They shook hands with the awaiting stranger.

"Arthur Zain."

He was nearly six feet, in his early forties, with a handshake that was reassuringly vice-like. There was something so indistinct about his features that she could have looked away for a moment and immediately forgotten his face. Ashy brown hair, hazel eyes that looked sleepy but flashed with a sharp cheerfulness. His build was hard, with broad shoulders and a lean waist. He wore lightweight tactical pants, a long-sleeved T-shirt and a pair of Merrells. It could easily pass for the outfit of an adventurous traveler.

"This is Adam Pichardo," he said, gesturing back to his companion.

Adam stepped up to shake their hands. He was an operator, through and through. Wiry muscle, too-long hair that spiked up in all directions, and wrap-around sunglasses pushed up on his forehead.

"At least neither of you got this glowing hay bale goin' on," he said, scrubbing his own blonde hair. "This'd be one of those days to blend in."

"We got gear for both of you," said Zain, "long as Booker got your measurements right."

They walked out to the jetty, where a sleek pontoon vessel bobbed in the water. The pilot onboard offered a hand as they stepped on.

He had dusky skin and a thick baby face, despite being in his thirties. His hands were the size of bear paws, his hair wavy black.

"I know it looks like a tourist boat," said the man, "but that's the point. And this is the fastest goddamn pontoon you've ever seen. Powertoon X-treme 3000. Sounds made up, huh? Ah, sorry, I'm Moaz."

They introduced themselves, and Moaz soon pulled out into open water.

When they were a few miles offshore, he killed the engine for a basic briefing. The ocean had begun to glow gold with the sunrise. From their seat compartments, Zain pulled out the load-outs.

Button-up shirts. Salomon shoes. A SOG SEAL XR folding knife for Henri. A Schrade fixed-blade karambit for Ridley. Tactical bags that looked like tourist backpacks. A pair of SIG Sauer M17s. Earpiece radios. Flashbangs. And two small pickaxes.

"You got rifles?" Henri asked.

Zain pulled an APC9K from his own gear bag. It was a compact 9mm rifle with an extended mag and a mini scope on the barrel, which didn't even reach five inches. He threaded a suppressor onto the end of it.

"My dwarfish little friend," he said with a grin.

Ridley holstered her M17, her own words echoing in her head.

I take the shot...

"Okay, listen up my new compadres," said Zain. "We're docking at Arwad and we're gonna blend in like a bunch of tourists. Did I bring nerdy glasses? Why yes, I did.

"This place isn't even fifty acres. Population 4,400. Threat number one: it's only two-and-a-half miles off the coast of Tartus, and Tartus is home to a vital Russian naval port. The whole city is fiercely loyal to that total gem of a human, that real *mensch*, Bashar al-Assad. So we don't want to play with them.

"We're on a recon and retrieval mission. You've met your unit members for the day. Moaz here was an Army Ranger that we scooped up for his prowess in all things rugged and manly. And he was born in Jordan and speaks fluent Arabic.

"Adam here was a SEAL who got picked up by Delta Force for being absolutely sick with a rifle and having some ultra-Spidey-sense when it comes to situational awareness.

"And I'm Zain, Green Beret turned Delta Force turned Ground Branch...served almost twenty deployments, Afghanistan and elsewhere. I speak a little Arabic and

Pashtun—badly. I love barbecue and bow-hunting and my family."

He grinned, looked over at them, and raised his hands.

"So, now we're all friends, why don't you guys tell us what exactly we're going to find today?"

"We have two objectives," said Ridley. "We need to get into the old citadel on the west side of the island to locate a hidden cache within the stone structure."

"And we need to locate this guy," said Henri, showing them a photo of Owen's university ID.

Each of the operators studied it closely.

"Friendly or hostile?" asked Pichardo.

"Complicated. He's in possession of an item that...that makes him hostile," said Ridley.

"What is it?" asked Zain.

She drew a deep breath. "It's a saber. It's this gold saber."

The Ground Branch guys exchanged glances.

"We know," said Henri. "If you'd told us this a few days ago, we would've looked like that, too. But having this thing makes him extremely dangerous. Use all the caution you have."

"It's got some kind of influence on anyone who holds it," said Ridley. "We need to remove it from his possession *without touching it.*"

"And do what with it?" asked Pichardo, sitting back and wrapping his arms around his chest.

"If we can obtain if safely, we take it with us."

"But really," added Henri, "don't touch it."

"So if we separate Owen Allchurch from the saber, he's a friendly," said Moaz, leaning on the wheel.

"Yeah," said Ridley. "He's with us."

And we really need him back.

"Okay," said Zain. "Let's go get your boy."

CHAPTER
THIRTY-NINE

_____

ARWAD, SYRIA

THEY ARRIVED on the tiny island of Arwad under the warm morning sun, sidling into a stream of locals who were meandering up the small wharf. There were few tourists in their midst, Syria having bottomed out as being a desirable travel destination.

Ridley and Henri went ahead with Zain, eyeing two noble portraits of Assad before they'd even left the dock. Moaz and Pichardo kept together, a dozen feet back.

There was always the odd Star Wars shirt or Liverpool kit even in these kinds of remote places, which amused Ridley. They passed scampering kids, by stalls that dripped with colored jewelry, hand-painted fans, and woven hats. There were miniature boats and sea-shell trinkets everywhere. These island people may have been close to the mainland, but fishing was their proud industry.

Henri longingly eyed some baskets of fruit as they went by. Moaz exchanged friendly words in Arabic with a few of the merchants on his way. Power lines tangled just overhead. Many of the walls were covered in graffiti, the steel doors of shops pulled closed.

Ridley attracted the most attention for her tall stature, though her coloring did help her to fit in a bit. By the looks that Henri was getting from many of the Syrians, they'd never set eyes on a black man in their midst before.

The Americans mostly just hoped that the tiny earpieces that each of them wore were going unnoticed.

As they wound deeper through the narrow streets, something began to feel wrong. The locals were darting about, their words fast and urgent as they gestured and shot nervous glances in the direction of the citadel.

"This doesn't look good," Henri muttered.

Moaz stopped to ask one of the women what was going on. She rattled off an animated reply in Arabic. He thanked her.

"There are Syrian forces on the island," he said once they'd moved out of earshot. "There's a rumor of a murder at the citadel, and they're afraid the rebels have gotten to the island. Looks like special company today."

"Shit," said Ridley. "That has to be Owen. If we lose that saber to the Syrian army, we're—"

She threw up her hands with a violent frown.

"We go now," said Zain. "Henri, go with Pichardo into the citadel. Find what you need, keep an eye out, communicate back. Ridley and Moaz, we take the outskirts, locate our target."

There was almost no one left on the street ahead, save the occasional boy running down an alleyway.

When they saw the citadel wall looming above them, they split into teams.

Henri and Pichardo entered the citadel, noting the security camera over the doorway. It was more likely than not to be broken, kept there only as a lazy deterrence. They stepped into an outdoor courtyard dotted with giant palm trees. There were doors all over the place.

"You know where you're goin'?" asked Pichardo.

"Yeah," said Henri, "when I see it."

The former SEAL looked skyward. "Great. Lead on, Indiana Jones. We don't got time to burn."

Where the domes split
In the tower that screams
It cannot stand
When you find what you seek

Henri had thought it strange that the Latin clue rhymed in English, which had make it easier to memorize.

They ran up the stairs onto the sprawling parapets. From there, they could see all the white rooftops of Arwad. The coast of Syria stretched ominously beyond a chasm of rippling blue.

"Domes..." said Henri, searching.

Pichardo pointed across the courtyard to two small white domes rising up above the citadel's mosque. Henri clapped him on the shoulder as they both broke into a jog.

The streets around the citadel were a labyrinth. Zain led the way through, staying near as possible to the great stone wall.

He and Moaz and Ridley were all itching to make this a tactical stalk. Every time they swept around a corner, she felt that ache to have a weapon ready. She could feel the M17 beneath her shirt, pressed snug against her back.

As they were coming up on an alleyway, they heard an exchange of male voices calling to each other in Arabic. Moaz put his arms out to stop them short until the voices faded.

"Soldiers," he said. "They're combing the area."

We're gonna find him first, you pricks. We're getting him first.

"P," called Zain quietly into the radio, "no sign of the target?"

"No sign of the target, boss. We're retrieving the item. Wait...oh, shit. We got a body here."

Ridley stiffened with dread. A cold crawled across her neck.

"Is it the target?" asked Zain.

"Stand by."

The wait was mere seconds, though it dragged like an hour.

"Negative. Unknown. Looks civilian, looks local."

If Owen killed a Syrian, we're so fucked.

"Copy. We're heading west."

Zain gave Ridley a look of relief as they moved on.

They circled around the northern end of the citadel. Ahead lay a rocky beach, bearing the ruins of some ancient Phoenician fortress. Zain motioned for them to disperse. He went for the upper beach. Moaz moved to the middle. Ridley headed down the coast.

Here they were exposed, conspicuous on a deserted stretch of the island, with Syrian forces prowling around. She knew the crash of the surf would swallow any calls for help.

Tidal pools and puddles reached across a long area of the shore. On the outer edge were a few broken pillars of massive cut stone. At least during low tide, they'd make for an excellent hiding spot.

Ridley headed out toward them, trying to dance over dry sections of rock. As she got nearer, something prompted her to draw her gun. She held the SIG tightly and rounded the corner of a huge colonnade.

Huddled against the base, facing out to the ocean, was Owen.

He was wet and ragged. Blood streamed from his scalp, down his neck, staining his shirt. His knuckles were scraped and bleeding. He looked like he was in shock.

But she could not see the saber. She circled wide, gun trained low, looking for any sign of the golden blade.

His eyes fixed on her. They were his own again.

"Hey," he said.

"Hey. You okay? What are you doin' out here?" she said, not relaxing yet.

"Running away. Where is this?"

She called into her radio, "Target acquired. He's *not* hostile, I repeat, *not* hostile. Western edge of the beach, behind the pillars."

Then turned back to him.

"Owen, you're in Syria. What did you do with the saber? What happened to it?"

She heard Zain and Moaz radio that they were on their way.

Owen looked confused. "Oh, bloody hell, it—I don't have it. I don't know."

"Did a soldier take it? Did you get into a fight?"

"No, I—what do you mean, a soldier?"

"Okay, rinse yourself off, you've got—" she said, then crouched down to take care of it herself. "You look like you've been in a fight."

She used her free hand to scoop salt water, washing away the blood with some extra scrubbing.

"Can you stand?"

"Yeah," he said, climbing to his feet, unsteady.

"We're getting outta here. We've got some help today, special forces guys."

"That's really cool," he said as she help-shoved him toward the beach.

She could see Zain and Moaz closing in from both ends, their heads on swivels for any arriving danger.

It arrived.

CHAPTER
FORTY

SHOUTS SPLIT THE AIR.

As Zain and Moaz converged to join Ridley, a team of Syrian soldiers burst out onto the beach. They were hollering commands in Arabic, rifles raised.

Moaz called back to them in Arabic, clearly trying to assure them they were no threat. But the commander had zeroed in on Owen, his bedraggled appearance, the wet blood staining his T-shirt. The commander stared down the barrel of his AKM, giving orders to Moaz as if he was an interpreter.

"They say he killed someone. That man in the citadel."

Another stream of Arabic as the unit crept closer.

There were four to match their own number, but their weapons were already drawn. It gave them the kind of advantage that couldn't be measured. Each of the Americans could have a pistol in their hands within one second, but that one second was deadly when a rifle already had sights on on you within a dozen meters. Zain and Moaz each had APC9K's in their packs, but those were inaccessible as long as they were out here in the open, at gunpoint.

"Tell them he was never in the citadel, he just got drunk and cut himself on the rocks. We're taking our friend to get medical attention and get him home," said Zain.

Moaz translated for the Syrians, who snapped at him. They took another step forward, bristling. There was another exchange in Arabic.

"I told him we're just tourists. We're just trying to get back to our boat before it leaves, but they're not very interested."

Trapped.

They could do nothing out in the open like this. These soldiers were coming for Owen.

Ridley whispered to Owen, "Kneel down. Put your hands up, but let them come get you."

"I can't—I didn't do it. Did I? Are they gonna kill me?"

But he knelt as she'd told him to, and raised his arms overhead.

As if on cue, Zain said quietly, "Make them close in. Moaz, on the sneeze."

What, the sneeze?

The Syrian commander yelled, gesturing with his rifle for them all to get down on their knees. Moaz played dumb, arguing for clarification.

The soldiers stepped closer, each of them staring down a different target. The Americans needed a distraction, and Moaz gave it to them.

As he was speaking calmly and slowly in Arabic, he hesitated mid-sentence, and then exploded with the loudest, best fake sneeze that Ridley had ever heard. It was so sudden, so surprising that every soldier's attention was briefly yanked to Moaz. That was the split-second they needed.

Zain snapped, swiping aside the long barrel of the AKM as he yanked his own gun free. He unloaded two rounds in the soldier's head from a foot away. Skull and blood exploded on him, but he'd already swung around behind the body-shield that was the dead soldier, and shot the next one in line.

Ridley lunged into the soldier standing in front of her. He had made the mistake of getting too close. At that range, *rush the shooter*.

The long barrel of the rifle made it nearly impossible for him regain his target, though he fired wildly into the air. She landed on him with her M17 drawn, planted the tip on his throat and fired twice.

Moaz had used the strength of his fake sneeze to double over. As all eyes had gone momentarily to him, the only weapon available in that posture was the Reapr knife in his boot. He never stood up so much as launched upward, ramming the blade into the soldier's jaw.

It was over in seconds. Blood spattered every one of them now. The sound of those gunshots had escalated the situation, though. Zain and Moaz pulled the short submachine guns from their packs. With suppressors and thirty round magazines on their APC9K's, they had gone full combat mode.

"There may be more. Move!" said Zain, then called into the radio, "P, back to the boat! We have four hostiles on the beach, deceased. Get your ass out, watch for soldiers."

"Copy!" came the staticky response.

Zain led them back into the labyrinth of narrow stone streets. They could hear locals calling to each other in alarm from open windows. The whole island would have heard the rifle fire. A woman in a hijab passed in front of them with her young son, and yelped at the sight of their advancing guns and bloody faces. She grabbed the boy and scurried away.

Syrians were no strangers to armed combat on their streets, to rebels with heavy weaponry stalking their enemies, but not here on Arwad. Word would spread like wildfire. It was a race to get back to the wharf.

The Ground Branch unit had just slid around the corner of the citadel wall when they heard a man's shout nearby.

"Soldiers!" said Moaz.

They moved faster, sliding through alleys and past gasping civilians. Some even yelled furiously at the armed strangers going by.

As they rounded a corner, they almost ran into a trio of soldiers in fatigues brandishing AKMs. They yanked themselves back behind cover, but the Syrians had spotted them. Shouts in Arabic were followed by a barrage of bullets.

"P, where are you?" called Moaz into the radio. "We're taking fire!"

The streets emptied. Zain stole a glance to be sure they were clear of civilians, before loosing a volley.

"At the wharf," came Pichardo's voice over the radio. "Got more hostiles on foot!"

Ridley reached into Zain's backpack just in front of her and pulled out a stun grenade. She yanked the pin—

"Eyes and ears!"

—and hurled it around the corner. It exploded with a shattering bang. They flowed out into the next bank of cover, into opposite alleyways, firing down into the haze of the flashbang. They heard a gargled grunt. One down.

Moaz fired a volley as the smoke began to clear.

Ridley slipped out and shot off three rounds. She saw one of the Syrians collapse. The last one standing flipped over a merchant's steel table and dropped behind it.

It was clear that Zain and Moaz had been working for a while as a unit. They advanced, covering for each other as if connected by a swinging wire. Ridley followed up behind them, a shield for the unarmed Owen and a rearguard for any threats from behind.

Finally, the remaining Syrian soldier looked over the top of the table to shoot, and Zain landed a headshot.

"Clear," he called back.

As they ran to the wharf, they heard more gunshots, and screaming.

They reached the open market on the harbor. Just ahead, Henri and Pichardo were trapped behind some concrete dividers. One Syrian soldier in fatigues lay dead in the square. More were firing on the Americans from behind the center statue and from inside shop doorways.

"Comin' up on your six," called Zain.

He and Moaz and Ridley and Owen planted themselves behind cover. Gunfire ripped over their heads.

"I found it," Henri yelled back to Ridley. "We got the next breadcrumb."

Two for two today, if they could survive and escape.

The Ground Branch guys called to each other to advance positions, each taking a turn to lay down cover. Pichardo had almost reached the small exit lane to the wharf.

"Go! Move!" Zain shouted at Henri over the gunfire.

He rushed to the next barrier. Crouching low, Ridley hauled Owen behind her. Pichardo had moved behind the concrete wall at the mouth of the pier, holding his position. He leaned out just far enough to hit the soldier behind the statue, who fell into the empty fountain below.

It was enough of a break to make a run for the wharf.

"Run!" she yelled to Owen, then burst toward the water.

She sprinted down the pier to the pontoon. If there was one

type of vehicle she could take on blind and drive with ease, it was a boat. Owen leapt in behind her. She gunned the engine as Henri rushed for them. Close behind, the Ground Branch trio came in staggered movements, firing back, staying low as the Syrians came after them.

Moaz was the last to jump aboard, blood seeping from his left hand. Ridley threw the throttle open. They surged out of the harbor, under fire.

The Syrians poured into a military speedboat and tore after the pontoon.

CHAPTER
FORTY-ONE

RIDLEY CUT THE WHEEL, veering as close as she could to the island's northern edge. They wanted nothing to do with the shore of Syria that stretched to their right, as far as they could see. The gunshots would have been audible in the port city of Tartus, and additional forces would no doubt be deployed within minutes. That was not a fight they could muscle their way through.

The Powertoon may have been a blunderous looking vessel, but there was a reason the Ground Branch unit had chosen it for today's mission. It was the fastest pontoon in the world, reaching speeds of nearly 80 mph. Against the Zhuk-class patrol boat of the Syrians, it had the clear advantage, except that the old Soviet boat had one ace card on board: a turret armed with two heavy machine guns.

Zain, Pichardo, and Moaz—despite his mangled hand—loaded fresh mags into their APCK9's, firing off the back of the boat, trying to steady themselves with the dipping and crashing of the wake. Ridley carved angles through the water, trying to slip the hail of bullets pouring out from the Zhuk.

The Mediterranean lay open and shimmering ahead of them. As the pontoon started to pull away from the Syrians, Ridley spotted something in the water. A thousand yards out, there was a dark spot, like a short pillar that had risen above the surface.

Submarine.

"Henri," she shouted above the roaring motor, "Russians?"

He got to his feet for a better view.

"It has to be!" he replied. "They've got a port right here."

As they raced closer, she steered wide. The sail of this leviathan rose up above the waves, a dark tower in the ocean. The sub would surely be coming in to dock, and the sound of machine guns above them would have put the crew on high alert.

The periscope swiveled.

"Hold on," yelled Ridley over her shoulder.

She had to slow a few knots. The pontoon was wide and flat, not suited to making sharp cuts. They nearly skidded across the surface as she pulled the wheel hard. Owen pitched to the side, vomiting over the rail.

The Syrians must have seen the submarine sail tower. They had stopped firing, but the Zhuk was still plowing through the water after the pontoon.

"Full speed!" Pichardo called up to Ridley.

Says a man trained on land.

Among other things, Ground Branch had been formed to execute covert operations in foreign territories. If operatives were compromised, the US government would deny any and all knowledge of their activities. They *had* to reach Cypriot waters. Cyprus had recently restored diplomacy with Syria, but if the Syrian army was found conducting military operations in their waters, all talks would go up in flames.

Ridley threw open the throttle again. The pontoon surged forward. The Syrians cut a wide perimeter around the submarine, but were able to maintain speed.

"Hold your fire," Zain yelled to his guys.

Here in the open water, they could outpace them. The military boat was made for patrols and defense, not high-speed chases.

Sure enough, the Zhuk began to grow smaller and smaller in the distance.

When the Syrian vessel had shrunk to a smudge on the horizon behind them, Ridley finally slowed.

Zain pulled out a medical kit from one of the seat compartments. He helped Moaz clean and bandage his bloody hand. Owen sat holding his stomach, looking like a wrecked man. He dodged over the side to vomit again.

Pichardo worked his way up to Ridley, leaning into her right ear to ask something. His voice was only a muffled garble.

"What?" she said, turning her left side to him.

"Do you want a break to catch up with your guys?" he asked.

She glanced back. Henri was trying to find Dramamine in the medical kit for their young Welsh charge. Owen's face was nearly gray, his damp clothes stained pink with blood. Looking at Pichardo, she shook her head.

They had executed the mission, achieved both their objectives, and made a messy but successful escape. The simple task now was shepherding them back to neutral territory. She wanted that one. She didn't want to do the tending. She didn't want to face Owen right now.

. . .

CYPRUS

They made land at Cape Greco, the southernmost peninsula on Cyprus. There were some vacationers on the cliff edge, a few sailboats floating on the crystalline waters. Ridley maneuvered the low cliffs to find an inlet where they could disembark.

Zain had radioed back to the island for a pickup. Two Toyota Land Cruisers were waiting for them, a couple of Ground Branch operatives behind the wheels.

They took Moaz in one to get to medical while Zain and Pichardo ran the pontoon back up the coast to its docking space. Ridley and Henri thanked them. These were the kind of ghosts to whom they had entrusted their lives for half a day, and would likely never see again.

After seeing off the Ground Branch guys, Ridley and Henri took the other Cruiser and drove Owen to a nearby hospital.

He was dehydrated, cut and scraped up, but hadn't suffered any serious injuries. They sat in the room as the IV fluids restored him. He was deeply rattled, but was trying to stave it off long enough to help them with the latest clues.

As Owen pored over the photos that Henri had gotten at the Arwad citadel, he kept shaking his head as if trying to clear it.

"I think it's—you know, it's not too clear. This one is damn difficult," he said, subconsciously touching his IV. "It's a castle on a river, and that's a basic diagram. No 'X' on it, of course. That stuff is silly. I just don't know where the castle is...give me a few minutes, I'm sorry."

"Yeah, sure, take those moments," said Ridley. "Can you tell us what happened to the saber in the meantime? Who took it from you?"

He shook his head, miserable.

"You don't remember running into anyone..."

"No, I don't even remember anything. You ever been blackout drunk? It's like that, I mean...it's all just missin' from my memory."

"Do you remember what happened up at the castle?" asked Henri. "The trickster jinn who thought he was Loki?"

"Yeah, and getting down to the car park, and seeing Rafael —is he all right?"

"Just a gash on his stomach. He'll be fine," said Ridley. "So you remember the jinn saying he served Maymun, a king?"

Owen nodded. "One of the seven, yeah."

"And that the saber was going to be used to free Maymun, or all of them?"

"Yeah...that part didn't sound good. I've no idea how. I've never heard of them bein' imprisoned."

"Yeah, that's definitely too bad," said Ridley, frowning in thought.

"You're all right," Henri said to Owen as he got to his feet. "Do you want anything to eat?"

"Bag of crisps?"

He nodded, and nudged his partner.

She looked up at him. "I don't care, anything with some calories behind it. Thanks."

As he stepped out, Ridley leaned forward in her chair.

"Owen. I'm sorry."

"You didn't do anythin' to me."

"I wanted you to come with us, but I shouldn't have let you. This was dangerous from the start. Stupid and selfish of me to put you in harm's way."

He looked alarmed by her distress. "I wanted to!"

"And you were an ace. You told us where to turn when the whole Order seems to have gone the other way, and you were right. You were—flippin' clever. Still, you shouldn't have been with us on the ground."

"But *I* insisted."

"You could insist all you want," she said with a wry smile, "but you weren't goin' anywhere with us if we didn't let you. So, I am sorry."

"But you came and got me," he grinned.

"Yeah. Yeah, we're glad that worked out."

"Portugal!" he exclaimed.

She blinked in surprise.

"The riddle. *Not of the Celts, not of the Visigoths, not of the Romans, not of the Moors, but of Gaia and portus.* Portus and Gaia: Portugal. I think all those people lived there at different times. And it all makes sense! Portugal was where the Templars fled to when they were being hunted by the king of France. The whole stupid Order of Raphael—" he said, waving a hand, "—it's all come back to Portugal."

Ridley laughed. "You are a gentleman and a scholar!"

He practically blushed. "I don't know where, though. Look up Templar castles on rivers."

She pulled out her phone and began to search.

"Ridley," he said quietly, "did I really kill someone?"

She stopped.

"You didn't. You never did any of it. The ifrit used your body. None of it was you. You never killed anyone."

He grimaced as if unconvinced, but nodded. She went back to searching. A moment later, Henri returned with a bag of chips for the invalid and a few hot pitas. His mouth was already full, forever the eating machine.

"What is this?" asked Ridley when he handed her one.

"Cheese pie. Delicious."

"I think we've got it, the next place," she said, biting into the small pie.

She held up the phone. On it was an image of a decrepit castle rising up along a shallow river.

"Almourol, Portugal."

"Is this the last place?" asked Henri.

There was a long moment as each of them considered.

"The saber was almost complete," said Ridley.

"There are seven jinn kings," added Owen. "I don't know how many pieces of the saber there are, but...each one had writing on it."

"And this would be the seventh shard, after the hilt," said Henri.

He sat down, chewing, deep in thought.

"Time to meet the ifrit, huh?" said Ridley.

"But you don't...you don't have the Seal of Solomon," Owen said. "You have to have that. You can't—we haven't been able to stop the ifrit with anything. It's why the Templars were looking for the ring. They knew—they *knew* that it was the only power that worked on the jinn."

"Okay, but they never found it. So you're saying that's curtains for us?" It came out more heated than she'd meant it to.

Henri spoke up. "What if this *is* the trail to the Seal? They wouldn't have just left breadcrumbs for the jinn. Maybe we're retracing their actual search."

"So...even if this ifrit completes the saber, goes to let out his master, we still have a shot to stop it?"

He looked at her. "We get the Seal, we can stop it all."

CHAPTER
FORTY-TWO

ROME, ITALY

TIAGO STOOD on the southern bank of the Tiber, pulling apart a *supplì de riso* with his teeth. He relished the way the deep-fried croquette steamed in his mouth, salty and rich. He gazed across the river at the looming Castel Sant'Angelo. It was beautiful to him that after nearly two hundred years, the giant cylindrical tower still dominated the skyline. Once the mausoleum of Hadrian, it was too good to be left unused by later Romans, who turned it into a hulking fortress.

It was then taken over by the popes. Of course it was, he thought, because they laid claim to everything in this city that their hearts of various shades desired. One of those popes had built a long stone corridor over the streets to connect the castle to St. Peter's Basilica. It was an escape passageway turned tourist attraction. A pope had even fled through it

234

while the rogue army of his rival, the Holy Roman Emperor, slaughtered nearly the entire Swiss Guard on the steps of the Basilica.

Religious strife had been so much simpler back then, he thought. Yet somehow, despite all their warring, the three grand faiths of the world had all survived. Each had its own perversions, and every one of them was blind.

The truth was so much bigger than they knew. Even the Catholics and Protestants, though they recognized the Triune God, had no idea how small their vision truly was.

And he knew that here in Rome, the Harlot herself rode upon the Beast. Soon enough, the purple and scarlet and gold and jewels would be ripped from her fleshly body, and more than a billion people would see true power in the hands of true believers. They would be free of the earthly kingdom that had claimed infallibility while it tortured its own followers, righteousness while it massacred its own cousins, and holiness while it violated its own children.

Tiago finished the *supplì* and wiped his fingers on a napkin. Beside him, Bruno leaned against a bench, absorbed in his phone. João, who was next to him, finished guzzling a water.

"You know, when you drink like a camel you piss like a race-horse," Tiago said to him with a dry smile.

"It keeps my skin looking fresh!"

Tiago took the empty bottle from him and tossed it in a rubbish bin with his crumpled napkin.

Bruno held up his phone, excited. "He got it."

On the screen was a photo of the citadel in Arwad.

After the misstep on Cyprus, they had raced to Saint Hilarion Castle. By that time, the local police had cordoned off the area, and the body of none other than a British constable was lying under a sheet in the parking lot. They were finally able to slip the swarm of searchers and reach the Queen's

Window, where they realized they were far behind the ifrit, and the Americans. They deciphered the clue to the next location.

Tiago had arranged their speedboat for the short trip across the Mediterranean, but just as they were about to depart from the northern coast, they received word of a skirmish on the island. The place would be in lockdown. Any suspicious-looking foreigners would end up in the rotting gut of a Syrian prison. There was no way to access the location they needed to reach.

Fortunately for Tiago, the Order had followers in almost every corner of the earth. The Americans had thought him to be in charge, but he was a trusted lieutenant and nothing more. For now, at least. He could make the calls to the ones who pulled the strings above.

That day, he sent out a missive by text, an urgent request up the chain of command: they needed a Raphael on Arwad.

He didn't know how high his request would go, or who would have to activate a trusted follower for this task, but within the hour he was instructed to go to Rome to wait with his associates. A member would be dispatched to the location and the relevant information would be relayed. It would take longer than if they'd pursued it on their own, but the option had been cleanly eliminated.

The order to go to Rome, though, had made Tiago nervous. Did they think he wasn't willing to do *everything* for the Order? He was savagely dedicated, and any thought of being diverted from the mission made him nearly sick to his stomach.

When he succeeded, it would be the greatest moment of triumph in the many long and dark centuries of the Order's existence. And it would be the ifrit that unleashed it all.

The Raphael that had been dispatched to Arwad must have been in Syria already. When the photo came through on the encrypted phone, it was exactly what they needed.

Tiago studied it in silence, waving away Bruno and João when they started to hover. After a moment, he smiled and looked up.

"We're going home. It's all coming home."

He handed the phone back to Bruno and glanced west across the Tiber, down the Via della Conciliazione. The dome of St. Peter's Basilica loomed at the end of it, bone-white against the flawless spring sky.

The Vatican would have to enjoy these last few days of world dominion.

CHAPTER
FORTY-THREE

THE LAST TIME Ridley had been in Lisbon, she was sixteen years old, sparking with youth but occasionally reeking of reckless stupidity. While small in the scope of European capitals, she'd felt a freedom in those narrow streets. There was something passionate about the aggressive artistry of their graffiti and the gorgeous melancholy of their music. The anguish and loss of all her young life seemed to come alive on those stringed guitars.

Today, as she climbed a steep cobbled lane in the bohemian neighborhood of Bairro Alto, she could smell fish grilling and egg tarts baking in the street cafés they passed.

Henri walked beside her, taking it all in for the first time. He never tired of discovering old cities and ancient buildings, silent testaments of history. Though being on mission usually meant they were working against a clock, he didn't want to lose this small pleasure. He may have been acting to save the world, but small moments of gratitude still carved meaning into his life.

They had left Owen at the airport in Cyprus with a ticket in hand. He was heading back to London, to his university life, and to some much needed rest.

"None of this will show up in your thesis paper," Henri reminded him.

"Keep your phone nearby," said Ridley. "We'll check in with you soon."

They left him in the security line and took a car back to Paphos. The Embraer Phenom 100EV was awaiting them on the open tarmac.

The ifrit would surely have not found it easy to go from Arwad to Lisbon. Even if it had made the journey to Cyprus, there were no direct flights from there to Portugal. Multiple tickets would have to be purchased. Layovers would have to be endured. The saber would have to be checked luggage. All the setbacks of traveling in human form would apply.

Considering those factors, they were certain that they had beaten the ifrit back to mainland Europe. Yet anxious thoughts still tugged at Ridley. This was their home country, after all, probably the seat of the Order itself.

How many other goons could Tiago call upon? Has he already set up traps? Who's on his payroll?

Every stop had left dead bodies along this trail, whether by their own hands or by the ifrit's or by the Order. She was determined that the next stop would be clean and efficient.

No more casualties. Well...no more innocent casualties.

Ridley and Henri stopped for a quick lunch at an outdoor café. After a few codfish cakes, some iberico ham with cheese and jam, and a plate of calamari big enough to satisfy him, they headed up a winding cobblestone street.

Halfway up, she stopped at a corner block in front of a shabbily painted green door.

"This is it."

They glanced at the intersecting streets. All calm, a few relaxed pedestrians and slow tram cars. A tuk-tuk disappeared around the corner.

Ridley pulled out her phone to play a track. Within seconds, she was singing along to Queen's "Somebody to Love."

Henri knocked on the door.

"You have a bluesy voice, Rid!" he said cheerfully, stepping back.

"Take a loooook in the mirror and cry—"

She had just started on the first bridge when the door finally opened. Behind it stood a slight, scruffy-looking man in his late twenties.

"Hello! You found somebody to love!" he said in a slight Portuguese accent. "Come in."

They stepped inside. He shut the door behind them.

The apartment was practically a jungle. There were plants budding on every sill, leafy shoots flowing down every shelf. Ridley took a moment to adjust. She just kept seeing more plants.

"Do you make everyone sing as a passphrase?" she asked.

He shrugged, with a surprisingly boyish grin. "It's more interesting, and I like Queen."

With his soft accent, it came out *Quinn*.

"I'm Cédric," he said, shaking their hands. "They don't tell me who you are, so you don't have to use names. I'll just call you six—" he looked at Ridley, "and seven."

"Double-oh seven," said Henri.

Cédric laughed, "Okay. Double-oh seven."

He's a character, for manning a CIA safehouse.

"They sent me your list," he continued. "I already have

some of it. Not everything, but if you want to wait, we can make a pickup tonight."

"Sorry, we don't have the time," said Ridley. "Do you have the car?"

"Yeah. How far do you need to go?"

"Eighty-five miles."

Henri added, "A hundred and forty kilometers."

"Yeah, I have a few options. I'll take you to the garage and you pick. But first, let's get your stuff."

Cédric beckoned them into the kitchen. He went to the microwave and punched a series of buttons. The double doors of the pantry suddenly swiveled outward. The shelves full of food rotated away, and from the back emerged an illuminated wall, stacked with an arsenal.

Henri gave him a very impressed thumbs up.

"That is the coolest hide I've seen," said Ridley.

"Thank you! I built it. It got stuck a lot in the beginning. But I have the Bravo AR-15, Viking sling, rail light, red dot, suppressor, everything..." he gestured to the rifle. "Ruger Precision, the Vortex Viper scope...that's a good one. You don't need any pistols?"

Ridley patted the SIG M17 at her appendix. "The benefits of flying private."

"Okay, cool. I also have your weird stuff."

Cédric pulled open a closet and hauled out a heavy duffel bag. He unzipped the top to show them the contents.

"Iron knives and salt blocks and a big set of tongs. And little pickaxes."

Ridley pumped a fist.

"This is the weirdest stuff anyone has ever asked for," said Cédric. "Not very James Bond."

"It's the weirdest stuff *we've* ever asked for."

"You need some garlic? A crucifix?"

Ridley gave him a mildly amused smile. "We do need that car."

"Okay. We pack this stuff," he said, tossing them an empty duffel, "and I'm ready to go. Only ten minutes from here."

They stashed the weapons, covering them with a layer of giveaway clothes that Cédric kept in a pile. Henri insisted on carrying the salt and iron. He tried in vain to make it look lighter than it was, but any keen eye would notice its heavy pendulous movement. Ridley was more content carrying their arsenal anyway.

One bag to take care of the ifrit. One bag to take care of the Order.

Twenty minutes later, the two Americans were driving north on the A1, Ridley behind the wheel. She'd given her partner low driving marks for his prodigious use of the car horn, and forcefully requested to take over.

"It's how you talk to other drivers in Haiti," he explained. "How else can you communicate?"

By the time they reached Almourol, the sky had turned an ashen gray. They drove past an airport and through an industrial stretch before reaching their isolated destination.

Castelo de Almourol was a medieval castle on a tiny island, really just a hill that was separated from the mainland by a stone's throw. The water was shallow enough to wade through. Sitting high above the Tagus River on a heap of granite, it served as the perfect lookout. It had once been a Roman fortification that was built up over and over by waves of invading conquerors: the Visigoths, the Berbers, and finally the Knights Templar.

Ridley parked near the shoreline. They got out of the car to a stiff, shockingly cold breeze. Fog had begun to hover and curl upward from the surface of the broad river.

"This is not very Iberian weather," muttered Ridley as they grabbed the duffels.

"Ifrits can't control weather, can they?"

"We would've heard about that before. This thing would have called down a tornado on us more than once already if it could...right?"

CHAPTER
FORTY-FOUR

***

Ridley and Henri donned the VTAC slings, strapping the rifles to them. Henri took the second duffel in hand.

They sloshed through the shallow water and trekked up the island. An eerie mist shrouded the castle. It seemed to get thicker as they climbed.

When they passed through the small main gate, they saw one main tower. Seven other smaller ones formed the exterior with extremely narrow parapets, not suited for any type of siege battle. The castle was so small that it looked more like a watch-tower than any type of defensive bulwark.

"Doesn't look disturbed at all," said Ridley, gazing around the quiet outer courtyard.

"I don't trust any castle anymore."

Henri led the way to the main tower, leaving the duffel at

the base of the stairway for Ridley. With his Ruger rifle, he trotted up the narrow steps to the top of the tower.

It had been a while since he'd taken up a sniper's position, but this was a damn good spot for it, atop a sixty-foot watchtower that overlooked the river. On a clear day, the view would have been spectacular. Right now, it was nothing more than a murky haze. Not ideal conditions, but at least it wasn't raining.

Below him in the tower, Ridley had counted and then double-counted the lines of stone on the floor. When she was sure she'd found the seventh stone by the seventh stone, she pulled out a pickaxe and began to hack into the mortar.

Once it was loose, she pulled at the slab until her fingertips were raw, finally getting the pickaxe into the crack. She levered it up and shoved it aside.

Beneath it was the cache that had lain buried for eight hundred years.

The golden tip of the saber was embedded in a carved niche in the rock. An urn was nestled into place beside it, and around the set was an array of writings and etched symbols.

"We got it!" she yelled up the tower.

"All of it?" Henri called back.

"Got it all."

Ridley started snapping pictures from every angle, and immediately sent them off to Owen. Then she grabbed a set of tongs from the duffel. She closed them around the saber shard and tugged. Then pulled. Then yanked, then levered. There was not a millimeter of give.

"Fuckin'...sword in the stone," she muttered.

The sharp golden tip could not be moved. Frustrated, she peered more closely at it, shining her flashlight down into the crevice.

There was one last line of script engraved in the blade. She glanced at the urn, then back at the saber. Once again to her frustration, she couldn't read Arabic, but she could tell like for like.

It was the same word on both, and one word was something she could figure out. She pulled up the encrypted search engine on her phone, and with painstaking precision, found the corresponding Arabic letters. She lined them up in the search bar and hit enter.

Zawba'ah

Cyclone

Ridley frowned at the urn.

Is that a name?

At the top of the tower, Henri had gone very still. His eyes were fixed downriver. There was something down there in the mist, floating on the water.

He looked through the Viper scope on his rifle.

It was a small boat, hardly bigger than a canoe, and impressively quiet. There was only one person in it, but he couldn't make them out through the fog.

"Rid," he called down, "we've got an unknown subject coming down the river."

"On the water?"

"Uh-huh. Small vessel, party of one. Four hundred yards out, not moving faster then ten miles an hour."

"Copy. Anyone from the Order?"

"Not unless someone went rogue in a rowboat."

Ridley emptied the duffel. She built a nest of little iron bars within the hole in the floor, placing each one carefully, making sure her hand never so much as brushed the urn.

"Three hundred yards," said Henri.

"Almost done," she said.

She hurried, using the pickaxe to grind away at a salt block, scattering the granules all over the saber tip, the hole, the floor.

"Touch that, fuckin' demon genie," she muttered under her breath.

Up top, Henri watched through his scope as the subject finally emerged from a patch of fog. He caught sight of their face.

"Oh, no."

He lowered the rifle on its sling. No, he would not take this shot.

Pulling out the SIG M17 from his waistband, he trotted down the stairs.

"It's a kid," he said to Ridley. "A teenager. He looks Middle Eastern, probably Syrian, given the circumstances."

Her eyes flashed with excitement. "It's coming for the last piece."

For a moment up there on the rampart, a thought had skittered through his mind. Would it all end if he shot this ifrit-possessed boy? If his body tumbled into the water and the saber sank to the bottom of the river, never to be completed, never to be found again...what would be saved by taking that shot?

Now, seeing the thrill in Ridley's face as they readied for the ifrit's landing, he felt the dark fingers of shame crawling over him. This creature would not drive him to murder a boy.

"Think this'll keep him from getting into it?" asked Ridley, looking over her handiwork.

He glanced down at the web of iron and salt. "Best we got."

"This is the last piece of the saber," she said. "I don't know what comes after putting the blade back together, but...short of getting our hands on that Seal of Solomon thing, this might be it, huh?"

He looked out the open doorway. He couldn't see the boat anymore.

"We don't kill him," he said firmly. "We don't kill this kid."

"If he's trying to kill you or me? Yeah I'm gonna kill him."

"But we don't kill him just to stop the ifrit."

She looked at him with narrowed eyes, realizing that he must have had that same thought.

"Okay, yeah." She pulled the M17 from her belt. "Definitely not."

They left the tower, weapons at the ready, and hurried up onto the outer wall. They each tucked into one of the narrow battlements on a small watchtower. It was solid cover with a sightline of the main tower entrance.

"*Leave it to the wrath of God,*" Henri whispered to himself.

Down the wall, Ridley clutched her SIG tighter.

Seconds later, a green-eyed Syrian boy walked into the courtyard.

CHAPTER
FORTY-FIVE

————

MUSTAFA DALI HAD ONLY BEEN hungry.

His mother had let him take lunch break outside the shop, demanding he return within fifteen minutes. He could go with his cousin, but only to eat and return. No wandering around the island, no taking a boat out, no flirting with the girls at the hat shop. There was a shipment of paint arriving midday, and he would need to pick it up from the harbor.

Thrilled to be free out in the open air, Mustafa grabbed the falafel wrap that she had made for him that morning, and charged off down the street.

He ran to the old citadel, where he knew his older cousin would be praying at that hour. Sure enough, Ayman was up on the eastern wall, kneeling on a small prayer rug, eyes closed, his hands lifted upward.

Mustafa had never understood how someone could be so devout as to pray five times a day without being reminded to do so by scolding elders. Ayman was only four years older than him but could already recite half the Quran. He loved the view from here. It was where he always took his noon prayers if he could.

This was not a time to disturb his cousin, so Mustafa dropped down on the parapet nearby, his back propped against the wall. He made no effort to be quiet about it, since he did secretly want Ayman to cut his prayers short. He had just dug into the falafel when his older cousin opened his eyes.

"You eat like a donkey," he said, rising to his feet and rolling up his prayer rug.

"I have to be back at the shop soon," said Mustafa through a mouthful.

"You have enough time to eat? Then you have enough time to pray."

He shrugged and took another bite. "Are you going to Tartus tomorrow for Ghassan's party?"

"Yes," said Ayman, squinting in the direction of the mainland.

"Can I come?"

"I'll take you if your father and mother say it's all right. I've been yelled at by Khala enough times, even before you were born."

"She'll say yes!"

But his cousin didn't respond. He was frowning at something down in the courtyard. Mustafa followed his gaze. A white man was starting up the steps, and he had something strange sticking out of the back of his shirt collar. Seconds later he emerged atop the wall, striding around the broad parapet.

Owen was heading straight for them.

ALMOUROL, PORTUGAL

Mustafa was slight of build. He wore a pair of scuffed Converse sneakers, black jeans, and a light T-shirt beneath a thin green track jacket.

And now, in one hand, he carried the golden saber.

His stride was resolute, and he didn't hesitate. He went straight for the steps up to the main tower.

Ridley and Henri watched from above. With his phone out, Henri zoomed in and snapped a photo of Mustafa. The boy hadn't noticed them concealed within the narrow battlements.

He disappeared into the main tower.

They padded down along the wall, along the narrow parapet, closing in toward the middle. Then they heard laughter from inside. It was so surprising and bright that the two of them exchanged a look of uncertainty. They crept a bit farther until they were facing the tower door, on level with it but separated by the small courtyard.

The boy emerged in the tower doorway, looking straight at them. Ridley and Henri both raised their M17s a few inches.

"You beat me here and you set a trap," he said in a mild Syrian accent.

His voice belied his soft appearance. He was really more of a young man, with the most startling, piercing green eyes that Ridley had ever seen.

"It would work against a lesser jinn," he said, "but you know what I am."

He smiled and turned around, facing into the doorway. Then he raised his arms, and a blast shook the tower like a sonic boom. It was a repeat performance of the ifrit's destruction of

Sainte-Chapelle. The force blew Ridley and Henri back against the wall of the parapet, scrambling to hang onto their weapons.

Mustafa had vanished inside the tower.

Henri froze, then turned slowly to look out at the river. He was listening.

"Do you hear that?" he asked.

"No," she said, turning her good ear outward.

She still couldn't hear anything, so she ran down the parapet wall to look out. Henri followed halfway, keeping one eye on the main tower door.

The middle of the river was roiling. It was not frenetic, as water in a pot would look at a boil, but almost as if there was something beneath it thrashing to get out.

"Henri, there's something in the river..."

But his attention was snapped away when Mustafa emerged from the tower. In his hand gleamed the saber. The only ragged line that remained on the blade was just near the tip.

All it needed was blood to seal the last shard, and it would be complete.

Henri pulled the Ruger rifle upward, about to set it against his shoulder.

Ridley had moved down the wall, closer to the tower, but she had not seen the ifrit-possessed boy reemerge. She was fixed on the disturbance in the river, which was growing bigger.

Henri had just settled his eye onto the scope and was looking for the boy in his sights.

He did not spot him in time.

A streak of movement caught Ridley's eye, and she whipped around. Mustafa landed in front of her, and a streak of gold came slashing down across her vision.

CHAPTER
FORTY-SIX

THE SOUND of a gunshot cracked across the courtyard.

Ridley leapt back as the saber hacked downward. She was just able to slip the greatest force of the blow, but not all of it. It sliced across her thigh. She felt a searing burn just above her kneecap as the Syrian boy lifted the blade.

The edge was now slick with blood.

Ridley stumbled out of range, looking squarely down the barrel of her M17 at his chest. A few yards down the wall, Henri had the Ruger set tightly on his shoulder, eyeing the hostile through his scope. Mustafa was thirty yards away, but he made no further move. He was holding up the saber, staring at it.

Where the shard tip had been added to the rest of it, there was a jagged line of brokenness. But as they watched, the line faded and vanished. The blood had restored the entire blade. The saber gleamed, whole and deadly.

It was all the ifrit needed. He jumped down from the wall.

It was a clean twelve foot drop to the courtyard below, but he landed like a cat. Dirt puffed out from beneath his Converse.

Physically impossible.

That's when Ridley finally heard it.

She looked over her shoulder to the river again. The roiling patch had become a storm, but unlike any other, it was not coming down from the sky, but up from the water.

"Henri!"

He climbed up on the parapet to get a look over.

The churning water began to rise. It couldn't have been a waterspout; it didn't reach the clouds. Yet it grew and grew until it was towering seventy feet above the surface. The column of water seemed to be boiling in place.

And then the ghostly likeness of a face emerged. It was huge, a grotesque spectacle as though some sort of monster was trapped behind a thick shroud. And it was facing them.

The urn...Zawba'ah.

Cyclone.

It surged forward.

"Down!" shouted Ridley.

They both dropped, huddling, clinging to the stone merlons that jutted up along the wall. A wall of water came roaring over the battlements. It crashed into the castle, hitting their backs with the force of a tsunami.

Stunned, they shook their heads free. Then they spotted Mustafa in the courtyard below. He had stood his ground, and he was bone-dry. He clutched the saber upright in front of his face.

Another colossal wave blasted over the stone walls. Henri was swept clean off the parapet. He tumbled in the surge, choking as he slammed into the inner courtyard wall. As the water sloshed away, he saw the ifrit-possessed boy backing away toward the gate, still clutching the saber as if he was a samurai. He was still dry.

Henri had only a second to glimpse it, but he watched as the water plowed apart around the saber, leaving Mustafa untouched. It was as if the blade was Moses' staff parting the Red Sea. And then another wave assaulted them.

Henri clutched his rifle and scrambled to the wall beneath Ridley, where the wave was coming over the top. Another one crested the wall. It seemed to hit with even more force, as if whatever monster lay within the river was growing angrier.

Ridley raced to the nearest stairs. Pieces of stone were beginning to loosen and shift. As she heard the next wave coming, she braced. A torrent of water came pouring down the stairwell.

Panic seized within her chest.

Tumbling in murky darkness...her ear shattered with pain...spinning to find the surface...

The wave broke, sloshing across the ground. She gasped for air and scrambled ahead.

When she reached the courtyard, she saw Mustafa edging out of the main gate, clutching his blade as though for his life.

Then she heard a thunderous crash, and turned to see the top half of the main tower leaning and crumbling. Pieces of stone fell onto the walls and the courtyards below.

"Come on!" she yelled at Henri, who was flat against the far wall for cover.

A tidal wave exploded over his head again. She ducked into the stairwell door, bracing a hand against each wall. As the crest subsided, she pushed the wet hair from her face and rushed out.

That one had taken stones off the wall, which were now

tumbling through the courtyard. She sloshed to the main gate as fast as she could. Henri ran after her, trying to avoid the falling pieces.

Another wave hit just as Ridley reached the main gate, but now they were exposed to the full force. It swept her through the archway, dropping her onto the sloping heap of granite below. It hurled Henri against the wall, knocking the wind from his lungs.

Gagging for breath, he crawled toward the gate. He had just pulled himself through and off to the side when the next one roared through. Stones thudded and crashed inside the walls. The castle had been built to withstand many things, but not a monsoon.

Henri spotted his partner clinging to the rocks below. He scrambled down and helped a limping Ridley toward the shore.

He saw Mustafa running up the hill on the mainland. The boy was well out of their reach, and now well beyond the reach of this river monster.

Henri and Ridley stumbled toward their car. The crash of waves had ceased, though pieces of the castle were still collapsing behind them. Still, they didn't slow or stop until they'd reached the distant safety of the vehicle.

Both of them dripped with water, their clothes stuck heavy and wet to their skin. Henri laced his hands atop his head, blowing out a sigh of relief. Somehow, the rifle was still slung to his chest. Ridley leaned two hands on the hood. She looked down at the SIG M17 still clutched in her grip.

She gave a breathless laugh. "Look at that. Training, huh?"

Then she glanced down at her thigh. There was a long, clean gash through her jeans. Blood ran with water down her leg.

"He got you," realized Henri, crouching down to check the cut.

It didn't really hurt yet, but she knew it would in a few minutes when the adrenaline wore off.

"You need stitches," he said, standing back up.

"We're not stopping for my cut. I'll take glue. There's some Dermabond in the medic pack."

He pulled off the rifle sling and went to open the trunk.

"Can we guess what that thing was?" he asked, rummaging for the medical bag.

"I internet-translated the urn in the tower. It had the word *Zawba'ah* etched into it. It means 'cyclone,' so..."

"The ifrit acted like he needed protection from it."

"Mo' jinn, mo' problems."

He gave her a look from around the open trunk.

"It's a...it's a Biggie lyric," she said.

"Yeah, I know. It just wasn't funny."

She holstered her gun. "So this is break point. He got the whole damn saber and we couldn't do shit to stop him, and now he's gonna go free some demon *kings* with it—wherever *that* is—and if that river jinn wasn't even bad enough to be their king...what now?"

Henri pulled out the medic pack. "Did the stash have another drawing in it? Another clue?"

"Yeah, of course," she said, pulling out her phone. "I got photos."

"So there's something else we need, then. The Templars didn't break the saber to pieces and bury it along a trail to help the jinn. They're pointing *us* to something else."

Ridley wagged the phone at him.

"Time to call."

CHAPTER
FORTY-SEVEN

Ridley and Henri drove north, just far enough to get out of the castle's vicinity. They stopped at a cheap roadside restaurant to call Owen.

He was at his small flat in Cambridge, unshaven, still looking slightly battered from the incident in Syria. It seemed that they'd interrupted a study session, but it was obvious that he was thrilled to hear from them. Professor White had given him a generous extension on his paper. It had been good for him to sink back into his graduate work, though the comedown from their escapades, discoveries, and peril had been trying.

At this moment, he was extremely interested to know why they were both soaking wet.

Owen's mouth hung agape as they recounted what had

happened with the river at Almourol. As shaken as he had been from his experience between Cyprus and Arwad, he couldn't believe he'd missed out on such a sight.

Ridley sent him the images of the last cache. He studied them closely.

"You said the name on the urn means *Cyclone?*" he asked.

"Yeah, I managed to get that much. I think the digital translator I used said 'Zawbah' or something like that."

"That's, ehm..." he trailed off, his eyes roaming the computer screen. "Yeah, that's the name of one of the seven jinn kings, *'Zawba'ah'*. And I think—I think maybe with what happened in Cyprus—maybe each of these imprisoned jinns in the urns are servants to different kings."

Ridley and Henri looked at each other, considering.

"So what was the thing in the river?" she asked.

"I think you ran into a big bad," he said. "So there are a few different types of jinn, remember? Like classes. The common jinn is at the bottom, mostly trouble-makers but they can't exactly upend the world. And then, *ifrits*—we're obviously really, really familiar with by now. They're more powerful than just a regular jinn, but then there's the *marid*."

He sat back in his chair, shaking his head in amazement, and went on.

"They're the most powerful, and their name might come from 'giant,' and they're tied to water. Like a water elemental."

"That sounds horrid!" said Ridley in a cheerful voice. "And exactly like the thing that just firehosed us."

"Owen, you have the photo of the saber tip? With that last Arabic engraving on it?" asked Henri.

"Yeah, you sent it. Pretty cool to see. It's the first photo of the saber blade we've got, yeah?"

"Can you figure out what that says?"

There was a long moment while he examined, typed,

browsed. A ginger cat had just sashayed in front of the camera when a look of triumph bloomed on Owen's face.

"It's the Arabic for *Zawba'ah*, the same jinn king. It's written on the blade, too!"

Henri exchanged a look of realization with Ridley.

"There were seven parts to this blade," he said. "Do you think each of the pieces had the name of a different king?"

"*Now* I do," said Owen.

"We know this thing wants to use the saber to somehow release all of those kings, and they've been imprisoned somewhere, yeah," said Ridley. "We *don't* understand what this is pointing us to. Templars still want us to find something, but the saber is already complete, all put back together. Humpty-Dumpty."

A grim thought came over Owen. "Who did he kill with this piece?"

"No one. He took a piece of me, just enough blood to seal it."

"Are you okay?"

"Just a cut on my leg. Thanks, though."

"Okay, just give me a moment," he said, absent-mindedly stroking the furry intruder on his desk.

They waited as he muttered to himself, sifting through some books, typing on the computer.

Ridley turned to Henri. "Let's bet, fifty bucks a take. Will we go by plane or car?"

"Plane."

"I say car. Where I can speak the language or no?"

"How many languages do you speak?"

"Eight, including English. Not like I sound like a native in all of them, though."

"That's absurd," he said, shaking his head. "Obviously I'm taking 'somewhere you speak the language.'"

"I'll take 'where I don't.' Need weapons or no?"

"Always need weapons."

"Damn, I'm on the same side."

Then they heard Owen exclaim over the video call.

"God, of course. Of course! The last place for the Templars' trail was the last place *for* the Templars themselves."

Ridley placed a palm out and mouthed to Henri, *Fifty bucks.*

"Where?" he asked, ignoring her.

"It's the Convent of Christ. It's in Tomar. It was built close to the river to be the last fortress against the Moors, and actually, when the king of Portugal let the Templars take refuge in his country, he let them turn the *old* Templar seat of power into the *new* Order-of-Christ-seat of power. It's an incredible building, beautiful architecture...I wish I could see it with you guys."

"What are we looking for there? I still don't understand," said Ridley.

He scrubbed a hand through his dark hair.

"Okay, so this is a bit mad, or a lot mad. It looks like...like there's a book there. Really, I guess they would call it a codex."

"A Templar codex?" she asked. "This is a real thing? This isn't a video game?"

Henri sighed as he looked up at the ceiling of the car. It almost sounded like delight. On the other end of the video call, Owen sat up in excitement, brushing the cat away from his screen.

"This is it," he said. "This is it! They're goin' to give you a way to get what you need. Bloody Templars..."

"What is what we need?" asked Henri.

Owen's hazel eyes were sparkling. "You need the Seal of Solomon."

CHAPTER
FORTY-EIGHT

LISBON, PORTUGAL

TIAGO NEEDED REINFORCEMENTS. He touched down in Lisbon with Bruno and João, his essential but depleted cadre. They were on the brink of finding the most valuable of Templar treasures. It had always been their purpose, since the first day they'd each joined the Order of Raphael.

For Tiago, it had been a journey across four decades. He'd grown up in a home that called itself Catholic, though they hardly ever saw the inside of a church. At the time, he hadn't thought of his life as dull, but when he was fourteen, the world seemed to fill with color for the first time, and everything before it faded like a dream. It was then that his uncle José, his mother's brother, spun him the most spectacular tale.

Over foamy cups of *galão*, sitting outside a café where mournful strains of fado trickled down the street, his debonair uncle told him the true story of the world. The Catholic Church was blind. The Jews were blind. The Muslims were blind. None of them had seen what was right under their noses, in every mythology story in ancient civilization after ancient civilization.

The god Yahweh was supreme, the maker of all things, but among the things he made were other, lesser gods. After the fall of Eden, the earth was divided into human tribes. Each of those peoples was given a celestial governor, a lesser god to teach and guide them in the ways that Yahweh had instructed. They were known as the Watchers.

But the gods were greedy, and when sinful humans began to turn their worship to the Watchers instead of to the One, the Lord above all the other lords, Yahweh was furious. He sent a man named Enoch to declare his judgment upon them, humiliating them by using a puny human to do so. Then Yahweh punished the Watchers for their pride, banishing them into the darkness of the earth until the day of judgment.

Angels were sent to keep them imprisoned. They were also sent to shepherd mankind, to pave the way for the redemption of humans when Yahweh would save them through his own sacrificial love.

Yet all was not clean, and remnants of the Watchers still prowled the earth. The powers and principalities of darkness were real, his uncle explained. They were not vague notions of evil. They were entities, beings who had wielded true power on this earth.

Tiago had listened in awe. His coffee had grown cold in his hands. The melodies of fado had faded away. It was as if someone had pulled back the curtain on a secret world that he'd always wished existed.

His uncle could see his young nephew enthralled. He went on.

Some of the Watchers had mated with human women, and their offspring had been giants, men of great renown. The superheroes of old were not myths, José said. Gilgamesh and Hercules, Goliath and Beowulf and Achilles. They were the descendants of the lesser gods. They became the peoples of the Anakim, the Rephaim, the Apkallu, and the Nephilim.

What happened to them? Tiago had asked.

José replied, *Yahweh sent a great flood across the earth. Don't you know anything of archaeology and mythology and geology? They all know this to be historical fact.*

Did any of the old superheroes survive? Are there any still here today?

An enigmatic smile spread over his uncle's face.

That is what we're devoted to, he answered. *Yahweh sent the angel Raphael to bind the rebellious leader of the Watchers, Azazel, in darkness. Then the Lord appointed Raphael to watch over the spirits of men. It's him that we follow. We're the disciples who carry out his mission on earth today.*

God told the angels to destroy the children of the Watchers, but let the righteous survive because they will worship Him alone, rightly. "The ones who were produced from the spirits and the flesh shall be called evil spirits on earth." *They will always rise up to do evil against the children of men and women.*

So we are the ones now who find those abominations that survived, those dark and corrupting spirits.

It was a fantasy tale come to life, the ultimate war that makes men's souls come alive. His uncle had trusted him enough to share this secret calling with him. Tiago never let go of it, and for the next two years, he would grill José about it at every opportunity. The only thing that his uncle demanded was that he never speak of this to the rest of his family. Tiago readily agreed. Questions streamed from him.

What have you seen?

What do you do?

Who's in charge?

How do you find these beings?

Why doesn't anyone else know about this?

When can I join?

José was discreet in every answer he gave, but as his nephew grew, he began to give him more and more of the pieces. To the last question, he finally gave an answer.

Sixteen. If you still want to join when you are sixteen, if you're obedient and keep the secrets, you can begin studying for your confirmation into the Order.

Tiago devoured everything they gave him. Some teenage boys hid pornography from their parents. He hid away the documents of the Order. His memory was a reservoir, and he could soon retell the history of the Order, recite the names of every Watcher, and tell the story of their fall as well as almost any of the actual Raphaels.

José was impressed with his nephew, but even more pleased with himself for having identified Tiago as the perfect recruit. He knew the Order would accept him.

A week after Tiago's sixteenth birthday, he was invited to Tomar, a small city east of Portugal. He was allowed by his parents to go on the day trip with his trustworthy uncle.

There, in the gardens of the Convent of Christ, he met four men and two women. He didn't understand how the grounds were empty that day, but soon he would realize that the Order held power in every hall of the Western world.

Under the gritty heat of that summer day, they put him through a rigorous test, showing no reactions to the answers he gave. In the end, he was confirmed and christened.

He was finally a Raphael.

While José was climbing the political ladder, Tiago was sent out on hunting expeditions. He was boosted at every turn of his real-world profession, making a career in the vagaries of the import/export business. By the time he was twenty-five, he was earning a six-figure salary. He could race cars and hunt big game and travel to his heart's content, but the only thing he ever really wanted was another sacred quest, another chance to affect the world, to raise up the Order.

His journey had begun, but it was not to be the same as his uncle's.

As good as he was at this work, at finding ancient relics, at following strange tales into the darkest wilds of the world, he was not given an open door into the hierarchy of the Order. He was a lackey, a worker bee, but he made himself undeniably the best that they had. They couldn't afford to lose him to the command structure.

Though José had always acted as his mentor, Tiago's bubbling resentment caused a rift between them. His uncle would not pull the strings any longer for his nephew. He wouldn't recommend Tiago to higher positions. He would not even introduce him to the mysterious new Grand Master, whose identity was kept as secret as their predecessor's.

Over time, that rift became a chasm of anger. By the time that José died from a stroke at the age of fifty-nine, it had been nearly three years since they'd spoken.

Yet his death changed nothing for Tiago. He was still the operations ace. In the last decade of work, he had decided to bring up his own protégés. Maybe if he could find a worthy replacement for his skills, they'd finally allow him to move up. He would finally be invited into the inner circle, to even know the identity of the Grand Master who ruled over the entire Order.

New recruits Bruno and João had come into his unit that very same year. They were capable and clever and loyal. That's why they were still alive despite all that they'd witnessed. This was a dangerous calling, and too many died along its path.

When they completed *this* mission, it would be the greatest accomplishment in the history of the Order. He would be recognized. Bruno and João would be recognized.

He was resolved. Now, all they needed was more men.

As they were waiting for their car at the airport, Tiago's phone buzzed with a message.

They're in Tomar

Of course it was Tomar. It all went back to the start.

CHAPTER
FORTY-NINE

———

TOMAR, PORTUGAL

THE GLOOM of Almourol had lifted. Tomar was pure beauty that late afternoon, warm and golden under a blue spring sky. Birds were chirping up a symphony all across town. Cream-colored buildings glowed under the sunlight, their old tile roofs shades of rusted red.

Ridley and Henri sat at an outdoor café table, their clothes finally dry. They had a map in front of them, along with a tourist guide to the Convent of Christ. He was eating a plate of steak, eggs, and fries, with a slice of chess cake waiting in the wings. Ridley watched in disbelief. There was nothing this man couldn't put away. She'd settled for the thing she had to think least about, *pasteis de nata*. The flaky and delicious egg custard tarts were everywhere in Portugal.

She'd begun to feel that gnawing anxiety in her gut again,

and it was putting her on edge, past the point of any appetite. Her leg jogged restlessly up and down.

Are they here already? Will it be Cornwall all over again?

Though it had been the ifrit who took an innocent life on the quay of St. Michael's Mount, the Order had enabled it. They had been protecting this creature on its quest, just wanting to be the first in line to seize the power it was trying to unleash in the world.

She checked her thoughts by checking her watch.

The Convent was too hot of a tourist site to infiltrate during the day. Especially on a day like this, it would be teeming with tourists. With so many potential witnesses, their excavation would land them quickly in handcuffs. The only plan of action was to wait for nightfall.

"Even if Tiago and his henchies made it to Arwad," said Henri through a mouthful, "Almourol was destroyed. They couldn't have found that last direction."

"It's stupid to wait, it's stupid to go," she muttered. "I love this job."

Tomar had begun as a Roman city but was eventually taken over by the Moors. When they were conquered by the Portuguese, the land was given to the Knights Templar, to the Grand Master, who built the Castelo de Tomar, and alongside it, at the end of a majestic aqueduct, the Convent of Christ.

The Templars grew the village surrounding the castle with attractive offers to peasants and immigrants. Over the centuries, the city became a pioneer of industry, with the business of textiles and hydraulics. Today, it was much more of a quaint tourist site for history buffs.

She glanced down at the stone tiled sidewalk. Even *it* was laden with crosses of the Order of Christ, the "new Templars." The entire city was steeped in the presence of the Templars. After all, it had been of their own creation.

And on this day, it was for treasure seekers.

After finishing their meal, Ridley and Henri headed up the street to the Sete Montes, the Seven Hills National Forest, where they'd parked their vehicle. The sun was slanting low through the trees now, but they still had hours to wait.

Ridley leaned against the hood, her long legs crossed at the ankles while she studied the layout of the convent.

"You must have memorized it by now," said Henri as he pulled a sweater out of the car.

"This is their home turf," she said. "Gotta think they know every inch of that place."

"Strange. The Order makes this place home, and they had to go hunting all over Europe and even Syria to find something that was actually right under their noses."

She dropped the map to her legs. "Where do you think the ifrit is now?"

He gave a long shrug. "That boy might have a hard time getting through borders. Maybe he'll have to hand it off to a vessel who's better positioned."

"Where could it be going, though? I mean, where on earth —on actual *earth*—would you imprison supernatural jinn kings that may or may not be those Watchers that the Order is so excited about?"

He squinted up at the setting sun. "I hope it's somewhere really hard to sneak a full-size sword into."

They waited until well after dark before driving up the winding road to the Convent of Christ. They parked in the empty lot of a nearby cafeteria, and waited. They wanted the town below to be asleep.

Ridley put some Alabama Shakes on the stereo. She'd always been aware of her psychological state before a basketball or volleyball game. If she had needed some juice to get into the right headspace and perform, she went with something like Jay-Z or The White Stripes. If she was too revved up, she came down to something like Labrinth or The xx. Occasionally, she would put on her headphones and just tune out to silence.

Tonight, she wanted her restless leg to calm down. When they finally stepped out of the car in the quiet of night, she was in a state of alert focus.

There was something big here, buried in this hub of Templar power.

They pulled a bag from the trunk. They'd had to restock after losing their last supplies in the tidal waves of Almourol. They'd packed a new pickaxe, crowbar, a lantern, rope, flashlight, gloves, and a bag of salt, just in case. Ridley had dubbed it "the murder kit." Henri eyed the salt and renamed it "the cannibal kit."

Ridley threaded a suppressor onto her M17 and pocketed the extra loaded mags. She slid the karambit into her belt. Then she slung the silenced Bravo AR-15 along her back. If the Order was here, there would be violence.

Demolish you all.

Henri had slung the Ruger around his shoulder and loaded up with extra magazines. He hoisted the tool bag.

"No, you can't carry this," he said before Ridley could confiscate it for herself. "You're more likely to be seen."

"Why?" she said, already offended.

He swiped his fingers across his cheek. "I'm always wearing camo paint," he said with a sly grin.

She was mildly irked by his point, but there was no argument. They headed toward the sprawling medieval compound.

Though the gates were closed and locked, there was no need for grappling hooks here. Parts of the grounds had shifted enough that it was easy enough to climb over the wall. When they'd lowered themselves down into the courtyard entrance, they slid into the nearby bushes to surveil the space.

Small lights illuminated the ancient rock walls, the stately hedges within the courtyard, and the old castle ruins beside them. Looming into the night sky, a thousand yards ahead, was the church. The curls and twists of the Gothic convent, accented as they were by the lights below, looked like some kind of fairy tale nightmare.

"Ten o'clock," whispered Henri.

Ridley's gaze slid to the left. There, prowling slowly along a wall near the front entrance of the church itself, was a dark figure. By their posture, it was evident they were holding some type of long gun.

So you're already here.

CHAPTER
FIFTY

—————

TOMAR, PORTUGAL

Ridley spoke under her breath. "They don't know the exact location, or they'd have found it all ages ago."

Henri cradled the rifle to his shoulder and peered down the Viper scope. "Another one, up in the bell tower."

They backed up to the wall, then moved along it across the courtyard. They dropped low for cover behind the neat hedges. The whole left side of the compound was thick with these hedges, a crop of shrubs, and even a few trees with enormous canopies. Using hand signals only now, they slid through the greenery.

They kept eyes on the figure atop the wall, just a dark silhouette that ambled back and forth clutching a gun.

As they approached on the flank, a narrow stairway led up into a crumbling section of the battlements. Ridley, with her

SIG in one hand, drew her karambit with the other. If she could avoid firing in this quiet compound, she would. Suppressors in the real world—unlike in the movies—didn't silence a gunshot. They only reduced it to a loud snap that would echo like hell across the convent.

She crept up onto the parapet, Henri behind her, still watching the bell tower through his scope.

The man ahead of them had his back turned, strolling away. Ridley quickly padded up behind him, clamped one hand around his mouth, and sliced the clawed blade of the karambit deep across his throat. She felt his muffled cries through her hand as she brought him down to the ground. They didn't last long.

Henri took aim at the bell tower lookout, and shot. The man atop it crumpled.

A small sound came from their left. They both jerked around to see the open cloisters of the convent, a magnificent gilded window on the end of the church, and a walkway on the roof in front of it. In the corner of that roof, a woman in dark tactical gear was lifting a bullpup AR-15 in their direction.

Henri dropped into cover to take aim. Given a full second to think, Ridley would have rather had her own Bravo AR-15 in hand. But combat often happened in the unconscious millisecond. She raised the pistol and fired, four rounds.

She had only a few exceptional abilities that had gotten her near the SEALs. Terrible at land navigation and not fond of High Altitude Low Opening jumps, she still had the physicality, the quick-thinking grit, unbeatable skills in the water...and marksmanship. Even at a distance of twenty yards, in the dark, with no time to set up her shot, it was a confirmed kill. The woman slumped to the stone.

Ridley dropped behind the stone baluster, scanning the rest

of the dark cloisters. There was no sign of movement, no reaction to the muffled shots.

"Clear," Henri murmured. "Go."

They had to reverse direction, head back down the narrow stairway, and then up onto the stone patio of the church.

The opulent carvings of the main entry were almost haunting in the accent lights, but those doors would be well sealed from the inside. Ridley led them around the other side of the tower. More cloisters led off to the right, down toward the gate they'd entered, but they headed for a smaller door.

Henri took the crowbar from the bag and cracked open the lock. They stepped out into another cloisters, weapons raised. The courtyard of the convent was dark and still.

Ghostly.

Ridley waved Henri through another door just to their left. He switched on the rail light under the barrel of the Ruger. The beam swept through the marble hall. This was the sacristy. An intricately painted ceiling arched high overhead, but there was nothing in the room anymore.

They headed to a narrow door at the other end, which led into a curving corridor. They swept it, and then entered the round church.

Henri's flashlight roamed the space. Even in the darkness, it was splendid. It had been built to resemble the Church of the Holy Sepulchre of Jerusalem, and it was not restrained in its imitation. Everything was designed to draw the eyes toward heaven. There were gilded alcoves, and saints on every pillar. Sumptuous paintings covered the walls, nearly to the ceiling. In the middle was a round charola, thick ornamented pillars rising up to form the sacred center.

Under it was a stone altar.

"That looks really heavy," said Henri.

"Kinda plain for this church."

He pulled off the VTAC sling and propped the rifle against a pillar.

"You take first watch?"

He'd gotten to know her well enough by now to make it a question, not a directive. Ridley nodded, stepping out of the charola to get a better sightline on the door. She strained to hear, as if the damage to her eardrum could be overcome if she focused hard enough.

Behind her, Henri had set up the lantern and gone to work. He took a pickaxe to one of the floorstones that edged the altar. *That* she could hear. Anyone within two hundred feet would hear the strikes echoing. But no one came through that dark doorway.

Finally, the strikes stopped. She heard a thunk below the floor, and some kind of grinding noise. Finally, she glanced back. Henri was straining to push the altar.

"Help?" he said.

Ridley slung the AR-15 over her back and dropped a shoulder against the slab. They strained and pushed, until the heavy piece gave way. Stone scraped across stone as the altar swiveled away.

Beneath it gaped a black hole.

CHAPTER
FIFTY-ONE

TOMAR, PORTUGAL

THE DARK CHASM was the size of a manhole, and stale air wafted up from it.

Ridley nearly laughed in astonishment. "This is unbelievable! They really did this shit. Secret tunnels."

Henri pulled a flashlight from the bag and shined it down. A narrow stone staircase wound into blackness. He looked up at Ridley.

"Ready?

She tossed a glance over her shoulder. Leaving the lookout position was not something she was comfortable with, but separating to send one of them into this ancient chamber alone would be stupid.

"Yeah," she said, grabbing the bag.

He grabbed the Ruger and started down. She climbed after

him. The stairs stretched for nearly two stories. When they landed on a dusty stone floor, Henri swept the flashlight over the room.

It was astonishing in its size, practically a cavern. There were painted murals all around, and two big free-standing pillars in the middle. Ridley pulled the lantern from their bag and went over to one of the walls.

"This took some work," she said. "Are these—these look like they're from the Bible?"

Henri peered across one section. "Yeah, but medieval style. They're telling stories. I'm not sure yet which ones..."

"Oh, wait!" Ridley thrust the lantern up to one portion. "I know this one!"

It was a dramatic scene of two women, one in anguish, one calm, standing before a throne. There sat a king of pure majesty, adorned in flowing purple robes and decked in gold. Beside the throne, a man in plainer clothes held a sword in one hand, and a baby in the other.

"It's King Solomon," she said.

"Of course," murmured Henri, now enchanted by the artwork.

He veered off to take in the rest of it. Ridley turned to survey the rest of the room.

"Well, it doesn't look like there's a book in here. Or one ring to rule them all," she declared, "but this..."

She took in the grand pillars. They were strange-looking things. They didn't reach the ceiling, so they looked oddly squat for the width of them. The most puzzling thing was the floor around both.

They were each ringed with a neat series of stepstones, each aligned perfectly to the others, each engraved with a symbol.

"Oh, boy. Henri. That's Hebrew. Each pillar has its own alphabet."

He approached the stones. "Oh, yeah it is. I took a year of Hebrew, a long time ago."

"What? Why?"

"To be able to read parts of the Bible in its original language."

This guy is a different kind.

"Well, your biblical moment has come. What are we supposed to spell on them?"

He glanced around, his eyes starting to get that puzzling-shine. "Something having to do with the stories...maybe."

Ridley's eyes settled on a section of wall where the fresco gleamed gold. She stepped closer to it. "Solomon built the temple, right?"

"The first one, yeah."

Knights Templar...temple...the Order of Solomon's Temple.

"There were pillars in the temple?" she said, turning back to Henri.

"Yeah, there were...two..." he drifted off, looking down, "and they had *names!*"

Ridley furrowed her brow. "I'm sorry, what?"

"It was really strange. They were people names. They don't explain why, either."

She was already pulling out her phone. "No service. Damnit!"

So close, and yet an absurd first world inconvenience crippled her here. She wanted to hurl the phone. Henri pulled out his.

"You have service?" she asked.

"No. I have the Bible app."

She could not help herself, chuckling. "Of course you do. This is your hour, Henri Michel."

He began to read. "*He set up the pillars at the vestibule of the temple. He set up the pillar on the south and called its name Jachin, and he set up the pillar on the north and called its name Boaz,"* he said, looking up at her. "1 Kings 7:21."

The moment he said "north", Ridley was already checking the compass on her Tactix Delta watch.

"That's north," she said, pointing to one of the pillars. "So how do you spell Boaz in Hebrew?"

Henri stared down at the stone alphabet, looking troubled. "I think..." he said, and began muttering to himself. "*Bet, alef, zayin*...no. *Bet, ayin, zayin*...I think. I'm not sure."

"If we get it wrong and giant spikes come out of the floor, we're going to have a hard talk about your study habits."

He found the *bet*, and stepped onto it. The stone depressed with a click. Both blew out a sigh of relief. To reach the *ayin*, he had to long-step. Another soft *clunk* under the floor.

"Okay," he murmured, and stepped on the *zayin*.

It locked in the down position. They heard a scraping deep within the far wall that made their hackles rise, but nothing moved. Nothing opened.

Henri actually laughed as he stepped off. His heart was nearly stampeding through his chest.

"Did you ever think you'd take an exam like this?" said Ridley.

"Multiple choice is really bad for the nerves," he replied, going to the south pillar. "Okay. Jachin."

He stepped for one: *yod*. Then another: *kaph*. Then he froze. She leaned forward, her eyes widening as she watched him.

"I know it's the *nun* but I used to get it mixed up when I wrote it out, with *vav*."

Ridley was about to tell him to take his time, but then remembered who she was talking to.

"Don't overthink it!" she said.

He took a smooth, deep breath, and stepped on the last stone. It depressed.

At the far end of the cavern there was another deep scraping. A piece of the mural shifted and rolled away into the wall.

Ridley and Henri looked at each other in astonishment.

"You Bible-reading, Hebrew-speaking, Haitian magician."

He stepped off the *nun*, shaking his head but grinning like he'd passed the test of his life. "I can't speak Hebrew. I can only read it."

"Oh, okay," she said, heading for the far end. "I take back your points, then."

He followed her with the flashlight, and they stepped through the hidden doorway.

CHAPTER
FIFTY-TWO

TOMAR, PORTUGAL

IT WAS a chamber like the first, but there was no artwork to be found on these walls. They were rough-hewn rock. The only things in the dark room were two colossal statues of brass. Ridley had never seen anything like them before. They loomed like a pair of sentinels.

Both gleamed in the light of the lantern. Human in proportion, they both stood at nearly fifteen feet tall. Each was wrapped in a massive set of wings, while another set of wings was unfurled behind. Their wingtips touched in the center, as though forming a protective arch between them. The feet on these creatures looked like the hooves of a bull.

Their heads were the strangest, though. They were simply rounded pieces of stone. Blank. Ridley felt an eerie sense of awe seep through her.

"Are these angels?"

Henri was staring up at them, almost reverential. "They're cherubim."

"Huh. I thought cherubim were really chubby."

"Like the babies on Renaissance ceilings?" He shot her a look.

"Yeah, like the greatest artists in the world have been portraying them for hundreds of years. My bad."

She knew this was all part of the tapestry of his faith, but she still felt a twinge of embarrassment. Ridley hadn't gone to college, and for all of her worldly savvy, there were significant gaps in her knowledge of the classics. She hated being caught out in ignorance.

I'll learn it. I'll learn it all.

"They're not like that," explained Henri. "They're described in a few places in the Bible, and they're strange looking."

Between the two enormous angels was a contraption, a set of interlinking rings.

"This would have been where the Ark of the Covenant sat, in the Holy of Holies," he said, "if this is supposed to be the Temple of Solomon."

"So what is this..." said Ridley, inspecting it.

There were two vertical stone rings, side-by-side. Then there were two rings within those, aligned horizontally. It looked like a primitive gyroscope. Along each of the thick rings was an array of carved animal faces.

"Animals," she said, "and one human."

She reached for one, and found that it rotated like a wheel. Henri glanced up at the blank heads of the statues.

"We have to arrange the faces," he said.

"Well, we can't do a guessing game, given the thousands of possible combinations."

He pulled up his Bible app again. "I can't remember where they describe it. There was a human, and a lion."

She glanced back at the door they'd come through. They were working on a countdown clock. The Order would certainly have found their dead by now, and would set about searching the grounds.

"Tick, tock," she said to Henri.

He was scrolling furiously. "Do you realize the amount of knowledge required to get through this? When they built this, you couldn't just bring a Bible with you. No one had their own personal Bible. You had to have memorized it, or brought a priest who had a Bible."

"No one expects the Bible app!" said Ridley in her best Monty Python voice. "But really, we gotta hurry."

"Ezekiel, okay, the vision of the cherubim! *And every one had four faces: the first was the face of a cherub—*"

"Wait, what?"

"*—second, human, third, lion, fourth, eagle.*"

"What the hell is a cherub face for a cherubim with four faces?"

She started turning the rings in frustration, looking for each of the four.

"No, I know there's another verse. Hold on," he said.

"Human," muttered Ridley, scrolling through the faces. "A human would be the front face. It would have to be."

She pulled one of the vertical rings around until a man's smooth, unshaven face looked out from the middle.

"Here," exclaimed Henri. "*The face of a lion on the right side.*"

She moved to the right of the contraption, spinning one of the horizontal wheels until she got the maned feline dead center.

"*The face of an ox on the left side.*"

"So 'cherubim' is another word for 'ox'?" she said, rotating the other horizontal ring. "Angels are wild."

"The Bible is wild."

She found the horned ox, then went around the back of the piece. "You said eagle?"

"Also had the face of an eagle."

Ridley found the eagle and pulled it to the middle. There was a heavy click under the floor, and they once again heard a scraping at the far end of the room.

A smaller opening than the last had formed in the rock.

"How many of these things?" said Ridley as they headed for it.

The next chamber was half the size of the others. In the center, a square, pockmarked plate of gold was laid flat against a sloping rock.

"Oh, look," breathed Ridley, looking around in awe.

Studded across the walls and the low ceiling were a dozen colored gemstones that sparkled in the lantern light. Henri stared about for a moment, then looked back at the sheet of gold.

"Okay. This is simple. It's the breastplate of the high priest."

Ridley ran her fingers over the indentations. There were four rows down, three across. "Don't tell me there's an order to them."

He sucked in air through his teeth, and cocked his head.

"All right," she said, setting down the lantern and pulling out her karambit.

She realized there was still blood on it from the guard atop the wall. Without flinching, she wiped it clean on the outside of the bag. Henri drew his own folding knife and they went to work, prying each of the stones out of the wall.

After they'd pulled every one and laid the stones out on the ground, the two of them stood over the pile.

"Do you know jewels?" asked Henri.

"Gems. Some, yeah."

She crouched down and began separating them by color. He went back to the Bible app.

"We have a translation issue," he said, frowning at the phone. "They do lay out the order, but there are six different ways to name the stones. They just weren't exact in the original languages, or the names we use are different than the names they used."

"Start me somewhere! Give me the ones that are the same in every version."

The puzzle began.

Ruby. The first slot.

Emerald. Sapphire. Amethyst. Onyx. Turquoise. Crystal.

Those were the easy ones to identify. Then, Ridley ran into the limits of her knowledge. *Beryl. Agate. Jasper. Topaz. Jacinth.* She had no idea what they looked like. It became a game of shuffling and reshuffling, waiting for that deep scraping sound of rock that would mean success.

Ridley felt like she could hear an actual clock ticking inside her head. This felt like a stupid game to be playing when there were enemies with guns somewhere above them. She and Henri were just beginning to argue over placement when she swapped a rust-colored gem with an orange-colored one.

Something clicked under the gold plate. She sat back and gave an astonished laugh of triumph.

At the far end of the chamber, a slab of stone rolled away.

"It better not be another puzzle," she said, getting to her feet.

Henri made it there first with his flashlight.

"Rid, this is it," he said, almost serenely.

She stepped into the next room. The only thing there was a slab of stone that looked like an altar, and atop it, something square wrapped in linens. They exchanged a glance. Henri reached out slowly to unwrap it.

Inside the linens was a book. It was twice the size of a common Bible. The leather binding was faded, the metal clasps just barely rusted.

The Templars' Codex.

Henri opened it carefully.

"Not as decrepit as I would have thought," he said, sifting through the pages.

The script was elegant, meticulous. They saw half a dozen languages as they turned the pages. Some had extravagant, colorful illustrations on them, of Templar knights fighting tremendous battles, being honored by kings, wedding great beauties.

Ridley frowned at the writing. "I can't read any of this. Old language forms, old script style...wait! That's the goddamn saber!"

Henri frowned at her. "I guess I'd have to agree it is God-damned."

There on the paper was the engraved golden saber. It was being held aloft by a Saracen leader on horseback as he and his army battled a force of European knights.

"Who is that?" she wondered, looking anywhere for writing she could actually read.

"It looks like Jerusalem," he said, noting the walled city in the background. "If I had a guess, I would say that's Saladin, with the saber."

"I've heard of him."

"Sultan of everything, great warrior. He defeated the Crusaders and retook Jerusalem to start the Ayyubid Muslim dynasty."

"But the Templars walked away with his sword? Bravo, Europe."

"I've never heard of him having a great sword before. I can't believe what's in here..." he murmured, almost caressing the ancient pages.

"We need shit about the Seal," said Ridley, glancing back at the door.

She was expecting to hear the sounds of alarm any second now.

Henri browsed through a thicket of pages, then stopped suddenly.

"Look—look! That's it," he exclaimed.

There was a drawing of a thick signet ring, on it, a six-pointed star encircled with ancient Hebrew script and symbols.

On the opposite page was a dramatic battle drawing, this one set well before medieval times. An Egyptian pharaoh was leading his army into Jerusalem, against the Temple of Solomon.

"Jerusalem is some kind of aphrodisiac to these guys, huh?" said Ridley, shaking her head. "Who is this one trying to take it over now?"

They turned the page to see another drawing, of a sword-wielding leader in Roman-style arms, with a familiar-looking face. There was some Old French script written below it.

"Is that Caesar?" asked Ridley, looking at the lead rider.

"I think...it's Alexander the Great."

She considered it, now very intrigued. "That's a twist."

He turned the page to a crudely drawn map of Egypt. Midway down the Nile was marked a city: KARNAK. Tucked within the binding was a folded piece of paper. It was an entirely different color and texture than the rest of the codex pages. Ridley picked it up and unfolded it.

It was papyrus, covered in hieroglyphics.

CHAPTER
FIFTY-THREE

TOMAR, PORTUGAL

RIDLEY GAVE A LOW WOLF WHISTLE. "Well, gee whiz and carry me out with the tongs. Did you think we'd be goin' to Egypt?"

Henri snapped a photo of the papyrus, of a dozen pages around the Seal of Solomon section and the illustrations of Saladin with the saber. He set them to upload through encryption.

She pulled open the bag. "Come on, time really has to be up."

Picking up the codex as if it was a baby, he placed it inside the bag and then zipped the thing shut. They headed back through the three chambers before pausing at the bottom of the long stairway. Turning off both lantern and flashlight, they would use only the barest of light that leaked down from the church windows above.

Henri slung the Ruger around his back and pulled his silenced M17 pistol from its custom holster. Ridley gripped her AR-15 at the ready. This time, she took lead, padding up the stone steps and emerging into darkness.

The round was empty.

They swept along the wall, back toward the sacristy. It was still empty as well, but when they neared its exit, they heard voices echoing through the cloisters ahead. Ridley stopped, holding up an instinctive fist in silence. She couldn't get a read on their location.

Too much echoing. This fucking ear.

She glanced back at Henri for his estimate, ashamed that she couldn't even determine the go-ahead. Furious at her handicap.

After a moment, the voices trailed away, and he nodded. They moved forward, clearing each other through a doorway. They stepped out into the dark walkway of the monastery. The voices were now in the main courtyard, to their right, where they'd taken out the sentinels along the wall. Ridley motioned to move straight ahead, keeping to the inside of the hall away from the open-air windows that would expose them to enemies on the other side.

They'd almost reached the far end of the cloisters when a dark shape moved suddenly in the doorway ahead. A flashlight seared their eyes as the man shouted.

Ridley and Henri shot just as the man's finger squeezed his own trigger. The sound of his M4 rifle split the night. Henri felt the heat of a bullet scorch by his temple, but the man's startle-response had thrown his own aim. Nothing of his hit on target, even as his own torso erupted with bullets.

Shouts exploded through the courtyard.

MOVE.

They swept into the next row of cloisters. Bullets began

flying, chipping the stone wall to their right, whizzing through the gaping window arches.

Suddenly one of the hostiles appeared in the small cloisters courtyard to their left, shooting upward. Ridley and Henri dropped below the stone wall. It was a hail from all sides, and closing in. There was no door ahead, only an open window.

Ridley knew what lay beyond it was an open ruin of the former castle, a one-story labyrinth of crumbling walls without roofs. It would be treacherous to get caught in there, with no easy exit. It was also their only way out.

"That's it," she yelled to Henri over the gunfire.

He motioned for her to go, slipping the bag off his shoulder. "Take it. I'll cover!"

She nodded. As he rose up to loose a volley down at the shooter in the courtyard, she grabbed the bag, bolted through the open window, and hit the ground with a bone-jolting thud. A second later, Henri dropped down beside her.

They wove through the decaying stone rooms, hearing the calls in Portuguese getting closer and closer.

The courtyard to the old castle opened up on their left. Both of them sprinted across it. Ridley was racing up the stairway to the parapet when shots burst the air just behind her. She dropped to the stone floor.

Henri, still below, took cover behind a low wall as four armed men swarmed into the courtyard. She scrambled for the barest of cover behind some of the stonework, dragging the bag with her. Ducking out, she shot down at the the dark figures in the yard. They were fanning out with precision, though.

Within seconds, she'd lost eyes on two of them beneath the canopy of a huge oak tree. They'd pinned Henri in a semi-circle.

There was a shout, and the firing stopped.

Why?

"Henri!" she yelled down.

"I'm okay," he called back.

From across the yard, they heard a roar. "Americans! You're not leaving with that codex!"

It was Tiago, and he sounded like a wounded animal.

Ridley quickly scanned the length of the wall. It would be at least a twenty foot drop down the outside, but there was no way for Henri to even get up to the parapet to make the jump.

"Finders, keepers," she yelled, stalling for some brilliant idea.

"You kill my men?!" he said, his voice shaking with fury. "I will put your head on a spike!"

They couldn't have known that the man atop the bell tower that night had been Bruno. The man that Henri had felled with a perfect sniper headshot was the same man who had asked Tiago to be the godfather to his son, who had surprised him with a custom humidor on his last birthday, who had served loyally at Tiago's side for the last thirteen years.

"You might escape, but your partner is dead." He was trying to control his raging anguish, to make the best rational call as a leader with a greater purpose. "Give me the codex and I will let him live for tonight."

Can't trust that *trade. There has to be a way out of this...*

"You don't trust me? I *will* kill you, I will slash your heads from your bodies, but not tonight. If I kill one American here and another escapes, I've brought terrible shame to the Convent of Christ, to the house of the Templars."

"Will you stop the ifrit?" asked Henri from behind his wall cover.

Ridley nearly scoffed, thinking her partner naïve for a moment, but when Tiago replied, she realized it was a clever bit to get him to show a card or two.

"Why would we want to stop it?"

"Then why do you want the codex? Why are you after the Seal of Solomon if not to stop this thing?"

"When that ifrit has finished its mission, there will be more important things for the Order to deal with."

Ridley leaned her head back against the stone. "You want the jinn king freed," she said, just loud enough that they heard. "They're the ones you want to control."

"The codex!" he snapped.

"Yeah, I have it," she said.

She had run every iteration in her head, and without a bazooka or the cavalry riding in, they weren't getting out of here with both their lives and the codex. They already had photos of the map, the markings, the writing around the Seal of Solomon drawing. And the loose sheet of papyrus was in her pocket.

He doesn't know about that piece.

They'd trekked and fought their way across Europe and the Mediterranean for this thing, been shot at and nearly drowned by a river demon. It was their only guide to the ultimate goal: the Seal. But now it was the only chip they had to play.

"Okay," she said finally, "I'll put the book on the top of the stairs here. When my partner gets up safely, we're out and it's yours."

She knew Henri would be chafing as he listened to this, but there was no objection.

"I'll come back to finish you," said Tiago. "Tonight, just the codex."

Ridley had to clench her teeth painfully tight to keep from unloading her ego on him. In her mind was a thrashing livewire of invectives.

Instead, she took the codex from the bag, holding it up for them to see. A flashlight beam hit it.

"The real thing," she called to them, then lay it down out in the open, on top of the steps beside her. "Now you let my partner walk up here."

"Go, American," said Tiago.

Henri left the cover of the wall. He held his gun at low ready, moving slowly. His eyes flitted from one hostile to the next to the next as he mounted the steps.

When he reached the top, he glanced at the codex, then at Ridley. She shook her head. He slid behind cover with her, and then they were off, racing down the parapet, climbing over the wall at its lowest, and rolling when they hit the ground with a vicious thump.

They raced for the parking lot, weapons raised, heads on a swivel.

"We just gave away all that?" exclaimed Henri as they rushed into the car.

"Oh, hell, no. Just most of it. Now we only need someone who can read hieroglyphs."

CHAPTER
FIFTY-FOUR

———

THE NEXT MORNING, the sun rose like a triumphant king over the Seine. Ridley had been up with the dawn, unable to sleep more than a few hours, and aware that she was probably going to regret it later.

There was no way that they were going to return to Lisbon. The eyes of the Order were seemingly everywhere within Portugal. How Tiago had even known that they were in the country, nevertheless at the Convent of Christ, was unsettling. So they returned to Paris.

Ridley had done some lifting, but had to limit it to upper body. Despite the sealing glue, the gash in her leg wouldn't take kindly to intense muscular pressure. She swam, then grabbed breakfast in the hotel café by the time Henri stirred in the adjacent room. He got up like a bear out of hibernation, showering off the grog while his partner set up their video call.

Owen was with Professor White in her campus office this time. They'd both received the photos of the codex earlier that morning. Each of them had notes already.

"D'you think you can get this back?" asked the professor. "The full codex, I mean. This is just such a small taste, and this sort of thing is a priceless—*priceless* find. It'd feature in any museum anywhere in the world."

"I'll certainly try," said Ridley with a convincing smile.

Retrieving the codex for the purpose of putting it in a museum came in at a thunderous last-place finish on the list of priorities.

Henri pulled up a chair beside her, scrubbed fresh and clean and smelling of the spicy hotel bodywash.

"I can't believe you really got it!" said Owen, beaming. "They left so many clues, and here it is...the whole Templar record in their own hand."

"So," said Ridley, "tell us about all these pages."

Professor White sat up, brightening into full teacher mode.

"This is the most remarkable find in the history of Templar study. Just truly...incredible."

She opened screensharing to display their photo of the page with the golden saber.

"Is that Saladin?" asked Henri.

"Very good! Yes, this is his sacking of Jerusalem, but the account here refers to this saber. I guess you're somewhat familiar with it."

Ridley saw Owen stiffen, his face going very still.

He held that blade. His hands stabbed someone through with that thing.

Professor White went on. "The writing doesn't say anything about it having supernatural powers, I'm sorry. Just a sword made for Saladin by his provinces. Gold is so soft I'm surprised it was good for any kind of warfare...but it *was* lost in the battle. A knight retrieved it and escaped, and added it to the treasures of the Templars."

"Things were just so magical back then," muttered Ridley. "Okay, what about the Seal?"

"Oh, yes, yes," she said, wriggling a bit as she sat up straighter and clicked onto the next screenshare. "*This* is a recounting of the Templars' search for the Seal of Solomon, and it's absolutely—*incredible*."

"Does it get us *to* the Seal of Solomon?" asked Ridley, one part amazed but two parts impatient.

Meanwhile, Henri was riveted to the history demonstration.

"Just hang on, then. Now, most of this is written in Latin and Old French and an antiquated version of Portuguese. Luckily, we're rather good at those things, but there are some sections here that are written in a code that looks...homemade. Unique? I've sent it just this morning to the best cryptologists I know. So please, put that on hold.

"As for the rest of it! You see, one of the great fascinations with the Templars is their riches, but not *just* theirs. Some people are convinced that during the earliest time when they headquartered at the Temple Mount, that they discovered the lost treasure of King Solomon. After all, it's believed by so many historians that the place where the Dome of the Rock and the al-Aqsa Mosque are now—*that's* the site of Solomon's temple, and his palace.

Henri glanced at Ridley. "He was wealthy."

"He was immensely, immensely wealthy," said Professor White, using two hands for emphasis. "Now, I've never believed that the Templars found anything there of great worth. It was long gone by the time they were in Jerusalem. And this illustration here—"

She pointed to the drawing of an Egyptian army led by a pharaoh on a chariot.

"This tells us what did happen to it. It's described below in old French script...I had to get another professor out of bed this morning for this...that this is Pharaoh Shoshenq, or Shishak as the Hebrew Bible wrote it out. He attacked Jerusalem just after Solomon died, and made off with his enormous wealth."

Now, Ridley was getting sucked in. Had she gone to college, she would have enjoyed a Professor White course.

"Mr. Allchurch did a bit of outside research to fill in some of the gaps here," she said, gesturing to her star student.

Owen sat up, rolling his traps out as if he was readying for a rugby snap.

"Yeah, okay. Pharaoh Shoshenq was buried in Memphis, 922 B.C. Now it's—there's sort of a gap here. Sort of a six hundred-year gap. The records in the codex don't explain it...I certainly can't, but you know who marched into Egypt in 300 B.C.?"

"Alexander the Great," said Henri.

Owen pulled up the next photo, of the sword-wielding leader in Roman-style garb who had looked so familiar.

"He was crowned in Memphis! And he built a chapel at Luxor, right near..." he moved to the map of Egypt that had been marked in the codex. "*Karnak*."

"So you think Alexander the Great ended up with the Seal— in Egypt—six hundred years after *that* pharaoh snatched it from Jerusalem?"

The longest treasure hunt in the world.

"That's what the Templars thought," said Owen.

She nodded. "Okay."

"That would explain something about the papyrus and the hieroglyphs," said Henri.

"But the Templars never found the Seal!" said Ridley, growing impatient again.

Professor White gave a look of confoundment. "All that's here is the hope, the certainty that they *knew* it was buried in Luxor."

"The Templars tried multiple times to invade and take over Egypt," said Owen. "They were never able to do it, and I guess they just...they were destroyed by the king and the pope before they could get to Karnak and finish the job."

"How did they discover all this?" asked Henri. "Alexander the Great to the Templars is, what—seven, eight hundred years?"

Owen's eyes gleamed. He sat forward, as though just about to open his magic bag of tricks.

"Oh, I love this stuff—okay, so...you know how Alexander the Great built Alexandria, and of course the great library there that burned? One of the biggest losses in history, honestly... Well, the last librarian in charge of it—before it was destroyed —was named Aristarchus. One day he found something interesting on one of the shelves. It was a papyrus, written in hieroglyphics, and he thought it was so important—so fascinating— that he put it with a stash of his *own* things.

"Aristarchus was persecuted and he had to flee Egypt around, near 200 B.C. He took this with him and he ran off, *to Cyprus!*"

Henri let out a chuckle of astonishment. Cyprus, the island of the Templars. The loop closed.

"We don't know what happened to his belongings, but the Templars found that papyrus when they took over the island. That's how this all started—how they became obsessed with searching for the Seal of Solomon," said Owen. "They found a papyrus that said that Alexander the Great had gifted it to the Temple of Amun."

He smacked the desktop in front of him as though resting his closing argument. Ridley had to shake her head clear.

"Anything more specific? 'Temple of Amun' sounds big to find a ring in," said Henri.

Professor White spoke up. "According to what the Templars wrote in the codex, it's there *on* that papyrus. God knows why they didn't want to copy out a translation for us on their own pages."

Within the Egyptian city of Luxor lay the greatest complex of temples in all the land, called Karnak. Today it was a sprawling center for tourism, with gargantuan pillars, mammoth gates covered in hieroglyphs, and towering obelisks.

Ridley shook her head in amazement. "You guys got these photos four hours ago and you just cracked a three thousand-year-old mystery."

Owen grinned and looked at Professor White, who was looking as if she'd just finished a divine meal.

"We're going to take you out for a pint," said Henri. "Fish and chips, bangers and mash, black pudding, steak and kidney pie—"

"That is cruel," said Ridley. "Get them a ribeye, some champagne."

"Well, that does sound lovely," said the professor. "Oh, and you're in Paris? You're really right in the heart of Egyptology. In Europe, anyway. You shouldn't have any trouble finding a translator for those hieroglyphics."

Ridley nodded. "As soon as you hear from the cryptologist, call us. Seems like whatever they chose to put in secret code might be marginally important."

"Immediately, I will," said Owen.

After they'd said their thanks and hung up, Henri stood, clasping his hands over his head. He blew his cheeks out in amazement.

"Do—you—realize," he started.

Ridley gave him a look of knowing, and rose with a sing-song under her breath, "We're off to see the wizard, the wonderful wizard of Oz..."

Hours later, Ridley and Henri walked the sunny streets of Montparnasse. There were few places more glorious in the spring than Paris. This arrondissement had once been the hub of bohemian and metropolitan creativity, where everyone from Picasso and Salvador Dali to Hemingway and the Guggenheims gathered.

Today it was more of a relic of bygone artists. Elegant sidewalk cafés were packed, but diners had to eat in the shadow of one of the city's few grotesquely modern skyscrapers. Of all the cities in Europe, Ridley had most wanted Paris to remain the same, preserving the architecture and aesthetics of the continental glamour girl.

As they were crossing one of the boulevards, they saw a small crowd of protestors thronged around an office building. Some were holding signs scrawled in marker: *END ZIONISM...FROM THE RIVER TO THE SEA,* and *LONG LIVE THE INTIFADA.* Others waved Palestinian flags and chanted loudly.

"Looks like that two-state solution idea is going well," said Henri.

"Something has dug a deep pair of claws into this city."

The last time that serious peace talks had been held between Israeli and Palestinian leadership, the PLO had turned away at the last moment. President Clinton had been furious, and felt played. Overnight, Jerusalem became ground zero for the bloodiest wave of violence that had been inflicted on the Jews in decades. As the French president tried to bring the sides together again, the pressure was nearly bone-splitting to not let the same thing happen.

Ridley and Henri left the furious shouts of the protestors behind as they turned down another street.

A moment later, they strode up to a door in the middle of a nondescript office building, and knocked.

"We're somewhere between the biggest cemetery in Paris and the catacombs," said Henri, looking around the fresh spring afternoon.

"The most morbid triangulation in Paris. I guess it makes sense."

The door opened.

"Good afternoon," said Claudine Gaspar with a smile. "*Entrez, entrez.*"

CHAPTER
FIFTY-FIVE

CLAUDINE USHERED Ridley and Henri into a space that looked more like The Office meets Indiana Jones than the regal, stuffy office they'd been expecting. It would make sense that INRAP's headquarters weren't much to look at. Their real work was spread out across every region of France.

"Would you like some coffee, or tea?" offered Claudine.

"No, thanks," said Ridley.

She gestured to a set of chairs in front of her desk. "Please, have a seat. It's a surprise to see you back in Paris so soon."

Since we set a jinn loose in the world that possessed one of your employees and wrecked an ancient monument.

"We didn't know we'd be back here this soon," said Henri, "but we need someone with expertise and we think you're the person to help us."

303

She straightened up with a real smile of delight. "I will try, certainly! What can I do for you?"

"We need an Egyptologist who can translate some hieroglyphics."

"Of course, yes, I can help you with that. Would you like to send a file to someone remotely?"

"No," said Ridley. "We'd really like to do this in person."

"Oh. Do you have a document that requires special handling?

"Yeah, with gloves and discretion."

"I see...I see."

Claudine's mind was racing. She hadn't expected to cross paths with these Americans again. She had played her part and brought their activities to the attention of the Order, but had no idea what had transpired since Tiago took up the pursuit.

Now these operatives sat before her with some ancient document, asking for her help in discovering its secrets. The opportunity was almost too good to be true. It was not one she could afford to botch.

"The French practically invented Egyptology in the modern era! We have an organization, Institut Français d'Archéologie Orientale, IFAO. It is a research branch that has a center in Cairo, you know, the French are very involved. We discovered Thebes for the modern world, and found the Rosetta Stone, and even translated hieroglyphics for the first time. The Cairo Museum itself is French!"

This was her life's work, so the arrogant puff of excitement over it was understandable.

Time to indulge her.

"It's exactly why we're here," said Ridley with a smile.

"There's a man with the institute who is one of our best. He works in Cairo but also teaches at the Sorbonne. I believe he's still here for the final exams. His name is Bernard Mariette, and he is just...*oh*, genius. May I make the introduction?"

"Please," said Henri.

"I do need to tell him something about the task," said Claudine. "Can you tell me a little about what you're looking at?"

"A papyrus, probably from the 300s B.C."

"Where did you find this?"

"That's not something we can share yet," he replied.

She nodded, trying to place any of this in the hunt for the jinn. "You, uh   you have the document with you?"

"It's in a safe location," said Ridley.

In fact, she had it wrapped to her own torso in a pillowcase.

"I see. *Alors*, let me call Bernard. Excuse me."

Claudine stepped into a back room. Henri watched her close the door for privacy.

"I don't trust her," he said.

"You tend to the 'not trusting,'" said Ridley.

"It's a useful quality."

He couldn't have known that his partner's own critical distrust had a fault line within it. Though he'd really never known his parents, she had lost a mother who had loved her, whom she had loved, who now only colored her memories. Ridley didn't even know it herself, but behind the smiling familiarity of any older woman, she was hoping to see a shade of her own mother.

"We don't need to share anything with her directly," said Ridley, "but I don't see any reason why we shouldn't be using her connection here."

"As long as this guy doesn't push with too many questions."

Bernard Mariette was a man fueled by questions. Only in his mid-forties, he was already one of the most accomplished

Egyptologists in the world. His career had been forged through a combination of brilliance, grit, obsession, and an exceptional intuition for discovering long-lost cultural riches.

They met him in his office at the Sorbonne, that monumental stone university that stood between the Luxembourg Gardens and the Seine. He was harried, in between teaching a class and handing off some papers to his teaching assistant. Normally, he would have said *no* to any visitors at this time of year, but when he'd heard from Claudine what her visitors were requesting, he nearly tingled with excitement.

No matter how many digs he'd been on, no matter how many papyri he'd translated or temples he'd excavated or relics he'd pulled from the sands, the thrill never faded. So he welcomed Claudine, Ridley, and Henri into his space, which looked like something between an architect's studio and an Egyptian temple.

"Where did you find the piece?" he asked, his Parisian accent so thick that it sounded like a parody.

"It was stuck in a very old book," said Henri.

Bernard took a swig from an oversized water bottle on his desk. "In Egypt?"

"In Madrid," lied Ridley.

She pulled up the photo of the papyrus on her phone. There was no way she was going to produce the original on the spot. He slipped on a pair of glasses as she handed the phone to him.

"Madrid? They have nothing of Egypt. One temple, one museum," he scoffed, peering closely at the photo. "Send this to me, yes? I cannot read it on here."

Ridley hesitated. They didn't want a digital, unencrypted copy of this on any civilian server. It would be all too tempting for a man who made his name discovering remnants of an ancient civilization, to share with the world a new finding.

"I can't do that," said Ridley. "We can't have any copies of this out there yet, but we can bring you the original."

The professor looked astounded with the offense. He gaped at Claudine.

Henri spoke quickly to smooth it over. "You're the only person we can trust to bring this to. We haven't showed it to anyone else yet."

"You need to understand, many people have believed in, uh...*contrefraires*..."

"Counterfeits," said Ridley.

He eyed her with a skeptical, Frankish respect.

"Yes. A lot of people think they have found treasure, but at the end..." he said, raising his hands, "they have nothing but a fake. Are you ready for that?"

"It's not fake," she said with a sure smile.

"They have some experience with antiquities," said Claudine. "They've been discreet, and I think they would know a fake if they see one."

Discreet like letting Sainte-Chapelle be blown apart in broad daylight...

Bernard smiled at them, as though they'd finally broken through his act.

"Okay! Let's fucking go, as you say?"

Henri burst out laughing. "Yeah, that's what we say."

Twenty minutes later, they met him in his lab. Ridley had pulled out the papyrus from within the thin pillowcase that had been strapped to her torso. They walked back into Bernard Mariette's office and laid it out on a long white table.

He donned a pair of surgical gloves and bent over the piece. Claudine stood on the other side, gazing at the papyrus with fascination. Henri was not happy that she was there, but there was no real way to kick her out without arousing too much suspicion, and potentially pissing off Bernard.

"Oh, my God," breathed the professor. "Look at this. It's perfect. How was this preserved?"

"Inside a book," said Henri.

Most of the papyrus pieces he got to inspect were decaying fragments. This was intact, still thick with a sturdy weave and clear ink.

"*Magnifique,*" murmured Claudine.

"This needs a carbon date," said Bernard.

Ridley decided to switch to French, as it would probably get better respect from him.

FRENCH: *"Can you translate it?"*

FRENCH: *"Of course. It's very clean, but what's the point of translating it before you know if it's real?"* he replied.

FRENCH: *"We believe the age, but we need to know what it says. Immediately."*

Claudine was listening with great intensity.

"This is absurd," said Bernard, shaking his head. Then he grinned, "But if this is a treasure map, I can pack my bags today!"

It was Claudine who laughed. "What a story that would be. I must leave for an appointment, but I *must* know what becomes of this! Please tell me when you've found what you're looking for."

Henri slipped a wary glance at Ridley.

CHAPTER
FIFTY-SIX

———

PARIS, FRANCE

RIDLEY AND HENRI didn't want to go more than a few blocks from the Sorbonne. They'd have preferred to stay in the lab while Bernard translated, but he'd kicked them out, claiming the need for total privacy and concentration. So they walked the few blocks to the Luxembourg Gardens.

On a day like this, the lush green lawns were filled with people lounging on blankets, stretched out on the grass, reading books. Thick banks of flowers stretched toward the Medici Palace, and colorful little triangles drifted about in the Grand Basin as visitors set loose model sailboats on the water's surface.

Ridley paced the gravel walkways. Henri had picked up a baguette stuffed with fried chicken and pickled veggies and some type of overflowing aioli. He'd gotten one for her as well, but she'd only taken a few bites before abandoning it to stroll back and forth along the promenade. His Spidey sense about Claudine had started to take hold in her own head.

"We're heading to Egypt, one way or another," she said.

"I'll send Booker an update when we get the translation," said Henri through a full mouth.

"He knows Egypt." She dropped down into a steel chair beside him and took another bite of her sandwich. "I know one of his guys there. At least I hope he's still there."

"Native?"

She nodded. "He knows it all."

Henri wiped his mouth, his eyes roaming over the vibrant park. "Where is this ifrit?"

They both ate their lunches in silence for a moment.

"The only place left for it is wherever it thinks those jinn kings are buried," said Ridley. "Do you believe that stuff, about the Watchers? Those things about God using angels and punishing the little gods..."

Henri shook his head more in bafflement than contradiction.

"This world is as big as hell and heaven," he said, squinting up at the flawless blue sky. "Think of how many stars are out there right now. How can anyone possibly know? How can anyone possibly imagine what goes on in every dimension?"

"You believe in the Bible, though, everything it says, right?"

"Yeah, but some of it is poetic, not literal."

"And it literally says that God imprisoned the bad angels in darkness."

He looked at her with a kind of earnest solemnity. "After all that you've seen...how can you explain the jinn without God? How do you know evil without good?"

"I don't—" she stopped herself to take a bite, time to think.

"I mean, like you said, how can anyone possibly imagine what goes on in every dimension?"

He chuckled. "Touché."

"I guess...maybe if we see the complete picture, maybe then it will make more sense to me. Then I'll see the proof."

"Maybe there could be better ways to find belief than seeing angry fallen angels let loose in the world."

She grinned, and bobbed her head to the side. "Maybe, but I won't mind if I'm wearing that Seal of Solomon like a proper diva in power, right?"

It was four hours later that Bernard called them back to the Sorbonne. His voice was brimming with a barely restrained glee. When they arrived, he was standing outside the lab chugging water from his supersized bottle. His eyes gleamed as he ushered them in.

The document was as authentic and well preserved as any ancient papyrus he had seen. The questions came shooting at them like a semi-automatic.

Where did you find this? How did you discover it? Did you know of its existence? Were there other antiquities with it?

Ridley and Henri slipped each of them as diplomatically as possible. They promised they'd credit him for the translation when their "private benefactor" took it public.

What exactly was Claudine's role in this?

She played no part in the discovery. There was no obligation due to her aside from gratitude for the referral.

"We'd appreciate it if you'd keep this private for now," said Henri, "even from Claudine."

Ridley added, "Do this for us and your department will be getting a funding upgrade next semester. You can continue that latest dig in—where was it again?"

"Saqqara," said Bernard, his eyes lighting up.

"It will get you through the next three years. So, now, what is it? What does this thing say?"

"It's a very specific account of Alexander the Great. If all the information is accurate, this was written by a priest at the Temple of Amun. He says it's the temple that Alexander built."

Bernard bent over the table, poring over both the papyrus and his translated notes.

"At Karnak," said Henri.

The professor looked up with a sly smile. "That's what I thought at first, the grand temple at Luxor. It's amazing. He was only in Egypt for six months, but he made a mark and built a shrine at Luxor. It shows him on the walls, shows him as divine. It would make sense that anyone thinks this is all about the Temple of Amun at Luxor, but—"

He pointed to a line in the lower half.

"This says 'oracle.' There was no oracle in the temple at Luxor."

Bernard pulled out a map of Egypt, pointing to the Luxor compound at Karnak, halfway down the Nile.

"Here," he said, "everyone knows about. It's on the Nile. It's magnificent. It has many, many temples and treasures. But here —" he continued, sliding his finger left, almost to the Libyan border. "This is Siwa. And here, Alexander the Great built a Temple for Amun-Re, when he went to visit the Oracle of the Oasis."

"What does it say about that temple?" asked Henri.

"Alexander brought treasure to honor the Oracle when he wanted to consult with her. He needed her to say that the gods recognized him as the divine ruler of Egypt. They wrote here that he brought a silver crown, gold armor, a painted shield, jewels and silver coins, and a powerful iron ring."

A volt of exuberance surged through Ridley. Henri had to fight back a grin.

That's it. That has to be it. It really exists.

"What did they do with it?" she pressed. "The treasure."

"This temple—this Oracle—they were not like the others," explained Bernard. "They did not want riches, to be grand like Luxor. They wanted to be simple, to give pure service to the gods. This writing...says exactly where they buried it, beneath the temple."

Ridley had to fold her arms tight across her chest to keep from throwing out both fists in victory. There had been no mention of this oracle in the actual pages of the Templars' Codex. They had marked Karnak on their map, and proceeded to launch crusade after crusade in an attempt to conquer it...the map that was now in the hands of the Order of Raphael. Only this papyrus tucked inside had the true location.

Henri turned to her with a smile, and said under his breath, "They're digging in the wrong place."

CHAPTER
FIFTY-SEVEN

It was one of those times when Ridley wished that Booker was in the same room as them. Instead, he was at home in his favorite leather office chair, a highball of Bulleit in his hand. Their encrypted video call was more of a storytelling than a debriefing. Henri was ebullient, thoroughly in his moment as he told their boss the story of Pharaoh Shoshenq, Alexander, the papyrus scroll, Cyprus, the Codex, and then the riveting cliffhanger: the ancient treasure was buried beneath the temple at Siwa.

"Eighty-nine percent certainty," said Henri, "that the iron ring buried with the rest of that treasure *is* the Seal of Solomon."

Booker had been listening attentively. "Ridley, you've got your guy in Egypt?"

She nodded. "Fouad. I already reached out to him."

"Then you know your way to Cairo. I want to say you're a step ahead of those bastards, but—" he said, leaning forward, which always meant a shift in seriousness, "we ran Claudine Gaspar's number into Bellerophon."

Bellerophon was the second-generation version of the most successful and insidious spyware ever created for cell phones: Pegasus. The wizardry of an Israeli cyber-arms company, Pegasus could install itself on any non-encrypted mobile with no more information needed than the target's phone number. It was "odorless," leaving no trace, yet it could see and take everything: emails, messages, contacts, photos, recordings, files, keystroke logs, internet searches, and location records. It could even activate the user's camera and microphone for real-time surveillance, without leaving any indication for the owner.

The program had been discovered a few years back—busted, really. The international outrage was ferocious, even though it soon became clear that dozens of countries had obtained the spyware and had been using it prolifically for their own ends. But inevitably, detection software emerged, and Pegasus was left behind the technological curve.

No successful spyware was ever truly left behind, though. It only faded, to be refined, improved, evolved.

From the ashes of Pegasus, Bellerophon had arisen.

And Henri had fed Claudine's number to it, unbeknownst to Ridley.

"She got a call this afternoon from Bernard Mariette."

"That son of a bitch," said Ridley. "Of course he lied to us."

"And the next call she made, within minutes of getting off the phone with him, was to an encrypted device. We had to dig on this one, but that's sort of our specialty, isn't it?"

He grinned, and it was clear he was pleased at having won this round.

"This number belongs to a man named Tiago Inacio."

Ridley's jaw went slack. Even Henri was stunned.

"What a coincidence!" said Booker. "They spoke for twelve minutes and forty-two seconds, and *that*, my friends...that is why you're neck-and-neck with this Order again. And Inacio's phone has a damn good encryption block on it. We had no luck getting Bellerophon onto it."

He leaned back in his chair and took a sip of his bourbon.

"Get yourselves to the land of the pharaohs, because they're surely on their way already."

When Henri knocked on Ridley's door twenty minutes later to catch their cab to De Gaulle, he found her in a fury. He stepped inside and shut the door.

"Claudine?" he said with a sigh.

"You went behind my back," said Ridley, jamming her dopp kit into the bag.

"I didn't betray you or lie to you."

"I'm your goddamn *partner*, not your subordinate. You deliberately kept something from me, and it was fucking important."

"Important because I was right to be suspicious about her."

"Yes, important because you were right!"

He was quiet for a moment while she shoved the last of her things onto the top layer.

"I didn't tell you, I'm sorry, because I didn't want to fight about something stupid. You made a trust call on Owen...and he got hurt. I didn't want you making another one."

That stung like an asp.

I fucked up twice. He's right.

"You should have told me," she said, trying to keep her emotions beneath a stony grit.

"I should have told you."

"Yeah, damn right."

"I'm sorry," said Henri.

They rode to the airport in near total quiet. Most of what they would have to say to each other couldn't be talked about in the presence of a third party anyway.

When they reached the gate with their carry-ons, Henri went off wandering. He returned with two bottles of Fiji water and a package of Starburst, which he handed to Ridley without a word.

Without a word, she took it, opened it up, and handed him the yellows. His favorites. They sat and chewed in silence.

CHAPTER
FIFTY-EIGHT

Smog hovered in a thick haze about the city. The edges of Cairo teemed with cars, motorcycles, buses, and tuk-tuks in a clamor of horns. The labyrinths of narrow streets were packed with vendors, using every square inch they could to hawk their wares. You could find almost anything in these alleys, from colorful galabeyas to knockoff Armani suits. There were cheap trinkets and ornate antiques alike in this maze of overstimulation.

The higher-end neighborhoods that bordered the river were dotted with elegant cafés, chic brand stores and sleek nightclubs. It was a cosmopolitan wonder for the wealthy and the tourists.

Yet, sandstone mosques from centuries past still towered. Palm trees still grew in thickets along the waterways. The Nile still flowed past high-rises and monuments alike, the queen of this ancient city that now thronged with ten million people.

Ridley and Henri waited for their contact at an outdoor café in Zamalek. She had visited Egypt twice as a civilian, what seemed like a lifetime ago. She'd been here once on government assignment, and it was then she'd met Fouad Elansary.

In the style of his people, punctuality was not a top concern. He wasn't a spy himself, but a skilled and friendly mercenary. His affinity for American culture had provided a way for him to fill his pockets. The man was also extremely fond of espionage and swashbuckling in general.

"Is this like Brazilian time?" asked Henri, already on his second cappuccino.

Ridley shrugged and lifted her hand up in the sunlight. "At least it's a *dry* heat."

Temperatures in the spring were bearable. It was eleven in the morning and nearly eighty-seven degrees already, but somehow baking in the sun in Egypt made Ridley feel more like she was part of the long dynastic tradition of the land, and less like a baking potato.

Today she wore a white t-shirt over tan capris, with an indigo scarf of thin cotton draped around her neck. Henri seemed perfectly at ease in the heat in dark jeans, a dark button-up, and a dark leather jacket. She could not understand how there wasn't even a bead of sweat on his brow. At least with his Caribbean complexion and her Mediterranean one, neither stood out like the light-skinned tourists they saw wandering around who just oozed "European/American."

"We should have gone to the pyramids this morning," he said. "We had plenty of time."

Henri had never set foot in Egypt before, and he was practically beaming at being in one of the greatest ancient civilizations on earth. He was simultaneously a bit cranky that their destination was not in fact the great temple complex of Luxor, but a sparse oasis in the western desert. His efforts to not get distracted by the great history at his fingertips had been obvious all morning.

"Maybe Fouad will have us ride camels to Siwa," said Ridley. "Very authentic."

"Do they really spit?"

"Yeah, grouchy beasts."

Just then, a huge Egyptian man came strolling toward them off the sidewalk. He was clean-shaven, with menacing black brows and the build of an NFL tight end. The sleeves of his button-up were rolled to his elbows, revealing forearms that looked like steel cords. At six-foot-six, he was the biggest Egyptian that either of them had ever seen.

He flashed a grin as Ridley stood up to greet him. "*Salamu-aleikum, sadiqi.*"

"*Aleikum as-salam,*" she replied, shaking his hand.

She knew barely a dozen phrases in Arabic, but managed the difficult accent without embarrassing herself.

"Fouad, this is Henri."

The men shook hands and said hello. Though Henri was still an inch taller than Ridley, somehow the combination of her next to this titan made him feel small.

"You look ready for Egypt, *habibi*" said Fouad as he took a seat, eyeing Ridley.

"I will always be ready for Egypt."

"So I'll see you here in August."

"What's in August?" asked Henri.

"The hottest time of the year," replied Fouad. "The tourists disappear, or they melt. It's very nice."

"You don't scare him," said Ridley. "He grew up in Haiti."

"Ah. Yes, your jacket...I could guess you're either carrying a bomb or you're a man of the Sahara."

Henri smiled. "Once upon a time, my people."

Fouad liked small chat laced with his own sense of humor. He would get touchy if pushed into business too quickly, so Ridley had learned to let him carry the conversation at his own pace. Once he got into the topic of business, though, he was a complete professional.

"It's a shame that she wasn't born three thousand years ago," he said to Henri, cocking his head toward Ridley. "She would be like Hatshepsut, build temples and palaces. They would make statues of her. The pharaoh queen."

"For the next pharaoh in line to destroy all traces of," she said dryly.

Fouad grinned, "You would come back to haunt them."

"Thank you. I'm very honored you feel that way."

"I'll take you both to her temple. It's beautiful. Awesome. Unbelievable."

"Next time. How is Aisha?"

"Acting more like a big sister than a little sister."

"*Oh, when she's angry, she is keen and shrewd! Something-something...and though she be but little, she is fierce,*" said Ridley, then looked at Henri. "His sister. And yes, I did play Helena once in 'A Midsummer Night's Dream' and that is literally the only line I remember. It comes in very handy when describing Aisha."

The big Egyptian laughed. "You'll have to tell her that over dinner one night. So, where are we going this time?"

"West."

"Faiyum."

She shook her head.

"My friend, there is nothing else farther tha—" he started, then sat back. "Siwa."

"Siwa. And it has to be today."

321

He looked between them for a moment. "That will cost more. You know it's dangerous there, too close to Libya."

The western border of Egypt was a precarious region. Given the instability in neighboring Libya, the government regarded it as an avenue for terrorists to bleed into their country. Yet many within Egypt believed the threat to be exaggerated, and they mostly used their lethal force to target smugglers.

Only a few years before, Egypt had used a cadre of French forces to assist them in unwittingly targeting traffickers in the western desert, an area of nearly 435,000 square miles. French intelligence used their surveillance capabilities to track down and relay the location of a convoy back to the Egyptian air force, which swooped in and destroyed nearly two dozen pickup trucks. The French believed them to be terrorist threats. Egypt knew them to be no more than civilian criminals. Most of them were young men, transporting supplies ranging from cigarettes, cereal, and makeup products to gasoline, drugs, or weapons.

Operation Sirli, as it was called, came to light in a series of leaked documents, establishing the complicity between Cairo and Paris in these executions. The French, after all, were the biggest supplier of arms to Egypt, surpassing even the United States. The relationship would have to be sustained despite the scandal. And none of the negative publicity made the Egyptian authorities any less heavy-handed in their policing of the desert region. That, in turn, put the smugglers on edge, ready for violence at even the hint of a threat.

It would be a long trip to Siwa, and a dangerous one.

"We need your best arsenal, too," said Ridley.

"What are we doing and who are we fighting?" asked Fouad.

It was a need-to-know briefing. There was no such thing as a friendly intelligence agency, only ones with allied goals, and there was certainly no such thing as a trustworthy mercenary, though Fouad got as close to it as anyone Ridley had ever known.

She and Henri took turns relaying their mission to dig out a small but historic treasure from beneath the Temple of Amun. They needed tools to do it, and manpower.

"We'll hire locals there," Fouad told them. "Less questions, less money, less time for them to think about it."

Then they described the hostile forces that would likely threaten the mission.

A religious order with arcane beliefs and fanatical dedication... financial means that allow them to get anywhere...international reach with well-placed connections...access to a supply of decently trained, highly equipped fighters...it's a race to Siwa.

The Egyptian gave them a canny look. "You're talking about the Raphaels, aren't you?"

Henri blinked in surprise. Ridley leaned forward with a thrill.

"You know them?!"

"They've been here before," said Fouad.

"Here—*here?* About this?"

He shook his head. "A long time ago. They were looking for something at St. Catherine's Monastery. I wouldn't go there. I don't know if they ever found it."

"Was it a guy with black hair, blue eyes, Portuguese?" asked Henri. "Looks like a James Bond?"

"It was a woman," said Fouad with a wry smile. "She was Indian, very smart. Very terrifying."

"What were they looking for?" asked Ridley.

"She didn't tell me! She just wanted a man—uh...a male escort." He chuckled at his own joke.

St. Catherine's Monastery was not Catholic, but Eastern Orthodox. It lay in the lower region of the peninsula, between the Gulf of Suez and the Gulf of Aqaba. The oldest continuously inhabited monastery in the world, it was just a little sandstone complex nestled at the foot of what is believed to be Mt. Sinai itself. It had been built in the sixth century, and claimed to have enshrined the place where Moses beheld the burning bush.

Now it was a UNESCO World Heritage Site. It was one of the most esteemed and sacred sites in the world, yet now it was one of the most dangerous. The library alone was a religious historian's fantasy, with more ancient manuscripts and rare codices than anywhere else in the world except for the Vatican. Given the value of its relics, it was probably a good thing that the journey there was so treacherous.

The Sinai Peninsula was a deadly trap, where Islamic militants waged war against the Egyptian army. This branch of the Islamic State called themselves Wilayat Sinai, and they claimed the blood of countless civilians and soldiers alike.

Maybe the Raphaels got beheaded, whatever they were looking for there.

"You have a list? Weapons?" asked Fouad.

Ridley slid a scrap of paper across the table.

He looked over it for a moment. "Why are you so fancy?"

Henri chuckled.

"Because I come to win," said Ridley.

Fouad slid the list into his pocket and stood up. "Go get some *ta'ameya*. You know it's better than that falafel thing the Zionists make."

She gave him a look, wagging a finger his way. He only smiled.

"Five hours. Meet me at Orman Gardens."

"We're driving through the night then?"

He shrugged. "You say it's a race. I bring you a camel."

. . .

Once Fouad had left, they took a taxi to the Cairo Museum. They'd studied as much as they could of Siwa on the plane ride here. Ridley had memorized the map as well as she could, and now Henri thought that a museum would be a welcome breath of enjoyment in this frenzied chase. They had nothing else to do but wait, and take in some of the most magnificent pieces of art ever discovered in this ancient land.

They had only just arrived at the building that glowed a burnt umber in the sun when Ridley's phone buzzed with an incoming call. *Professor White.*

"Hello?

"Ridley!" said the professor, "The cryptologists came back to us, and they've got it. They've got it! They figured out the lot of that Templar code."

"Yes! Send it to me?"

"Of course, yes, but...are you sitting down?"

CHAPTER
FIFTY-NINE

"I DON'T THINK I need to sit down, Professor White," said Ridley, beckoning Henri to come away from the entrance.

She planted herself between the reflecting pool and a small sphinx statue. Her partner leaned in close, his curiosity piercing.

"You know the first headquarters of the Templars? Where they were founded?"

"Jerusalem, right?" she asked, glancing up at Henri.

She wanted him to listen in on this but couldn't risk putting it on speaker.

"The Poor Fellow-Soldiers of Christ and of the Temple of Solomon. Yes, Jerusalem. The Temple Mount, in fact. It wasn't just that they wanted to reestablish themselves on a holy site that they believed held the original Temple of Solomon, but they *also* needed to show themselves to be victors—to conquer the Al-Aqsa Mosque of their enemies."

"Right, yes, I think I recall this," said Ridley. "What does that encrypted writing say?"

"My dear, they believe that they know where the seven kings of the jinn are imprisoned in darkness for a thousand years, or some sort like that. *A thousand years* is probably not literal, but...it's in the ground beneath Solomon's Temple itself."

Her gaze lifted to Henri's. "You're saying...they mean the kings are imprisoned beneath the Temple Mount."

Henri's eyes grew wide.

"That's exactly what they say here! Frankly, they sound very certain, beyond mere speculation."

Ridley's voice was flat, stunned. "This boy—the ifrit—wants to release them...from beneath the Temple Mount."

On the other end of the line, she could hear a few papers being shuffled.

"That golden saber of Saladin that—that Owen had quite a bad experience with—that was—*is*—engraved with the names of each of the kings. The Templars also call them here 'Watchers.' They believe them to be the manifestation of biblical fallen beings. Some sort of divine governors that were punished by God."

"Yeah," said Ridley, "we got that connection."

"But the, uh..." Professor White started, clearing her throat, "there's an unfortunate part here. I don't know how they could possibly know this, granted, so take this with a pinch of salt. Anyone who *claims* the full saber and goes to release the Watcher-kings will have one clear window of power in which to do it. It's the day when all of the major religions overlap their holidays, and that's—well, that's this year. Passover, Easter, Palm Sunday, Ramadan."

"You're fucking kidding me."

"That's the end of the week," said Henri, piecing together what he could overhear.

"Are there instructions, tips, anything that they left us to stop this thing?"

The professor sounded rueful. "They placed all their hopes in the Seal of Solomon. Those kings would be *so* much more powerful than any other jinn, even this ifrit. There's nothing these chaps believed they could do, except...wield the power that God was supposed to have given to Solomon, in that ring."

Ridley paced, blowing out a deep breath.

"We're going to get it. We're going today to get it," she said.

"Then I suppose you'll go to Jerusalem?"

"We will *teleport* if we have to."

Professor White promised that she and Owen would keep poring over the texts. She'd let them know if anything new arose. Ridley thanked her and hung up.

She looked at Henri. Between them filled a chasm of dread.

"Shit," declared Ridley.

"And when I see the blood, I will pass over you...and no plague will destroy you when I strike the land of Egypt."

"You always know the backstory."

The Temple Mount. Only the most incendiary place on earth, and this ifrit was going to unleash a supernatural chaos upon it during the most sacred week in the Jewish and Muslim and Christian calendars.

Ridley and Henri both stared off across the courtyard, the city, the flawless blue of the sky above them.

Ridley and Henri ditched the Cairo Museum. They went instead to the Orman Gardens, and found a deserted thicket away from anyone else. From there, they called Booker.

The most fateful update I've ever delivered.

He was in his office at Langley, and like the veteran heavyweight that he was, he took it soberly.

Jerusalem was already a tinderbox. Peace talks between the prime minister and the PLO hovered on the horizon as a possibility, so violence crackled through the city like static electricity. If someone was to disrupt the Temple Mount in any way, no matter who was responsible or why, the intifada of 2000 would pale in comparison. Blood would paint the streets. Body parts would have to be swept from the asphalt.

When Booker put a hand over his mouth to process their news, Ridley felt the gravity compounding in her own mind.

"Okay. This really escalated," he said.

"And we're putting a lot of stock in an old piece of jewelry to do anything about it," said Ridley.

"There aren't any more promising options out there. Haven't we all seen stranger things?"

"I did see the TV show."

"Kids...no, I did, too. Great stuff, very spooky. Took me back to the great-and-Reagan-eighties."

"Old man," said Henri with a small grin.

"Hey now, you want me on that wall. You *need* me on that wall."

Ridley chuckled, loving his Jack Nicholson rendition.

Booker straightened up and shifted serious again.

"Look, at face value, we've got a rogue Syrian male who's intending to hit the Temple Mount on Ramadan-Passover-Easter. I'll meet with Conway today—I know he's in the office—and I'll be on a plane to Jerusalem by tonight."

Ben Conway: Deputy Director of the CIA's National Clandestine Service. He was a former Marine with a prematurely gray beard and a booming voice to rival Booker's own bass tones. Though he had a cynical edge, he was surprisingly reasonable, willing to listen to even the more outlandish undertakings of the Osprey Division.

"We'll get there as soon as we can," said Henri.

"You go out into that godforsaken desert and get that damn ring, and you don't think about anything else right now. I'll see you in Israel when you've completed your mission."

"Sir, yes, sir," said Ridley.

"And you're taking an arsenal, right?"

"We gave Fouad a list."

"Well, Fouad always gets the list," said Booker.

"If we run into the Order out there..."

Henri finished his partner's thought. "We bury them in the sand."

As they hung up with Booker, they felt a moderate sense of reassurance. He was competent, dogged, and most importantly here, persuasive. He'd walked into Conway's office with some preposterous stories before, but still held the seasoned director's full trust. And they were going to need everything to prevent a meltdown in the Holy City that would send violence shattering across the globe.

By this time, Henri was of course hungry again. They had enough time to grab some *ta'ameya* and *sobia*—a bottled coconut milkshake—from a street vendor, before getting back to the Gardens. They bagged an extra two servings for Fouad.

"Do you think the boss has a new lady?" asked Henri as they sat on a bench, eating the falafel-like wraps.

She squinted and see-sawed her head in thought. "I dunno. He did seem kinda chipper. He even pulled out that *A Few Good Men* quote."

"That *was* good."

She nodded. "Very high marks for delivery."

They were wiping their hands clean when a Nissan sedan pulled into the lot and parked. Fouad climbed out.

"You fit that whole list into a four-door?" said Ridley, getting up to greet him.

"I had to do it. No trucks across the desert," he replied. "You'll look like a smuggler and they'll bomb you straight down from the sky."

"And 'no beards' or they think you're a terrorist, right?" asked Henri.

"My man!" grinned Fouad, impressed. "That's right. Ahh...I love this country."

"Can you eat while you drive?" asked Ridley, holding up a plastic bag.

"Will you feed it to me?"

"If you want to be covered in tahini sauce, yes. Yes, I will."

He took the bag from her. "We go now. I want to get past some of these checkpoints before it's completely dark."

"Take us to the desert."

CHAPTER
SIXTY

———

FOUAD DROVE through the night on a mix of energy drinks and willpower, while Ridley and Henri took turns sleeping. The big Egyptian enjoyed their tactical ritual of watchfulness, as he always had at least one of them to talk to.

The desert was ghostly at night. They passed a tourist bus and a couple of other vehicles, but nothing that looked threatening.

"They always drive overnight," Fouad told Henri. "Too hot out here to drive the whole day. If your engine gets too hot, you're in shit."

"Tourists. Never there in the movies, always there in real life."

"It's okay. Not too many."

They had to stop at four checkpoints along the way. Little

more than a police van sitting along the dark road, Fouad was nonetheless compliant and gregarious. He explained to the armed guards that his passengers were tourists from Canada. That seemed to calm their nerves, as Americans would require a police escort across this stretch of smugglers' road.

The government took great care to protect tourists, especially Americans. The tourism industry brought in over twelve billion dollars a year, and employed millions of Egyptians. Not since 1997 had there been a serious attack on tourists in the country.

That day had darkened Egypt for years, when six members of a Sunni Islamist group arrived on the steps of Hatshepsut's Temple one morning in Luxor. They opened fire on the hundred foreigners there visiting, stalking them deep into the temple, hacking them to death with machetes. The massacre lasted nearly an hour, and by the end, fifty-eight foreign nationals lay dead alongside four Egyptians. The youngest was a five-year-old child from England.

Understandably, tourists balked at the horror. However, terrorism within Egypt dropped dramatically afterward. Gone were the sympathies among the general populace for any sort of grievance that these militant groups espoused. Switzerland, which had lost three dozen of its citizens in the attack, later determined that the operation had been financed by Osama bin Laden.

Despite the special care that the Egyptian government took with Americans these days, Ridley and Henri preferred to travel on other passports when and where they could. Canada was a sturdy alternative. It was unremarkable, non-inflammatory, and culturally similar enough to the States that it was an easy pass. Fouad flashed their fake passports.

The guards waved him on. Not one of them had any notion of the armory that lay under the floorboards of the backseat.

They arrived at the outskirts of Siwa just as dawn began to glow on the horizon behind them. The narrow dusty highway ran straight through the salt flats, pools of crystalline water on both sides of it stretching as far as they could see.

As they drove through the dim streets, a donkey cart rolled past them. A middle-aged couple were opening up their bakery, and the sweet smell of toasting *mahlab* wafted through the open windows of the Nissan.

Ridley was awake in the front seat, taking it in. The grandeur of Egypt's history loomed everywhere in this country. Though Siwa had Wi-Fi and beauty salons and gas stations, it still somehow seemed like they had stepped into an ancient civilization. Despite the millennia that separated them from the pilgrimage of Alexander the Great, it felt as though they were treading the very same dust.

Still, it was the Order she was on the lookout for, scanning every vehicle and peering down every street.

"We go to the temple first and find the place you want to dig. Then we get breakfast," said Fouad, rubbing his eyes, "and we hire some local diggers."

"You know your way around?" asked Ridley.

"There's not too much to know. Desert. Oasis. Fortress. Temple. Fatnas Island. I'll take you there for a strawberry milkshake."

Fouad had been here once before, as a teenager on a whim with his friends. They'd grabbed backpacks, borrowed his uncle's car without asking, and gone out to see Cleopatra's pool, to float in the electric blue of the salt flat lakes. It had been worth the hiding he'd received when he got back with the car.

Now, he drove them through a forest of palm trees until they reached a clearing. Before them rose a rocky hill, and atop it, the remains of an ancient sandstone structure.

The Temple of Amun.

They stayed wide of the tourist office that was yet to open. Fouad parked under a thicket of date palms, and they geared up.

He grabbed a Colt 1911. Henri holstered a Glock 17 into the small of his back. Ridley tucked an HK USP into appendix carry. She grinned when she saw that her Egyptian friend had even procured a karambit for her, the size of a raptor claw.

"Prince among men," she said, sheathing it along her belt.

"You're so bloody. So deadly everywhere," joked Fouad.

Fully armed, they then hiked up the small hill, each step both thrilling and disheartening. They were so close to the final discovery, but this was not just a temple, it was an entire complex of crumbling sandstone and winding pathways.

Do we really know where to dig?

Henri pulled up the decoded instructions from the Codex. "The translation says it's in a chamber well, between the outer courtyard and the inner sanctum."

"The hypostyle hall," said Fouad as they trekked up to the small temple itself. "We're not going to destroy this place, though..."

He was a mercenary, but he was also a proud Egyptian. He would dig for treasure and plunder a tomb or two, but he balked at the idea of desecrating the physical structures that upheld such majestic history.

"We're digging down, not taking walls apart," assured Henri.

Their shoes crunched against the grit. They reached the top of the complex as the sun was rising over the salt flats like the sun god himself. They stepped into the remains of the temple, and Henri's eyes went wide. The ceiling was long gone, but most of the walls were intact. They could still make out traces of a once-great mural and the faint etchings of a pharaoh's cartouche.

The three of them passed into the hypostyle hall, their eyes sweeping the antechamber. Ridley went to the left, to a hole in the wall that looked like an enormous mail slot, and peered in.

"Gentlemen, these are the droids we're looking for."

It was a descending chamber, something of a narrow well-like structure that dropped down nearly six feet. There was a bigger opening on the other side of the wall for access. Henri and Fouad came over to take a look.

"We can dig this," said Fouad. "It looks easier than I thought."

"Don't say things like that," said Ridley. "We're going to end up in a tunnel to Hades."

Henri wondered aloud. "Could it really have been here the whole time? Over two thousand years and it's just, right here."

Fouad shrugged. "It's just rock below. There aren't many archaeologists who come out here to dig into a rock."

It's here. It's right below us. This damn ring better be magic.

"Let's go get our diggers," said Ridley.

CHAPTER
SIXTY-ONE

———

A FEW HUNDRED yards from the temple was a small school beside a hospital clinic. A few dozen kids scampered about before class began. They were playing soccer in the dust, hollering to each other in the hot morning sun.

Fouad had decided to pay one of them to be a lookout. He spotted an older boy approaching on a bicycle and pulled him aside before he reached the schoolyard. He offered the kid six hundred Egyptian pounds to play hooky.

The boy, who said his name was Mohamed, gaped at the large man. It was the equivalent of nearly twenty American dollars, more than any child could make in Siwa in a week. Ridley and Henri had stayed well out of sight, wanting to keep their distinct profiles in the area as low as possible.

Fouad handed the wide-eyed Mohamed half the fee, and a burner phone with his number pre-programmed in it.

"Watch the temple area today. If you see a group of men arrive, and they don't look like the tourists you see here every day, you call me that instant," he instructed. *"You're a good boy. You're making a lot of money for your family today."*

Mohamed rode off for the entry to the temple grounds. Fouad drove Ridley and Henri a short way to a little café on the edge of the salt flats. It was nothing more than a thatched hut serving mint tea and—to their surprise—strawberry smoothies. They camped at a little table while Fouad drove off into the flats to recruit some day laborers.

As much as the aquamarine pools out there were a social media fantasy photoshoot, the plains were in fact a mining site. Mountains of salt were transported from there back to the city each week. And miners were just the type of workers they were looking for. Fouad just needed the Americans to stay behind. The sight of foreigners, especially a white-ish one, would jack up the price of any hire.

They watched the Nissan cross the flats until it had disappeared behind mounds of salt. Henri sipped a mint tea while Ridley slurped on a smoothie. The flavors were slightly tainted by the scent of manure occasionally wafting from a nearby horse stable.

Waiting was horrible. Ridley's leg was bobbing up and down. Despite the lack of sleep, she was wired. A torrent of thoughts was rushing through her head.

Passover in Jerusalem...the carnage...where is the ifrit right now? Who's the boy he has possessed now? Has it already jumped to another? How will we find it if it has?

Owen would kill to be here right now...he's not because I made the wrong call. Claudine — that treacherous bitch. People are dead because of her. That's my fault, too.

This goddamn ear. That goddamn wave.

I'm not going to lose our mission to this self-righteous Portuguese prick.

Henri was pensive and quiet. She finally hauled her brain out of the rapids of her own anxiety. She picked up some small stones from the ground, targeted a hole in the ground a few yards off, and lobbed one. *Swish.*

"Free throw contest," she said, handing some of the stones to Henri. "Shoot."

He took them with a smile of surprise. "But you played basketball. I played soccer."

"So kick it."

Henri placed a stone on the top of his toes, then flipped it up with his foot and kicked it. It skittered inches wide of the hole.

"Soccer ain't shit," she said.

"The waiting is awful, huh? Okay, Kobe. Let's see who can get it farther."

Ridley didn't need any more prodding. She stood up and hurled a stone as far as she could. They watched it disappear in the sun-blasted distance, completely lost to sight.

"Huh," she said, hands on her hips. "I assume that went really far. The farthest it could physically go, in the world."

He stood up and punted his stone. They both squinted as it vanished into the light-colored ground.

"I won," said Henri, sitting back down to take a sip of his tea.

She got to her feet and kicked her last stone, just as he had. It arced into the sky, indistinguishable from his.

"That was a winning Super Bowl field goal," he said soberly.

"Rematch when we can actually see the results," she replied, grabbing her smoothie.

They sipped their drinks in silence for a moment.

"Kinda funny that we were both assigned this because we

speak French," said Ridley with a smirk. "How you like me now?"

She gestured to the Egyptian desert sprawling before them.

Henri laughed. "Doesn't this always happen with Osprey?"

"It beats working on a Navy carrier. By a *lot*."

"Beats wandering around the White House grounds."

The older man who had sold them their drinks shuffled away from the hut to feed his cart donkey. A warm wind swept through the palms.

Ridley felt a strange pang of eeriness. She looked around, eyes sweeping the forest of palms behind them. Only the old man and his donkey.

But then something appeared in the distance, coming out of the salt flats. Two light-colored SUVs. She sat up at alert.

"Henri."

He followed her eyes to the vehicles heading toward them on the long, straight highway.

"How long has Fouad been gone?" she asked.

"He said to give him an hour. It's been..." he checked his watch, "forty minutes."

"That's them. They're coming."

"Bad feeling?"

"I feel like Spiderman right now. Or Cassandra."

She jumped up and dialed Fouad, but it only rang and rang. "Pick the fuck up, Fouad!"

"And we have no car," said Henri, now on his feet.

He saw the donkey by the cart, and gave a nod toward Ridley. She shook her head.

That little trotter will be slow as shit in a bag.

Just then, a breeze wafted the stench of manure their way. She looked upwind and spotted a horse out in the paddock.

Henri saw her thoughts before she said a word. "Ah, okay. Yeah, I can ride...a little."

Only minutes later, they had saddled two of the scrappy desert horses. With no sign of the owner, they mounted up and galloped off toward the temple.

CHAPTER
SIXTY-TWO

———

RIDLEY STEERED her mount through the groves of date palms. She'd ridden a thousand times along the rugged shores of the Greek isles, but this horse was a backbiter, probably running only in an effort to shake her off. She tried to keep her direction straight, weaving around the thick trunks and ducking heavy fronds.

Henri tried to keep pace, unsteady as he was atop his horse. He had only ridden a handful of times in his life, but not one of those had banished his nervousness around the big animals. And horses could feel that fear.

He began to fall behind as Ridley tore through the dense thicket on her mount, until he'd lost sight of her completely.

She burst out at the back side of the rocky hill and skidded to a halt. The light-colored SUVs were already parked at the front.

Ridley felt her phone buzz. Wrestling with her horse to keep still, she pulled it from her pocket.

Fouad.

"They're here," she said over the phone. "Come to the temple right now."

His astonishment was genuine. "*What?*"

"Load up for this."

"I speed. Fifteen minutes."

She dismounted and drew the HK USP from her back. Keeping cover within the palms, she moved around toward the entrance. There was Mohamed on his bike, eyeing the complex nervously while dialing on the burner phone they'd given him.

When the boy saw Ridley approaching, he was about to call out. She put a finger to her lips, but beckoned him to her. The boy rode into the thicket.

Shit, I can't speak Arabic.

She pointed to her gun, then to the temple complex with a questioning face. He nodded vigorously, wide-eyed. She began to count on her fingers, pointing to herself, then him, then pointing up to the temple again. He raised six fingers, then seven, then shrugged. Ridley nodded, clapped him on the shoulder as a thank you, and gestured for him to get out of there. Mohamed grabbed his bike and pedaled off, glad to be out of that place.

Hoofbeats sounded behind her, and Henri dismounted. He was hugely relieved to have made it on horseback, but now seeing his partner at alert, he pulled his Glock.

"Six or seven hostiles," she said quietly, "armed, obviously. Fouad is on his way."

"Surveil, wait to engage."

They circled the edge of the palms until they reached the

front. They kept their guns low and discreet, but as they approached the entrance lot, they spotted the lookout.

He was leaning against the driver's door of one of the SUVs, his gaze roaming the access road they'd just come through themselves.

Lazy sentinels only think of one approach.

Ridley and Henri didn't want to shoot here and give away their position to a superior number of the enemy. They could take one man silently.

They motioned to each other, arguing about which of them would take him with a rear naked strangle. Henri won.

Seconds later, Ridley walked casually up toward the back of the SUV, rounding the trunk. The lookout jerked his head up, his hand giving a short spasm toward his waist. Pure gun reflex, but he stayed it, because this attractive, Amazonian-tall woman with the friendly expression was flashing her most irresistible grin.

"Hey, are you American?" she asked.

"No, but I speak English," he replied.

It was just enough for her to realize he wasn't Portuguese himself.

Eastern European?

But she wouldn't hear his accent again. A pair of dark arms folded around his neck from behind, strangling his outcry. He scrabbled and clawed at his assailant's hands and face, but the technique was perfect. Within seconds, Henri's arms had cinched off his carotid artery. His face went red, then purple. His struggle went limp and his eyes rolled back. Henri held on for an extra moment. This was not for sport.

Finally, he dropped the limp body of the lookout to the ground. The man collapsed in the dust. Ridley knelt down and yanked the firearm from his side holster, another Glock. Then she slammed the butt of the pistol against his windpipe. He wouldn't get his breath back through a crushed trachea. They rolled the mercenary under the SUV, then turned back to the temple.

The walls of the complex were too elevated and too high to see anyone inside. They would have to take the outer stairway up, then pass through a narrow hallway in the first building to enter the grounds.

"We have to go," said Ridley. "Fouad's too far out to wait."

"We don't have the firepower. He has our stash."

She yanked open the back of one of the SUVs. Inside was a tangle of supplies, rope and shovels, and a long black Pelican case.

Opening it, she murmured with a smile. "Oh, my darling."

Inside was a Blaser R93 Tactical rifle, a sleek German beauty with a pistol grip, bolt-action, and a Nikon scope. Beside it were two short loaded magazines.

She looked at Henri, whose eyes had lit up. His hands floated toward the gun with some deadly magnetic force.

"Okay, let's go now."

The morning sun was starting to sear. They swept up the temple steps, through the small corridor, and into the grounds.

Once inside, Henri crouched down behind a high wall on the front parapet, clutching the Blaser. Across from him, Ridley dropped low behind the crumbling stone barrier.

In the ruins of the courtyard below them wandered three of the Order's mercenaries. They were dressed like militant tourists who didn't want to seem too martial in appearance but still couldn't give up their fatigues. Khaki cargo pants, tactical boots, and either heavy-duty button-ups or long-sleeved polos with too many sleeve pockets. One of them carried an AK-47, another had a GROT C16 FB-M1. It was a new version of a Polish modular rifle.

Henri thought it was a bit excessive to have brought to the

Egyptian desert, but the man wielding it probably had a great affection for such a toy, and would probably jump at the chance to fire it.

The third man below was climbing around the edge of the courtyard where a slope of ragged rock met the upper wall. A handgun was tucked into the back of his belt.

On the far end, at the highest point of the complex, three more men wandered in and around the remains of the small temple. One of them carried a rifle, probably another GROT, but from this distance, Henri couldn't make it out. The last two were surely armed as well with holstered handguns.

Henri wanted a closer look at the men in the temple. He couldn't see Tiago, but from here, raising the barrel of the rifle would likely catch the light, and he didn't trust the brittle stone wall in front of him against high-powered incoming shots. There was a very tall, narrow tower on the corner of the entrance, but none of the cut-out windows faced into the complex.

A sniper's nest is what he wanted. He motioned to Ridley that he was going up a level to get behind a thicker barrier. She nodded. Keeping low, he scurried up to a higher wall and got set.

Henri had taken a thousand shots more difficult than this, at a thousand yards in low light. His partner would wait on him to fire first here. He'd have a clean sightline with the element of surprise.

There were only five rounds per magazine. He had extras stuffed into his back pockets, but having to reload was the bane of a sniper's existence.

Resting his eye against the scope, Henri slowed his breathing, centered his aim, slid his finger around the trigger, and squeezed.

CHAPTER
SIXTY-THREE

———

THE RIFLE SHOT shattered the complex.

One man's head burst in blood as he spasmed back and fell limp to the ground.

Shouts of alarm exploded as the mercenaries scrambled for cover. Henri slid the bolt forward, locked it, and aimed again. This time he was searching for the GROT-wielder in his sights, but the man was keeping low beneath a wall along the steps.

Below him, Ridley loosed a volley. A hail of bullets came flying at them, biting into the worn sandstone. She realized she had no angle on any of their targets.

Just as another rifle shot cracked the air, she made a dash to her right. It was the only path to advance behind cover toward the temple. Two against five. It was all or nothing now.

She saw a flash as GROT took aim at her from the stairs, but

347

yanked her head behind the wall as his volley smashed the rock around her. Ridley slid along the ground until she reemerged a yard down the wall, firing downward.

She moved against the wall, starting to move down the side parapet, exchanging volleys.

Henri had just changed magazines and regained his sights when one of the men up in the temple area tried to relocate. It was a foolish choice. Henri hit him with the first shot.

Two down. Four more.

Ridley knew she had six left in the chamber. They were all for the man wielding the GROT. She scampered another yard down the wall as he started to back up the stairs, trying to find new cover. His foot caught on the uneven steps. It was the only mistake she needed as his rifle slipped.

Four shots, rapid-fire. His chest and throat tore open, and he stumbled back with a gargling noise.

She rushed forward, staying low. Halfway to the temple now, and she could hear the sniper shots cracking off. Henri would get the last mercenary standing in the courtyard. They needed to end this firefight as fast as they could.

But where's Tiago?

Henri hit the cheek of the hopeless last man who had ducked for sparse cover in the courtyard. Then he slung the Blaser over his back, drew his Glock, and *moved.*

The two mercenaries at the far end had withdrawn into the temple. He could see Ridley advancing, only a dozen yards away from them now.

Then the floor in front of Ridley disappeared. The wall structure wasn't connected to the next, and an eight-foot drop lay below. Drop or leap. She leapt, out into the open.

The last two men did not waste their enemy's total exposure. The stone behind her exploded, but it seemed no louder in her ears than her own galloping heartbeat.

She landed hard on the other side, skidding behind the ragged wall, her arm and hand scraped bloody. Across the courtyard, she spotted a glimpse of Henri as he raced along the high wall cover, toward the back of the complex.

As he drew their fire, she moved again.

Only thirty feet from the temple...

The mercenaries were calling to each other between volleys in some Slavic language she couldn't understand.

Henri appeared across the courtyard. They'd cut off the angle so that from within the temple, the Slavs had no sightline unless they bodily exposed themselves. Ridley holstered her nearly-empty HK and drew the dead man's Glock. She checked the barrel, then motioned for Henri to move in. He nodded. This would surely end in close quarter combat.

They both moved, dropping down from the walls onto lower ground. Henri had to cross a concealed lower level to reach Ridley. When he came up behind her, they formed a seamless unit. She took lead.

Weapons raised, they closed in on the outer temple walls. The gunfire had stopped. The only sound now was their own shoes crunching softly against gravel.

They both flattened themselves against the outer wall, listening.

Silence.

Ridley motioned: *go.*

They swept into the outer temple courtyard. Empty. They rushed to the outer walls as a barrage of bullets roared toward them. The mercenaries were holed up in the middle section, the hypostyle hall.

Combat, as much as it was about skills, reactions, and composure, fell under the shadow rule of predictability: openness to all possible actions your opponent *could* take funneled into the anticipation of likely actions that they *would* take. Most creativity in combat was really just stupidity trying to wear a cape. But every now and then, some action would be so unanticipated that it left the enemy in the lag, just far enough behind with a stunned reaction that they were momentarily caught on the back foot.

Whoever these mercenaries really were, they had not brought enough ammunition into the complex for an all-out firefight. One of the mercenaries was pressed against the wall on the other side of Ridley, just a few feet of sandstone between them, and his last magazine was empty.

Desperation made people do the unexpected.

The man lunged around the corner, with one hand yanking Ridley forward into the hall. His other hand shoved down the top of her Glock. She tried to wrestle away her wrist, to twist the barrel toward him. He slammed an elbow into her jaw.

Henri stepped forward, trying to get a clean shot on the attacker, only to spot the second mercenary, gun raised. He swiveled to shoot, exchanging fire before having to draw back into cover. He couldn't shoot at Ridley's assailant without hitting her.

Still struggling to redirect the barrel of the gun, she bulled into her attacker. With one arm wrapped under his armpit, she hooked her leg onto the inside of his, lifted, and pivoted his torso. It was a brutal throw.

He slammed to the ground with a grunt. He was shorter than Ridley, but thick with muscle, and by pure strength he was gradually gaining control of the Glock.

She tried to go for an armbar in order to break his elbow and snatch it from his grip, but she had to keep one hand on the barrel to keep it pointed away from her.

Behind Ridley, Henri and the second mercenary were blazing volleys at each other across the sanctuary.

She yanked her wrist suddenly, the barrel slipped toward

him, and she squeezed the trigger. The bullets exploded next to his ear, chipping off rock shrapnel that sliced his face. Enraged, he tried to shove her aside. She had to post an arm out to stop herself from falling. As she did, he moved to get up. She leapt to her feet as he went to stand, both still gripping the Glock barrel that burned in their hands.

With a ferocious whip of her neck, she slammed her forehead into his nose. Blood burst across his face, and his grip loosened just enough. With two hands, she jerked the gun free and unloaded three shots into the center of his collarbone.

Before he had even hit the ground, Ridley wheeled about to find the last man. She unleashed a volley at the jutting edge of the wall he was hiding behind. He slid out to return fire. Henri shot twice. They heard a thump, and it was quiet.

He swept forward, into the inner sanctum, and put one more into the head of the dying mercenary. His skull snapped against the ground, then went still.

Ridley drew in a deep breath, then let it out slow and smooth.

Henri stepped back out to look at her. "Clear."

There was a shout in the courtyard.

They jerked back against the walls, guns at the ready.

"Rid! Henri!!"

It was Fouad. Henri raised his arms in sarcastic disbelief.

"Up here!" Ridley yelled back, relaxing again.

Neither holstered their weapons, even when Fouad came tearing up the stairs and into the temple. He'd passed a trail of bodies by the time he reached them, and his expression was stony. Looking down at the two dead men on the ground though, he broke into a grim chuckle. He muttered something in Arabic and shook his head.

"So, maybe we need to dig some extra."

"You got the diggers?" asked Henri.

"They're here, outside the entrance. We heard the gunshots. You're going to have to pay them extra."

"If they help us with the bodies, it's double."

"Wait," said Ridley, feeling a sharp sense of alarm. "Where's Tiago?"

CHAPTER
SIXTY-FOUR

———

THEY WERE certain that the squad of Eastern Europeans had been with the Order of Raphael, but it was the first time that they'd encountered anyone apart from Tiago. It wasn't sitting well with Ridley. The possibilities spun through her head on shuffle.

Whether Tiago had died, been replaced, or sent an advance team, it hardly mattered. They had to work quickly.

Fouad had brought three miners out from the salt flats, who had taken a long lunch break to put in a shift for this stranger. He had offered them an entire week's pay for their time, which had gotten several enthusiastic volunteers. Given the size of the chamber in which they were digging, he only needed three of them.

He had chosen a small, wiry young man who moved with

brisk energy, who would fit well into the space. Another, broad-shouldered and tall, who would be fit to haul up the rocky dirt, and the third was a man with calloused hands and a hard, apathetic expression. The less curiosity they had for this job, the better.

Fouad first paid off the ticket office outside the temple complex. No tourists today. Then he directed the miners to the shaft in the temple with their equipment.

Meanwhile, Ridley and Henri went around the courtyard. They stripped each of the mercenaries of their weapons and hauled the bodies into a pile. There was nothing incriminating or even telling on any of them, though that was expected. Given their weaponry and their behavior, they were clearly professionals who wanted to stay anonymous.

"Scouts?" wondered Ridley aloud as she ejected the magazine from an AK-47.

"They must have been. Tiago wouldn't miss finally finding the Seal," said Henri, "and these guys had no digging equipment."

He pulled out a satellite phone from one dead man's pocket. He tried to activate it, but it was password protected.

"Then he's on his way here," she said.

She picked up the GROT C16 FB-M1, admiring its sleek build.

Henri hoisted his rifle again. "I'll post up at the front. You keep an eye on the dig?"

She nodded.

Henri settled on the front wall with the Blaser. Ridley went back to the temple, where Fouad was crunching on a bag of Tiger chips while the miners tunneled downward in the tight space.

"We don't know how far down," said Ridley, folding her arms as she leaned against the wall beside him, "but damn, I hope they're the fastest shovels in the east. And the tightest lips in Egypt."

He gave her a look, *not likely,* and held out the bag of chips. She took a handful with her less scraped palm.

She also realized that her thigh was hurting with a burning ache. The gash left by the ifrit's attack in Tomar must have taken a hit during her hand-to-hand fight with the mercenary. Glancing down, she saw a small, dark stain along her quad.

I don't have time for this.

Even as she ate the chips, her stomach was fluttering. At first she wondered if it was the tide of adrenaline washing out, but then realized the feeling was building rather than receding.

All of the destruction of the past few weeks, all of the ifrit chaos and death that had been strewn across Europe...all of it could be stopped by what lay under the ground, only yards from where they stood now. It had to work. The ifrit's powers were real, as she had witnessed with horror again and again. The saber had some kind of dark magic welding it back together with blood.

Why would the Seal not *have supernatural power?*

The Templars had sought it for two hundred years. Lifetimes of struggle, pilgrimages and bloodshed, supplications and crusades, and they had never been as near to it as Ridley was now.

For the next forty minutes, the miners dug at a furious pace. Henri sent her a text SITREP—situation report—from the front wall.

Clear here

Ridley and Fouad pitched in to shovel away mounds of rocky dirt.

A sheen of sweat started to glisten on her skin, mixing with the dust to create a muddy grime. She was just wiping away a smear when they heard a muffled shout from the dig-shaft.

The small, wiry miner was deep into a J-curve beneath the temple, but he popped his head out to yell up to them in Arabic.

"They found a chest," said Fouad, his eyes lighting hungrily. "It has hieroglyphs on it."

"You can read those, right?" she said.

He gave a scoff of pride. "I'm not a philistine. All treasure-hunters in my country learn hieroglyphics."

"Oh, yes. My mistake."

The miners began to dig out the chest. It took them about fifteen minutes to free it, then strap it up securely and haul it up out of the shaft. They finally set it down for Ridley in the middle of the inner sanctum.

She went down on one knee. It was no bigger than a carry-on suitcase. Fouad crouched beside her, rubbing off the dirt so he could make out the small engravings.

"*Power of the gods*—that sounds good—*the conqueror of the world comes with the treasure of—from—the wise king. It rules over the demons of fire.*"

He drew back. Ridley looked up at him.

"That's the one."

The two of them heaved off the heavy stone lid.

A ripple of awe passed through everyone in the temple. Inside the chest lay a pile of dull gleaming treasure. A golden goblet lay in a bed of silver coins. Gold and ivory necklaces and bangles were half-buried in the heap.

But she didn't see the iron Seal.

There was a rapid exchange of words amongst the miners. Fouad snapped at them in Arabic, and they immediately fell quiet.

"Do you want the treasure?" he asked Ridley.

"Give them a pile each," she muttered, pulling out handfuls of coin.

Fouad gathered up the silver as she dug down, swallowing a sense of panic.

No...no...it has to be here...

She tossed out jewelry and shekels and pieces of silverware with increasing urgency, until she'd almost reached the bottom. There was a small canopic jar made of carved limestone. The top of it was a likeness of some pharaoh in the striped Nemes headdress. Ridley opened it and shook out the contents. There was nothing but a wad of folded linen inside, but it was heavy. She unwrapped the tattered piece.

And then in her hand lay a huge iron signet ring. A six-pointed star was encircled by an ornate edging.

"Cracker Jack."

She was holding the Seal of Solomon.

CHAPTER
SIXTY-FIVE

SIWA, EGYPT

RIDLEY SENT A MESSAGE TO HENRI.

Got it

Fouad gave an even distribution of the silver coins to the miners, who scrambled eagerly for their shares. He shoved the rest of the gold and ivory pieces into one of the dirt sacks and slung it over his own shoulder.

There was no time or efficient way to remove the dead bodies from the complex. The shootout earlier had certainly been heard by neighboring residents in Siwa. Whenever the East Europeans were found and possibly identified, it's likely they'd be linked with terrorism coming across the border. Mercenary work was just that shady. They could link it with anything.

Ridley had wrapped the ring up tightly in the linen, shoved

it into a pocket, and zippered it shut. They met Henri outside and loaded the collected arsenal into the Nissan.

Fouad peeled out of the parking space and sped off down the dusty streets of Siwa. When they broke through the forest of palms, they picked up the long highway east, that cut through the waters of the oasis. A bus and a pickup truck passed them heading into town.

"We might have eliminated the advice team," Henri announced as their nerves began to ease, "but if they were the muscle hired to keep us out, their boss won't be far behind."

"This Order thing..." muttered Fouad, shaking his head. "Egypt has enough problems of its own. We don't need their problems."

Ridley patted him on the shoulder. "We're here to get rid of your problems."

But all she could really think about now was Jerusalem.

The Seal of Solomon was bulky in her pocket.

Is there really power in this thing? I don't feel any power. Does someone have to be wearing it on their finger? Does it have to fit?

They had almost reached the salt flats, where rectangular pools of aquamarine were clustered in grids to their left and right. It was then that two vehicles appeared, heading toward them, toward Siwa. White Land Rovers.

"Those look too nice," said Ridley, a sharp edge creeping into her voice. "Don't those look too nice?"

Henri muttered rapidly in Creole, then said, "I can't see the drivers."

Fouad didn't need any prompting. If the Land Rovers encountered them on the straightaway between the shallow pools, they could block off the single Nissan sedan. Only water surrounded them. He sped up.

The Land Rovers seemed to respond. They surged forward, just as Fouad reached the salt flats. Closing in, a hundred yards.

"That's fuckin' them," said Ridley.

Henri grabbed the GROT C16 FB-M1 from the back and passed it up to her. He pulled out his own Glock to check the magazine.

Fifty yards. The Nissan was holding speed. The second Land Rover began to lag back from the first.

Ridley and Henri braced as they closed the distance.

The first Land Rover veered suddenly toward them.

Fouad had been expecting something aggressive. His reflexes were on a hair-trigger. He swerved to the right, onto the salt flats, tires skidding as he tried to straighten the vehicle.

The second Land Rover pulled off, going straight for them.

"You have a shot?" Ridley asked Henri.

He slid his window halfway down in the back, and aimed his Glock over the top. He fired off a volley at the oncoming second Rover, as the first was backing up for another attempt at them. A few bullets found their mark in the metal body.

Fouad peeled around one of the salt pools as the Rovers returned fire. The back window exploded. The second Rover was coming off the road toward them. Ridley lowered her own window, swiveling in her seat to get a clean sight on it, but she was jolted off it when Fouad braked and swerved.

They skidded a tight corner around the edge of a pool. The second Rover followed. It was more agile than the Nissan. They weren't going to be able to outrun or outmaneuver these.

Ridley braced the barrel of the GROT out the window and fired on the first vehicle. As good a shot as she was, tires were so difficult to hit that they were usually a waste of ammo. She was betting that these cars would not be bulletproof, so she aimed high. The semi-automatic rifle kicked off in her hands, and one of the back windows shattered. The man behind it spasmed back, clutching his arm.

They spun and drifted and sped in a predator dance through

the grid of water and sand. Dust rose in vaporous clouds around them. Bullets sheared through metal and glass. And once, just as they veered away from the first Land Rover, Ridley thought she caught sight of Tiago in the passenger seat. She unloaded a volley his way, but with the lurching of the Nissan, hit nothing.

Fouad eyed the second Rover coming up on his rear, threatening to ram. He braked, fishtailing just enough to butt out against their trunk. The hit sent the Rover tires wobbling. They couldn't recover in time, and pitched forward into the shallows of one of the pools.

"Nine o'clock!" shouted Henri as he opened fire out the left window.

In the split second of confusion, Fouad glanced back at Henri. He wasn't familiar enough with military terminology to register what his passenger was saying, until Ridley yelled.

"Your left! Go, go!"

The first Rover was roaring straight at their flank. Fouad couldn't peel off because of the pools on either side. Unless he could outgun their pace, it would be a direct T-bone hit.

Fouad floored it.

It was too little, too late.

Henri and Ridley wrapped a hand around their seatbelts just as the Rover smashed into the rear side of their sedan. The Nissan lurched sideways, skidded across the sand, and toppled into a basin of crystal blue water.

The bottom was no deeper than the deep end of a pool, but it was big enough to swallow the Nissan. Water gushed into the vehicle. Clutching the GROT, Ridley pulled herself out of the open passenger window. She checked to see Henri and Fouad both extricating themselves. Then she kicked hard upward, buoyed easily by the liquid's density.

She broke the surface. Salty water poured from her as she stumbled into the shallows to stand, rifle raised. The Rover had stopped by the edge. The occupants were already out and in position, their barrels trained on her.

"Tiago!" she yelled, squinting through the sting of salt water, through the glare of the high sun.

Henri and Fouad sloshed up into the shallows. Henri's Glock rose out of the water, dripping and already trained on the nearest Order member, but the Egyptian had emerged without a gun in hand.

Shit. We're outnumbered.

Tiago stepped forward on the white salt bank. He cradled a bullpup X95 rifle in his arms, aimed straight at Ridley.

"You almost drove right by us," he said, in genuine relief. "Thank God!"

"That's not who's helping you," snapped Henri.

"Well, today, you're helping us, too. Because you must have killed all the men I sent ahead, and you're leaving Siwa, so you must have the Seal."

Ridley could feel it in her pocket. Her pants were now soaked and clinging to her. She realized the outline of the ring must be visible to a keen eye.

"We dug for it and didn't find it, so we figured it must be at Karnak after all," she said. "Nice to cross paths like this, though. And your mercenaries were shit."

The occupants of the second Land Rover, that they'd run off into the pool behind them, came jogging up, weapons raised. Tiago gave them an order in Portuguese. Then he looked back at his enemies with an expression of annoyance.

"You put it in my hand or we kill you and take it from your hands. You're not this stupid, are you?"

Henri glanced at Ridley. He knew that it burned his partner deeply to be beaten like this. First, the Codex. Now, the Seal. Stuck in a pool of water, surrounded by nearly a dozen guns, there was no coming out of this one on top.

She gave her partner a look of acquiescence, and lowered the GROT. Unzipping her pocket, she took out the wad of wet linen wrapped around the iron ring. Tiago's eyes widened, but she didn't budge. This loss felt scalding to her.

"Put it on the ground," he said.

She waded up to the edge and placed it in the dust, then stepped back, too furious to even speak.

Tiago went and picked it up himself. He returned to the Land Rover and placed his bullpup on the hood. He delicately unwrapped the linen, and finally saw the Seal.

For a full thirty seconds, he stared at it, turning the thing over in his hands. João came up to him, equally awestruck, and the two spoke quietly in Portuguese to each other.

When Tiago turned back to his captives, the look on his face bore an almost sublime, transcendent triumph.

"It would raise too many questions if Americans were found dead in Egypt, especially CIA, which I assume you are. It would be a lot better for us if some Americans ended up in an Egyptian jail because they killed one of its citizens in a smuggling trip that went bad."

João stepped up to the water and shot Fouad twice.

CHAPTER
SIXTY-SIX

SIWA, EGYPT

It seemed that no one at the hospital in Siwa spoke English.

Ridley and Henri had arrived in a whirlwind carrying an unconscious Fouad. All three of them were soaked with water and blood. Henri had tried to communicate in French and Ridley had tried Greek, to no avail. At least the wounds on Fouad were obvious, as they acted out a gun firing, then pointed to the bulletholes. The attendants nodded and fired out rapid Arabic calls to each other as they wheeled him off down a hall on a rickety gurney.

Finally, a nurse arrived who spoke some shredded English. His name was Omar, and though it took nearly five minutes to explain that the patient had been shot by someone, they were finally able to relay it.

Within a few minutes, Omar brought back word that Fouad

was receiving a blood transfusion. The bullets had just missed his vital organs. The doctor was sure that he would stabilize within the hour.

Ridley and Henri couldn't stay at the hospital, but they left a thousand US dollars for Fouad's care if Omar would call them with updates at the number they left. Though he was bewildered by these foreigners and deeply suspicious of their behavior, the Egyptian nurse gave his word that he would. He took the money discreetly, and they left before any authority figure could show up with questions.

Their only vehicle was sunk and they were too low on cash to buy a substitute. All they could get was a pair of bus tickets for the overnight trip back to Cairo.

At least by the time they boarded, their clothes had dried into stiff salt cakes. Exhausted, Ridley and Henri passed out on each other's shoulders. Both slept through the night, only awakening when the sun rose over the pyramids like a burning ember.

CAIRO, EGYPT

The bedraggled pair got off the bus into the hot, dry morning. Cairo hadn't slept for thousands of years. The pungent smells of the city wafted past them, donkeys and trash and belching exhaust, all mixed with the scent of baking bread and spiced meat.

It felt like a betrayal to return without Fouad. For Ridley, it felt like this ancient city of millions was missing a piece of life. She and Henri stopped at a mid-level boutique shop that had a section of European clothing. They walked out with a bag each, then took a cab through Tahrir Square to a generic tourist hotel overlooking the Nile. On the way, she grilled their English-fluent driver on how to say, "*May I please speak to...*"

After they checked in, Ridley showered first, scrubbing off the crust of salt that had caked her skin for hours. She washed her thick hair twice to be rid of it all. She didn't even mind the sting of hot water against her cuts and scrapes. She needed the scalding cleanse.

She dressed in a fresh pair of jeans and the long-sleeved navy blouse she'd bought. She tossed a new ivory-colored scarf over her shoulders. It would come in handy to be able to veil herself should they encounter any unwelcome eyes. Then she attached the karambit sheath to the waistband of her new jeans. She slid the blade into it, and arranged the tail of her shirt for concealment. No matter how many guns she had to give up along the way, the karambit stayed.

While Henri showered, she phoned the hospital in Siwa, asking in her new practiced Arabic, "*May I please speak to Omar?*" but the stream of Arabic she got back left her bewildered. She asked a few more times but only got longer, more irritated responses. She hung up in frustration.

Then she made the call she'd been dreading.

When Aisha picked up, Ridley felt an acid wave of anxiety break against her. Then she spoke.

An hour later, she and Henri waited for Aisha in the central courtyard of the Cairo Mall. The floors rose above them in layers of sweeping glass and shiny brass. Shoppers teemed through from every direction.

"Ridley," came a clear, gentle voice through the din.

They turned.

"Aisha," said Ridley.

Henri nearly gaped at the woman coming toward them. With Ridley and Fouad's references to her little ferocity, he had been expecting someone barely over five feet, but he realized that both his partner and the Egyptian were giants. Everyone probably looked small to them. Aisha was no less than five-five, slender, and magnificently self-possessed with a scarf draped over wild brown curls. Henri was nearly dumbstruck by her eyes, though. They were captivating pools of darkness, and very, very canny. *Keen and shrewd.*

Aisha gave Ridley a brisk but heartfelt hug.

"I know, you think—we're in Egypt, surrounded by the most amazing history in the world, and you want to meet in a mall?" she said. "But it's air-conditioned, and I like Starbucks."

"It's your world," said Ridley, raising a deferential hand. "This is my partner, Henri."

He had recovered himself enough to greet her professionally, with the light, brief handshake he'd learned was appropriate for men and women in this country.

"Hi, Henri."

"Hello. I'm so sorry about—"

"I know."

"I'm—" Ridley started awkwardly.

"I'm hungry, too," said Aisha, placing a hand on her arm. "You want a *ta'ameya*? You liked those, didn't you? And I called the hospital. Fouad will be okay. They said the bullet missed his lungs."

Ridley nodded. She had told Aisha the basics over the phone. She'd given her the number of the hospital in Siwa and Omar's name. Still, they had left her brother behind, shot on a job they'd hired him for. She had every righteous reason to be furious with them. Maybe she was, but Aisha only showed her emotions when she was ready to use them.

They picked up some *ta'ameyas* in the food court and found

a table by the fountain, where their voices would be drowned out by the ambient sound of running water. Ridley couldn't touch her pita yet.

"We'll arrange a private ambulance service," she told Aisha. "As soon as he's stable enough to move, we'll get him back to Cairo for the best care."

Aisha regarded her for a moment, the look on her face inscrutable. "You know I understand what my brother does for a job. The whole thing is a risk, and then he adds big, stupid risks to that because danger is actually what keeps him alive. Until one day, it will bite its master. I know why you couldn't stay there."

Anger flared in Ridley...*the sight of Tiago, only yards from her, calmly ordering the execution of Fouad.*

"You know why we couldn't stay?" asked Henri, a bit too sharply as he glanced at his partner in concern.

Aisha took a bite of her pita. "Oh, no, Fouad didn't tell me what you were looking for. Of course you didn't give him the details, but he did tell me why you needed so many weapons. The Raphaels shot him, yes?"

"You know about them?"

Aisha gave a sober nod, in bracing contrast to the cheeky look that had come over her brother when he'd spoken of the Raphaels.

"I know what he knows, but you know Fouad. He sees everything like a game he's playing, but he never seems to care about the set of rules in use."

Maybe that's why we get along...

"It's not the first time he got shot, but it doesn't mean that I'm not going to find these people and take off their skin," said Aisha, wiping some tahini from her mouth. "Tell me, did you get what you were looking for?"

Ridley answered quietly, "Yes, but then they took it from us when they shot Fouad, so...no."

Henri leaned back in his chair, needing a reset. He had been eating his *ta'ameya* in silence, but for the whole conversation he'd been a conflicted mix of beguiled and agitated. Aisha was bewitching to him beyond reason, and it was unsettling him. Yet his frustration over losing the Seal was growing into a beast whose fangs were tipped with fury. He had to steady himself with a prayer for peace.

"Where are you going now?" asked Aisha.

Ridley leaned forward on the table, finally able to start eating her own lunch. "Israel. Our flight leaves this afternoon."

Aisha paused, and looked between them. "Jerusalem?"

Henri spoke up. "Why?"

"Is that where the Raphaels are going, too?"

"Yeah."

"Then Allah save you. That city is about to burn."

CHAPTER
SIXTY-SEVEN

———

THE FLIGHT from Cairo to Tel Aviv took less than two hours. It felt like a day.

Ridley spent the flight in a mood, churning through the tidal peaks and dips of the last twenty-four hours. No matter how impressive their takedown of a mercenary squad had been, no matter how precise their locating of the ancient treasure had been, at the end of the day, it had only culminated in two things: the wounding of Fouad, and failure.

We're just following along with and occasionally helping these radical pieces of shit.

Failing everywhere, but along the way finding out just enough to know how significant the next failure will be.

The thoughts burned.

They're going to help this thing tear apart the most sacred and fragile city in the world. And so far, we're doing no better than tagging along. We need to send this thing back to hell, and the Raphaels with it.

The spiral of thoughts sent her fuming, but by the time they touched down in Israel, she'd dispelled every vapor of such self-condemnation. Every thought turned back to stone resolve. This was the end of the line. This was where they stopped the Order of Raphael.

This was where they stopped the ifrit itself.

Booker came by for them at their seaside hotel late that afternoon.

They had called him from the airport in Cairo, where Henri grimly relayed the incidents of the last few days. The major bullet points were enough at that point. The details would be laid out in person that evening.

So when their boss climbed out of the passenger seat of a black chauffeured sedan to greet them at the hotel door, both Ridley and Henri were gauging his face for any sign of the mood. Doubtless he was unhappy, but he had a long spectrum between "unhappy" and "raging disappointment."

It was the nature of their work. There were almost no clean operations, no routine missions, no ordered plans of action. Osprey ran "investigative dynamic quests," as Booker himself had once put it. There was almost always an X factor, something that didn't behave by the rules of the natural world.

"Director Gadot is ruthless when it comes down to it. He's not an easy man to understand. He can be proud, but in his position...I can't imagine all the factors he has to work with. He's also not a—a *believing man*," Booker told them along the way. "We have to frame all this for him as being about what the *enemy* believes. Trouble's comin' whether this stuff is true or not."

"Does Gadot know about the Order of Raphael?" asked Henri.

"No. Frankly, if we get to the point of them being a factor? Means the sky is falling anyhow. We've got no intel on them that makes them a threat to the Israelis."

"As long as they don't mind me ending Tiago on their territory," muttered Ridley.

They drove the rest of the way north through Tel Aviv in relative silence. The city was a vivid metropolis during the day, but at night the streets began to glitter and pulse with life. Ridley had been there only once on holiday, in her fierce and sleepless youth. The beaches were hot, the food heavenly, and the men and women tanned and beautiful. The place had dazzled her.

Now, she felt like she was passing the circus on her way to the police station. Now, they were carrying the weight of a threat that could split the world.

Their car glided past the lush sprawl of Yarkon Park, through the bright apartment towers of Ramat Aviv, until they finally arrived at the nondescript, industrial-looking headquarters of the Shin Bet.

As the three Americans climbed out of the sedan, they were met at the entrance by a woman wearing gray pinstriped pants and a black turtleneck. It was office-professional, but since she'd pushed the sleeves up her forearms, it gave the impression that she wasn't all too comfortable with it.

"Director Douglas," said the woman, extending her hand. "I'm Agent Nakav."

Booker shook her hand. "Good evening. Thanks for meeting us here. My operatives, Ridley Samaras and Henri Michel."

Nakav shook their hands in turn. Her tumbling dark hair

rivaled Ridley's for thickness. She looked to be in her forties, and everything about her was sharp and aquiline.

"I hope you had no trouble at the airport."

For the first time on the entire operation, Ridley and Henri had traveled with a diplomatic pass-through. It provided streamlined relief.

"No trouble," said Henri.

"Well, Director Gadot is waiting," said Nakav, and she led them into the building.

Despite the escort of the Shin Bet agent, they all had to show identification to pass through security. Ridley had gone without the karambit for this outing.

They headed up a few floors on the elevator, down an austere hallway, and finally, to a conference room. Nakav requested their cell phones, which she placed in a secure Faraday locker. No electrical signals could penetrate it.

As they stepped into the conference room, Ridley and Henri exchanged a glance of bracing solidarity.

On the far side of the table sat a woman in her sixties, so thin that the blazer she was wearing hung off her shoulders like they were a coat hanger. Her hair was short and spiky white, her face inscrutably drawn.

Sitting at the head of the table was a man in his late fifties. He had salt-and-pepper hair that looked windswept, and a square, weathered face that could have belonged to a French movie star of the 60s. He wore a suit but no tie, a silken scarf wrapped in a twist around his collar.

They both stood to greet their American counterparts.

"Avi," said Booker with a broad smile, shaking the hand of the director.

"This is Director Avi Gadot," said Nakav, making the formal introductions. "Director Booker Douglas, from the CIA's National Clandestine Service."

"It's not 'Director,' please. I'll be happy if you call me Booker."

"Is that for Booker T. Washington?" asked Director Gadot.

"Yeah! Yeah, it is. First time someone from a foreign country has ever noticed that."

Nakav went on diplomatically. "These are agents Ridley Samaras and Henri Michel. Please meet the Director of Arab Affairs, Yael Goldwirth."

The bleak-looking woman shook their hands. Even with a smile, her face barely lost its severity. "Pleasure," she said.

"Please sit, everyone," said Director Gadot, motioning as they took their seats.

Nakav went to sit beside Goldwirth, across from the Americans.

Ridley reached immediately for the water bottle in front of her and began chugging it.

"Sir," said Henri, "I don't understand. I don't want to be rude, but is this really a matter of Arab Affairs?"

Gadot raised his brows but allowed Booker to take it.

"We've done preliminary briefings already. The last known hostile you encountered was Syrian. Despite his age, doesn't matter if he's Palestinian or not, he's gonna be seen by Israelis *and* Arabs alike as Arab."

"You've only just come in through Tel Aviv. You haven't been to Jerusalem yet," said Goldwirth, her voice calm and dispassionate. "It's combustible right now."

Gadot leaned forward. "Booker says the threat is to the Temple Mount. The day of Passover."

Ridley nodded.

"That's right," said Henri.

"It's not the first time for the Temple Mount. Have you ever heard of the Jewish Underground?"

"No," said Ridley, thinking that it sounded like a terrible name for a band.

"Terrorists. They were around in the early eighties. Completely fanatical and violent as any of the PLO. Thank God there were so few of them. They planted bombs on Arab buses, but they were a bit stupid, and eventually were caught.

"It was then that we found this little plan—these bus bombs we know so well in Israel that leave our streets littered with brain and blood and bones—those weren't their real objective. They had planned to blow up the Dome of the Rock."

Ridley gave a polite grimace as his eyes fixed on her. He was a very good storyteller, his voice drawing them in like this was some ghastly bedtime fairytale.

"It was not an idea. It was a plan. They had detailed locations for each set of explosives, and had even calculated the weight of the materials they would need. It was the luckiest the Shin Bet have ever been. We had no idea of it before we caught them planting bus bombs. You can imagine, no? If Jews had blown up the Dome of the Rock...it would be total war. Not between Israel and the Palestinians—no. Not just between Israel and the Arab states," he said, shaking his head, then his voice quieted, "but every Islamic state in the world would rise up against every Jew they could find, to the ends of the earth."

Booker had leaned back in his chair, fingers curled against his mouth. "What did they want?"

Gadot chuckled darkly. "Villains like in the movies. Stupid and wicked. They wanted to bring about the War of Armageddon! If I remember that kind of nonsense...bring the Messiah who would create a Jewish kingdom and build a Third Temple and whatever else."

This got a mocking half-smile from Goldwirth across the table.

"Isn't that always so?" said Gadot, then looked more seriously between Ridley and Henri. "Is that so with your threat?"

There's no such thing as a friendly foreign intelligence agency.

Ridley always remembered this. There were more allied agencies, ones more trustworthy and those less so, but the ultimate interest was selfish, as it would always and should always be. A country should always prioritize the interest and well-being of its own people.

"That's what they believe," said Ridley, "and if this individual reaches the Temple Mount, they're going to unleash hell."

"Individual? You believe it's only one?" asked Goldwirth.

"From our experience," said Henri, "they deploy one at a time, like...a tag-team."

Director Gadot uncapped his water bottle and began to pour into the cup in front of him.

"Well, I'm sure you must know, but the Israeli government —" he said, sitting back and taking a small sip, "does not govern the Temple Mount."

CHAPTER
SIXTY-EIGHT

"WHAT DO YOU MEAN," said Ridley. "You don't control it?"

"Agent Samaras, we don't *govern* it. Do you know anything about our affairs here?"

There was the sharpness of Gadot. She should have done more homework on this. Israeli politics were labyrinthine on their own. Mix in the Arab relations and it could take years to fully understand.

"We've made concessions for peace, again and again and again," he said. "One of them was giving up control of *our own* holy site. The Temple Mount. Jordan has had dominion there since '67. They appoint members of the Jerusalem Islamic Waqf, who also have oversight of the Al-Aqsa Mosque. But everything religious is under the direction of the Grand Mufti of Jerusalem. And *he* is Palestinian government."

The tangles...

"But the IDF has gone into the Temple Mount before," said Booker.

His brow darkened. "I've been there. Ariel Sharon decided to visit the Mount in 2000. There were hundreds of police and Shabak and Special Forces undercover, Border Guard, his own security team...but the Palestinians were almost choking on their rage. It became a riot. We were overwhelmed. We barely got Sharon out of there alive. They were thirsty for the blood of Jews. The intifada began.

"We thought the Muslim clerics would help us calm the crowds, but instead they made a call to take up arms. Young Palestinian men climbed up onto the edge of the Temple Mount and started throwing rocks down on the Jews who prayed at the Western Wall. So police and Border Guard agents had to go in to put down the mob. Dozens of ours were wounded. Dozens of them died."

He rubbed his forehead once, as if wiping away the memory of that brutal showdown.

"I don't command the IDF, the police, or the Border Guard. I'm only the director of the Shin Bet. All I can do is give them the intelligence and make my most urgent recommendation."

The Shin Bet, or Shabak, was the nickname of the Israel Security Agency. The Mossad was one of the most famous intelligence agencies in the world, akin to the CIA, while the Shin Bet was more similar to the FBI. Like any organization that dealt regularly with terrorism, they had a storied history of both breathless success and brutal violations. They had been vital in dismantling the masterminds behind the plague of suicide bombings. They gathered the intel and created operational files for the Special Forces to act on.

Director Avi Gadot was one of the most powerful men in a country that lived on edge, under the threat of attack at all times. The valley of the shadow of death could be found here. Despite their significant world presence, their Western democratic values, their technological triumphs and military excellence, the people of Israel lived in danger every day. The decisions that the director made could quickly tip a crisis into a full-blown catastrophe.

"Do you know how many threats we see every week? Booker, look, Passover is in two days," he said. "Our prime minister is trying to talk to the PLO for the first time in over twenty years. We can't afford to shut down the Temple Mount for something this vague."

"It's not vague," said Henri, insistent. "We've been tracking him across Europe for the last week."

"Do you have communication intercepts? Any digital trail? Dossiers?"

"I have some dead bodies and a budding scar myself," said Ridley.

Booker cleared his throat and sat forward. "This is a low-key terrorist operation. They've left almost no digital trail. But my people have interacted with this suspect *personally* over the last week, and his associates. Look, I understand, we're in your territory. What can we do?"

Gadot exchanged a look with Goldwirth, who spoke next.

"Our government doesn't control the grounds of the Temple Mount itself, but we do control access to it. There's a balance. If our forces are thought to be too restrictive, the Islamic worshippers will revolt. If they attack our forces and are beaten back, those images will fill broadcasts around the world. You know how it is, to see only the second half of a fight that's been provoked."

"It would bury Prime Minister Shalmi's olive branch," added Gadot.

"We don't need a mass crowd kept out," said Ridley, unable

to stop herself from jumping ahead of Booker. "It's not a bunch of rioters trying to get in. It's just one person. Probably."

"You gave us a photo. Isn't he Syrian?" asked Goldwirth in a calmly withering tone.

"We believe so."

"Where did you last have contact with him?"

She hesitated for a second. "Portugal."

"Syria to Portugal...to Israel."

"He was trying to find something that he believes is going to create chaos on the Temple Mount."

"Did he find the something?"

"Yes."

Ridley couldn't see Booker squirm, but she felt the accusatory writhing of failure in her own gut.

Goldwirth and Gadot knew the answers to these things already. Booker had briefed them in advance, or they wouldn't even be sitting in this room.

"There's no intel on the method," said Gadot.

Booker leaned back in. "It's variable. The French combed every inch of Saint-Chapelle, and they still haven't figured out how the attacker did it. But that's the damage we're talking about. That's chaos."

"That attacker is in French custody," said Gadot.

"He also says he has no memory of the attack, but it looks like when he was caught, the mission was handed off to someone else, to go create chaos somewhere else."

"And you say that was London. The royal attack."

"You know what happened to the radicals who tried to blow up the Dome of the Rock those years ago?" said Gadot. "The Knesset released them all."

His face hardened. He looked at Goldwirth and Nakav.

"You're sure that this attack won't happen *before* Passover?" he asked.

"Ninety-nine percent," said Ridley. "He believes he's following some ancient command."

"And you think this has nothing to do with Islam?" asked Goldwirth.

"Their beliefs are—" Henri started, "they're complicated. They overlap historical teachings of the three major religions."

"It won't matter," said Goldwirth, exchanging a glance with Gadot. "Violence on the Temple Mount means Jews will be blamed."

Gadot must have been satisfied enough to make his first move.

"This goes to the Commissioner. They guard the access points, and they have the units that can go undercover as Arabs. Bar-Lev is like your Teddy Roosevelt. He speaks softly and carries a big stick. He also hits very hard with it."

David Bar-Lev was the Commissioner of the Israel Police, a national force with highly specialized counterterrorism units. He answered directly to the Ministry of Public Security. Unlike the United States, the collaboration between the Shin Bet and the police was regular and fluid.

Director Gadot stood, prompting the others to do the same. Since he'd made up his mind, there was no point in wasting more valuable time at the table.

"This is the first time in my career that Americans have come to the Shin Bet instead of the Mossad," he said, reaching to shake Booker's hand. "We won't forget. Agent Nakav will be available to you, whatever you need here."

In other words, she'll be keeping an eye on us.

"We need to be in on the operation," said Ridley with sudden force. "We need to be on the ground."

Gadot and Goldwirth both stared as if she'd asked for a seat on the supreme court.

"No," said the director.

"You'll want to reconsider that." Booker's great voice rang with both authority and assurance. "You know the threats to your nation every day, every week, every year, but our country knows darkness, too, and I'm telling you, this threat is unique. You can't have a more valuable asset on the ground than these two. You can attach them to a Shin Bet agent, to an IDF unit, armed or unarmed, whatever. But you're gonna want their eyes and expertise with this particular enemy."

It was clear that Gadot respected his American counterpart, but he was a tough read otherwise.

"I'll talk to Bar-Lev. Meanwhile, Nakav knows the best places for food in the city. Tell her if you need anything."

No more persuading. The meeting was adjourned.

As the Americans collected their phones from the Faraday locker, Ridley murmured under her breath to Henri.

FRENCH: *"Do you think the Order is in Jerusalem already?"*

FRENCH: *"Maybe. They have no reason to be in Tel Aviv,"* he replied.

FRENCH: *"They have the Seal. If they find this boy before Passover, they could force the jinn to act,"* she said.

Henri looked at her. He felt Nakav glancing at them, clearly not pleased that they were speaking a foreign language, obfuscating her friendly surveillance.

FRENCH: *"You think of the worst things,"* he said. *"You really make a good spy."*

She rubbed her thigh where the ifrit had slashed her. It still ached from when it had re-opened during her scuffle at the Temple of Siwa.

Nakav interjected with a polite smile. "I've called the car for you. Would you like to go somewhere for dinner? Back to the hotel?"

Booker looked at his operatives, then at the Shin Bet officer.

"Agent Nakav, I'd really appreciate your help, if you could point us to the best archaeologist in Jerusalem."

If it was a surprising request, Nakav didn't let on. "I know the one. And you might be delighted to know, she's also American."

CHAPTER
SIXTY-NINE

BOOKER WENT BACK to the hotel with Ridley and Henri. He'd been staying two floors above them. Since they'd called him from Cairo, he'd been setting up their meetings with the Israeli officials.

"You both look like something the dog pulled from a gutter," he said as they stepped onto the elevator. "Take a bath, get some room service. If I call you later and I'm not waking you up from a Rip van Winkle sleep, you're demoted."

They were admittedly a bit delirious with fatigue. The urgent intensity of their meeting with the Shin Bet, on top of the adrenaline whirlwind of the last week, had sapped them.

Agent Nakav had gotten in contact with the American archaeologist. Thankfully, the woman happened to be in

Jerusalem that day, not out in the country on a dig. She would meet with them late tomorrow morning.

When Ridley got back to her own room, she trudged straight to the bed and collapsed face first. She'd intended to order a steaming hot dinner to her room and study a map of the ancient web of streets surrounding the Temple Mount.

Instead, she sank into sleep, enveloped peacefully by the plush blanket.

Hours later, an urgent jingle woke her. She fumbled for her phone in the darkness.

"Hello," she mumbled.

"Doing your assignment to the letter, Rid. I'm so proud of you," came Booker's voice. "We're meeting with Bar-Lev and Gadot at IDF headquarters tomorrow. It's only across town. Conway will be joining us. He's up to speed. Seven a.m. Look fresh, be fresh."

"Yes, sir."

He hung up. She set an alarm for five a.m.

When she woke again, dawn was seeping over the horizon. Ridley did an improvised bodyweight workout in her room. She thought it would energize her for the day, but she hadn't even realized the accumulated beating that her body had taken over the last week.

This is nothing after BUDs. The best are sharp, strong, ready for anything. Embrace the grind or you won't be any better than the others.

Afterward, she showered, dressed, and got down to the lobby with more than an hour to spare. Henri found her at six o'clock at a table in the corner. In front of her was a coffee and a plate piled with yogurt, olives, hummus, pita, and an omelet. But instead of eating it, she was huddling over a map of Jerusalem.

She looked up as he arrived.

"You must be in a fantasy," she said, gesturing to the buffet lining two entire walls of the dining room. "But hurry up, you're late."

He wasn't, but Ridley was the player who went to basketball practice an hour early just to work on her free throws.

Henri lined up for food, but quickly found himself bowled over by the Israeli etiquette. There wasn't any, just as there weren't any real lines. It was just a shapeless, sharp-elbowed free-for-all. He felt deeply uncomfortable pushing through a crowd of retirees, but he would go hungry that morning if he didn't.

He fought to finally get two plates piled up with almost every type of food in sight, then slid into the chair across from Ridley.

"You know how Tiago is fucked up?" she said.

He snorted into his fruit juice, but nodded. "Yeah."

"And he wants to destroy all the 'fake religions' that don't believe what the Order of Raphael preaches? Look," she said, pointing to the map, where she'd drawn an uneven triangle.

On one end was the Al-Aqsa Mosque on the Temple Mount. Just beneath it bordered the Western Wall. On the farthest of the triangle she'd marked the Church of the Holy Sepulchre.

"That's about five hundred meters," she told him.

Henri met her eyes. There was a piercing gleam to them, and he realized what she was showing him.

"If the ifrit releases the jinn kings, these Watchers, *from* the Temple Mount...and Tiago has the Seal to command them—" he started.

"What do you think he'll command them to do?" she finished.

Henri looked stricken. He leaned back and took a robotic bite of pastry. "Oh, shit."

She'd never heard him swear before.

"How did we not see this before?" he wondered aloud.

She threw up her hands. "The magic of maps."

"We thought he just wanted general chaos and power..."

"Passover. Easter or Palm Sunday, whichever one it is. Ramadan. What more chaos could you create than destroying three of the most holy places in the world, of the three biggest religions, in the most holy city on earth, on their holiest holidays?!"

Ridley realized she'd gotten loud, and quickly brought her voice down.

"But I've been sitting here trying to figure out how we can secure these places, and...we can't."

"The only security is getting the Seal," said Henri.

"But the ifrit is step one. The Seal doesn't even matter if he can't release the jinn kings to begin with."

Henri leaned forward, with a rebel glint in his fox-like eyes that she'd never seen before. "The Shin Bet and the IDF carry a watch list every day. They've got the Syrian kid's picture. No doubt he's made that list."

"Okay, we gotta go," said Ridley, checking her watch. "Can you please Hoover your plate? *Plates?*"

"I'll finish two before you finish one."

It was a losing bet, but at least it would make her fuel up sufficiently for the day. Make anything a competition.

By the time he glanced up, she was wolfing down the last of an omelet.

. . .

Booker had skipped breakfast for a bout with his distressed intestines, but he met them in the lobby with a coffee in hand. They hurriedly told him their new theory. He was appropriately stunned, and appropriately grave. Henri went fairly quiet after that, his mind swirling with the looming devastation. Ridley was so ready for action that she was nearly twitching.

Agent Nakav picked them up with that graciously impersonal smile and drove them across the city to the Camp Rabin military base. She flashed ID to pass through, and a moment later pulled up to a square high-rise building, the Matcal Tower.

There they were ushered to a conference table in what looked more like a war room than a conference room. There was a wall of digital screens, and water bottles set out at every place beside individual dossiers.

Just behind them walked in Ben Conway, Deputy Director of the National Clandestine Service at the CIA. He was Booker's boss, someone that Ridley and Henri had only interacted with a handful of times.

Conway was a big man, just outsizing Booker himself in height and shoulder width. He was a former Marine who still carried himself like one despite a bad back. He sported a thick beard, salt-and-pepper hair, and a sonorous voice.

"How was your flight?" asked Booker, giving him a hearty handshake.

"Overflowing with concerns," he said, "but that's why I'm here."

That moment, they were joined by Director Gadot, Director Goldwirth, and a trim, grizzled man in his fifties who looked like he'd been formed by hard clay and bar brawls. He wore a uniform of the IDF and an expression of grim focus. He introduced himself as Commander David Bar-Lev. He was accompanied by an assistant, a gangly but attentive young man.

Bar-Lev was intent on hearing everything the Americans had to say, so they went through their intel again. He'd gotten a brief overview from Gadot the night before, but now he dug into the business with sharp, urgent questions. The assistant took notes on seemingly every word. Henri pressed the matter of the Passover timing.

Then Ridley spoke up.

"We analyzed the data we've gathered with some of the statements made by one of the suspects, and we believe the chaos they want to create on the Temple Mount is a diversionary tactic. Or a prelude. There are three actual targets: the Al-Aqsa Mosque, the Church of the Holy Sepulchre, and the Western Wall."

Gadot's jaw went slack, but a look of fury sparked in his gaze. To think they'd withheld this from him in their meeting the day before. Goldwirth's eyebrows climbed at least an inch, and the assistant's pen froze. Deputy Director Conway actually leaned forward to get a better view of Ridley saying this. It was only Bar-Lev whose expression did not change.

"With individual actors or explosives?"

She hesitated. *A giant malevolent genie?*

"We don't know."

"The Western Wall, on Passover," said Gadot.

Booker spoke, "We realize there will be a lot of worshippers there tomorrow."

"*Birkat hacohanim*," said Bar-Lev, his voice quiet. "It begins in the morning. Tens of thousands of people in the plaza. It already takes more than two thousand officers to secure the area. The Church of the Holy Sepulchre will have thousands of Christians for mass. Muslims from all over the world will be at Al-Aqsa for Ramadan."

It was in line with what they'd imagined, but sounded worse when he laid it out.

"The CIA stands with this assessment?" he asked, looking directly at Conway.

Conway had always been fair, but in all the years Booker had worked in the NCS, he'd never known the man to place a firm foot where the ground was still unknown. Ridley's heart nearly caught in her throat for the agonizing seconds it took him to respond.

"Given what's happened in Paris and London in the past two weeks," he replied, "and given the nature of the potential consequences here, we consider this a threat of the highest order."

She exhaled. Bar-Lev gave a curt nod.

Henri spoke up. "We gave you a photo of the suspect who's heading to the Temple Mount to trigger the attack, but—uh—we have another suspect. He's a Portuguese named Tiago Inacio. He's going to command the attack on the places of worship."

CHAPTER
SEVENTY

WHILE BOOKER and Director Conway stayed behind to coordinate with the Israelis, Ridley and Henri had an appointment to keep.

As they walked with Agent Nakav to a gray Mercedes-Benz sedan, Ridley's phone buzzed. She pulled it out to see a text from Aisha.

He's home. He'll be okay.

Ridley nudged Henri and showed him the message. He breathed out a little puff of relief and lifted his eyes to the sky.

Nakav drove them the hour to Jerusalem, a cagey but cheerful tour guide through the countryside. Her grandparents had made *aliyah*, escaping the pogroms that threatened their lives in Russia to move to the land of their ancestors. The gratitude that exuded from their granddaughter was almost tangible. She recounted the time that Jews had been murdered in nearly every Arab nation after the outburst of rage following the reestablishment of their nation.

"There's only one place that's safe for Jews in the whole world," she said, then added dryly "where we only have to worry about stabbing attacks, café bombings, and rockets raining down on us from Gaza."

Like all young citizens, Margalit Nakav had served in the IDF, eventually becoming a combatives instructor. When her service was up, she doggedly pursued a career in the Shin Bet. They were extremely selective but she was determined to prove her worth. After receiving a dozen rejections, they finally afforded her a chance. She excelled, a masterful reader of body language, so much so that they took to calling her *chozeh*. The seer.

"So why take you out of the field to be our escort?" asked Ridley.

Nakav glanced at her, and of course.

She's reading us.

"I know Israelis. I know Arabs. I know this city and all its rhythms and violence and acts of worship. You'll be happy to have me, I promise you."

She grinned. Frank but not completely honest. Ridley couldn't help but like her. They all had jobs to do, and they each served their own country's interests. For today and tomorrow at least, they aligned.

Henri was fairly quiet in the back seat. His face, though it could split into that broad, contagious smile, could also turn to granite when he withdrew into thought.

In that moment, no one could have known the Bible verses that were slipping through his mind.

As they finally arrived in Jerusalem, Ridley felt a surge of something she'd never experienced before. It rattled her. As politically embattled as this city was in the modern world, it was *the* city of ancient cities, the epicenter of faith for billions. There was no other like it in history.

The sidewalks teemed with people. Traffic clogged the roads. Within the crowds mingled yarmulkes and baseball caps, prayer shawls and headscarves. On nearly every corner were pairs of soldiers, wearing full combat protection and carrying M4s.

"Have you been here before?" asked Nakav after they'd passed through a checkpoint.

"To Tel Aviv, once," said Ridley. "Not Jerusalem. Henri?"

She eyed her partner in the backseat, hoping to pull him out of his reverie.

"Oh, here? No. It's...it's overwhelming."

"There's no place like it in the world. You'll have to come back," Nakav told him. "If we're all still standing after tomorrow!"

A few minutes later, they pulled onto Salah Ad-din, a dingy street lined with tiny shops, whose awnings were lined with Arabic and English. No Hebrew in sight. Across the road from a drab pizza parlor stood what looked like a squat Italian villa. It was set back behind an iron fence, but the entry gate was wide open. Across the top of it was printed in bold white letters:

W.F. ALBRIGHT INSTITUTE OF ARCHAEOLOGICAL RESEARCH

Nakav pulled in.

The institute was small, though there were plenty of people milling about, talking animatedly, studying in corners surrounded by books.

Agent Nakav knew where she was going, and a moment later, was knocking on a half-open office door. A placard outside read, EMILY AUSTIN.

The door swung open. On the other side stood a woman in

her forties, with copper-blonde hair and a spatter of freckles across her cherubic face. She flashed a broad smile.

"Hello again!" she exclaimed.

"Hello again." Nakav greeted her with a kiss on the cheek. "Emily Austin, meet my pond-hopping friends-for-a-day."

She looked at Ridley and Henri with an open expression of delight. "Americans? What do you say we go for a drive?"

Before they could respond to the abrupt suggestion, she'd grabbed a hat and a pair of sunglasses from her desk. And they were off.

Introductions were made as they climbed into the Mercedes. As they drove, Emily directed Nakav south through the Muslim Quarter.

"Margalit told me you'd like to know about the Temple Mount? Archaeologically speaking." She twisted around in the front seat to talk to them.

"Yes, please," said Henri. "In short, if you could."

"No such thing as a short history when you ask an archaeologist," Emily laughed, "especially when it comes to the most contested thirty-five acres in the world."

She was clearly excited by her work, but Ridley was struggling to keep her thoughts on the topic of history.

Where is Tiago this minute? Who is the Order calling on for their expertise? They must be here, now, in this city.

She forced herself to concentrate as the American archaeologist launched into her lesson. Over the next ten minutes, Emily Austin laid out the tumultuous and tragic tale of millennia.

According to Jewish history, the site of the Temple Mount was the place where God commanded Abraham to sacrifice his son Isaac in an act of devotion. It was later the grounds on which King Solomon built the First Temple to the Lord, made of gold and cedarwood.

When the Babylonians tore it down hundreds of years later, it was rebuilt by King Herod as the Second Temple. That was later demolished when the Romans sacked Jerusalem in a savage display of dominance.

For Muslims, it was a holy site not only for Abraham, whom they regarded as a prophet, but because they believed it to be where Muhammad ascended to heaven. Their legends told that he had been transported from Mecca to Jerusalem in the same night by a mythical winged creature. When he landed on the Dome of the Rock, he was escorted to heaven by the angel Gabriel.

"It's the MVP of land on earth," muttered Ridley as they headed into a valley.

"You are so right about that," said Emily, then pointed for Nakav. "Would you turn in here?"

They parked and climbed out of the car. A short distance away, a small dig site was set up. There were nearly a dozen people working on it, some kneeling in the dirt, some sifting through bags of soil with meticulous care.

"We're in the Kidron Valley," said Emily, moving buoyantly as if she was about to give the lecture of her life. "Over there, the Mount of Olives."

They looked to the east.

"And up there, other side, that's the Temple Mount."

Ridley and Henri looked up the steep hill beside them, stepped with walls. They could see the thick stone perimeter around the top.

"Okay," said Ridley. "Not the best view of the place."

"Sorry, Ms. Austin, but we—" Henri started.

"Oh God, please just call me Emily."

"—we have some questions. It's why we came to you."

"You want to know what we're doing here with this awful

view?" she asked, then gestured to the little archaeological tent nearby.

"The Islamic Waqf—they run the place—did a little grounds work back in the nineties. First they decided to make Solomon's Stables—this incredible vaulted underground place next to the mosque—into a prayer hall. So they added electrical wiring and tiled the floors. It was *very* likely where the Templars kept their horses when they ruled Jerusalem, instead of Solomon."

Ridley and Henri exchanged a wondering glance.

"But three years after that prayer hall construction," continued Emily, "the Waqf decided to make an 'emergency exit.' Except they actually turned it into a massive entrance. And you know how they dug into the earth to excavate? *Bulldozers.*"

She spit the word from her mouth as if it was poison. Propping her hands on her hips, she gazed up at the Mount looming over them.

"Fucking bulldozers. That was precious earth—*invaluable.* It should have been gone through with a toothbrush. I don't think they were incompetent, either. I think they *wanted* to destroy any evidence of pre-Islamic history there. I mean, the Grand Mufti himself says the site has never once belonged to the Jews and that any records of the temple are fake."

She snorted in derision. Nakav's expression had gone dark as she squinted upward.

"Anyhow, we're standing here because I wanted to show you where archaeologists have to go to find the literal *tons* of earth that they dumped. Right here. Into the nearest 'ditch' they could find. God, it makes me mad."

Ridley looked at the little dig site. There seemed to be absolutely nothing there.

"Have they found anything?" she asked.

"Coins. Pottery. Some shards of ancient glass. You can tell it's not from a beer bottle because of the bubble formation, you know?"

"Has anyone ever dug under the Temple Mount to excavate it for real?" asked Henri.

Emily screwed up her face. "A tiny bit in the early forties, by the British. It was mostly survey work done of the cisterns and tunnels nearby, though. The Waqf sees everything as a desecration, and since they're not going to be giving the land back to Israel *ever*, that's pretty much it...a goddamn gold mine of history and heritage sitting right there! I mean...that's where the *Ark of the Covenant* sat. Allegedly."

It was tale of woe and grievance all around.

"On the Temple Mount, what's holier," asked Ridley, "the Al-Aqsa Mosque or the Dome of the Rock?"

"Well, the mosque is—I mean, it's a *mosque*. Outside of Mecca and Medina, it's the most sacred in the world. The Dome of the Rock is a shrine, so it really just houses a massive slab of rock called the Foundation Stone. Muslims think it's where Muhammad was taken for a divine ride. Jews—and Muslims—and actually Christians—think it's also where Abraham was going to sacrifice Isaac."

Something sparked in Henri's face. "Is there anything under the Foundation Stone?"

"You can go under it, yeah," she nodded. "People go into this little cavern to pray. It's just for Muslims, though, so...you can't. Unless you are...?"

He shook his head.

They had never wanted to open up this line of questioning with Nakav present, but as she had become their "minder" for all purposes, there was no way to shake her, to have this conversation in private without arousing intense suspicion.

Here goes. The Shin Bet are about to think we're crazy.

"Emily," said Ridley, pulling the woman back to focus, "have you ever heard of the seven kings of the jinn?

"Um, I've heard of jinn, sure. Mythology stuff."

Henri took a step closer. "Have you ever heard of the Watchers?"

"Were those the fallen angels, from the Book of Enoch?"

"They say God threw them into the earth, bound them in darkness until the end of time."

"Yeah, I'm a little familiar. We do study *some* ancient texts, have to know context and all for these ancient civilizations if we want to really *understand* them."

Ridley looked around the narrow, rocky valley. "If someone believed those things were imprisoned on the Temple Mount, and that they needed to be set free...where would they go?"

For the first time, Emily's face went still. She glanced at Nakav, as if realizing suddenly that the presence of a Shin Bet agent should have indicated this wasn't some exploratory academic visit.

"Well..." she started, as though suddenly venturing onto a spidering ice floe, "I know about the Temple Mount. I entirely believe—I mean I *know*—that it was the site of the First Temple. I can't say if Abraham really took his son there to sacrifice him or if Muhammad really spent his final moments there. I've never heard of any association with the jinn, though."

Nakav was reading her hesitation. She was also watching the Americans with intense focus. This was not a matter that had entered the briefing. It was getting religious now, which meant that it was only getting more hazardous.

"What if they were the same thing as the Watchers?" pressed Henri. "Have you heard of that linkage?"

"We're not gonna quote you in an academic journal," said Ridley, getting annoyed with Emily's reluctance to speak, when clearly there was something going on behind the woman's eyes. "We're just exploring ideas and ancient legends."

She doesn't want to say anything crazy because Nakav is here.

Emily propped her hands on her hips again. "I read one thing, once, when I was just starting in the field, but it was such an obscure and unreliable text that I just thought it was *weird* and moved on. Mostly religious myths, nothing concrete, nothing physical for me to go after."

"So...?" prompted Ridley.

"It said that fallen angels were chained in darkness beneath the great stone," she said. "The Foundation Stone. The Dome of the Rock."

Henri nodded as though his worst fears were confirmed. Ridley blew out her cheeks, glancing up with dread at the walls above them.

There it is. The only place worse than that would be inside the Al-Aqsa Mosque itself.

"Great, thanks," she said to Emily. "We came to the right archaeologist."

Ridley flashed a bland smile at Nakav, whose eyes were inscrutable. Now the Israeli agent knew what they were really looking for, and where they would have to go.

CHAPTER
SEVENTY-ONE

"THE DOME OF THE ROCK?!" exclaimed Booker over the phone. "Why couldn't it have been the Gaza Strip, somewhere less provocative than that?"

Ridley had left the restaurant table she'd been eating at with Henri and Nakav to make the call. She was now standing in the empty bathroom, the only place she wouldn't be overheard. It wasn't that the Shin Bet agent was untrustworthy, but Ridley had been burned on this mission already by overtrusting.

"Pro:" she said, "the place will be so crowded with foreign visitors because of Ramadan that it'll be easier to infiltrate. Con: the place will be so crowded with foreign visitors during Ramadan that it will be fucking *hard* to find this boy. Or whoever the ifrit has gotten its claws into now."

"There's a debate on," Booker told her, his voice growing softer, more deliberative. "Because this threat is against the Muslims, the Jews, and the Christians. Gadot wants to call an emergency summit, confidential, with the three faith leaders of the city. If they can understand it's against them all, maybe there's some hope they can keep their own people from going after the others for revenge. He's in the 'talk to your enemies' camp. It's the only way he believes Shabak can keep a lid on things.

"Bar-Lev is *not* that guy, though. He doesn't trust the Grand Mufti to not weaponize this. If they give him a forewarning, he'll try to leverage it, spark another intifada. It would be the perfect excuse."

Ridley paced the tile. "What do you think, *jefe*?"

"I'm with Bar-Lev. Don't open this thing up. It's a need-to-know basis. We all just do our jobs."

"What about Conway?"

"He's a hard-ass, but he's also trying to be a diplomat. He's hesitant, but I think he'll come down with Gadot and try to make it a collaborative effort."

"The complications..."

"You don't have to tell me," he said. "We're meeting in an hour to duke it out. But in two hours, you need to be at King Saul Boulevard. Nakav's under orders to get you both here. We're working with the best of the best on this, and I'm demanding you and Henri be embedded. You're the only ones who understand this thing." Then he grumbled, "Unprecedented, yeah, but I'll fight like a honey badger in a beehive. A unique threat takes unique tactics."

"Anything else we need to know going into this?" she asked.

"Not that you struggle with this," he said dryly, "but be blunt. They don't offer here, especially not to outsiders. If you have to ask, you have to know *who* to ask. Don't push outside your rank, but don't get pushed around. I'll have your back."

She sighed. "I'll do my best, Mr. Douglas."

Two hours later, Ridley and Henri walked with Agent Nakav into a completely unremarkable office building on King Saul Boulevard.

She led them to a small conference room on the second floor. The sconce lighting was low, with gray carpeting, black tabletops, and a bay of computer screens along the far wall. There was a tech setting up at the desk who studiously ignored them.

At the bigger table, a man in his late thirties leaned back in an office chair. He was tapping his fingers on a thin folder in front of him. He wore a rumpled button-up that revealed taut forearms. Unlike any other military official they'd seen, he had a short, scruffy beard. With his dark and curling hair, he looked more Arab than Jewish.

He looked up when Ridley and Henri stepped in, but before they could acknowledge each other, Booker, Bar-Lev, and Gadot appeared behind them.

"Said," said the Israeli, sweeping past them to the head of the table, "meet the CIA. Booker. Ridley. Henri."

He gestured to the Americans, with no need to add last names.

"And you know Director Gadot, Agent Nakav. This is Master Sergeant Said Atashi. He's Ya'mas."

The dark-haired man stood up and leaned across the table to shake each of their hands. His smile was surprisingly infectious.

Ya'mas. They were *mista'aravim*, which roughly meant, "those who live among the Arabs." They were the primary

402

undercover unit of the Border Guard, a faction of the Israeli National Police. Their job was to masquerade as Arabs, to sink into the whirlpool of rage that made up certain Palestinian neighborhoods, in order to take out the masterminds and moneymen who directed terrorist attacks on the nation of Israel. They were the lightning squad, men of guile, wits, and astonishing courage. There was no more decorated squad in the country during the intifada than this scruffy, multiethnic band of operators.

Everyone took their seats, and so began *another* briefing. It was clear that Said Atashi already had a full grasp on all the intelligence they'd provided. Bar-Lev was not there to run the operational planning, but to support whatever the Ya'mas needed to execute their plan.

Booker asked the technician to pull up the photo of Tiago Inacio onscreen.

"The Portuguese is certain. He'll be there. The other suspect—"

The tech flipped to the photo Henri had snapped of Mustafa Dali in the Tomar castle.

"—probable, but there's a real chance the mission may have passed to another."

"And you believe it's not a suicide bomber," said Atashi.

Henri spoke with assurance. "He's not there to blow himself up. He believes he's there to smash open the Dome of the Rock, that there's some ancient power inside of it."

The master sergeant glanced at Agent Nakav. "That's different."

"The thing we know he'll be carrying—he *has* to have," Ridley said, "is an engraved golden saber. Whatever else he has on him, we can't say."

"No one can get into the grounds with a weapon," said Atashi. "*Magavnikim* secure it so tightly."

"So how did they ever get those Molotov cocktails in during the riots?"

His eyes fixed on Ridley. The point bristled.

"We've shut down access for Muslims before," said Bar-Lev. "I considered it, but if we do that tomorrow, Jerusalem will bleed and burn. There will be no Jews there on the Mount anyway. Passover, everyone is at *Kotel*. We segregate on Jewish holidays to prevent riots."

Kotel: the Western Wall.

"The best of times, the worst of times," said Atashi dryly. "Ramadan and Passover and Easter Sunday."

The Jerusalem Ya'mas unit had been on the Temple Mount plenty of times before. They could melt into a crowd of worshippers and tourists better than anyone in the country. But it was the capability of this undercover team to function on only a fraction of intelligence, deep within enemy territory, that made them ideal for this operation. Other counterterrorism teams would want to get within ninety percent of total intelligence coverage. Ya'mas needed only half that. They could adapt on the move, as fluid as water.

"We'll need all teams," he continued. "Deploy at every gate. Send in *ha'dovrim* first, with 'international tourists' also."

Ha'dovrim were "the Speakers." They were the secret ingredient of the Ya'mas, operators from the minority populations within Israel that didn't need to be schooled on the ways of Muslims in order to blend in. They didn't have to fake the Arab dialects, culture, or customs. They had known it all their lives.

Ya'mas recruited the overlooked, the Druze, the Bedouins, the Circassians, the Christian Arabs. These "Speakers" were the first element in place on any operation.

Ridley knew the time was now. "Henri and I are going in as tourists."

Bar-Lev just looked at her. "No."

"We have to be on the grounds," she said. "You said international tourists. There are more here right now on pilgrimages than any other time. There's no reason we couldn't be among them, and plenty of reasons why you would want our eyes up there."

"It's fourteen hectares and you don't know your way around," said Atashi.

"I know the space. I've been studying the maps for hours," she said.

If there was one thing a unit commander in Ya'mas appreciated, it was the dedication to studying maps. Every operation required them to know the area streets until they could navigate every curve and alleyway blindfolded.

Henri joined in. "Both of us blend in. You can hear my accent isn't American. I can pass for West African with my French."

Ridley gestured to her own Mediterranean complexion. "Greek? Italian? Spanish? I can look any one of them and speak any one of them."

"We don't take foreign intelligence agents undercover!" said Atashi.

"You wouldn't be taking them into the unit," interjected Booker. "They're visiting the Temple Mount like a thousand other people on the holiday. Give them an earpiece and let them wander."

Atashi threw up his hands and looked to Bar-Lev in disbelief. A muscle flexed in the Commissioner's jaw. He looked from Atashi to Gadot, who had been remarkably quiet.

"Ya'mas is part of the Border Police, but they answer to the Shin Bet," he said for the sake of the American guests. "I won't sign off on it. It's up to them who they trust in the field."

Nakav's brows rose in anticipation, just waiting for the

whole thing to go down. Gadot pondered his gaze on the table-top, until he finally spoke.

"We're not the Mossad. We don't collaborate with foreign agents."

Then he looked across the table at the sober intensity of Booker, Ridley, and Henri.

"But you may visit the Mount tomorrow, as long as Sergeant Atashi gives you a disguise, an earpiece, and you do every damn thing he says."

Atashi glared at Ridley for getting this concession, but he respected the Director.

"Report at 0430 hours. Agent Nakav will bring you to base."

CHAPTER
SEVENTY-TWO

THAT EVENING, Ridley and Henri picked up chicken shawarma from the corner shop. They went to her room at the hotel to pore over every detail of the Temple Mount that they could get their hands on. They had requested the layouts of the Church of the Holy Sepulchre, the Western Wall, and the ancient tunnels within it. Agent Nakav had given them satellite maps, photos, and videos of the areas.

"Thank God he's not heading for a mosque," said Ridley, sitting cross-legged on the bed as she held her pita with both hands, leaning over a computer tablet. "We'd have six to deal with on the grounds."

Henri pointed to the image. "There's the one Emily Austin was complaining about. They built it underground in the nineties, where Solomon's Stables used to be. It's why they dug out and dumped all that earth in the valley below."

"This really *is* ground zero for all the wars of belief," she muttered through a full mouth.

"The streets of this city have flowed with blood more than probably any other place in history."

Ridley looked at a detailed map of the tunnels running just inside the Western Wall. "They actually have a spot where they think the Holy of Holies was? Wasn't that where the Ark of the Covenant was? We've all seen Indiana Jones."

"It's not really—it wasn't *in* the tunnel. It was up in the Temple. I guess that's the closest that Jews can get to it now." He shook his head. "Just amazing. Walled out of their holy site when there's plenty of space for everybody."

"So they just go down into a tunnel to pray at this alcove they think is close to where the Ark was? Okay," she said, perplexed. "I guess that's the idea of the whole Western Wall, anyway."

He looked out at lights of the Old City, barely a mile from where they were staying.

"Do you think it's gonna be the Syrian kid?" asked Ridley.

"No, but I didn't want to say that right out."

"Really?"

"You need ID to get in. That kid wouldn't have left Arwad with a passport."

"That is...a good point."

There was a silence between them as they continued sifting through the visual materials. Finally Henri finished his shawarma. He sat back, wiping his fingers with a napkin, and looked at his partner.

"In Paris, you asked me if I believed in the Watchers."

Ridley looked up, giving him her full attention. "Yeah. You gave me a shitty, evasive answer."

"It was thoughtful and uncertain, but now I'm asking you, after all this. Do you believe that there are supernatural beings under the Temple Mount that can be set loose on this city?"

Specifically chosen words.

She didn't like the words that came out of her mouth next, but she felt unable to say anything else. "I've seen little supernatural beings set loose all over the continent. It wouldn't be an honest thought if I shut out the idea of there being a *big* supernatural being. Or seven of them."

He nodded.

"Do you think…" she halted in the squirms of her own wondering. "Do you think God's going to help us tomorrow?"

Henri was surprised by this, like a child asking before bedtime if God was bigger than the bogeyman. It was more endearing than he could have expected, and a grin crept across his face.

"He made the Seal of Solomon, so we know he provided at least one way. But I'll still be asking, an awful lot. Without ceasing."

She took this, but didn't reply, giving a barely perceptible nod before going back to the tablet. They spoke little for the next fifteen minutes as they finished up.

Henri finally grabbed his bag and went to the door. He pulled it open, then paused on the threshold. Lowering his head ever so slightly, he murmured over his shoulder.

"Blessed be the Lord my rock
Who trains my hands for war
And my fingers for battle…
For the Lord your God is the one who goes with you…
And our struggle is not against flesh and blood."

The quiet resolve of his voice, the vulnerability of asking for this help, gripped Ridley. She couldn't even respond before he looked forward again, and walked out of the room.

For a moment, her mind spun with visions of demons and angels and the lava-skinned jinn that had broken free of that urn in the bowels of the Louvre...of the riddling jinn in Cyprus whose voice rattled with malice.

What could these Watcher-king things look like?

She burned with curiosity, yet also knew finding out would mean they'd failed to prevent the enemy's mission.

Ridley buried herself back in the material to spend another half hour studying. She didn't want to find a foot of ground tomorrow that she hadn't seen coming. Wondering about these Watchers, these jinn kings, would do nothing for her. The recon, the operational planning, the geographic awareness; these were the ways she prepared. Leave the praying to Henri, the kind of person that God would actually answer.

She finally had to give it up and take a shower. Four-thirty was going to come up fast. Sitting out on the balcony as her hair dried, she tucked in a pair of earbuds. Tel Aviv pulsed with energy, but Jerusalem nights were sleepy. There was a reverence to the quiet, to the lights glittering across the darkness.

Ridley put on the velvety thud of Gang Starr. That muffled sound of music in her right ear, she'd never gotten used to. She gazed out at the Temple Mount. The Dome of the Rock gleamed on the skyline, a golden beacon.

34 acres of stone. The most combustible place in the world.

Melancholy surged through Ridley, as though a profound yearning had unfurled within her. Nothing had ever felt sacred to her before, but there it was, this sense of a vast majesty, a power that outshone human understanding.

The words of the rap felt inadequate. All words did. She put on *Clair de lune*, and as she watched the ancient city shrouded in night, she saw the dead and wounded that they'd left strewn about in their pursuit.

The sergeant in England, shot dead in the Temple Church...the pub owner in Cornwall, his throat slashed open by the ifrit...Rafael, cut down on Cyprus...Owen huddled on the Syrian shores, covered in someone else's blood...Fouad falling backward into the water, his chest oozing blood...

This would be the end.

If the Watchers were chained in darkness until the day of judgment...

Tomorrow.

Tomorrow.

The graceful chords of the piano flooded her ears.

CHAPTER
SEVENTY-THREE

JERUSALEM, ISRAEL

DARKNESS STILL LAY thick over the city when Agent Nakav picked up Ridley and Henri the next morning. Cradling a coffee that smelled of cardamom, she seemed unnervingly fresh. Three minutes into the ride, she tossed them each a scarf.

"We trust the CIA. Enough to trust that you'll blindfold yourselves."

It was understandable and somewhat quaint, how low-tech this coverage was. There was no way that the Shin Bet was going to give them a guided tour to the doorstep of the most elite undercover unit in the city. They complied, tying on the blindfolds.

Ten minutes later, they were standing in the home base of Ya'mas.

There was nothing sleek about it, with its linoleum floor

and shabby leather couches. It smelled faintly of cigarette smoke and spiced coffee, and looked like a boys' club. The waste bin nearby was overflowing with empty cans of energy drinks.

Sergeant Said Atashi greeted Nakav. She was clearly part of the family. The frostiness that Atashi had shown to the Americans the day before seemed to have thawed considerably, and he now welcomed them to the unit with the respect of a peer. He probably didn't feel it, but saw it as nonetheless important to set an example for the rest of his team. The operation was the only thing that mattered now, and he wasn't going to jeopardize a moment of it with petty jurisdictional disputes.

He introduced them to the rest of the undercovers. In the kitchen, a short, barrel-chested man with a shaved head and the look of an old Italian mafioso was making a feast of *shakshuka*. Yoav was a Sephardic Jew, Jerusalem-born, with an almost insane level of courage. He kissed Nakav on the cheek, then in broken English, he insisted that they eat breakfast with the team.

"Heart of a lion," said Atashi as they turned away, "hands of Julia Childs."

He introduced them next to Orel, a shaggy-haired Ashkenazi, and Tal, a striking Arab wearing a cross necklace. They had been cleaning their Glocks at the coffee table, but each of them rose to shake the Americans' hands.

"Thing One and Thing Two," Atashi chuckled. "Maybe there is hope for Jews and Arabs."

They moved to the long table, where a blond, light-skinned man of almost shocking beauty was bent over a computer. He got up to greet them in English shaded by a faint Rus accent.

"Hello, nice to meet you," he said.

Atashi introduced the operative. "Semion. Semmy. Came the whole way from Ukraine to play a woman in disguise. And oh my God, he's the most beautiful woman you've ever seen."

He roughed up Semion's hair like he was the family Golden Retriever, then led Ridley and Henri through another door. There they stood in the midst of a costume department that could rival that of a film set. Makeup was stacked on two vanity tables. Lights glowed around the mirrors. There was an entire bookshelf dedicated to hats and headwear of all types. Two full racks of clothing lined the walls. At the back, a swarthy, broad-shouldered young man was scrawling on a whiteboard in Hebrew.

"Aron," called Atashi, and the man turned. "Our embeds, Ridley and Henri."

He nodded coolly to them. "Hello."

"This is Aron Abada. He's our best Persian." He gestured to Aron, speaking quickly in Hebrew, then added, "Put them on the board."

Aron responded in Hebrew, seemingly annoyed, but finally complied, writing out more Hebrew script.

"In English," snapped Atashi.

He wiped the marker clean and put down their names as instructed.

At that moment, a rangy man with sleepy eyes entered. He carried a black suit and a checkered black-and-white keffiyeh.

"Izhak, meet the Americans," said Atashi, waving between them.

"Nice to meet you," said Izhak in rich basso tones as Ridley and Henri introduced themselves with a handshake.

He exchanged a few quick words with his sergeant and then moved off.

"You speak other languages?" Atashi asked them.

"Just French and Creole," said Henri, who then looked at Ridley. "She's a whole Rosetta Stone."

She sighed. "Greek, Spanish, Russian, French, German, Italian, Dutch."

Atashi lifted his eyebrows, leaning forward in disbelief.

"Not all *very* well," she said. "I moved around a lot as a kid and I wanted to talk to everybody."

"Oh, my God. You should be working for us all the time."

"Sorry to say, no Arabic and no Hebrew between us."

"We're not the Duvdevan. We don't have to go into Palestinian neighborhoods trying to pass as locals. Jerusalem is full of nationalities. It's the *most* difficult city in the world to police, but here we can be tourists, students, Orthodox, anything."

Atashi looked over the room, as if brainstorming.

"Henri, only speak French. You can be a Haitian. Exotic but it won't raise any flags on the Mount. Plenty of black Muslims. Trousers and a button-down and obviously you don't need any makeup. Check that rack," he said, pointing to one.

Henri went over to browse. "Do you have anything orange? Green? Yellow?"

Atashi's brows furrowed in puzzlement.

Ridley whispered loudly, "He's a little fussy about his clothes."

"Haitians like bright colors," Henri said. "I look good in orange."

"Welcome to Israel," said the sergeant. "We don't. The Islamic Waqf has been making some Christians and non-Muslims wear yellow head coverings to mark them. We would like you to not stand out that much."

"Why yellow?"

"For humiliation, to try to dominate. The Baghdad Caliphate and the Mamluks—hundreds of years ago—made all non-Muslims wear yellow. The Nazis made Jews wear stars of yellow." He gestured to the entire supply of wardrobe. "There's no yellow here."

He turned to Ridley, looking her up and down with a frank gaze.

"I know," she said. "I'm tall."

"You're a giant. I bought you clothes last night."

She nearly blushed in surprise.

They turn over every stone they see.

"You look Greek," he said. "How is your Greek?"

"I'm half-Greek, and I half-grew up there. My Greek is wholly perfect."

"You have a fake Greek passport with you?"

"Yep."

Booker had supplied them with a proper stash, one for every occasion. Spanish, Greek, Canadian, and American.

Atashi yelled something in Hebrew toward the other room. A moment later, the Arab with the cross around his neck stepped in.

"Tal, she's going to be Greek." Atashi turned to Ridley. "Only Muslims are allowed into al-Aqsa and the Dome of the Rock. We don't go in there undercover, you understand? Except today we have that problem, and we need eyes inside. *Your* eyes, they tell me. The guards will ask your parents' names, where you're from, and if they doubt your faith, ask you to recite something from the Quran. You're going to be a new convert.

"Tal is our best 'Muslim.' You're his bride, learning your new religion. He's going to give you a phrase to memorize and recite in Arabic. It doesn't matter if you sound bad saying it. It will help you get past them."

Tal smiled at Ridley, his enormous dark eyes warm and open.

"Don't worry. I'm a good husband," he said with a wink. "Just remember to walk a foot behind me."

That'll be the hardest part.

From the kitchen, they heard Yoav call for mealtime.

. . .

Breakfast for the team was delicious and efficient. It lasted no more than ten minutes, and afterward, it was time for wardrobe. Henri ended up in a simple white button-down and black pants, with a white mesh prayer cap—*kufi*—on his head. Ridley changed into navy slacks and a long-sleeved gray crew neck. Over it, a white patterned robe and a scarf with shades of blue embroidered in a stunning pattern.

"Wear it like a *shayla*," said Tal, arranging it gently for her. "Loose style."

He'd taken off his crucifix necklace and draped it on the table. As he blacked his beard and slicked his hair back in front of the mirror, he drilled with her on *Ayat al-Kursi*. Known in English as the Throne Verse from the second surah of the Quran, it was the best known and most memorized verse in the Muslim world. It would be perfect for a new believer to have memorized.

Ridley felt every gear in her head working in overdrive to grasp it. Her skill with languages amazed Tal, but she was nowhere near satisfied. For the rest of the morning, she'd be turning over and parading the words around in her head.

"Now," said Tal, turning to her when he was done with wardrobe, "do you want a Glock or a Beretta?"

She sighed. "Now *this* is one of my languages. Glock. Please."

A moment later, she had the 9mm tucked into her waistband, well covered by the robe.

The team gathered in the briefing area for the last rundown, and Ridley hardly recognized some of them. It took her a moment to realize that the old, bent, shaky-voiced man beside her was Izhak, now wearing the black suit and keffiyeh, moving with a cane. Atashi stood before them in a simple polo shirt and jeans, helpfully speaking in English.

"Every officer in the city has these pictures," he said, pulling up the photos they'd supplied of the Syrian boy and Tiago Inacio. "Do not try to take them alone!"

It was an aggressive, audacious plan of action.

The Western Wall plaza had just about all the security they could cram into it. An increased number of officers would be posted at the Church of the Holy Sepulchre. All of them would have memorized the faces in those photos.

Every Ya'mas operator on the Temple Mount would be armed, and have a discreet mark on their passports that would signal the Border Police guards to fake the body search and wave them through. Each of them would have a thin black bala-clava tucked away in a pocket with big silver lettering 'POLICE' written on it in Hebrew and English. If things went bad, they would have to break disguise and pull them on.

The target's destination was the Dome of the Rock.

The team assembled in this room was only one part within the unit, but the other five would be deployed with the same briefing, the same intel, and the same plan of action. The master sergeants had devised it together only the night before. Their last-minute readiness was extraordinary.

As he wrapped up, Atashi's voice grew soft but steely. "We've walked through the blood of our people on these streets. Only we know the kind of work it takes to keep Jerusalem safe, to keep our children from being blown up and our wives from being shot. But I tell you the truth...you haven't seen a mission like today. At every cost, with the last breath we have, we protect the Dome of the Rock. Or hell will come to earth for the Jews."

CHAPTER
SEVENTY-FOUR

A COOL BREEZE swept the stones of Jerusalem as the sun rose. It was the kind of spring morning that promised a blanket of warmth by midday.

The Old City was already thronged with people. White shawls and yarmulkes, hijabs and checkered keffiyehs, scarves and wooden crucifixes formed a teeming mix. The presence of the armed forces was conspicuous. Young men and women in green and gray uniforms, decked in full body armor and carrying M4 rifles, had their heads on swivels. Their eyes roved the crowds as they milled about their patrol spaces.

At the Church of the Holy Sepulchre, mass would begin at 8 a.m. At the same time, the gates to the Temple Mount would open. Only a few minutes' walk from there, at the Western Wall, a prayer session would begin at 8:45 a.m.

419

Each of the operators would arrive at an assigned gate. The lines at each one were thick, awaiting the opening on this blessed day of Ramadan.

For the Ya'mas teams, it was the riskiest, most perilous time to slink in undercover, for only Muslims were allowed on the Mount during sacred holidays. This was well abided by non-Muslims in Jerusalem, as a sign of respect but also for fear of being set upon by a furious mob. The Border Guards still kept an eye out. However, they would not be stopping anyone whose fake passport carried the distinguishing mark of the undercover unit.

Henri and Izhak were assigned together. The Israeli agent tottered about in flawless old man disguise. To ensure that Henri never had to answer any questions in English from the Islamic police inside, they'd determined that he should only speak French while on the grounds.

So they'd paired him with Izhak, a Ya'mas team member who also could speak French fluently. It might deflect attention from the American operative if he was seen to be assisting an old man in his pilgrimage to the holy site.

They waited together in the crowd, with Izhak shuffling and shifting his weight on the cane.

Ridley and her "husband" Tal stood at the Gate of the Tribes on the northern side, as a devout Muslim couple would, with her standing just barely behind him, her *shayla* draped over the thick braid of her hair. She could feel the mass of bodies shifting around her in anticipation. Electricity coursed through her limbs. Her gaze roamed discreetly over the crowd.

There was no sign of the Syrian boy. No sign of Tiago.

The rest of the Ya'mas teams had melted into the crowd. Every one of them had a tiny earpiece, so small and discreet that the Americans found it nearly impossible to believe. She'd last seen Atashi toward the front, in his jeans and sky blue polo shirt, having blacked his hair and beard.

Communications would be kept sparse, essential transmissions only. Even for the Speakers, the most fluent and integrated Arab team members like Tal and Aron, the number one rule for survival in Ya'mas was to keep verbal interactions to a minimum. Fortunately for them all, a vast spectrum of nationalities had assembled at the Temple Mount today.

Ridley and Henri had both felt great relief in not having to venture far beyond their native identities. Yet they, too, would avoid speaking whenever it was possible.

Tal glanced back at Ridley. He looked no more nervous than a man waiting in line for a matinée. He carried a small prayer mat rolled up under one arm. When he saw her look, he leaned back and began to murmur assuringly.

"*Bismallaah ar-Rahman ar-Raheem*
Allahu la ileana illa hu
Mal Hayyul Qayyum..."
In the name of Allah, the Beneficent, the Merciful
Allah, there is no god but he
The Living, the Self-subsisting, the Eternal...

She closed her eyes and joined him, reciting the long verse under her breath. She hitched and stumbled in parts, but pulled out the ending with confidence. They finished it together word for word.

"*Wa la yeuduhu hifzuhuma wa hu wal aliy ul aziym*
Saddaqallah hul Azim."
For he is the highest and most exalted.
Allah, the Most High, speaks the truth.

At the front, the gates to the Temple Mount opened.

. . .

The crowd of Muslims at the Iron Gate began to loosen and disperse into the courtyards. One man in the midst was wearing a disguise worthy of Ya'mas. He wore a white *kufi* prayer cap over his thick black curls. His cerulean blue eyes had vanished beneath brown contacts, and the light shade of his Iberian skin had been tinted with olive-tone foundation makeup. He carried nothing but a Quran. On his right hand, he wore a massive iron signet ring.

The plaza below the Temple Mount brimmed with Jews who were facing the Western Wall. It was as close as they could get to worshipping at the temple that Solomon had built as the house of the Lord, three thousand years ago.

On one side of the partition was a sea of men in white prayer shawls and *kippahs*, in black suits and fedoras. On the other, the women in a flood of dark skirts and headscarves. Many read from *siddur* prayer books, rocking softly as they poured out their pleas to God. On a balcony above the plaza, a priest called out the melodic blessing, which rang sonorously over the loudspeakers. The crowds echoed back the chant.

At the Church of the Holy Sepulchre, Christians streamed into the ancient house of worship. A line of white-frocked priests marched in a stately procession, carrying aloft an ornate cross, pillar candles, and a Bible. Incense wafted upward to the domed ceiling. Along the edges, dozens of cameras and phones captured the procession on video. Several in the crowd held candles themselves.

Those gathered were dressed in every style of clothing, from every corner of the world. A hushed reverence settled over the worshippers. The faint chords of an organ filled the chapel as they sang a solemn Latin hymn.

At the intelligence headquarters, Booker observed the satellite feeds on a wall of screens. He stood with Director Conway, who had been given a special permission from the Minister of Defense to oversee the operation. Agent Nakav was nursing another coffee in the back. Bar-Lev stood over a bank of computers like a sentinel with a headpiece on.

On each screen there was a different satellite thermal image. One of the Western Wall, one of the Church of the Holy Sepulchre, and one of the Temple Mount. Each of the Ya'mas operators, including Ridley and Henri, were marked by the signal emitted from their earpieces. They showed as little dots of green amidst the thousands of white heat signatures.

On the northwestern corner of the Temple Mount, four women in black burqas advanced in line at the Gate of Bani Ghānim. Three of them were friends. One was only hovering close enough to pass as part of the group.

Women in burqas were rarely alone when visiting the holy site. To an Israeli officer, a lone figure clad head-to-toe in black was a red flag. Anyone could be hiding under those flowing black robes, and anything could be concealed under them.

For this woman, it was camouflage by association. Beneath the robes was Chadia Yaseen, a Jordanian woman of thirty years. Yesterday was the first day since her betrothal that she had ever acted without her husband's permission. She was the wife of Musa, a cold fundamentalist to whom she had born four children.

Yet it was not her own thoughts or desires that had driven

her from the northern hills of Jordan to the dense, roiling streets of East Jerusalem.

Only the previous morning, she had been shopping with two of her young children when she'd had to lay her bag down on a bench. It was only for a moment, but when she turned back around, a young man was leaning over it. She yelled for his attention, but he bolted, slipping into the crowds of shoppers before she could scold him any further.

She went over to her bag to see what he had stolen from it.

Nothing. He'd taken nothing. But when Chadia lifted the bag, she saw the strangest sight beneath it.

A golden saber.

The blade was shorter than a man's torso, but gleaming with the most beautiful Arabic script she'd ever laid eyes on. How could anyone have left such a treasure on purpose, with a stranger?

She bent over and touched the hilt.

CHAPTER
SEVENTY-FIVE

RIDLEY FELT a flush of adrenaline as she and Tal stepped into the Temple Mount together.

Everything suddenly looked sharper. The scent of roasting meats from the city below smelled stronger. She could hear the chatter around her, though she couldn't understand a word of the guttural Arabic.

They began their meandering walk across the stones toward the glittering dome. Ridley had prepared as best she could for the size and grandeur of the place, but it was a remarkable thing to stand in the midst of it. It was an enormous space, but as more and more people poured into the grounds, she recalled what Nakav had told them about the estimated attendance for the day: 200,000. It was nearly inconceivable.

They passed by the Museum and the stubs of Corinthian

pillars scattered throughout its courtyard. The great green doors of the Al-Aqsa Mosque itself were just opening.

"Those were Solomon's Stables," said Tal, pointing down a wide stairwell to another mosque that had been built into the earth.

All the worship and brutality and sanctity and gore that this place has hosted...

She silently pleaded a prayer—half to herself, half to the God that Henri was sure of—that no one in the crowd would start something that day.

Violence often followed the flood of Ramadan. Rocks, Molotov cocktails, batons—they used anything that could be launched in fury at Israeli police. The Israelis would have to storm the Mount in order to quell a riot, and tempers would boil all over again just because of their presence.

Not today. Please, not today.

At the moment, the crowds were surprisingly casual. Plenty of the visitors were dressed in jeans and T-shirts, chatting on their phones or taking photos.

Ridley and Tal wandered past the fountain, where Muslims would wash their feet at ornate faucets before going to worship. Past it was a grand stone staircase. Above that rose the golden dome.

Ridley spotted Henri fifty yards off, in his *kufi*, lingering for a moment in the shade of an olive tree so that the impeccably disguised Izhak could rest, as an old man would.

She scouted the work crew that was transporting carpeting and tools into the Dome of the Rock beyond them.

"Time to worship," she said softly to Tal.

"Wife. Let's go to the shrine."

They ascended the steps, passing under the majestic Qanatir arches, and walked to the Dome of the Rock.

However many hundreds of photos and videos that Ridley

had seen of it, she was not prepared for the beauty of that exterior. The delicate marble pillars, the lattice design in cobalt blue and vivid green, the calligraphy of Quranic verses that encircled the upper edge in elegant script. It was the oldest work of Islamic architecture still standing in the world, and what a monument it was.

Her awe lasted about four seconds. Then her eyes settled on the door, where a line had already begun to shuffle along the ropes.

I will get into that building.

They joined the line. Within a minute, were standing before the guard. He had a deep furrowed brow and a look of boredom on his face already despite the early hour. But once those eyes settled on Ridley, he stood up straight, narrowed his gaze, and beckoned her over. She started to move, and then realized she would have stepped right in front of Tal, her "husband."

Shit! Way to almost blow everything for a damn gender role.

Tal walked up with her and began speaking to the guard in Arabic. The guard responded, clearly questioning him and throwing glances at Ridley. The man's voice didn't rise, and he wasn't speaking quickly. His expression hadn't changed much. All of the signs boded well for Ridley, but body language was always more difficult to read in a culture so unfamiliar.

Tal's gestures got bigger, his words flowed faster. The back and forth intensified, until finally the guard turned his eyes to her.

"Passport," he said in a thick Palestinian accent.

Ridley pulled the fake Greek one from her back pocket. He inspected it for a full twenty seconds.

As though he can read Greek...

"What is your father's name?" he asked.

"Alexios Apostolakis."

There were always tricks to remember your cover story.

Swap your father's name for your brother's, and use your grandmother's maiden name. Easy to recall.

"What is your mother's name?"

It didn't matter how far undercover Ridley went. It didn't matter how well she had baked in her cover. It always stung to imagine a fake mother, as she had spent a lifetime trying to imagine her real one.

"Zola Papanikolaou."

Her grandmother's middle name and man from whom she bought her favorite ever horse.

Give him the tough pronunciations. He'll leave them alone.

"Vasiliki, you are married? You are Greek Orthodox?"

She affected a Greek accent as she answered him in English.

"I am Muslim," she said humbly. "*Ash-hadu an la ilaha illa Allah, wa ash-hadu anna Muhammadan Rasulu-Allah.*"

Her mimicry of the pronunciation of the Shahada was so good that Tal had to keep himself from gaping. He managed to give a proud smile instead. That had to have done the trick.

Except the guard handed Ridley back her passport and said firmly, "No. No entry for her."

They were stunned. Tal's indignation was genuine as he spat a stream of incensed Arabic back at the man.

This can't be happening. No.

Whether he doubted her marriage or her conversion or was just being a pissant, she couldn't tell, but she played on her true distress.

"*Bismallaah ar-Rahman ar-Raheem*

Allahu la ileana illa hu

Mal Hayyul Qayyum—"

She had lifted both palms to the sky and lowered her eyes, but her heart was thundering as though she was galloping at breakneck speed into the most sacred verse in Islam.

It was long. She felt the chains of guttural sounds catching in her throat at times, but this had to be good. Her skill with language was the reason Osprey had found her. It was the second thing Booker ever knew about her. It was why she'd been chosen for this mission. It was her only way into the most important place on earth today.

Finally she came to the ending, and spoke the words with triumphant, reverent confidence.

"Wa la yeuduhu hifzuhuma wa hu wal aliy ul aziym
Saddaqallah hul Azim."

The guard's brows had risen a few millimeters. Something had shifted to her side.

"Please, we traveled so far. I want to worship here with my husband," she pleaded.

He didn't respond immediately. For that moment, she was frozen in dread. Then he gave the slightest jerk of his head toward the door.

Tal and Ridley thanked him, but he had already moved on to the next in line.

They stepped into the Dome of the Rock.

CHAPTER
SEVENTY-SIX

———

THE HOLY SHRINE was surprisingly casual. There was a wall of cubbyholes in the entrance to leave shoes, but Ridley and Tal preferred to keep theirs in hand. They padded around the red and beige carpet in their socks.

A young boy in a Chelsea football shirt scampered by. Friends chatted with each other. Many took photos and video on their phones.

The interior was nothing less than gorgeous, with its gilded arches and green marble. A few people had taken up chairs along the outer ring of the space, and each of the Byzantine pillars along the edge had a book display at the bottom. Several of the more contemplative Muslims were already reading from the holy texts.

For the American and the Israeli, every single one of them

430

was a potential threat. As Ridley's gaze roved over a family, the dark thought slipped by that even a child could be under the possession of the ifrit. Tal knew nothing of the jinn. All that Osprey had shared with Ya'mas was that their *targets* believed in these supernatural beings.

Maybe I should have told him? He's Christian. If Henri believes it...but Henri had to see it for himself. Not every Christian believes the same things. But shouldn't he know at this late hour? If it's true, he'll see what he needs to.

The torrent of considerations evaporated just then, as they reached the carved mahogany railing in the middle. There under the dome lay a slab of rock, lumpen and pale.

The Foundation Stone.

Whether Abraham had actually prepared to sacrifice his only child, whether Muhammad had truly ascended to heaven, this place was wholly real.

"I thought it would be like a rock you could find in a back-yard," Ridley muttered to Tal. "That is really, really, very big."

His gaze was transfixed on the stone. Then she realized that for all his time in this land, in this city, he had never before been allowed to see this place. He whispered a prayer to himself in Arabic, and quickly snapped his attention back to her.

"You go down," he said. "I'll walk around up here."

She nodded and walked down along the wooden rail, to a short marble archway flanked by gilded columns. Ridley passed under it, down a short stairwell, and stepped into the Well of Souls.

The cave beneath the Foundation Stone had been turned into a chamber of prayer. It was small, barely twenty feet long with a low ceiling. The floor was carpeted, and each of the four corners had its own small shrine. It had been wired for light, so dim lamps cast ragged shadows across the walls.

It was still so early that there were only half a dozen people in there at the moment. Most were women. One even had a baby with a terribly cranky wail. Ridley lowered her head and went to kneel in one of the corners.

Every one of the women wore a veil. Some had only the head covering of the hijab, some the niqab that drew also across the face. No one looked suspicious, all relaxed on the carpet, with the baby crying and people kneeling.

After a moment of proper reverence, she got to her feet and started back up the stairs. As she climbed the steps, she passed three women descending. Two of them were in niqabs, one was in a burqa. They were chatting with each other. Ridley dismissed the possibility.

The ifrit is a lone wolf.

She walked on by the trio, barely brushing by the woman in the burqa.

Beneath that black fabric, the golden saber shifted against Chadia Yaseen's leg.

A voice over the radio purred in Ridley's head:

"Potential sighting, the Portuguese. Dome of the Spirits."

At that, she leapt up the last few steps.

The Dome of the Spirits was a small gazebo only a hundred yards from the Dome of the Rock.

"Prince, do you have eyes?" she asked quietly over the earpiece.

Henri's call sign for the day was "Prince."

"We're at the Dome of the Chain. Going to the Spirits," came his reply.

One of the two Americans had to confirm the identification.

The Dome of the Chain was one of the other small buildings surrounding the Rock. Though Henri and Izhak were marginally closer to it than her. She knew this was her post for a reason, ground zero for the entire mission, but she was nearly pawing the ground to be first there.

Ridley was eyeing the door, trying to keep from fidgeting herself straight toward it, when Tal walked right across her eyeline.

"It's calm in here," he said.

Despite the tranquil observation, there was an edge to his voice. She shot him an anxious look, her jaw clenching as they awaited Henri's next transmission.

Izhak the old man shambled across the courtyard. Only the keenest observer would realize that he was moving at about twice the speed he'd been able to muster throughout the entire morning. The American knew the layout of the Mount, but still Izhak led. He couldn't help it. This was his city. These were his people at risk.

A few hundred Muslims were milling about the courtyard as the pair approached the Dome of the Chain. It was an open arcade of elegant tiling, domed ceiling, and ornate marble columns. Under and around it were more than a dozen people.

Henri's eyes scanned rapidly across the lot. *Girl...too tall... woman...too skinny...boy...*

Two men were standing in the slanted shadow of the pillars. One was young, baby-faced with a scruffy beard and no mustache. The other was a man just under six feet tall, with thick black hair and olive skin. He was looking down at his phone, saying something to his younger companion. When he lifted his head finally to glance around, Henri caught a full look at his face.

Where once he would have seen that shade of startling blue, now there was a pair of deep brown eyes. Yet it was undeniably him.

Tiago. And on his right hand, he wore an enormous iron ring.

The sight of the Seal sent a fiery surge of adrenaline through Henri.

"I have eyes on," he said, leaning in to give Izhak a stabilizing hand. "He's here, Dome of the Chain, and he has a friend with him."

"*Confirmed,*" came Bar-Lev's voice over the radio. "*Prince, hold your position. Emir, flank him.*"

"Emir" was Atashi's call sign. It was time to tighten the lasso.

In the Dome of the Rock, Ridley dropped her head low and let out a triumphant hiss.

Cut that goddamn Seal off his finger.

Tal gave the slightest nod to the positive report, but his eyes were still roaming.

Ridley shook herself back into the moment, turning her attentions back to surveillance. Tiago was the second piece. They still needed the first.

Between Henri and Izhak, the Israeli was far better versed in the skills of undercover work.

Henri had wanted to get closer, but Izhak had to warn him off and keep the distance. None of the intel suggested that Tiago would be using or detonating explosives, but the Temple Mount was itself a powder keg right now. They couldn't risk any sudden, overt action in the middle of the courtyard.

So Henri stayed back, cooling his sniper's instinct to pull the trigger when he had the target in his scopes. Instead, he pulled out his phone and began taking photos of the surrounding buildings.

He spotted Atashi in his sky blue polo coming around from the north side.

"In position," came the master sergeant's voice over the radio.

Just then, his camera aim landed on Tiago, zoomed in. The Portuguese turned and looked directly into the lens.

Dread trickled through Henri's gut.

The baby-faced companion looked straight at him across the courtyard, pointed, and yelled, *"Jesh! Jesh!"*

Jesh: "army" in Arabic.

Over the radio, every operator heard the shout. It may as well have been a grenade.

In the Dome of the Rock, Tal's entire body tensed.

"Get out of there!" came Bar-Lev over the radio.

He seized Ridley's arm and his eyes shot to the door.

"No," she said.

"They're gonna kill them!"

"They're making chaos to use it! Their mission is still on!"

He glared at her. "You don't understand what's about to happen."

"No, I don't," she said, "but neither do you."

They could hear more shouts outside, confusion roiling into anger. Within the dome, heads began to turn in alarm.

The Well of Souls had emptied almost completely for the commotion. One older man was kneeling in a corner, his prayer unperturbed in stubborn piety.

The only other person, the woman in a burqa, bent down and began to rip at the edge of the carpet. She peeled it all the way back to the ancient tile floor, where a faded geometric pattern encircled an eight-pointed star.

Vexed by the disturbance, the older man finally peered over his shoulder. It was only in time to see a flash of gold sweep across his vision.

Blood spurted from the man's throat. He collapsed with a gurgle of astonished pain.

Chadia Yaseen ripped the veil off her burqa. She looked at the saber, now dripping red, and the ifrit within her shuddered with ecstasy.

She knelt in front of the star, and with two hands clutched the saber above it. It dripped scarlet beads onto the tiled floor. She lowered it until the tip was about to hit.

Yet before the blade even touched the surface, the stone floor *cracked* beneath it.

The cry that poured from her throat was not of anything that Chadia had within her. It was as old as the earth below, a millennium's worth of wretched faith and tormented devotion. It was the furious roar of the end of days.

She plunged the saber into the cleft stone.

CHAPTER
SEVENTY-SEVEN

IN THE COMMAND center at headquarters, Booker could see the rush of white silhouettes swarming into the courtyard of the Dome. In their midst were the signature green dots of the Ya'mas operators.

He found himself gripping the back of a technician's chair, staring at the screen, willing Ridley and Henri to melt away to a secure location.

Beside him, Conway watched with hands on hips, jaw clenched. Bar-Lev was snapping orders to the Border Guard police who were manning the gates. He was summoning reinforcements to the Mount. He was putting the rest of the city's officers on alert to the hostile activity brewing there.

Just when Booker thought his stare might burn a hole

through the monitor, something caught his attention on the left of screen.

The Dome of the Rock was quaking.

"What is that?" He pointed, straightening up in dread. "*What is that?!*"

Ridley and Tal felt a rumble through the carpet, and then the floor began to shake.

"Oh, my God," she said, though hardly a sound came out.

"They're here!" exclaimed Tal.

He dashed to the railing, looking across the Foundation Stone for the cause. Ridley turned to the steps she'd just come up. She yanked on her shoes and ran to the archway, pulling the Glock from the small of her back.

There, in the Well of Souls below her, knelt a woman in black robes. Her face was now bare. Her hands were wrapped around the hilt of the golden saber, and its blade was buried deep in the shattered floor. The walls of the cave were shaking.

The moment Ridley appeared on the stairs, the woman looked up. The shine of her eyes was inhuman.

"Let go!" shouted Ridley. "Stand up!"

She realized the woman probably didn't understand English, but the jinn had always been able to communicate in any human language. The ifrit knew what she was saying. Ridley also knew it wouldn't care.

"Stand up!" she yelled again, this time hearing a crack in her own voice.

Her trigger finger had begun to squeeze when the ifrit-possessed woman let loose a scream.

It was a sonic blast that lifted Ridley clean off her feet. The force of it hurled her back into the rotunda, slamming her into one of the marble columns. She crumpled to the ground.

For a moment she wondered if her back was broken. Her ears rang with a muted tone, like she was underwater. Panicked visitors were running to get out. Ridley fumbled to pick up the gun that had clattered from her hands. She gripped it tightly, even while knowing it was useless here.

She thought she could hear Tal yelling somewhere over the buzz in her eardrums, but then the entire place came apart.

The Foundation Stone, that colossal slab of holy rock, split clean through the center. She stumbled to her knees to see what was coming.

From the violent crack in the stone burst forth smoke, a billow of colors and textures and a beastly chorus of sounds. The dome above it all exploded outward.

Then the miasma of horror began to divide itself, and separate forms appeared. Before Ridley's eyes, they became the monstrous titans that she had never wanted to believe in.

One was a vaporous white being. It had no features, only a gauzy mask that seemed to stream out behind it like mist.

There was a black-skinned being with a glowing seal on its chest and horned armor across its shoulders. Where its head should have been was an eruption of horns, split open in a volcanic blaze.

The third was a frenzied mass of burnt feathers and curling ram's horns. Blinding sparks of sulfur were bursting all over its noxious form.

The next was a beautiful, terrible sight. Its hair flowed like smoke, a giant pair of black wings was folded on its back, and its skin was like the night sky. It glittered with stars and nebulae. Fiery constellations glowed all over it.

Another was a ragged beast that looked as if it had risen from the depths of the sea. Its form looked to be nothing more than swirling smoke, a cyclone itself, and it dripped water that never seemed to hit the ground.

She saw next a being with red leathery bat wings. It had three glowing yellow eyes, the body of a muscular male human wrapped only in a scarlet sarong. Its skin rippled like lava, and in place of its hands were flaming torches.

The last of them was the sight of a nightmare. The thing was sinew and bone wrapped in the scaly skin of a black mamba. Its had massive taloned hands and webbed wings with spikes top and bottom. Under the smoking shroud it wore was a face that Ridley would never forget. A pair of beady eyes glowed impossibly gold. Beneath them, a snout protruded, something between a crocodile and a baboon, baring teeth that could surely tear apart flesh and bone.

They're loose. I failed. I didn't see her. I saw her and I didn't know.

Every last person still within the Dome was stricken with horror. These seven unearthly creatures rose, roaring and shrieking, flexing every limb and wing with their new freedom.

Ridley drew herself up to stand, the gun hanging slack in her hand. There was only one weapon that meant anything now.

Outside, the mob was swelling. The cries of accusation from Tiago's baby-faced Arab companion had stirred up rage, but it was confused by who exactly he was pointing at. The distance between them and Henri was too great to specify.

The turmoil gave him and Izhak the chance to slip away. It only looked natural for anyone helping an old man to get him safely out of an angry crowd.

On the other side of the courtyard, Atashi affected outrage himself, shouting simply to blend in. It would only be moments before this fury turned to violence. The people might not have a defined target, but they would find an outlet. As with almost every time, it would certainly be aimed at the nearest Jews. The Border Guard would be sucked into the Temple Mount yet again.

Atashi scanned the crowd for the locus of aggression, trying to scout where his operators were in this mess.

But then the Dome of the Rock exploded.

There was no fire, no smoke. It seemed as though it had simply burst from the inside. Chunks of tile, wood, and gold plating rained down into the courtyard. The crowd broke, running for cover as howls of shock echoed across the stone.

Henri was at the Qanatir arches, looking desperately for Tiago in the melee. He would be the only one not surprised by what had just happened.

Next to him, Izhak pulled off his shawl and ditched the cane. The time for moving at the pace of a frail old man was over.

Then Henri saw him—just a glimpse, rushing through the stampeding crowds.

"Target acquired!" called Henri. "Moving south toward Al-Aqsa."

He ran. Izhak rushed after him, but was soon pulled into the surging crowd. Angry rioters bulled toward his face. He tried to admonish them as an old man would in Arabic, but he had lost sight of his American partner.

Henri was on his own.

Inside the Dome, Chadia Yaseen emerged from the Well of Souls and stood at the rail. She gazed upon the destruction. She looked up at the seven kings of the jinn in awesome wonder, and lifted her arms to them.

"*Malakiun!*"

She climbed onto the cracked Foundation Stone, dropped to

her knees, and prostrated herself. Every one of the towering beings looked down at this beseeching human.

It was the one with the golden armor and head that looked like lava spilling out of split horns that moved toward her. It lifted its hands, and Chadia flew up into the air, suspended in fear.

When it spoke, Ridley was stunned as to how she could understand it.

"Leave the vessel," came a voice that seemed to scrape and echo through the building.

Chadia seized up, then spasmed and plummeted to the Foundation Stone in a crunching heap.

What was left in her place, floating above, was the ifrit. It was that same vaporous black that Ridley had seen in the basement of the Louvre. Its murky skin was gashed with molten fire, its eyes blazing out of darkness.

It gazed up at the jinn king as though it was looking upon God himself.

"You have brought us back into bondage," came the shattering voice again.

"No!" shrieked the ifrit. *"I freed you to rule the earth! I have the saber!"*

The rest of the colossal beings circled around to look down on the ifrit mid-air. Ridley had never seen anything so terrifying.

"Solomon is here. You have made us slaves again."

From the faceless head of the jinn, liquid fire erupted in a show of wrath.

The ifrit's limbs stretched out into the form of the Vitruvian Man. Then it began to scream in agony as they stretched farther, and farther. The smoking skin cracked into rivulets of lava, and then it burst.

Ridley flinched, but the bodily pieces of the ifrit seemed to evaporate in the air. Within seconds, there was nothing left of it.

Then something hollered within her head.

There has to be something more to the saber than just splitting the Stone.

She bolted back down into the Well of Souls. The walls of the cave had cracked and partly collapsed. She could no longer see where the saber had impaled the floor. Dropping to her stomach, she had to crawl and reach, scraping the back of her hands on jagged rock, until she finally felt the hilt.

She yanked the saber out from the debris and scrambled back up the steps.

What the hell do I do with this?

She scanned the rotunda quickly for Tal, but couldn't find him. This place was lost. The only battle now was for the Seal of Solomon, and it was the jinn king itself who had recognized that it was here.

Ridley ran to the side door and burst out into the courtyard.

Into mayhem.

CHAPTER
SEVENTY-EIGHT

JERUSALEM, ISRAEL

THE STONE COURTYARD was strewn with the wreckage of the golden dome.

Worshippers had scattered in terror, but now anger began to billow out from the crowds. Confusion was giving way to blind fury. The oldest sacred site in Islam had been desecrated in front of their eyes. It wouldn't be long before that fury sparked violence. Ridley could already hear roars at the gates, surely aimed at the Israeli guards.

She had heard Henri's call on the radio calling them to the Al-Aqsa Mosque. Clutching the bloodied saber in one hand, a Glock in the other, her scarf fallen down about her shoulders and smudged with rock-dust, Ridley sprinted across the courtyard and down the steps.

There they were.

444

Henri stood with his back to her, pointing his Glock at the baby-faced Arab. The man was holding a young girl at knife-point. The child was clawing at the man's arm, her eyes flared wide with fear. Yet the hostage was only a distraction to keep Henri at bay, to keep him from getting to Tiago.

The Portuguese—now dark-eyed and olive-skinned—stood a dozen feet behind his companion.

Ridley tried to flank Tiago at a distance, hoping to remain unseen, to take him by surprise. His young accomplice wouldn't murder a little girl if he thought it would get his boss killed.

"Don't!" Tiago yelled at her. "You kill me, that little girl dies with a knife in her neck."

Ridley didn't even have to look at Henri. She could feel how steely his grip on that gun was.

Tiago raised his hands to the sky. There was the massive iron ring that he had stolen from them in Egypt. He wore the Seal of Solomon.

"Al-Ahmar!" he shouted. "Azazel!"

From the Dome of the Rock rose the three-eyed jinn king, its red leathery wings pulling it upward through the shattered roof. Summoned.

What had been bewildered discord on the Temple Mount suddenly gave way to true pandemonium. Heads craned upward. First there was a ripple of silent disbelief, and then the screams of horror grew into a cacophony.

The creature flew to them, and came to hover over Tiago. It had obeyed the call, but its grisly red face rippled with anger.

A king, made a slave again. He hates his master.

When Tiago spoke in English, Ridley knew it was for them to understand what was about to happen.

"Destroy the church."

Al-Ahmar / Azazel shuddered. It turned to glare down at Henri.

"Believer," its voice rumbled in a wicked taunt, *"try to stop me."*

Henri was deeply spooked. It even shook Ridley. Though he wore an Islamic prayer cap, this thing knew he was of the church, that his faith was in Christ.

With a powerful stroke of its leathery wings, the creature launched itself into the sky, where it shimmered into a translucent haze. Its three yellow eyes turned toward the Church of the Holy Sepulchre.

Henri wavered. Here, he held the culprit, the commander of this chaos, at gunpoint. There, he had been taunted with an invitation to stop—somehow—the destruction of the church. Of course it was a trap, a diversion, but he felt an overwhelming, almost burning urge to stand within that church as a demon rained down upon it.

Ridley saw his gaze flit from Tiago to the jinn as it drifted west on the wind. She knew what he wanted.

Before either of them could act, Tiago called upward. "Maymun! Gadreel!"

He was calling them each by two names, that of the jinn legend and that given to a Watcher.

They could scarcely have blinked in the moment that this creature appeared, looming above Tiago, facing the Americans. It was the most gruesome of them all, the seventh. Its scaly obsidian skin, its bat-like wings, that snout that bristled with fangs. It glared down at them with beady yellow eyes.

"Tear them apart," Tiago said.

The voice of this one was a rasping hiss that chilled their bones. *"We cannot touch the woman."*

"I command it!" he exclaimed, clenching the fist on which he wore the Seal.

"Her blood is in the blade. We cannot touch her."

Tiago went livid, so angry that he seemed to forget Henri as a target. "Blind her! Wreck her path!"

She locked her eyes back on Tiago, over the barrel of her gun. Henri was the sniper with a rifle. She was the sniper with a handgun.

The monstrous creature pulled back its lips, its horrible gaze fixing on her. Her stomach lurched. For the first time, she felt a riptide of fear starting to drag her under.

"My bullet's as good as yours," she said, trying to sound brave to her partner. "I'm safe. Go!"

Henri seemed to snap into motion, and shouted into the radio, "Evacuate the Church! Now!"

He turned and sprinted to the nearest western gate, the Mughrabi. It would be the run of his life.

The jinn spread its talons wide and hissed. The sound was so loud it almost stunned Ridley, and she was immediately grateful to have already muffled hearing on one side. From the thing's hooked fingers poured acrid gray smoke.

She looked at the baby-faced terrorist, at the girl with panicked eyes that he clutched at knifepoint. He was distracted for only a second, watching to see exactly where the smoke was coming from.

Now, or I lose it and she dies.

Ridley squeezed the trigger.

The gunshot cracked the air. The man's head shot backward. The girl screamed as he collapsed behind her, a bloody hole punched through his temple. She ran off as the smoke wrapped itself around Ridley.

It was bitter, and something in it was burning her skin. She'd lost sight of Tiago in the miasma, but over the sound of her own choking, she heard his voice call out.

"Al-Abyad! Asbeel!"

She could not see the ghostly white jinn that rose above her, but she heard the next chilling words of the Portuguese.

"Tear down the temple wall."

He had barely finished his sentence before Ridley was shouting into the radio, "Evacuate the Western Wall! Clear it out now!"

She heard the terror in her own voice.

"Paladin, what's your location?" came Atashi through the earpiece.

"Outside Al-Aqsa," she replied, trying not to gag on fumes. "The smoke."

She tried to dodge away from the fog, to find her way out of its putrid, blinding cloud. Yet wherever she moved, it seemed to follow. The rattling hiss of the jinn was somehow coming from every direction.

The screams and howls of the Temple Mount had moved farther away, as the terrified mob had run from the sight of these titanic, supernatural beasts.

Ridley swung the golden saber wildly about, just hoping that the blade reached Tiago. She hacked and coughed, her eyes starting to water, flailing in the darkness.

It's me or no one. I stop him or they set the world on fire.

She couldn't see it when Asbeel the White One drifted to the western side of the Temple Mount. She couldn't see it loom over the holy Jewish site. She could only hear the cries of shocked terror echoing up from the plaza. She couldn't see the top row of stones tumble down into the courtyard.

She could only hear them smashing onto the ground below.

CHAPTER
SEVENTY-NINE

HENRI FELT as if his lungs were going to rip through his chest. He'd never sprinted so hard in his life. The pounding of his shoes against the stone streets thundered in his own ears. His prayers to God were now just garbled, desperate pleas for help.

He'd heard the pandemonium over the earpiece, the chaos on the Mount. He'd heard Bar-Lev clearing the way for him to reach the Church of the Holy Sepulchre, telling all officers to let him pass. He'd heard the commands to police everywhere to mobilize reinforcements for the Temple Mount.

Then he'd heard the call from Ridley to evacuate the Western Wall...and then the screams from the plaza behind him.

The Old City was in complete tumult. Israelis were some of the most stubbornly resilient people on earth. They lived on a knife's edge in a city that demanded eternal vigilance. They had seen bombings and stabbings, shootings and car rammings every year of their lives. Yet this was something they had never seen before, and a sense of panic was surging through the people.

The streets were a din of confusion, some people scurrying, some stampeding. Henri barreled through them, his heart raging. He had no idea what he could do against this fallen Watcher, this jinn king, but he would stand in that church and hold the pillars together with his own hands if it was the last thing he could do.

In his peripheral vision, he saw a massive shadow flit above the buildings. Just as he glanced up, it vanished over the rooftops.

He didn't know he could run any faster, but in that moment he did.

Every breath Ridley drew felt thinner than the one before. The bitter smoke was coating her lungs and burning her throat with every cough. She couldn't find her way out of this gray vapor.

She heard Tiago's voice. It sounded a mile away.

"Borqaan! Boraqijal!"

What's left?

"Destroy the mosque."

Of course. Oh my God. Al-Aqsa.

The Order of Raphael wanted to set the world on fire.

She couldn't get enough oxygen. Her vision began to dim. She wobbled. Then she stumbled. She wouldn't let go of the saber, so her knuckles smashed against the stone as she crashed to one knee.

The smoke began to dissipate.

"Why are you stopping?" said Tiago, somewhere nearby. "Don't let her go!"

The grating hiss of the jinn's voice replied, *"We cannot touch her. We cannot harm her. Her blood is in the saber."*

Then the supernatural smog began to clear, and she could see. Her eyes landed on Tiago.

He was barely a dozen feet away, flushed with exultant power, listening to the screams of hundreds of thousands of people.

Behind him, the beautiful creature who looked like the night sky had spread its wings over the mosque. The blackness beneath was absolute, like a living darkness that was oozing over the building. The earth quaked beneath it.

For a moment, Tiago took his eyes off of Ridley, who was gagging for air, broken and collapsed on the ground. He couldn't resist looking back to the grandeur of this destruction. It was the religious apocalypse he had always dreamt of.

Ridley's eyes were clogged with burning tears. Her lungs were scorched by the smoke. Her body ached from the ifrit hurling her into the marble wall of the Dome. But she only needed those few seconds.

Her gaze narrowed on the Seal, and she lunged.

The golden saber slashed once through the air with all the power she could muster. The blade sliced through skin and sinew and bone, and the lower half of Tiago's forearm fell to the ground, spurting blood.

He screamed, as much from shock as pain. Before he could register it all, Ridley had dived for the severed limb. She snatched it up and rolled away.

The warm flesh was so slick with blood that she struggled to keep hold of it. Over the sound of his blood-chilling wails, she pulled and yanked at the iron ring, until finally it slid free of the deadened middle finger.

"No!" he cried, charging at her.

She stumbled back out of his reach, shoving the ring into her pocket. He was a wreck, clutching the stump of his arm in desperation and agony. He swung for her. This time she side-stepped, and rammed the saber into his gut.

It went clean through, the gleaming tip appearing out his back. His face froze in horror. The golden blade dripped with blood.

Ridley felt a tide of relief break within her. She yanked the saber free and watched Tiago crumple, groaning in agony.

"It is finished. You can't st—"

She didn't want to hear his monologue. She raised the Glock and shot him in the head.

The layers of smaller stone above the Western Wall had been demolished. The ghostly titan of Al-Ahmar / Asbeel hovered above the chaos. It seemed to radiate pleasure as it began to tear out the gargantuan slabs of rock beneath them. They crashed into the plaza below, some thudding into the broken ground, some tumbling and smashing worshippers as they tried to flee.

Shrieks of agony and panic filled the Old City.

Henri nearly skidded into the courtyard of the Church of the Holy Sepulchre. There were a dozen Border Police there already in full body armor, clutching their M4s. They raised their rifles as he came charging forward.

"No, no!" he shouted. "I'm call sign Prince! With Ya'mas!"

A sergeant seemed to register that this was the operator their commander had given a clear order for. She told the others in Hebrew to stand down.

Christian worshippers and tourists were streaming out of the building, ushered on by some of the guards. None of them had yet seen what was coming, what had been unleashed on the Mount.

"How many still inside?" Henri asked the woman who had recognized him.

"We don't know," she said. "There are a lot of sections inside."

He knew that much. The ancient Church was a disorienting labyrinth of territories. It was divvied up amongst the Roman Catholics, the Greek Orthodox, the Armenian Apostolics, and even the Copts and the Syrians. Each area had their own ceremonies and their own visitors.

"We have snipers on the roof, reinforcements coming," said the sergeant. "There's no way for someone to get near the church."

"You don't understand," he said, but had no idea how to adequately warn her.

He didn't have the time to anyway.

Two rifle shots cracked the air above them, and shouts of alarm came through the Border Police radios. The guards on the ground were quicker into combat mode than anything he'd witnessed in the Secret Service.

What they could not have expected was the colossal shadow that spread across the courtyard. They looked up.

Darkening the skies was a monster. The jinn king had appeared, its red wings unfurled, its three eyes burning yellow.

The cries from those below, both Israeli guards standing their ground and civilian visitors fleeing, rang with terror.

The courtyard exploded in gunfire. Every one of the bullets reached their target, but none of them hit. Azazel bellowed, but it was not for pain. It was reveling.

The creature raised its two hands that burned as torches,

and flared them toward the front of the church. The windows shattered. The balcony ladder that had been stuck in place for three hundred years burst apart. Flaming splinters showered to the ground.

Screams echoed from inside.

"Get them out!" yelled Henri to the stricken guards.

He could not watch a massacre unfold in a house of God. He ran into the church.

The fallen Watcher, the jinn king, landed on the famous dome, and tore off the roof.

CHAPTER
EIGHTY

———

Ridley was regaining her breath.

Her eyes began to refocus, enough to see the cataclysm around her. She could hear Ya'mas operators calling their positions and movements over the radio, Bar-Lev responding from headquarters with organizing commands.

Thousands of Muslims had surged to the gates, overwhelming the Border Police, who were caught between trying to fight for their lives and trying to orient themselves to the supernatural horrors rising behind the crowds.

The three remaining jinn kings had ascended from the Dome of the Rock. They towered about the Temple Mount, a trio of awesome horror, looking upon the wreckage as if considering where to strike.

In front of Ridley, Maymun / Gadreel had settled onto the

ground. There seemed to be something slithering under its black-scaled skin. It took a step toward her, its spiky wings dragging along the stone. She had never seen anything as malevolent as those eyes staring at her.

Hell exists.

She shoved the Glock into her waistband and yanked the big iron ring from her pocket. She slid the Seal of Solomon onto her middle finger.

"Stop!" she yelled at the creature in front of her.

But it kept advancing, its snout gleaming full of predators' teeth.

"Stop!" she called again, her voice rising with genuine fear.

"Your blood is in the saber. You are a servant. You cannot command the Seal."

The words struck like sledgehammer in her chest.

This can't be happening.

Beyond the creature, Ridley could see the walls of the Al-Aqsa Mosque cracking. Worshippers fled from it. The titanic night jinn circled above them.

She could do nothing. There was no one nearby to shove the ring onto. She looked down at the golden saber in her hands, now slick with the blood of Tiago. It was pure desperation that sent her mind spinning.

The saber had brought these things up from darkness. The saber was also protecting her. Sealed into it were the restrictions and protections of this other world. It had been worth nothing and had no power of its own before the ifrit had pieced it back together and stabbed it into a holy place.

Henri had been right. He had known of the Watchers. His faith had recognized them, the fallen chiefs of God's appointing.

The Seal may have been the bridle and reins, but the saber had given them their freedom, had somehow broken the chains of banishment that had held them in darkness for millennia.

Destroy the saber.

Perhaps it would destroy all chances of imprisoning them again. Perhaps it would doom the earth to their carnage until the last of days. Perhaps it would do nothing.

The jinn had demolished the Dome of the Rock. The Al-Aqsa Mosque was being ripped apart. The Western Wall was crumbling. The Church of the Holy Sepulchre was surely being demolished.

Destroy the saber. Where?

She turned to the west, and ran as fast as she could.

Henri was tearing through the Church, hauling out frightened tourists and priests who had huddled for safety. Some of the Border Guard had gone in as well, and were directing everyone toward the exit.

Just as he reached the rotunda, Henri stopped.

An avalanche of stone and gilded vaultings crashed to the floor of the Holy Sepulchre. From where the ceiling had been, now sunlight poured in. Chunks of the dome fell onto the Aedicula.

The ornate shrine in the middle of the Church had been built hundreds of years ago to shelter the tomb of Jesus, as more and more pilgrims came to visit the site. What lay within it was nothing less than the revered place of the resurrection, the whole foundation of the Christian faith. Henri could not process the scope of this.

He yelled for the remaining civilians who had crammed together under cover. They scrambled toward him as he half-shoved them toward the doors.

Azazel appeared above, above the shattered ceiling.

Henri had no weapons against this. He dropped to his knees and placed a hand flat on the stone floor. There was nothing left for him but this.

"Stop this," he whispered. "Protect your church. Give me help. Put your hand on Ridley."

His murmurs rose into the cacophony of the Old City.

As Ridley sprinted down the Mughrabi Gate into the Western Wall plaza, she saw the true devastation.

The stones were splattered with blood and bone. Pieces of clothing stuck out from under massive slabs of fallen rock. The stampede of panic had left dozens injured or unconscious. Some of the visitors were trying to drag others to safety, away from the wall.

Above it all hovered Asbeel, its face nothing more than streaming white gauze as it took apart the sacred monument stone by stone.

Just go. Don't watch.

She ran, around the back of the plaza, relieved to be ignored in the melée despite the sword she was wielding. Ridley sprinted to the entrance of the Western Wall tunnels. With every officer pulled out into the plaza, it was unguarded.

She entered the labyrinth at full tilt. The obsession with studying maps for an operation had saved her life more than once. Today, it could save more.

The tunnels were illuminated, all the crags in the unhewn rock and sections of sleek chiseled walls between them. There were narrow passages and wide cisterns, modern railings and cut-out stairways. She ran through the Crusader Church, turned into the madrasah, and then hit a long hallway. It glowed a faded gold from the small lamps along the floor.

Just ahead. It was just ahead.

Then something reached her nose, a smell that made her snort in disgust. She looked up in dread.

It was the same acrid smoke of the jinn king on the Mount. She whipped her head around. A dark front was billowing down the tunnel toward her.

Ridley bolted down the stretch.

She was nearly there when she saw what was coming toward her from the other end of the tunnel. A cloud of of smoke was filling it from floor to ceiling.

Oh my God.

She knew she had another speed in her, and it was for this moment. Something in her reached for overdrive, and she shot through the narrow passageway as if running from death itself.

And then she glimpsed it, and skidded to a halt.

In front of her was the alcove of the Holy of Holies. She had only seconds to find out if this would work at all.

Ridley stepped into the space. She stabbed the tip of the saber between the cut stones, and yanked.

A piece broke off. She pulled it out and went again. Another shard snapped. She had to use two hands to pull it out of the tight crevice this time, slicing her palm open on the slippery blade.

Smoke was rushing toward her from both ends of the tunnel, the stench growing stronger. She could hear the rasping hiss of the jinn echoing closer.

Another snap. Another. She tossed the shards to the ground. Again.

Smoke billowed into the alcove, blinding her, burning her skin and throat. She fumbled to jam the stunted blade back into the crevice.

Finally it slid forward. She tore it with all her strength, and the saber broke.

Seven pieces.

The hiss of the jinn king grew into a shriek that pierced her ears. It was pure agony. Ridley clenched her eyes shut and bent over, holding her head, choking on the bitter smoke.

Suddenly, it faded. The furious howl grew more distant, until there was nothing left of it at all.

Ridley opened her eyes. The air was clear. The golden shards of the saber lay strewn across the floor. Her fingers dripped blood. The jinn king was gone.

Kneeling on the floor of the Holy Sepulchre, Henri's muttered prayers had become a full-throated beseeching of his God.

Sweat glistened on his brow as windows shattered above. Jeweled lanterns crashed to the floor. Stone columns split and toppled. Flaming candles tumbled from their holders.

Azazel was climbing into the dome, its blazing eyes fixed on the shrine of the tomb below.

"You are stronger," said Henri. "Put these creatures back in darkness. Keep your church," he shouted, eyes squeezed shut against the dust that wafted through the rotunda. "Stop this thing!"

A blast of light erupted. Even through his clamped eyelids, it seared Henri's vision like a phosphorus bomb. He winced as it shone and burned into his retinas.

Above him, Azazel roared as if blinded. It reeled backward, up toward the open sky. Its cries grew wild in rage and torment.

There was one last bellow, and then it was quiet.

Henri opened his eyes, still seeing the residue of the astonishing flash.

"My God."

He looked up, blinking his vision clear.

The jinn king, the Watcher, was gone.

CHAPTER
EIGHTY-ONE

JERUSALEM, ISRAEL

NINETY-TWO PEOPLE HAD BEEN KILLED in Jerusalem that day.

Most of those deaths were accounted for at the Western Wall, where worshipping Jews had been crushed by the massive stones. Some had died on the Temple Mount, Muslims killed under the collapse of the Dome of the Rock and the Al-Aqsa Mosque. The Christians at the Church of the Holy Sepulchre had fared only slightly better, mostly due to the advanced notice to evacuate. Three people had died due to the human crush of a panicked stampede.

One had been found on the Mount with his arm severed. He had been shot in the head.

The Defense Minister of Israel was the first to address the country that morning. It was clear that he had no idea what to say about the supernatural causes. He still hadn't shaken the dazed look in his own eyes, though he made strong statements toward the Muslim and Christian communities as well as the Jewish, condemning the violence that had been done against them by "foreign actors."

Of course, there was no covering up the appearance of those attackers. They had shown themselves to tens of thousands of people that day. Within the hour—within minutes—there were shaky videos flying across the internet of the apocalyptic-looking beings. The news exploded, from religious zealots of all faiths to conspiracy theorists who salivated over the spectacle.

The violence in Jerusalem did not, in the end, look anything like what they had feared. There were some low-level outbursts of stone-throwing and fist-beatings, but each community was so rocked that there seemed to be no ready-made response at hand. The streets were hushed.

Despite the daze, people had almost immediately begun to clean up the sacred sites. Restoration of the physical structures would be long, but the spirit within the city of Jerusalem would not be long bowed. Blood was scrubbed from the ground. Stones were hauled off. Broken tiles were swept away.

Bus fees were waived. Taxis drove for free. Food was offered at sidewalk cafés for no cost. Homes were opened to the wounded and distraught.

Ridley had emerged from the Western Wall tunnels bloody and dusty, her eyes rimmed red. The scarf she had been wearing was now tied like a sash across her chest, carrying the clanking pieces of the saber.

She'd rushed into the plaza, toward the groans of the dying, and tried to stabilize as many of the wounded as she could. She had no more medical knowledge than the basics of a special forces soldier, but she had worked as long as she could, until Atashi found her there.

Instead of pulling her away, he knelt down and helped splint a young man's leg. No officer in Israel could turn away from a scene of bloody terror, and too many of them had seen too many of these.

They spent an hour in the plaza, a scene of groaning masses amidst the destruction. They helped wherever they could.

Ridley called for Henri repeatedly over the earpiece. They couldn't raise him, and her fear began to rise with every failed attempt. Finally they got a sergeant on the radio, the woman who had been posted at the Church of the Holy Sepulchre with her unit. She claimed to have seen him rushing into the building just as it started to crumble.

She looked at Atashi, who had heard the report over his earpiece.

"Come on," he said, getting to his feet.

She knew the way, but let him lead through his own city. She only demanded that they run.

They reached the church within minutes.

Their jaws nearly dropped when they rounded the last corner. That ancient holy building, which had stood for over a thousand years, was mutilated. The domed roof was gone. A number of soldiers had formed a chain to lift the wounded out through the door. The exit had been partially blocked by collapsed stone.

They called out that the last of the injured had been evacuated, then backed away from the door. It was then that the officers who'd been inside climbed out over the debris.

There was Henri, stepping into the sunlight. He was so covered in dust that he looked like a stone statue himself. His Islamic prayer cap was gone, and one sleeve on his white button-down had ripped through. Streaks of sweat left darkened trails down his forehead.

Ridley burst forward, and finally he saw her.

He clamped his partner tightly into a hug. It was the kind of hug that grasped for life, even as the scrapes of death still burned on the edges of their minds.

When they pulled back, she grabbed his head with both hands.

"We fucking did it."

He dropped his chin and laughed in relief. "What did you do?"

She pulled off the scarf she'd tied up as a satchel, and opened it for him. Inside lay the golden shards of the saber.

He clapped her around the back of the neck.

"God with you," he said, shaking his head again in disbelief.

It was another hour before Ridley and Henri regrouped with the rest of the Ya'mas operators back at their station. Tal was so relieved to see his momentary partner that he pulled her into a bear hug. He was very concerned about her getting stitches for her sliced hand.

Izhak had been battered by the mob on the Mount when he was separated from Henri. They'd fractured his cheekbone and left him with one eye swollen purple, and possibly a torn ligament in his knee. Aron and Semion designated themselves to take him to Shaare Zedek hospital, but he put them off. It would be crowded with people in more dire need than he.

The first thing Atashi made them all do was drink a bottle of water. Then he called on Ridley and Henri. The after-action report was theirs to deliver.

He sighed. She drew in a deep breath.

How to tell this story...

CHAPTER
EIGHTY-TWO

ALEXANDRIA, VIRGINIA

THERE HAD BEEN nothing on this level of worldwide shock and devastation since the attacks of September 11th.

Every national leader in the world was trying to get Prime Minister Shalmi on the phone. The call from the American President Voller came early. He wanted to be first on the scene not because of his country's alliance with Israel, but rather to beat everyone else to it, to be seen as the most important of them all.

Shalmi took his call, but at the time, neither of them had any idea that there had been American operatives embedded with Ya'mas that day, or that they had been the ones to alert them to the attack, and to end it.

It would be the Deputy Director of the CIA's National Clandestine Service who would brief him later that evening on their covert involvement. Ben Conway had never spoken directly to

Voller before, and by the frothing tantrum of his response, he resolved to avoid doing so again at all costs.

Voller demanded the firing of "whatever bonehead" had directed CIA employees to work with the Israelis, and then demanded the firing of "the idiots" themselves who had worked on the ground that day. He was furious to be made a fool of, and supremely concerned that Shalmi would have known about this before he did.

Conway had no intention of telling the president who it was that had sent his operatives on this mission. Voller wouldn't remember to follow up, and he had no idea that Booker Douglas or the Osprey division even existed.

And in the end, it was clear that Booker had been right from the beginning. He had no way of knowing what the mission would become, nor the stakes involved, but he always seemed to have a nose for these things. He also seemed to select just the right operatives for each undertaking.

Twenty-four hours after the attack on Jerusalem, Ridley and Henri were sitting in a stately conference room with the Man in Black himself, CIA Director Jude Fraser.

They had prepped with Booker that morning in his office, recalling the timeline, sorting their files on Tiago Inacio, Claudine Gaspar, and their own involvement with the Israeli special forces.

Once they'd gotten their records in order, Booker sat back in his chair and folded his arms with an ample sigh.

"I've seen a lot of things in this work that I never wanted to believe," he said, "but *that*...that was the most goddamned thing I've ever..."

He set his mouth to brooding, and shook his head slowly.

"Literally God damned," said Henri.

"Almost had me diggin' out my Bible for the book of Revelation, lookin' for the right part."

He looked at Ridley, who hadn't spoken.

"Samaras. You're gettin' time off. I want both of you to talk to somebody."

"I am talking to somebody," she replied with an overly radiant smile.

"Don't talk to me. I'm backlogged years on talking about my own stuff. Sorry I don't know any therapist who could take someone needing to talk about supernatural demon genies without calling a mental institution. So I mean a priest or something."

"I know a few nightly show hosts who'd love to hear my story of the demon genies," grinned Ridley, pushing back in her chair.

Henri gave her a look.

"Cut that out," said Booker, his tone changing. "We get through today, and you all take the next few weeks off."

He couldn't make them talk to anyone, at least not be real with anyone. Ridley played witty and cool in his office, but one day, she would have to reckon with the dimensions of this world and its supernatural realms. At least Henri had some faith by which to process it all. Booker wouldn't press the matter today, though. It was not the time.

Minutes later, Deputy Director Conway came to the office. To their great admiration and gratitude, he was a man who believed that responsibility lay with leaders. The higher up you went, the heavier the duty, the more accountability was required. He had never micromanaged Booker, but was ready to act as a shield for whatever repercussions might rain down on them from the top.

Conway was not, however, an easy man or a permissive boss. As he sat with them in Booker's office, he had first congratulated them on the fulfillment of a mission, on their perseverance in discovering the imminent danger and preventing a full-blown, worldwide cataclysm.

Then he excoriated them for the public spectacle.

Osprey was one of the smallest and most covert divisions in the agency. It functioned only in the shadows, to confront threats that the rest of the world could hardly comprehend. What had happened in Israel was nothing short of an international catastrophe. There was no explanation that the authorities could offer that would both satisfy and reassure the public.

Theories had run wild. Every news and talk show and podcast in the world was talking endlessly about it. Was it a foreign attack perpetrated with holographic drones and explosives? Was it a false flag attack meant to sabotage peace talks between the Israel and Palestine leadership? Or was it in fact supernatural, exploding people's preconceived understanding of the spiritual dimension?

None of these things boded well for stability in any country. The spectacle could not be covered up. In many ways, it felt like the world had cracked.

There was nothing that Ridley or Henri could say to this. It was true, and they had failed to contain the threat. They had only barely stopped it, and not before monstrous damage had been done.

It was the most disastrous success in the history of the Osprey division.

So they were reminded when they then faced the man at the top.

Director Fraser had earned his nickname both for his affinity for Johnny Cash's *Folsom Prison Blues* and his commitment to wearing all-black suits. He was known for his striking intelligence, the crafty type that knew how to climb ladders that others couldn't even see. They had never met him before today, but felt the gravity of his presence before he'd even spoken.

In his dry, gravelly voice, he surprised them all by first addressing the operatives.

"Congratulations. You saved the world and you fucked up."

There would be no commendations handed out, but he listened to their accounts of the mission, often sniping in with questions or comments on their methodology. He was demanding as any boss they'd encountered, with more than a few shades of "politicking" thrown in.

After that, he went to Conway and Booker. He demanded a full reporting of Osprey's last ten years of operations.

Booker's jaw nearly dropped. If there was one thing he hated about his job, it was paperwork. This was going to bury him for months. This division would no longer escape a more involved oversight. Now that Fraser had realized the magnitude of what they did, he was not going to let them slide back into the shadows.

After three hours of intense grilling, the Director of the CIA adjourned the meeting.

When Ridley finally walked out into the parking lot, she looked up at the sky and breathed in the fresh air. The canopy of robin's egg blue above her, the breeze that swept back her dark hair, the scent of cherry blossoms...the whole of spring seemed to revive her.

Henri swung his keys around in his hand. He gazed out at the gleaming sea of cars in the lot and blew out a long breath.

They looked at each other across the pavement.

"So," she said, "do you believe in the Watchers?"

He cracked into a laugh, the first smile of the day for either of them.

"Which one was your favorite?" he asked.

"Oh, the one that attacked the mosque. How pretty, huh?"

He nodded. "That was a beautiful jinn, can't argue."

They were quiet for a moment. Neither moved for their vehicle.

"What do you do now?" asked Ridley.

"Eat my weight in pizza. Take an eighteen-hour nap with my cats. Go to church. What about you?"

"Take my dog out for ice cream. Maybe climb a mountain. Watch all of *The Thin Man* movies. Who knows how long it'll be before we get called back."

Osprey was not a team in the sense that Ya'mas was. For each mission, Booker selected two agents that he thought would be best for the assignment. The pairs were mixed and matched. It wasn't always a hit, but this time, Booker had gotten it right. A partnership thrown together for their proficiency in French ending up in a city where neither of them spoke the native language to engage in a spiritual battle that one of them hadn't even believed existed a month before.

I'll see him again.

"If you..." Henri started, then paused. "If you want to talk about any of this sometime...you know I get it."

She didn't. She wouldn't. But she hadn't the heart to tell him.

"Race you back to Alex?" she said brightly.

Alexandria was a clean half hour from Langley.

"Car against bike?" he smirked.

"I'm fast. Somewhere between a snake and a mongoose. And a panther."

He arched a brow.

"It's—it's from *The Office*. You should watch TV more."

"You should have installed a booster on your bike."

In fact, she had no need. She roared her Indian Scout bike back into Alexandria that afternoon a full minute ahead of Henri. All was well.

Maddie greeted her at the door. The little mutt could not have wagged any harder as she leapt up to reach her owner's face with boundless licks of affection. She'd practically exploded with joy the night before when Ridley had picked her up from the neighbor's apartment.

Later that night, the pup lay snuggled in at her side in a deep sleep. The witty banter of Nick and Nora Charles crackled from the black and white screen of the TV.

Ridley had tried to turn her brain off, strolling out for ice cream down the block, ordering Pad Thai for delivery, and sinking into the pillowy embrace of her comforter to watch the antics of the best private detective couple in film.

Yet for all her exhaustion, she couldn't fall asleep that night. Her hand throbbed. Her ribs ached. Anxiety crawled through her belly as she kept replaying all of the things she should have done better. Her head was a mad kaleidoscope of burning wings, demonic faces, and crushed limbs.

When she finally dreamt, she was back on the Mount, putting a bullet through Tiago's head.

When she woke up the next morning, however, she wasn't bothered.

But there was still something that needed doing. She hated loose ends.

CHAPTER
EIGHTY-THREE

PARIS, FRANCE

Claudine Gaspar got home from work late that evening.

She hauled her bags onto the kitchen table and began unloading groceries. She'd stopped for a loaf of fresh rye, a bottle of Syrah, a brick of Gruyère, a carton of heavy cream and a slab of pork belly. She'd promised Franck that she would make him quiche Lorraine when he returned tomorrow from Switzerland, having made his biggest acquisition of the year. He had always preferred it with Gruyère instead of Swiss cheese, and pork belly instead of bacon.

"Valerie?" she called down the dark hallway.

No answer. Her daughter was rarely to be found at home in the evenings when there was the entirety of Paris to attend to, but she called out each night just the same. A mother's hope.

After putting away the ingredients, she poured herself a

glass of Syrah and grabbed a box of crackers from the cupboard. Franck was insistent that she start eating more protein and dairy, fearing that she'd develop osteoporosis like her mother had. He was probably more afraid of having to take care of her if she broke a hip, than worried about the pain she would experience herself.

Nonetheless, theirs was a mildly happy marriage. At least they rarely rowed, and she had never gotten even a whiff of infidelity off him. Still, Claudine was glad to have the apartment to herself.

Knocking her shoes off, she turned on a light and settled down into the couch with a sigh. After thirty-three years of marriage, there was still a precious relief to these moments of solitude.

She had just taken a deep swig of her wine and chased it down with a salty cracker when she felt a slight breeze drifting in from behind her. She turned.

There on the threshold of the balcony door was the silhouette of a tall, statuesque intruder.

Claudine yelped, scrambling from her chair and spilling Syrah across the carpet. The shadow stepped inside.

"Ms. Gaspar," came that full voice with the throaty edge. "It's actually rewarding to scare the shit out of someone when they're holding a glass of wine."

The intruder moved into the dim cast of the lamplight, and the gaping Claudine found herself facing off with the American agent. She had a thin pack strapped to her back.

"Oh, my God!" she said with a laugh of feigned relief.

"Really?" said Ridley, picking up the box of crackers and popping one in her mouth. "Which god?"

"What are you talking about? What are you *doing* here?"

"You sit down."

The sudden hardness in her voice was menacing. There was

no use in playing it lightly for Claudine. She slid into the nearby chair.

"So I'm sure you saw the news!" said Ridley. "Did you happen to see your compatriot on any of those viral videos?"

"My what?"

She enunciated to a snarl. "Tiago."

"I haven't watched any of those videos on the internet."

"*Bullshit.* Do you even know who it was you were betraying when you sicced him on us?"

Claudine was silent. The dumb innocent act had evaporated. It was replaced by a seeping defiance.

"You should really always know who it is you're making an enemy of," said Ridley.

"Are you just here to show me your temper?" asked Claudine. "What do you want?"

Ridley lowered herself onto the edge of the couch, though in no way did she relax.

"I want to know who the Grand Master is."

At this, Claudine burst into real laughter. "Are you crazy? Even Tiago Inacio didn't know who the Grand Master was."

"Oh look, you know his full name."

"Why pretend?"

"That's a good way to be thinking," said Ridley. "You people who believe in Raphael seem to be everywhere. I don't really get it, the failed offshoot of the failed Templars, but somehow you've got your fingers in everything, don't you? Every country...enough money to fund these little excursions looking for treasure that you think will destroy the world..."

That provoked genuine scorn from Claudine. "You think the Order of Raphael wants to destroy the world? You are never going to find the Grand Master. You're really an idiot."

Ridley hurled the box of crackers against the room so violently that the older woman flinched.

"You know, I'm not really enjoying our chat right now," she said. "I don't think you realize what I've been through in the past few weeks. I *know* you don't realize how much blood I saw spilled because of Tiago and his angel-worshipping henchmen."

The glint in her eyes was new, and it was frightening.

When Claudine spoke again, it was quieter, more humble. "This is honest. I do *not* know who the Grand Master of the Order is. His real identity? Or hers. Nobody knows this."

"Then how does he or she have so much fucking power?"

She looked at Ridley as though she was simple. "You don't believe in anything, do you?"

"I've recently come into a very strong belief about jinn. Watchers. Whatever."

"Then you have a tiny little peek. What's out there..." said Claudine, almost dreamy as she gazed out across the city. "We barely understand our own world. We've been here longer than we think. We've mingled with gods we don't even know. The truth is beautiful, incredible. We *want* people to know the order of things. We *want* them to know who guards the heavens, and the darkness. All other things—"

She waved a hand.

"—are lies."

Ridley had not come for a soliloquy, no matter how enchanting the accent was that delivered it. She felt again the scorch of shame for having trusted this woman.

"Tiago is done," she said. "I want the next in line. Give me the name."

The silence from Claudine was equal parts haughty and fearful. When finally she spoke, her voice was flat.

"I can't do that."

"Well, funny you should say that. So, Franck is scheduled to fly Swiss Air, taking off from Zurich at seven-thirty tomorrow morning. Currently he's staying at the Widder Hotel. Room eight.

"Valerie is at Fréquence right now with Sandrine and Léa. It's pretentious, but she seems to love it. Went four times last month. She drinks too much, you know, but very responsible. Never drives after. Always calls for an Uber."

Claudine stared at her, frozen.

"Which one will make it home and which one won't?"

Ridley hated this role, but she played it like Meryl Streep. All that mattered was that the person across from her believed it.

"I'll write it down," said Claudine, utterly subdued. "Do you have a pen?"

"I am the pen. Tell me."

"Andreas Colby. He's a real estate developer. He owns a football team in England and an American football team."

"Does he know you?"

She nodded.

"I can't tell you how much you'll regret it later if you're lying to me now."

"No, I promise. He was part of the Order before me. I'm just..." she said, lifting her hands, "an archaeologist."

"Oh, don't kid yourself," said Ridley, getting to her feet. "In this business, you guys fire the starting gun."

She resettled the strap of her backpack and headed to the door.

"Where's Tiago?" asked Claudine, jumping to her feet.

"Somewhere in the Israeli dirt. With a bullet in his head."

Ridley walked out of the apartment.

Claudine stared at the door as it shut behind the American. She looked down at the burgundy stain bleeding across the carpet, the glass that lay in violent repose next to it. She clutched her hair and breathed out a huff of astonishment. Then she rushed into her office to open her laptop on the desk.

It was gone.

Ridley strode down the Canal Saint-Martin, glittering with the café lights that lined the waterway. The laptop in her bag thudded gently against her back with each step. They already had everything on Claudine's phone through Bellerophon. Now they would have everything on her computer.

Ridley could smell garlic on the breeze, with cigarette smoke and rotisserie meats. For a moment, she almost envied the diners who looked so carefree chatting over the patio tables. So they had seen their city attacked. So some otherworldly creatures had demolished some old buildings. Life went on in the city.

She had one last stop to make in Europe before heading home. Pulling out her phone, she typed up a message.

I'm heading back through London tonight. Want to grab a pint?

Less than a minute later, her phone buzzed. She read the reply from Owen.

Buying a train ticket this second! Fish and chips are on me

Ridley smiled and tucked the phone away. Some damages might be repaired after all.

ACKNOWLEDGMENTS

To Mom and Dad. No gesture and no words could ever suffice. You gave me life, you saved that life, and you supported so many of my ventures that I can't imagine what I would have made of this life without your help.

To my siblings, who are so loyal and talented and tremendous that I wouldn't trade one of you. Not even one!

To my nieces and nephews, who have made my life so much brighter, and reminded me what it's like to live in imagination.

To Karen, who has seen the peaks and valleys firsthand. Your belief and support has been boundless. This book wouldn't exist without you. I am immeasurably grateful.

To Remy, because even though she can't read, she's my most constant companion. Anyone who knows me knows this.

To Paul, whose friendship and partnership have been invaluable to me over the years. You have made me a better writer, and I can't wait to see the adventures that lie ahead.

To Joe, who is 'my people' for life. I would be a poorer friend without you. You've opened up worlds of storytelling for me, sharing art and inspiration and insight.

To Sarah, the friend I've known for as long as I can remember. You're the kind of friend worth knowing for a lifetime.

To Ubisoft and Melissanthi Mahut, for creating a character that enthralled me, and inspired more than a little bit of Ridley.

And for E, who is still — always — alive in everything I write.

But most of all, for Granjan. I miss you.

ABOUT THE AUTHOR

Ox Devere is a pseudonym for writing duo Parker Jamison and Paul Kimball. It's an ode to the most famous pen name of all time.

Parker worked in the film industry for years before finding her way back to her first love: books. She now puts her love for thrilling and cinematic suspense onto the pages of globe-trotting novels. A connoisseur of cocktails and cookies and SIG Sauer, she trains in Brazilian jiu-jitsu and lives outside of Boston with a Border Collie mix who is probably smarter than her.

Paul went from warehouse work to film sets to producing academic curricula. He wouldn't say that he's an adrenaline junkie, but he loves motorcycles, firearms, and action movies. His favorite cocktail is an Old Fashioned and his favorite place in the world is sitting on the front swing overlooking his family farm. He lives in Maryland with his wife and two feisty little mutts.

Made in United States
North Haven, CT
19 January 2024

47678613R00296